Light in the Forest
a family saga

JuliAnne Sisung

ISBN-13: 978-1544841304
ISBN-10: 1544841302

This is a work of fiction. Characters and incidences are the product of the author's imagination and are used fictitiously.

Published July 2015 by JuliAnne Sisung

Books by JuliAnne Sisung

Curse of the Damselfly
Sophie's Lies

The Hersey Series
Elephant in the Room
Angels in the Corner
Light in the Forest
Place in the Circle

The Idlewild Series
Leaving Nirvana
The Whipping Post
Ask for the Moon

Acknowledgments

Thank you to my family for their unique character flaws which continue to provide interesting fodder for my imagination: to my brother, Mark Jessup, who relates his real comic excursions with flair and fantasy; to my sister, Jackie Downey, who also stomps her foot to get her way, and for loving my words; to Mom, Esther Mathia, for my devotion to fiction and for guiding my reading choices as a young girl, against my wishes.

Thanks to Larry Hale for editing this novel, and most especially, thank you for *not* loving my words.

All of your roles are necessary to my work, and I thank you from my heart.

Thank you, David Thompson and Mid-Michigan Community College for your encouragement.

Thank you to Hersey for being a wonderful home town memory.

Cover by Boris Rasin

Foreword

The hills around Hersey were barren of tall white pines. These majestic trees were once plentiful, but by 1917 the logging industry had felled them and guided the skeleton logs down the Muskegon River, a Landmark stamp smacked solidly into their raw ends. They stopped briefly at the saw mill to become construction lumber and then went on to provide building material throughout the country. Michigan was a logger's paradise, providing more lumber than any state in the union, and its hills were plundered and pillaged as a result.

From a distance and looking west toward the white steeple of the Congregational Church, the Village of Hersey still looked lush and green as new growth peppered the hills. Up close it was evident most of the terrain was not fit for farming, though many still spent their hard-earned money trying to cultivate the hilly, inhospitable ground, eventually giving in to hard reality and finally giving up. The land around Hersey was meant to be what it had always been -- hills of white pine, tamarack and scrub oak -- home to white tail deer, raccoons, coyotes and opossum.

In 1917, Hersey had only one automobile and no telephones. Autos streamed by, but time forgot the small village in its quiet, out of the way corner of the world. People still depended on telegraph and the Big Rapids or Reed City newspapers for information about the world. Some young men left the area for the money Mr. Ford was paying his workers -- an unheard of $5.00 a day -- more than twice the normal automotive wage. But most came home again, unhappy in a city without two rivers enfolding it and bereft of anyone who'd call you by your given name or people who would offer you water when you walked by on a hot, dusty day.

News of the war was a dark cloud hanging over the village. When the Lusitania was sunk by a German U-boat in 1915, every adult expected to contribute to the war effort in some way. When the call finally came in April of 1917, it had been a fact of life for a long, long time. In May, conscription became a reality, and men began to leave the hills of Hersey for those of Europe. Women began to enter the work force, and the world changed.

Eventually, war ends and there is peace, but peace comes in many forms; when there is no war; when loved ones are near and well; when you become comfortable with your past; when the present is cause for a steady heartbeat; when you leave your future up to karma and stop fighting it. Or, when you forge your future and accept what you've made even though it doesn't look like what you envisioned.

Chapter One

Fall 1916

Kate rolled over, her eyes still closed in a drowsy half-sleep. When she stretched, her foot came up against a hairy leg and she froze. There was a man in her bed! When she opened her eyes, she saw Mel and remembered. How many times would she wake, scare herself, and then smile thinking of the night before? How many times would her mind play tricks making her think she still slept alone in her small bed at the cabin?

It had been a month, and she still awoke with a start, sensing someone in her bed. His hefty frame took up much of it, and she frequently shoved him with a foot against his hip just for the fun of it. He wasn't really taking up too much space, but he didn't know that.

"Will you give a girl some room?" she complained with a glint in her eye.

Before he fully woke and was aware, he moved over to lie on the edge, barely hanging on. He knew he was large and was afraid of rolling on her and breaking something. When she had maneuvered him far enough, Kate gave a gentle little push and Mel landed on the floor with a loud thump and a groan.

"What?" she asked, wide eyed when he peeked over the mattress at her, accusation in his eyes. "What's the matter? What are you doing down there?"

Mel jumped onto the bed, pinned her to the mattress and kissed her soundly. "Your punishment, my dear, for shoving me out of bed. While I was still asleep, no less." He kissed her again, sliding his lips down her neck as she struggled in mock distress. "For shame," he chastised.

"I didn't do anything. You must have been dreaming and fell out of bed," she responded, her eyes clear and falsely innocent.

"If I'm dreaming, I don't want to wake up. You're here and I'm happy."

"What a sweet talker." Kate's arms wrapped around his neck and pulled him closer. They were married in September, and Mel not only took on a wife after more than forty years as a bachelor, but he opened his arms to her four daughters as well. He'd loved Kate his entire life, and she wondered what she had ever done to deserve this wonderful man.

Many moments later, he smacked her bottom as he lifted his long body out of bed. Kate smelled fresh coffee brewing, the unmistakable scent of bacon wafting up the stairs, and heard the sounds of Mel's mother, Laura, moving about in the kitchen. She'd have breakfast done by the time they got downstairs as she had been doing for her son his entire life.

Mel's father died many, many years before, and after his brothers and sisters married and moved on, it was Mel and his mother, together. He worked the farm, and Laura kept the house. Theirs was a companionable relationship, respectful and loving. It may have been lonely at times, but it was easy and quiet.

Now the house also held Kate, three of her four daughters, and two dogs. Well, one wolf and one dog. Wolf disliked references to himself as a dog.

Kate snuggled back on her pillow and watched Mel splash water on his face and neck. She admired his tall, muscled frame, still strong in his forties, still handsome with his sun weathered skin. He grinned at her in the mirror, not minding that she was openly admiring him. Liking it very much, in fact.

"You look like a Cheshire cat," he said with a satisfied smirk.

"I feel like one, and it's nice, but I'm coming. I'm getting up," she said with a moan and a decidedly catlike stretch, then throwing the covers off.

2

He strode over and yanked them back up to her chin. "Stay in bed if you want. Sleep. You've earned a rest."

"I have children to feed, remember?"

"Yes, and I have a mother just dying to be a grandma to them."

"I'll be down in a few minutes," she told him.

When Mel left the room, Wolf bounded into it and onto the bed. He wasn't happy about being relegated to the hallway outside the door since he'd always slept by Kate's side, and any morning he could find her still in bed he would leap on it to stand over her with his nose in her face and one brown eye rolling in clarification of his discontent. He had two distinctly different colored eyes: one soft brown, one devilish, lupine blue.

"Get down you great oaf," she said with a groan. "I still love you."

Wolf moved off the bed slowly and turned back with a doubting look. 'I'm not sure I believe you. Prove it.'

"We'll go to the cabin today. Would you like to go see Harley?"

A single thump of his thick silvery tail accepted her offer.

Kate brushed her long, still blonde tresses and tied them back with a ribbon, washed her face and dressed, ready for the day.

"Let's go, Wolf."

In the kitchen, Laura was frying potatoes, and Jeannie was helping. Kate poured a cup of coffee and offered to help but was refused, as usual.

"Sit, Kate. This is my pleasure, really. Just talk with me a bit."

It felt odd to sit there idle, but she had grown accustomed to it in the last month. Laura really seemed to enjoy the rhythm of her morning chores and the company Kate and the girls provided. Her moves were mechanical and effortless, and Kate would likely be in the way if she insisted on helping.

She looked around the neat room and at copper-haired, ten-year old Jeannie, Kate's youngest daughter, who had

3

attached herself to Mel's mother soon after they'd moved in. If Kate couldn't find Jeannie, she only had to look for Laura to find her daughter hovering nearby. Jeannie would be with her or with the chickens and calves, her second loves. Her first love was the huge fur ball she called Poochie, who followed her around with blind love and devotion only a mutt can give.

It was a peaceful kitchen with yellow walls and bright chintz curtains, a place where you wanted to be, to gather in with your family and friends. Through the large windows over the sink, Kate saw a bright sun rising, and trees were more golden than red as the end of October rolled near. Kate thought of fall at the cabin and could smell wood smoke coming from the hearth and the earthy scent of damp forest.

"If I can help, please let me. I'm used to being busy," Kate said, sipping her coffee and watching Jeannie emulate Laura by wrapping the ties of her apron around her waist and knotting them in front.

"I know you are, Kate. It's a perfect time for you to take a little break. Enjoy it. You've worked so hard all these years."

"So have you, Mrs. Bronson."

Laura turned to Kate. "When are you going to stop calling me Mrs. Bronson? Jeannie already calls me Grandma. Don't you, Grandchild?" she asked, and sunshine crossed her face as she glanced at Jeannie. "What a gift you are," she told her.

"I'm a gift." Jeannie giggled. "Wait til I tell Harley."

Kate laughed. "You guys and your alter egos. Urchin, Spinner, Angel, Cookie. How many things are you two?"

"We're lots of things. Just ask Dr. Crow."

John Crow was the doctor who had healed Jeannie's leg after it had been crushed by an automobile and subsequently grew infected. He'd told her she was a tough cookie, and Jeannie thought he had called her a real cookie, like oatmeal or molasses. Cookie stuck, along with the many names Harley had given her and others had given Harley. It was a game they all played.

"But I think it's Kat who is the urchin," Kate mused. "Where is she, by the way? I'm sure Becca's with Mel but where is your other sister?"

Jeannie shrugged and gave her mother a blank look. Laura said she hadn't seen her all morning.

"Think I'll go rouse her. It's time she was up and about," Kate said and left the room. Moments later, she returned with a sheet of paper in her hand and a stunned look in her eyes.

"She's gone," Kate said in a voice filled with bewilderment and something close to fear.

"What do you mean, gone?" Laura asked. Confusion and disbelief flooded her face.

"Gone . . . Packed up and left." Opposing thoughts ricocheted in her head, like 'Kat just went to the cabin. That's what her note said. It's only a few miles. Kat knows the area well. Anything could happen to a young woman alone on the road. Anything!'

Kate's thoughts traveled back to when she herself had been accosted, almost raped. Her faithful dog had died trying to protect her. Kate's face went white with the mental vision and she grasped the back of a chair to keep her knees from buckling.

"I've got to go. Watch Jeannie for me, please?"

Laura nodded and Kate fled from the room. She found Mel and Becca in the barn and showed him the note from Kat.

"You want the buggy," he asked, "or just a saddle?"

"Just a saddle. Kat and I can ride double coming home."

"You want me to go?"

"No. Keep an eye on Becca and Jeannie for me, please."

"You're sure?" he asked, knowing how much Kate was trying not to be afraid. He put his arm around her shoulder and squeezed. "She's fine, Kate. You know that. She's probably already at the cabin having breakfast with Harley."

Kate nodded, knowing he was right, but her knees still felt rubbery. "Saddle your mare for me, please? She's fast." She'd left her own mare, Kitty, with Harley so he could go back and forth between the cabin, town and Mel's farm. He

5

still schooled the girls and spent time with Ellen at her house and with Verna at the saloon in Hersey.

"Let's go, Wolf," she called as she climbed on the mare.

Wolf ran ahead a bit but kept turning back to check on her, making sure she was following and safe. When she rode into the clearing where the cabin sat in the middle of a white pine forest, Kate felt her breathing slow and a sense of peace enfold her. Justified or not, the world felt better when she was there. Magnified problems became minute, petty irritants drifted away on earth scented breeze.

The door to the cabin stood open, and Harley was in the opening with an arm around Kat's shoulder. He was smiling, but Kat was watching warily, wondering if trouble was about to descend.

"Welcome," Harley said. "Coffee?"

Wolf squeezed by them, checked out the corners, and quickly curled up in front of the hearth, his normal place.

"Please. Thank you, Harley. Sit, Kat. We need to talk."

"I'm not going back," Kat said with quiet defiance. She shook her head slowly back and forth in emphasis, and her straight, honey blonde hair swung with the movement. Kat wasn't a tiny girl; at fifteen she was already taller than Kate. She was all lean muscle and tanned from the summer outdoors. She had pronounced cheek bones and blue eyes which sometimes turned green. Kate frequently wondered where Kat had gotten the dark lashes and coffee colored brows setting off blue-green eyes. She was striking to look at, and it was enhanced by her enigmatic demeanor.

"Why?" Kate asked, wondering how she had missed clues to what was going on with Kat. "What's so wrong about being at the farm?"

She was trying hard to understand her daughter. Kat was different than the other girls. But truthfully, each one was different from the rest. Each was unique, though Kat was the most unusual; pragmatic, terse, honest to a fault, and blissfully unselfconscious. She had a kinship with the woods and preferred being there alone. It wasn't dislike for her family. She loved her sisters and the rest of her family, but she was more at home in the woods. The forest was her family, and she was happiest in it. She was also happiest near Harley.

"Nothing. I just want to live here," Kat said.

"But we live at the farm now, Kat," her mother said gently.

"No," Kat said, calmly but firmly. "You do."

Kate pursed her lips, making an effort not to say anything she'd regret, not to be frustrated with her daughter, but it was difficult. "We need to be together, Kat. Families live together."

"Not always. Rachel doesn't live with us. Hasn't for a long time."

That was true. Rachel, the oldest of her daughters, had gone to take care of Eldon Woodward after he fell and broke his leg. She'd stayed on after he recuperated because he needed help and he enjoyed her youthful company. She also loved living there -- in town -- in his beautiful home.

Kate didn't know how to respond, so most of what came out was stilted half-nonsense. "I'm trying to be fair, Kat. But help me here. I want what's best, but I don't want to lose you."

"I'm not lost, Ma. I'm right here. Harley's going to teach me about forest herbs, where to find them in the woods. I want to learn. Dr. Crow is going to teach me how to use them to help heal."

Kate was stunned and it showed on her face. She looked up at Harley who stood leaning against the cupboard. He shrugged and nodded a bit, acknowledging Kat had asked him about the herbs.

"What do you know about this Harley?"

"Kat asked if I was familiar with medicinal herbs, and I told her I knew a bit. I could identify them and distinguish between healing herbs and poison or harmless ones."

"Did you know about her coming here today?"

He shook his head. "But if she wants to stay, that would be fine with me. You must know that, Kate."

"I didn't leave the room," Kat said, listening to them talk around her.

Kate gave a begrudging little smile and lifted her hands in defeat. "Okay. For now." She was not giving up on having her family all together. She told both of them it was temporary, a trial.

"And there are rules," she added quickly. "You need to ride over once each week, to spend the day with us, and you must not walk the roads alone in the dark. Ever."

"Ma, that's silly."

"Which? The visiting or the walking?"

"The walking . . . I'm not afraid of the dark."

"I mean it, Kat, or the deal is off."

"Okay. Deal," Kat said, and a real smile lit her face. She got up and gave her mother a rare spontaneous hug. "I'm going to unpack."

Kate sat back, stunned at what she'd agreed to. She looked around the room at what had been her home for so many years. It still felt like it.

She'd found the cabin when she was a young woman, when it was covered with vines and the door hung from one hinge, when mice and spiders and who knows what else nested there. She had cleaned and repaired it, found solitude there with her dog, Bug. It was where she had lived with Mark, raised her daughters for several years, grieved over Mark's death, and learned to love again.

She understood Kat's feelings about the place. She loved it, too. When she moved to the farm with Mel, she'd been happy Harley was going to live here and take care of it, keep the woods and critters from encroaching again.

She noticed the suit hanging on a peg by the door. The clothes had always been there, a reminder. She always assumed they belonged to the man who owned the place. Kate had taken care of them for twenty years -- in case he came back. It was her acknowledgement she didn't really own the cabin. It belonged to someone else.

Her feelings were mixed. She was losing Kat to the woods. A small part of her wanted to live here, too, and it made her feel guilty. How would she ever explain to anyone she'd prefer to live in the tiny forest cabin than in Mel's six-bedroom farm house? She couldn't explain it to herself. She would have to adjust, learn to love Mel's house. He was worth it, many times over.

She drank coffee with Harley and then went to Kat's room before she left. It was the same small room she'd used before they moved to Big Rapids, one they had added onto the cabin's original two.

"You could use the bigger room, Kat. No one else is using it."

"This is fine. I like mine."

Silence lingered, not uncomfortable, but feeling like more might be said if they waited a moment. Kat looked at her mother with something approaching maternity.

"It's gonna be alright, you know," she said.

"Yes. I know. You're right."

After a moment, they walked out together. Kate hugged her daughter, and Harley watched from the cabin window. Her eyes were strangely dry, and Kate wondered why when so many feelings were running rampant through her. Shouldn't she be crying? Shouldn't she be desperately unhappy to leave Kat?

"Damn!" she spouted and then added, "sorry."

"No, you're not, Ma," Kat murmured, having heard her mother apologize for swearing her entire life.

"Yes. You're right again. I'm not," Kate said, grinning finally and believing her words this time. "This is really what you want?"

"It is."

Kate threw an unladylike leg over the saddle, waved to Harley, and called to Wolf.

"I'll see you later for Becca and Jeannie's lessons," he shouted from the doorway.

Kate nodded and kicked the mare gently. She let the horse find the way home -- she knew it well -- while Kate tried to comprehend the events leading her to this place. She suddenly remembered John Crow's name. 'How had he come to be a part of this?' She whipped the mare around and galloped back into the clearing, Wolf following with eye rolls over her strange behavior. 'We were just here, Kate.'

Both Harley and Kat came out to meet her.

"What does John Crow have to do with this?"

Kat gave a sigh and explained. "I watched him while he tended to Jeannie, and we talked about herbal medicines."

"And?" Kate prodded.

"I asked him to teach me, and he said okay."

"That's it? Just -- Okay, I'll teach you?" Kate asked, still trying to grasp all of the morning's new knowledge.

Kat nodded and Kate sat on the horse befuddled, unsure what to say next. 'Aaarrrgh!' came to mind. What she said was, "That's nice. Can we talk about this later?"

Kat nodded again, and Kate rode off. Still dry eyed. She even laughed. "It's a good day, isn't it?" she said to the doe ambling down the lane in front of her. It turned its head to look back at Kate, moved off to the side a bit, and nibbled at grass while it waited for her to pass by.

"Do you have children?" Kate asked as she drew near.

'Sure, one or two each year,' the doe responded.

"Girls are a problem, aren't they?"

The doe gave her a knowing look and went back to grazing.

"Right. I speak whitetail, now," Kate said.

Wolf gave her the second eye roll of the morning.

No one was in the barn when she unsaddled the mare. She took her time, brushed her down and rewarded her service with fresh oats. When Kate walked in, they were all at the kitchen table and looked up expectantly, waiting to see Kat follow her into the room. Mel got up to fix her a cup of coffee and pulled out a chair.

"Sit. Tell us what's going on," he said, concerned Kat was nowhere in sight.

Kate looked at the faces around her, felt their various worries and fears. She smiled to let them know she was alright with what they were about to learn, and she was.

"Kat is going to live at the cabin with Harley, at least for a while. It's where she needs to be."

Becca and Jeannie accepted the news without distress or any obvious unease, like they'd been expecting it.

"She'll come with Harley for lessons, won't she?" Becca asked.

Kate laughed because she hadn't even considered Kat's schooling. "Dummy," she said out loud, then added, "Not you, Becca. Me. I hadn't thought of that. You're a smart girl."

Mel looked like he was the least accepting of the arrangement. He had pushed back his chair and was looking at them carefully. One by one, as if he could read their minds if he stared really hard.

Becca and Jeannie had heard enough. They knew their sister was in good hands with Harley. Satisfied with the news, they ran outside eager to pounce into the orange and yellow leaves turned into crisp, colorful piles. Laura recognized it was time to leave, too, and made an excuse to follow the girls.

"Do you want to tell me what this is all about? Does Kat hate me -- or living here, at the farm? Did I do something?" Mel asked. Hurt had become the color of his eyes.

Kate covered his hand with hers. Mel didn't deserve to be injured by the family he'd been so good to.

He was there for them when Mark died. He helped them survive afterwards even against Kate's determined desire to do it all by herself. He had given much to them over the years and asked for nothing in return. It pained her to see his uncertainty now.

"This is most definitely not about you, Mel. You have to accept my words. Kat needs to be near the forest. She feels out of place here."

"Out of place among her family, people who love her?" he questioned.

"No. That isn't right," she argued with herself. "She isn't out of place here. She is in place there. In the woods. Like you are with your cows."

"I see. Yes . . . I do. I understand."

Kate nodded. "She knows she can see us whenever she wants, but she's happier there. She promised to spend time with us -- and she'll be here for lessons with her sisters."

"Are you alright with this?"

"Strangely enough, I think I am. As long as I know Kat is happy, not lonely for us and nearby, I'm okay. She said she wants to learn about herbs and healing, and both Harley and John Crow were going to teach her."

This time, Mel looked at Kate like she had lost her mind.

"Really," Kate responded quickly. "That's as much as I know for now, but it's what both Harley and Kat said. I don't know when Kat talked to Dr. Crow, but he has apparently agreed."

"Well, if you're okay, I'm okay. You really are, right?" Mel asked again.

Kate nodded and Mel got out of his chair, kissed the top of her head and gave her a hug. He stood behind her chair for a moment pondering his step daughters. Becca was the one he thought he understood because she was a farmer at her core, in her heart. She loved his cows like he did. The rest of the girls were complete mysteries.

"I'm going back to the barn to finish chores. The girls there are pretty simple."

Later in the day, Harley drove up in Kate's old buggy, and Kat was with him. Kate's eyebrows lifted when she saw her, and hope grew thinking Kat had changed her mind about living at the cabin. It was soon squelched when Kat said she was collecting her things. She couldn't carry everything with her when she'd left.

Becca and Jeannie had their lessons and Kat gathered her things and put them in the buggy. Kate followed her out.

"Kat, I'm curious about something. When did you talk with Dr. Crow about herbal medicine?"

"When he came for your wedding."

"Hmmm. I didn't know you were interested. How will that work with him in Big Rapids and you here?"

"Harley will collect herbs with me. He has knowledge of the plants. Then Dr. Crow will come show us what to do with them."

Kate nodded, but she didn't really see how it could be that simple and said so.

"It won't happen all at once, Ma. Stuff doesn't all grow at the same time, and some of the preserving processes are long."

"This is really nice of him to do, Kat."

"Well, I'll go to Big Rapids sometimes, too."

"Not alone, Kat. Never alone. Promise me."

"Well, maybe I'll find me a wolf," Kat said with a wry, little smile.

Kate wondered where this young *woman* had come from! It was like talking to a strange adult; trying to get them to do what you tell them. Just because you tell them.

Kat watched her struggle and let her because in the end there wasn't anything else to do. She knew her mother well. She'd chafe at her inability to make something happen, stomp her foot, swear, apologize for swearing and move on.

"Damn, Kat! I don't know about all this," she said, kicking at the buggy wheel. "Sorry."

Kat grinned again and knew they were more than halfway there.

Jack Bay rode in as Kat and Harley were preparing to leave and Laura talked them all into staying for milk or coffee and cookies. Laura's molasses cookies were hard to refuse, and Harley rubbed his big belly with glee when she brought them out.

"You make me a happy man, Mrs. Bronson," he told her, his cherubic smile lighting up the room.

"It's Laura, Harley. Please, call me Laura, and I would bet you've not been anything but happy a day in your life."

"That's true. I'm a happy man. In fact, happiness can be a way of life if you choose to make it that way. I'd tell you more about it, but I see Kate's eyes warning me, and I don't have any moonshine in my hand."

"Since when did that ever stop you, Harley?" Jack teased.

Jack Bay was Kate's brother-in-law and was dark, slender elegance. He brought a shadowy past with him from Boston where he left a legal practice to swing an axe in the woods. He and Mark had been like brothers for a variety of reasons, but mostly because they both came from backgrounds described as questionable. Their past was a bond. No one but Mark knew why Jack had quit his practice and left the east coast. He kept his personal information to himself, and his dark eyes and menacing brows discouraged questions.

Jack had not strayed far from Kate after Mark's death, and being near Jack had always felt good to her, familiar and loving. He helped her through many dark days. He did it without asking permission, so she couldn't refuse.

She didn't get to see him as much since the lumber camp moved to Petoskey, and she'd been hoping he'd find work nearer, maybe hang his lawyer shingle out again.

"What brings you out our way," Kate asked him. "Not that we aren't happy to see you. I miss you."

"Well that's why I'm here, 'cause you miss me," he said with a grin. "I heard you were pining for me."

"Your ego's bigger than you are, Jack!" Mel told him with a playful smack on his back. "What's the news in Hersey? Everybody doing okay?"

"We're all good. Things are getting even hotter in Europe, though. Don't know how much longer we'll stay out of it."

Mel nodded. Most of his corn and wheat had been going across the ocean to feed soldiers, and he tried to keep up with the news. "I heard one of the Jackson boys signed up to fight with the Brits. Got tired of waiting."

Harley shook his head, for once unable to be cheerful or come up with anything to combat the feelings of dread war talk produced.

"I am happy I don't have sons," Kate said, looking at Jeannie and Becca munching their cookies and Kat leaning against the wall watching. "Never thought I'd say that."

"Well, I didn't come out here to make everyone unhappy. I have good news. Your Ma finally said she'd move in with Ruthie and me. We're going to get her things this weekend, if you're in agreement, Kate."

"You're kidding! She finally bent that stiff back of hers? What did you say to change her mind, Jack?"

14

"I used my persuasive charm. She couldn't resist."

They all agreed the move was good. Ellen Hughes was sixty-five and had lived alone for a long time. She had been determined not to be a burden to her children, and Kate wondered if she wasn't well and avoided mentioning it, not wanting to be a problem to anyone. Well, she'd go find out for herself.

"I'll come in and help her pack. Are you moving her on Saturday?"

Jack nodded, said he had to go and went to get hugs from the girls. "Ruthie will be happy to see you all."

Chapter Two

Saturday was a typical cold, late October day. The sky was overcast and teemed with Canadian geese in multiple v-formations heading south. Their honking glee about flying and moving to warmer weather and sunshine spilled over to the shivering earthbound. Kate thought she might like to be going with them as she rubbed her fingers together trying to warm them.

Jeannie climbed into the buggy next to Wolf who claimed the place by Kate, and Poochie gave them big sad eyes for being left behind. Becca had decided to stay at the farm to help Mel, and she called to Poochie, waving from the milking parlor door as they left.

"Ma, I think Becca's crazy wanting to milk cows instead of going to see Grandma and Aunt Ruthie. Oh yeah, and Rachel," she added as an afterthought.

"Well, she does love those cows," Kate said with a laugh and grinning at Jeannie, "most likely more than us."

Jeannie's copper curls were burnished bronze in the dull light. She looked like a ten-year-old pixie with her orange freckles speckling her nose and cheeks and her startling blue eyes alive with fire.

"It's okay, cuz now it's just us, and I like that. Well, us and Wolf. But he's part of us."

When they got to Kate's mother's place, Ellen met them outside and proudly said she had the packing all done. Kate grinned and told herself she should have known. Ellen most likely started ten minutes after she decided to move.

She hugged her mother, reflecting again about how small her frame felt. Each year she was more slender, more fragile. The hand on Ellen's shoulder rested on more bone than flesh.

"You could have waited for my help, Ma," Kate told her, not really scolding but letting her know she wanted to lend a hand if Ellen would take it.

"I didn't want help, Kate. I needed to do this myself. You, of all people, should know what that's like," Ellen said, and a tilt of her head said even more. Her words were gentle but strong and pushed Kate to move forward.

Kate walked into the kitchen and was shocked by its stark barrenness. It was a wasteland, empty of life; the counter canisters Ellen left out for quick use had vanished. Knickknacks, prized and lovingly cared for treasures, were gone. No towel was carefully folded and hung to dry, no cookie jar sat in its special corner. The absence of possessions came in like a flash, like a bolt of lightning, and she stopped. Ellen was behind and bumped into her.

"What are you doing, girl? You all of a sudden quit moving and I crashed into you."

"Sorry Ma. It was just . . . I saw . . . well I didn't see anything that I was expecting to see. It startled me. It looks . . . strange, so empty."

"It does, doesn't it," Ellen said, an inscrutable look crowding her smile. Kate wasn't sure how to read it. Didn't really want to know what it said, but knew her mother was tougher than she was; Ellen's strength was clear.

Jeannie pushed past them and spun around in the middle of the room. She ran up to the loft and then back down. "Where is everything?" she asked, concern drawing a frown on her face.

"It's packed up, Jeannie, ready to go to your Aunt Ruthie's house where I'm going to live now."

"Why? Why don't you stay here? I like you living here. Don't leave," Jeannie said, more honest in her questions and demands than either her mother or grandmother. They were burdened by old memories and new needs.

"Well, I liked it, too, but it's time to move."

Kate went to her mother and put an arm around her shoulder. "I liked it, too, Ma. We all did."

"Yes, we did!" Harley said from the open doorway. "Wow! You've been a busy girl. Thought I'd come help but you beat me."

Ellen gave Kat a big hug and Harley a real smile. He and Ellen had formed a remarkable relationship from the beginning when she made him take off his clothes and wait in a sheet for her to wash and dry them. He sat on the steps wrapped totally in white, his golden curls shining in the sunlight and told her family Ellen couldn't wait to get him out of his clothes. He neglected to say it was because they were filthy and the only ones he owned.

As their friendship grew, he teased her into spiritual discussions, and they spent delightful hours at her kitchen table lightly arguing. Harley could get away with saying things to Ellen no one else could. She accepted it from him with a deceptive frown.

"You can help, Harley. All those boxes need to be hauled to Ruthie's and up her stairs to the spare room." She pointed to the far wall which was lined with neatly stacked boxes, all labeled and tied with twine.

"Are you all ready, then?" he asked. "Everything is packed?"

"Everything I need or want," she said curtly.

"You're sure?" he prodded.

"Yes, you old fool. I told you; I have everything. What's wrong with you?"

"Ma, are you alright?" Kate asked, concerned about Ellen's brusque behavior towards her old friend.

Kat sat on a box shaking her head at them. She knew what Harley was getting at, probably before he did.

"Well, since I was a might parched from the long drive, and since this is kind of a momentous occasion and could use a meaningful toast, I thought maybe a jug of Will's moonshine might still be sitting around in a cupboard. Especially since that isn't something you'd need or want."

Ellen cuffed the back of his head and grumbled under her chuckle.

"You old coot. It's right here," she said, and went to the cupboard to retrieve the jug. "I knew we'd need it left out."

Harley took it from her and held it with reverence. "Thank you my friend," he said and began another of his infamously long toasts.

"Here's to the times we've all had in this house, the heartwarming and the heartbreaking, and here's to walking bravely into the future and the change it brings, and . . ."

Ellen's foot tapped on the bare wood floor, a staccato sound echoing in the empty room, and was loud enough to halt the flow of Harley's words. Kate laughed at the wounded look on his face and her mother's elevated eyebrows.

"Mrs. Hughes, are you trying to tell me something? I was coming to the important stuff."

"You just love the sound of your own voice, Harley Benton," she responded, teasing but knowing it was at least partly true. Maybe mostly.

Harley continued, "And here's to making this move out of love, because you know that's what it is." He sipped and then passed the jug to Ellen who to Kate's surprise held the opening to her lips and took a healthy swallow.

"Wow, Ma. You didn't even choke on it. Good for you."

Kate sipped, too, as they sat at the table Harley made for them years ago and reminisced. They passed the jug a couple more times, talked about special moments they each held dear and looked around at empty walls that had held such vast amounts of living.

Kate had first laid eyes on Mark, her first love, in this house and had accidently dumped water on him in this very spot. She'd eavesdropped on her parents' conversations when they sat here talking by lamplight, and she lay in the loft above them. Ellen had dressed her husband for his funeral as he lay on this table. Kate had done the same for Mark.

Ellen ran her hand over the smooth, polished surface as she thought about the most difficult time in her life.

"I love this table, Harley. It has served us well."

"It holds many memories in its boards, and you've treated it well. It looks as good as the day it came into this house." Harley paused, thinking. "Where will it go? Can it fit in Jack and Ruthie's kitchen?" he asked.

When Ellen shook her head, Harley said, "Well, how about this? It can go to the cabin. There's room and Kat and I will take excellent care of it, just as if you were doing it yourself. What do you think?"

Ellen beamed. "That's a wonderful idea! What do you mean by you and Kat?"

Kate gave him a 'Not today, Harley, please' look. He stumbled a bit in explanation but was able to satisfy Ellen. They loaded the boxes into both buggies and headed to Jack and Ruthie's house. Harley, with permission, brought the jug so he could propose an appropriate toast once they were finished unloading and had things in their proper places.

It was evident Ruthie was excited to see them all; her cheeks were flushed and her eyes sparkled. Jack watched her animated chattering and was happy for her. When it ran down, Jack asked if they wanted to see Ellen's rooms.

"Rooms?" Ellen asked, "as in plural?"

Jack nodded. "We have plenty, and I think you'll like having a space of your own, more than just a bedroom. Come on. I'll show you."

Upstairs were two good sized rooms, freshly painted in pale yellow. In the center of each were colorful and welcoming braided rugs.

"I took the furniture out, Ellen, because I thought you'd want your own here. I hope I was correct," Jack said.

Ellen's face lit up in surprise. "That is wonderful! It's perfect, and I thank you so much. I'll feel happy with my own things."

"In fact, I've borrowed Mel's wagon to bring your stuff over. It's right outside. I'll go now if that's alright with you and then you can start putting your stuff away."

Ellen went to Jack and gave him a huge hug. "You've made an old woman happy," she told him.

Jack and Harley hauled the furniture she'd told them to bring while Kat, Kate and Ruthie hauled the boxes upstairs. It was afternoon before they were finished unpacking, and

Ruthie was putting the vegetables in with her pot roast when Mel strolled in with Becca.

"I didn't know you were coming," Kate said in surprise.

"I didn't know either til Jack showed up to borrow the wagon right after you left. I'm surprised you didn't pass each other on the road."

"Good timing. You're a little late for the work," Jack teased.

"Well, I got to thinking . . . hmmm . . . one chubby old man and one weak, scrawny one . . . I'd better come along and get the job done. No telling how long it will take them if I don't."

"Who're you kidding?" Harley asked. "You knew I was about to make a toast and you couldn't resist. You couldn't stay away."

Mel groaned and turned as if to leave. He cupped a hand to his ear. "I think I hear my mother calling me."

But Ellen reached up and grabbed his ear, pulling him further into the room by his ear lobe. "No you don't, Son-in-law. This is my celebration and you're staying." When she released him, she crossed her arms with a satisfied smirk on her face. "Can't tell you how long I've wanted to do that."

Kate sent the girls to get Rachel, and Ruthie brought out glasses and the wine she and Jack had made when wild strawberries were plentiful last June. She fixed lemonade for the girls and set it all out on a lace tablecloth in the dining room. She moved a vase with dried flowers to the center of the table and put out napkins. It looked pretty, and she was obviously excited and proud to have everyone in her home.

Kate looked harder at her sister and recognized how much hosting this gathering meant, how important it was to have her mother living in her home. Jack put his arm around Ruthie and held her still for a moment.

"You're like a hummingbird. It's all good. Let it be," he said gently.

"I want it perfect," she responded with a nervous smile.

When the girls came back with Rachel, they had Verna with them. Kat had refused to go by the saloon without running in to get Verna. If they were having a family gathering, Verna was going to be there, too.

"Kat went in the saloon?" Ellen shouted over the greetings.

"She did," Verna answered, pride puffing her chest.

Kate refused to look at her mother, Kat ignored them both, and Ellen gracefully let it go. Ruthie gave each of the girls a glass of lemonade and Jack poured wine for the ladies and himself. Harley held the jug out at arm's length in ceremonial pose, waiting for quiet, intense anticipation a fire in his eyes.

Jack sidled up to him, grinning. "You live for these moments, don't you?" he asked, only half joking.

"No. Living is what brings me to these moments." Harley looked around the room at his adopted family, and a thought occurred to him. Out of all of them, only Ellen, Kate and Ruthie were at the Hughes house when Mark first brought him there. And that's what he said.

"Here's to the three of you who greeted this hobo on my first day in town. Ellen was one of those and she created the other two, Kate and Ruthie. A lot of living has, as always, brought change."

A low groan interfered with Harley's words, and Ellen scowled. "Don't interrupt," she scolded. "Harley is saying something."

"Has he brainwashed you, Mother?" Ruthie kidded.

Harley cleared his throat. "As I was saying, a lot of living has turned these three, Ellen, Kate and Ruthie, into the rest of us here today. A genesis has occurred. It's apparent that Ellen is the creator of all who stand before this aforementioned hobo." He turned to Ellen and raised the jug towards her. "Here's to Ellen, the creator."

"That's blasphemous, Harley, and you know it," Ellen said. "I should have let them interrupt you."

"And you know I don't blaspheme, my dear Ellen. You created those two girls and that led to this. And . . ."

"Drink, damn it!" Kate said, then added, "Sorry." This time she meant it because the look her mother gave her made her feel like a girl again, and she'd been bad. She took a sip of wine to cover it, and breathed again when she could, when Ellen quit looking at her.

More toasts were made, and they all went to see Ellen's new living quarters. The rooms were cozy and familiar with her pictures on the walls and her personal treasures displayed on the tables and dressers. "I'll be happy here," she said to them all, "so please don't worry about me."

Ruthie had food out and the table set. Not everyone could sit around the table, but they either stood or took their plates to the living room to eat. Kate found a space next to Rachel on the settee in the living room and settled in.

"How are things at Eldon's? Is he doing well in this chilly weather?" Kate asked. "Do you need some help bringing in a supply of wood?"

"We're doing fine."

"I still miss you, Rachel. You know you could have your own room at the farm if you wanted," Kate said softly so others wouldn't hear.

"Mother, I don't. Sorry, but you know that." Rachel pushed her food around on the plate, tried a bite, and then pushed it around some more.

"Are you feeling all right?" Kate asked, thinking her daughter didn't seem herself, and she looked peaked. "Do you have a bit of a bug?"

"I'm just not hungry, lately."

Kate ate and tried to make small talk, disturbed. Having a conversation with her child shouldn't be so difficult. She continued to try and said, "How long have you been not hungry? More than just today?"

"A couple of weeks. I just have a sick stomach. That's all."

"Well, if it's been that long, I think you should see a doctor. I'll come in tomorrow and take you."

"No, I'll be fine. Don't do that."

Kate nodded, not knowing what else to do or say. When dinner was finished, the girls took care of the kitchen while the adults either sat in the living room or took a walk in the cold, evening air. Kate, Wolf, Mel and Harley set out to walk

Verna home. On the way, Harley handed Verna off to Mel and took Kate's arm.

"I want your woman for a few minutes, Mister," he said to Mel, letting them walk a few steps ahead.

"How's everything with Rachel?" Harley asked.

"Other than not feeling up to snuff, she's okay. It's strange that we can't have a conversation anymore though. I hate it."

"What do you mean by not up to snuff?"

"Not hungry. Feeling sickish, I guess."

Harley puckered his face up, scrunching his eyes in thought. But he wasn't diagnosing Rachel's illness. He was wondering how to tell Kate her daughter was pregnant. She had all the signs, and he was surprised no one else could see them.

When they neared the saloon, he asked Mel to go on in with Verna for a minute. Mel questioned with his eyes, but did what he was asked after getting a nod from Kate.

Harley was quiet for a moment, waiting for insight on how to begin, and Kate waited patiently. Then he took a deep breath.

"What I'm going to tell you, you're not going to like, will shock you, and might not even be true, but I think it is. Do you want to hear?"

Kate stepped back and looked involuntarily for Mel -- for support, sensing without knowing that she didn't want to do this alone anymore. But for the moment, she had to and she nodded. Wolf moved against her leg, alert to her distress.

"Then here it is because there is no gentle way to say this. I believe Rachel is with child."

Kate crossed her arms and leaned back against the saloon. She stared at Harley, like a stranger who had told her a horrible joke.

She stood there breathing, but she didn't know how because there wasn't any air in her chest, only a deep, painful drumming. Harley put his hands on her shoulders and told her to stay where she was. He went into the saloon and came out with a tiny glass filled with brown liquid.

"Sip," he said. "I'm so sorry."

Kate sipped and felt heat slide down her throat, land in her belly and lie there like molten lava. She felt like she wanted to throw up. Maybe she had what Rachel had. Maybe they were both sick. When she sipped again, it warmed her and brought her back to her senses. She wasn't sick and neither was Rachel.

"Oh, my God," Kate said. "You're right. She is. Why didn't I see it?"

"Because she's your little girl. Because you didn't want to."

"Oh, Harley, what are we going to do? How could this happen?" Her eyes filled and tears spilled, flowing down her cheeks, icy streams in the frigid night.

Harley's heart broke watching her. She had been dealt a bad hand for too many years, and she'd been strong through it all. It didn't seem fair to pile on more, especially when she had turned the corner toward a safe and sweeter life. A lump grew in his throat the size of an apple making it impossible for him to respond to her questions. His eyes watered, and he let the tears fall after he'd taken Kate in his arms and held her there. They slid down his face privately.

He breathed deeply and then held Kate at arm's length, looking directly in her eyes.

"You've never been in a saloon before, have you?" he asked.

Kate looked at him like he'd forgotten what he'd just told her.

"Harley, you know I haven't," she said, irritated by the question.

"But you've always wanted to, haven't you?"

Kate nodded, still wondering if he'd lost his mind.

He held his arm out to her and then patted her hand when she took it. She didn't have a clue what he was doing, but she trusted him.

"Let's go."

They stepped together through the door of the saloon, and the men, many whom Kate knew, turned to see who was coming in. There were gasps, sharp little intakes of breath, when they recognized Kate. She walked boldly and determinedly up to the bar where Mel and Verna were standing, silently watching. A quizzical smile lifted Mel's lips as he raised his glass to her.

"Congratulations," he said. "You've finally done it."

Verna said, "Damn, good for you!"

The barman came and asked what they'd like to drink, and Kate lifted her shoulders in confusion. "I don't know."

"Do you have any sherry?" Harley asked. When the man nodded, Harley told him they'd each have one.

After the drinks came, they sipped silently, everyone but Harley wondering what was going on. When they could stand it no longer, Verna asked.

Harley said, "We needed a bit of a lift, and this was just the ticket. We all need to do things we've set aside for another day. We say *someday I want to . . .* Well, at some point in time that day has to come. Today's the day for having a drink at Sadie's Saloon."

Sadie, herself, came from the back and waddled over to the group. She hugged Mel and whispered in his ear, nodded to Verna, hugged Harley, and stood back to stare at Kate. "I knew you'd get here one day. This one's on me," she told the barman.

"Thank you, Sadie," Kate said. She turned and left them to their drinks. Her broad back jiggled with the black fringe she was so fond of wearing. She thought it disguised her multiple rolls.

Mel watched Sadie walk away then looked from Kate to Harley and back again. He knew Kate's face too well. When he tilted his head to look closely at her, it spilled out in a gush of whispered misery.

"Rachel wasn't feeling well, and she wouldn't talk to me or let me take her to the doctor, and then she wasn't eating, and Harley wanted to talk to me . . ." Kate took a deep breath, so deep there was concrete anticipation over the end of it. "And Rachel's pregnant."

Both Verna and Mel backed away from Kate, from her words. Like Rachel's pregnancy was catching, even from a distance or by proxy.

"That doesn't make me a leper. You don't have to move away from me," she said, only half kidding.

Mel collected himself, unsure why he'd stepped back, and put his arm around her.

"Are you sure about this?" he asked.

Kate nodded. "I wasn't, but I am now. Harley is right, and I don't know why I didn't see it like he did."

They talked for awhile, pondering why this had happened and then what to do about it. They sipped their drinks and Kate finally looked around at the interior of the saloon she'd wanted to see since she was a girl pressing her nose against the dusty window to peer in at all the men. She'd longed to be inside, not outside looking in, but a saloon was not for respectable women. 'Damn respectability,' she told herself.

"Well, how do you want to handle this?" Mel asked. "I need to get home for milking. I can take Jeannie and Becca with me. You'll probably want to talk with Rachel before coming home?"

Kate nodded and Harley said, "Why not take Kat with you, too, and I'll wait here for Kate so she won't have to make the ride alone. I'll pick up Kat when I drop off Kate. Does that work for you both?"

Kate nodded again, dreading the conversation with Rachel, wanting to go on pretending this hadn't happened and let it go away, disappear into the night.

It was dark when they left the saloon, and they were quiet on their walk back. Wolf nudged close to Kate's leg again, sensing discord, needing to feel her presence. When they got to Jack and Ruthie's, Mel put his arms around Kate and kissed her softly.

"I'm going to hitch up, and then I'll be in to get the girls. I love you, Kate."

"I love you, too."

Chapter Three

Rachel

They sat on Eldon Woodward's porch swing, shivering in the frosty cold. She came right out with the question because she didn't know how else to proceed, and Rachel denied it. When Kate persisted, it took several minutes before Rachel admitted the truth. She'd been intimate with Charlie for several months, and she wasn't sure, but thought her last period had been about six weeks ago.

Kate tried to hold her daughter's hands, to let her know she would be by her side all the way, but Rachel pulled them away, her back stiff, her face stony.

"Charlie and I will handle it. We'll get married and everything will be wonderful. We'll have a fine house and nice things." Rachel shook her long, dark curls and raised her chin.

"Are you saying Charlie knows he's going to be a father?" Kate asked.

Rachel shook her head. "Not yet. I wasn't even sure, but if you can see it, I probably am."

Kate was stunned at Rachel's casual manner, her lack of any thought or concern about the baby she would have, any feelings of remorse over her actions. Kate thought back to her youth and knew she would have died of embarrassment had she been in a similar situation.

"How will you live? Have you given any thought to that? Charlie works his father's farm. He's a school boy," Kate said, growing stressed with the direction the conversation was taking.

"He'll get a job," she responded, antagonism flooding her tone.

Kate sat back, warning herself to go slowly, to consider Rachel's youth, her innocence. 'You were young once,' she told herself and took a couple of deep breaths.

"You know you don't need to marry. You can have the baby and come live with us. We'll raise the child together."

"Mother! Charlie loves me. We're going to have a wonderful life . . . and we won't be poor," she added.

Kate sighed softly, breathed in slowly. "Have you thought about when you'd like to get married? Soon would be best."

Rachel lit up and looked briefly like a young woman should when thinking about her wedding. "Yes. Will you help? I'll have a white dress and a lace veil. It'll be beautiful."

"Certainly, I'll help," Kate said. "Rachel, you need to talk with Charlie. Perhaps I need to talk with Mr. and Mrs. Tate."

"No! This isn't about you!" Rachel snapped. "I'm not a child. I'll talk with them."

Kate took a few more deep breaths trying to remain calm. She wanted to be helpful, not hurt her child. "Well . . . Then you talk with Charlie in the next day or two, and I'll be back on Tuesday to talk with you. Does that work?"

Rachel nodded, and Kate sat immobile, frozen in indecision. Rachel was living in a dream world, thinking if she wanted it badly enough or said it loudly enough, it would come true. Kate was conflicted and countless thoughts ran through her muddled head.

"I love you very much," Kate said to her daughter's shoulder. "Do you know that?" She could see a flicker of connection in her profile and an imperceptible nod of assent. "I'll see you in a couple of days." She patted her daughter's hand and gave her an unreturned hug.

When she left the porch, Wolf was by her side, and soon Harley came out of the shadows and joined them on the walk back to where the buggy waited. Kate climbed up and onto the seat with a weary body, drained mind, and sorrowed heart. Harley pulled a thick, wool blanket from the bucket in the back and wrapped Kate from head to foot in it as Wolf snuggled close. He clicked to Kitty, and she moved down the road, her old bones creaking in the chilly night. She was happy to be going home.

"Have you been waiting long? Are you frozen?" Kate asked.

"No, I figured you'd be finishing up about now and left Jack and Ruthie's just a few minutes ago. I gather it didn't go as well as you would have liked."

She shook her head. "She's living in a dream world. I don't understand her."

She recounted the conversation briefly, and Harley listened without comment. Kate asked if he'd said anything to the others, and he shook his head. "That's yours and Rachel's to do. I'll be there, of course, if you want or need me."

"You always are, Harley. Thank you."

They rode in silence, both deep in thought, while the stars came out and the moon finally rose to guide them. If Kate chewed her nails, she'd be doing it now, except that would mean taking her hands out of the warm blanket.

She snuggled down deeper and watched her breath frost the wool hovering near her mouth. It would be winter soon. She wondered what winter would be like in Mel's big house. Certainly different than at the cabin where it was sometimes a battle to stay warm, but likely not as cozy either. She hoped she'd find a way to be useful there. She needed to feel worthwhile, like she was contributing. It was hard to be superfluous, unnecessary.

There's too much going on, she thought. First, Kat moves back to the cabin, then Ellen gives up her home and moves in with Ruthie, and now this.

"My brain is mush. I don't want to grow up."

"Too late. You're a big girl now," he said. "You even had a drink in Sadie's! You've wanted to do that since you were -- oh -- probably no more than six. How'd you like it?" he asked, turning his rosy face to her.

Kate gave him a satisfied smirk and nodded solidly. "That was a great idea."

"It was, wasn't it? It won't be long before the whole town will know Kate Hughes Ramey Bronson, twice married, mother of four and former school teacher, was drinking in Sadie's. They'll say they knew you were a hussy all along."

"You're right," she giggled. "They said it before. Wish I could hear them now. Oh well, someone will fill me in on the nasty stuff."

"Agatha Pennington will lead an upright, virtuous, righteous mob to drum you out of town."

"Bring on the multitude, Agatha!" Kate shouted. "I'm ready and waiting."

They pulled up to the house and Harley put his hand on Kate's arm to keep her with him for a moment longer.

"Kat's fine with me, you know. She's happy and doing what she needs to do, so don't you worry about her."

"I know she is, and thank you. For everything. But I do miss her."

At the door, Mel hugged her, kissed her closed eyes and then her lips and propelled her to their room, turning out lights on the way.

Chapter Four

Winter 1916

Kat spent the morning splitting wood and piling it around the corner nearest the door where it would be easy to get to and easy to shovel a path to when the snows came heavy. Kat knew this winter would be a hard one; all the signs she read said so. Acorns hit the ground hard, like a hailstorm, and 'acorn hail' means a harsh winter.

She and Harley took Kitty into the woods and hauled back several seasoned trees, ones that had been down for a couple of years or more and would burn without smoke. Combined with what was left in Kate's woodpile, they thought they had enough to last the winter.

Harley stocked the cupboards with staples and the outside cellar with winter vegetables that would keep well underground. Kat watched it all with a keen eye, wanting to be sure she wasn't taking the food from Harley's mouth by living here. She wouldn't be a drain on him or anybody else.

"You want to go into the woods with me today? Before the snow falls?" she asked, throwing the last piece of wood on the pile.

Harley stretched, put a hand on his back as if holding it would make it feel better. "Sure I do. What are you after?"

"I found some Chinese skullcap."

"How do you know that's what it is?" he asked, testing her a bit.

"It had tiny purplish flowers late in the summer, and it's about three feet high. It looks like a tiny cap where the flowers were."

Harley nodded, impressed with Kat's knowledge. "Lead on. But you know the leaves carry the medicinal properties. What are you going to do with the winter stalks?"

She nodded understanding. "Dig up a root and plant it at the edge of the woods so I can keep an eye on it when it blooms. Maybe test some dry leaves if there are any on the stalk."

"Test? On who?"

She grinned. "Maybe you. It's for aches and pains, like arthritis. I don't have any aches, but you must."

"And why must I?" he said, teasing.

"Because you are older than these hills, and old people have aches and pains . . . and you were holding your back."

"And how old do you think I am, miss?"

Kat studied him, tilted her head to one side and looked him up and down. Harley watched her assess him and was tickled. This no-nonsense daughter of Kate's was nothing if not methodical.

"It's hard to say because you don't have the normal wrinkles, and you have extra body fat."

"Excuse me. I am fat?" he asked, trying out a wounded tone.

"That's not what I said, but . . ." and she started off towards the woods. "Coming?" she called, turning back to look at him briefly, her eyes twinkling.

Harley laughed and trudged off after her. This was their life together. This was one of his joys. Kat had a sharp, inquisitive mind and did not suffer fools lightly. She was determined but moved quietly, tender but seldom showed it, and only spoke when she had something to say. She didn't need much, but she'd take a wolf like her mother's.

She wanted to heal, and she wanted to do it with natural remedies gathered from the woods. It's where she'd always wanted to be since she was a little girl. Years before, Harley had made a trap so she could gather and study insects and small rodents. She'd been doing it steadily ever since. When the girls found wild, wounded or abandoned critters, Jeannie and Becca mothered them, and Kat studied them.

When they were well into the woods, Kat showed him the plant she'd told him about and dug it up after he agreed with her identification. "I think the dried leaves are usable," he said, becoming more involved in the day's activity. "They're probably just not as potent. Do you know it's also used to control asthma and hay fever? But we have no one to try it on."

They walked back, enjoying the sounds of the forest and each other's company. Big, fat flakes began to fall and stayed where they landed, coating their shoulders and the top of their heads. Harley stuck out his tongue to catch them as they fell, and Kat laughed at his antics.

"How come you never grew up?" she asked him.

"Why do you say that, because I catch snowflakes with my tongue?"

"That, and because much of the time you seem like a little kid."

Kat was only half teasing. He was like a boy. But he was also a sage with incomparable knowledge and wisdom, and those who knew him well could never fathom the source.

"Well, Kat, unlike me, you have never been a child. You were born old."

It was her turn to play offended. "Excuse me. Are you calling me old? I'm fifteen."

"Did you call me fat?"

"No. I didn't *call* you anything. Your recollection is faulty."

Harley shook his head. "I have taught you too well, young lady. Now you're a smarty."

He blew the snow from his shoulder into her face, and she laughed.

It was a world of white when they got back to the cabin. They quickly dug a hole at the edge of the woods and planted the Chinese skullcap, pulled off the dried leaves still clinging to the branches and took them into the house with them.

Dinner was a joint affair. They usually cooked and cleaned up together. When they were done, they'd read near the lantern or talk in front of a warm fire in the rocking chairs Kate's father had made for her. Harley thought she would want them with her at the farmhouse, but she declined, saying this was where they belonged. She'd visit them here.

Kat looked good in the rocker. The chair fit her personality, solid and smooth, clean lines, burnished with glowing depth and beauty. Like Kat.

"I'm going to make up a few peppermint fennel tea packets for Rachel for her morning sickness. Lemon balm and chamomile, too, and a lavender and chamomile mix for her bath. She'll probably get them confused and drink her bath mix."

Harley laughed. "That'd be better than me taking a bath in my moonshine. What a waste that would be. How is your sister doing? I haven't seen her in a while."

"Rachel is acting bizarre, crying if you just look at her. John said if she takes a warm bath in lavender and chamomile at night, she'll sleep better."

"Where will you get the herbs?"

"He dropped them off for me at Nestor's. I picked them up the last time we were in town."

Harley was thoughtful. The other girls took the news of Rachel's pregnancy with aplomb, but sometimes it was hard to read this one.

"What do you think about all this, Kat?"

"What? Rachel having a baby?"

Harley nodded, watching her face.

"She's going to have a baby," Kat responded with a shrug of her shoulders.

"Well, I guess it's good she's getting married when she is," Harley said, wanting to know Kat's thoughts on the subject.

"What if she doesn't? What if she has the baby and raises it herself? Women raise kids alone all the time. Look at Ma. She raised four by herself."

Harley considered what she said. Of course Kat was right, but it certainly wasn't the recommended way, and it would be a particularly difficult row to hoe for *this* single mother. "Sometimes it's unavoidable," he told her.

"Well, I wouldn't get married just because I was pregnant. That's dumb."

"I'm inclined to agree with you, Kat."

She was silent for a bit, thoughts evident in the wrinkle of her brow. "Rachel will make a terrible mother," she said.

"And why do you think so?"

"Because she's self-centered, shallow and impractical."

"Let's hope she grows up between now and then. And perhaps you can help her out, my practical friend," he said with a warm smile. "She'll need lots of it."

Christmas came and went, and Kat's 'acorn hail' winter had settled in. Below zero temperatures plagued Michigan, along with record snows. Kate understood on those snowy, freezing cold days, Harley and Kat would stay home and the girls wouldn't have lessons.

Charlie joined the family at the town Christmas tree ceremony and together, he and Rachel lit their own candle. The rest of the Tates were there, too, and if there wasn't obvious joy in the wedded union, there was at least acceptance. Jack had gotten Charlie on at Landmark Lumber, and he was riding to Petoskey with Jack each week and coming home on weekends.

When Eldon Woodward got the news Rachel would be getting married, he cried thinking she'd leave him. He begged Rachel to stay on as his housekeeper, and said he'd let Charlie live there, too. There was plenty of room and Eldon did not want to lose Rachel.

She was much more to him than employee. She was his companion, his surrogate daughter. He even purchased her wedding dress and provided a small reception in his home for her and Charlie. Kate tried to discourage him from doing it, but he was insistent, and so was Rachel.

"Eldon," Kate had said. "Rachel is my responsibility, not yours. We can have a wedding supper out at the farm."

The three of them were talking at Eldon's kitchen table. Rachel had served coffee with elegant little tea cakes on a lace covered silver platter. Linen napkins waited by fragile china dessert plates next to cups with handles so tiny you couldn't get a finger through to lift the cup. Kate gave a tired little smile at the clear statement Rachel was making. She wanted this. All of it.

"And that pretty, print lilac you have, Rachel, we can fix it up with some lace and a veil. Or I can ask Mel for money for fabric and we'll make a dress."

Rachel sat stiffly after pouring the coffee. "I want the one in the catalog, Mother. Eldon and I picked it out. He wants to buy it for me. I can't see what's wrong with that."

Eldon reached a deeply veined, red-knuckled hand out and patted Rachel's. "You will look beautiful in it, my dear."

"Yes," she replied with a shake of her long dark curls. "I'll be elegant in that dress, and there is no reason not to get it if Eldon wants to buy it," she repeated. "You're just being stubborn, Mother. And I want the wedding as well as the reception here, not at Mel's," she'd added with more than a little frost in her tone. "Eldon's home is more suited to holding a fashionable gathering, and, anyway, this is where I live."

Kate was shocked and bewildered by Rachel's response and didn't have one of her own. She crossed her arms and was silent, took several deep breaths and tried not to be angry or hurt. It didn't work. She wanted to shake her daughter until she shook some sense into her. She was acting like a brat, and Kate wondered about the origin of her flawed behavior. Had she spoiled her daughter? If not, then who had?

"What is it you would like me to do then?" Kate asked, reigning in her frustration and trying to be helpful. But it was hard because she didn't want to help. She wanted to cry, and tears weren't going to happen. Damn it!

"You can set it up with Reverend Daniels to marry us here instead of the church. If he won't then I guess we can do it there. But it will be cold on the ride back here afterwards."

"Have you thought about a maid of honor and who will give you away?" Kate asked, uselessly hoping common sense and a good heart might help her choose Mel to give her away.

"Kat and Uncle Jack," she said, and Kate nodded, acknowledging Jack was a good choice. She would have liked it to be Mel because it would have made him so happy, but that was a pipe dream and Kate knew it. A pie in the sky.

Kat reluctantly agreed to stand up with her sister, even to wearing a dress picked out by Rachel. She drew the line at anything too fancy, and Rachel agreed as she wouldn't want to be outshone by her sibling. In a couple of weeks, they were ready, and the first of Kate's four daughters was married.

The Congregational Church was stunning in the snow, a white portrait of purity. Its tall stained windows glowed deep indigo and brilliant ruby against a colorless snowy landscape, a stark splash of color in a world of white. The bell rang in its soaring steeple, muffled by the falling snow. In the church tower, John Nestor pulled the bell rope and wondered how a wedding could feel empty, joyless. He didn't know, didn't understand, but it did.

Rachel looked beautiful in her white dress with dark, glossy curls streaming down the back, and Jack was stylishly handsome walking her down the aisle. He talked to his old friend, telling him how beautiful his child was and how he wished Mark could be here in Jack's place. Kate thought of him, too, and the lump in her throat grew.

On her way to meet Charlie at the altar, Rachel thought of her father; her heart ached to have him by her side, and her memory teased about his handsome elegance and how they would look together.

Chapter Five

1917

It was March, and the harsh winter showed no signs of abating. Most folks hovered close to their home fires and became inwardly thoughtful or outwardly verbose. Those who lived with people they cared about grew more devoted and tender with them. Others, who harbored hostility or rancor, grew more bitter and ornery. Hard winters had various effects and few were reprieved from its heavy hand. A sense of humor helped stave off the cabin fever that drove people to brave storms with a visit to Sadie's or Sunday church.

Poochie died, and Jeannie grieved with big, tear filled eyes that broke the hearts of everyone who looked at her. They found him in the barn, his massive head lying on his paws. He looked like he was asleep, and at first Jeannie refused to believe he wouldn't wake up.

"He can't die," Jeannie told them. "He's mine. I need him." Tears fell in streams for days, and she avoided talking to everyone. Harley made a casket for him, and Mel used a pick axe to dig the grave.

"Do you want to say anything to him, Jeannie?" Kate asked at Poochie's funeral. "Or would you like to say a prayer?" She pulled Jeanie to her, tried to console her, but her mother was not what Jeannie needed.

She crossed her arms over her slender chest and pursed her lips, looked down at the hole in the ground like it, someone, God, had betrayed her. She didn't understand and was mad. She sucked in breath, hiccupped trying to get air, and couldn't bear the pain.

"I love you, Poochie. You need to wait for me in heaven. Do you hear me?" she yelled through her sobs, then turned and ran from them.

Kate found her in her room, face buried in her pillow. She sat next to her and watched as pain wracked Jeannie's body. She rubbed her back and waited.

"We all loved him, Jeannie, but you most. And he loved you the best, too. You'll miss him like I do Bug. It's hard."

Jeannie didn't respond. Couldn't.

"It will be alright, you know, sweetie. You'll feel better. I promise."

"No!" Jeannie gasped. "It won't be. You don't understand. I love him!"

"I know. Believe me, baby, I do know." Kate pulled her into her arms and rocked, her own tears dampening copper hair, mingling with her daughter's.

"God, living is hard, Jeannie. It is just plain hard."

Kat and Harley went to the farm when they could and did lessons with Jeannie and Becca, but when winter interfered, Kate took over schooling, and they hunkered down in the cabin, enjoyed the solitude. Given Kat's quiet nature and Harley's easy adaptability, they spent hours without conversation, each without need for noise, but they could also engage in spirited academic and philosophical discussions. They were a matched set and were contented.

They studied the books on herbal medicine John Crow had dropped off, and Kat was absorbed by the multitude of cures growing in her woods. She was learning from Harley as they read at the table or sat in the rockers soaking up heat from the hearth fire. They grew closer each day and found new respect for one another within the confines of the small cabin.

Kat wrote voluminous notes about what she would pick in the woods when spring came, and what she wanted to do with each herb. With Harley's help, she ordered seeds from a catalog to plant in small pots placed on window sills with southern exposure. When the ground warmed, she'd have seedlings ready. On the day they picked them up at

Nestor's store, she asked him how he managed to buy things without having a job.

Harley tilted his stocking capped head and peered at her. Kitty was pulling them easily through the snow on their sled, and they were covered to their chins in a warm blanket. He contemplated how best to respond to her question, even if he should respond. Eventually, Kat questioned his silence.

"Are you thinking or deliberately not answering?" she asked.

"I'm pondering."

"You don't have to answer, you know."

"I do . . . have to answer that is," he said, "but I don't have to satisfy your curiosity about my financial affairs. However, I believe I will."

"I have wherewithal, and I am very careful. If I'm not, I'll have to leave the family I've come to think of as my own and go find work. That's not a choice for me. Does that satisfy your inquisitive mind?"

Kat nodded and thought. "Then, I should get the seed money from Ma."

Harley laughed and bumped her shoulder with his.

"I don't think your seeds will cause me to have to look for work."

"But it's not right," she said. "I should get a job."

"You have one, Kat. It's studying so you can be a healer. That is your work."

After they picked up the seeds and a few supplies at Nestor's, Harley dropped Kat off at Woodward's to check on Rachel.

She opened the door when Kat knocked and her face lit up seeing her sister.

"I'm so glad to see you. Did you bring more tea packets for my stomach and bath herbs?" She was holding her back like it ached and rubbing her stomach at the same time. "God, I'll be glad when this whole thing is over."

"Can I come in first?" Kat asked. "And yes, I brought you more packets. They must be helping, huh?"

"Some, but nothing, absolutely nothing can help this gigantic stomach." She plopped down in the kitchen chair, groaning as she sat. "I am so fat. Charlie even said so."

She was five months along and acting like she could give birth at any moment.

"Well, what does he know? He's never been pregnant."

"He knows I'm not very attractive to look at. That's not too hard to figure out."

Kat shook her head in mild disgust. "Come on, Rachel. You're going to have a baby."

"I can't believe this is happening to me. This isn't the way it's supposed to be," Rachel moaned.

Kat didn't respond. What was there to say about the way things should be? Or shouldn't be? Life was pretty much what you made of it because you can't control events. Events happen. You can only control what you make of them. She didn't bother to share her thoughts with Rachel because she knew how her sister would respond. She'd whine, and Kat had little patience for whining.

She boiled water, put a spoonful of fennel and peppermint in to steep and sat down to wait. She explained the different packets and warned Rachel to pay attention to the notes she'd written on each. "This is medicine, Rachel, so treat it that way."

Rachel nodded and sipped at the hot drink Kat handed her. "Thanks, Kat. I'm really sorry to be such a pain. I'm just miserable."

"I know that. You'll have your baby soon, and it will all be worth it."

Rachel nodded again, but Kat didn't see a smidgeon of sincerity on her sister's face and worried about the child in Rachel's womb. She passed it off as the melancholy pregnant woman experience. "I'll drop off some rosemary for you before I head back to the cabin. That might perk you up."

"God, Kat. How can you stand living out there all by yourself? I'd hate it, and why are you studying all this herb stuff?"

"I'm not alone. Harley is there, too," Kat answered.

"Well, you might as well be. He's just an old man. A silly old man."

"Harley's wonderful, Rachel. He's a part of our family."

"He's a hobo. He doesn't have a stick to his name."

"I'm going now." Kat got up and walked across the kitchen, stopped and turned back. "And I study herbs to help heal animals. People sometimes benefit from it. Like you."

"Wait, I'm sorry," she said to Kat's back.

"Don't get up. I can find my own way out."

Kat fumed as she walked to Sadie's where Harley was visiting with Verna while he waited to pick up Kat, giving her and Rachel time alone. Without a thought, she pushed through the door, and heads turned her way, surprise evident.

"Don't worry about it," she muttered to anyone and everyone who appeared to be shocked at her presence in the saloon, and strode over to the table where Verna and Harley sat. Harley got up and pulled out a chair for her, doing an admirable job of not showing his own surprise.

"Want a root beer?" he asked her.

"Sure. Hello, Verna."

"Hi, urchin," she answered with a favorite nickname she'd given to Kat years before. "Good to see you."

"When are you going to come see us at the cabin?" Kat asked.

"How 'bout today?" She turned to Harley, "I'm off til Friday, so I can stay for a bit if I'm not in the way."

"I don't know. Will she be in the way, Kat?" Harley asked.

"Probably, but what are you gonna do?" she answered with a twinkle. Kat didn't grin broadly, but her eyes smiled at full volume. She adored Verna, and it was written on her face.

"Everything okay, little chick?" Verna asked.

Kat nodded and sipped at her root beer. "Better get your winter woolies on, Verna. It's going to be a cold ride."

Verna left them to gather her things and Harley tried to read Kat's face. He was only successful in knowing everything wasn't *okay*, and he knew Kat would share only when she was ready, so he let it go. He patted her arm and saw her struggle.

"Don't be nice," she said, swallowing hard and breathing deeply.

Harley laughed loudly. "My God, girl . . . If I had a penny for every time your mother said the same thing to me, I could buy you a wagon load of seeds. You are your mother's daughter, without a doubt."

Kat shrugged, shaking her head. "Was there *ever* a doubt?"

"No. There wasn't."

"Well then, why are you telling me something we all know?"

Harley laughed again, louder this time, and was still laughing when Verna came back.

"Let's go," she said, "and you can fill me in on the way."

As they left, Kat said, "Harley seems to think there is some doubt about my parentage."

"That's not what I said, Kat."

"Yes, you did."

"Why are you filling this girl's head with nonsense?" Verna asked.

Harley stashed Verna's bag in the back and tucked the blanket around them. When he was in and covered, he tried to explain.

"I merely said she was her mother's daughter."

"Well, why would you feel the need to tell her that? Was there ever any doubt?" Verna teased.

"That's what I said, Verna," Kat said.

"Oh Lord, I need a sip of moonshine."

Verna leaned back, reaching a hand into her trousers pocket, and magically produced a flask. She pulled the stopper and took a sip before handing it to Harley. "Your wish, my command, and all that silly stuff."

"You are a savior, sweet woman."

"Yes, I am," Verna said with a satisfied grin.

Over the next several days, Kat planted her seeds in eggshell halves saved for this purpose. They sat on shelves

Harley made and hung in front of the south windows, four shelves for each window. She sprinkled them frequently, making sure the surface remained damp so the seeds would sprout. She and Harley discussed what they could do with the grown plants, from the roots to the stems, flowers and leaves.

Verna watched, enjoying the view of the two of them engaged in their work. She even cooked dinners for them, loudly proclaiming if they told anyone, she'd resort to violent retribution.

At night, they watched the fire and talked. Kat finally mentioned she'd walked out on Rachel, but didn't say why, only that she was miffed at her. "I already told Harley I don't think Rachel is going to be a good mom. I'm even more convinced."

"Well, my friend," Verna said, determined not to voice her questionable opinion of Kat's sister, "she might not, but you're going to make a very good Aunt. None better."

Chapter Six

Kate sat rocking in the kitchen near the crackling hearth fire. Red, blue and orange tongues licked at the ironwood logs and hissed at the dampness of the wood she'd added. A toe gently moved her back and forth, a soothing motion, one she loved to pamper herself with when she sat in front of the fire at the cabin. She missed those rocking chairs but chose to leave them at the cabin with Harley. It felt like they belonged there. She could visit, sit in one and feel her father's arms wrapped around her again. She tapped the floor again to increase the comforting movement and stared at the flames.

The mending in her lap sat untouched, and thoughts moved through her head without form, meandered around her mind like a slow stream through a meadow. She thought about Rachel, due to give birth in about three months. 'I'll be a grandmother. God, how did that happen?' Two of her daughters lived away from her, with other people. She didn't know how that had happened either.

Like everyone, she was eager for spring after a cruel winter. But it hadn't been so harsh in Mel's house. The walls were thick, and wind sounds were muted. Cold wasn't noticed until you went outside to bring in wood or take care of the animals. Window panes still frosted over like they did at the cabin when the temperature dropped, and it dropped a lot this winter. Sometimes she missed the cozy feel of the cabin in the middle of a snow storm. Spring was coming, though the April fool's joke had been six inches of snow. Ha, ha, Mother Nature.

Mel stomped in, banging wet snow from his boots at the door. "You look far away and comfortable, sweetheart."

"I am," she said, laying her head against the back of the chair and looking up at him. "Did Becca stay with her girls? She does love those cows."

Kate smiled up at him as he ran a hand over her hair.

"I'm just in to get a couple of hot drinks. It's pretty nippy for April. And yes . . . she does. She's really good at it, too, like she's been doing it her whole life. I swear she gets more milk from those girls than I do."

Kate set milk to heat for hot chocolate and poured coffee in a thick cup. Mel sipped and said, "I'm missing you. Are you okay?"

"I am," she said with a soft smile, and wrapped an arm around his waist. "You?"

"Yes, I'm more than okay."

She handed him the mug of hot chocolate and he gave her a soft kiss, lingering there for a moment.

"We'll be about another hour," he said, his breath warm on her lips.

Kate closed the door behind him, sending a drift of cold, snow laden air into the room.

Wolf opened his eyes to look at Kate, berating her for the chill.

"I couldn't help it. It's cold and snowy outside," she told him.

Wolf had followed Kate home from the woods years before and had instantly grown used to comfort. He was mostly timber wolf and guarded Kate with attentive care. He was also adamant about his expectations. He liked warmth, untainted by cold drafts.

The house was unusually quiet.

Mel's mother was in her room, trying, Kate thought, to give her some space in a house shared by two women. Laura was happy for her son, had wanted this marriage to happen many years ago, and Kate thought they'd found a peaceful partnership in the house. They cared for one another, liked each other, but Kate felt she was an interloper in Laura's kitchen. It had been Laura's home for more than forty years. How could she not feel proprietary about it? And Kate still missed her own small kitchen at the cabin.

Mel and Becca were still milking the large herd. They'd been up and out of the house long before the sun rose. Twice a day she tagged after Mel when he headed for the milk barn. She'd taken to farming life like she'd been born to it. Mel cared for her like she was his own, and although he loved all of Kate's daughters, there was a special place in his heart for this thirteen-year-old girl who loved his herd of milk cows, his other girls. Like Mel, she would warm her face against the side of a cow while she milked, smell the musky scent of her hide and love every serene moment.

Jeannie, too, loved living at the farm, but what she liked best was taking care of the small animals. She fed the chickens and helped take care of the youngest calves. There were at least a dozen cats in the barns, and Jeannie made sure they had milk every day. Mildred, the woodchuck, was still around, but she lived in Jeannie's room most of the time, away from the rest of the animals.

Jeannie was in heaven with all of them, except for three old mascot geese who chased her, squawking and opening their wide beaks to snap ferociously at Jeannie's legs. She checked carefully when she stepped outside, looked right, left, then right again, and ran quickly to the barn to escape them. Mel heard her shrieking as she flew into the milk parlor one day, and he tipped his stool over backwards leaping up to save her, thinking something was deathly wrong. He grinned when he saw the geese and she told him the problem. He gave her a stick and showed her how to make the geese run from her instead of the other way around.

"You're in control, Copper Top. You just need to show them that."

"I'll like being the boss. I never am."

From then on, Jeannie strolled deliberately around the yard waiting for them to act up so she could be the boss again. She'd never been in charge before because she was the baby. It was fun.

Of all Kate's girls, Jeannie had the least recollection of her father. She knew Mel much better and had feelings for him akin to those of a child for a father. She'd been climbing into his arms since she was little, when Mark was still alive, and much more so after he had died.

"What's wrong with me," Kate asked out loud. "Why all this remembering?"

"I'm not sure," Laura said, coming into the room as Kate spoke.

Kate laughed. "I was talking to myself again," she said with a self-deprecating grin. "I do that a lot."

"So do I," Laura said. "Especially when I'm thinking things through. Are you working out a problem?" she asked. "Maybe I can help."

"No, no problem. Just kind of reminiscing. So much has changed. It's a little hard to grasp it all at once."

"I know, Dear. You will take hold of it, though. Change is hard, but most often, well sometimes anyway, it's worth the trouble."

Kate started to respond, but they both gave a yelp, startled by the banging on the door. When they opened it, a red-faced Jack came in, stomping snow and asking for Mel.

"He's milking, Jack," Kate said. "Come in. Is something wrong?"

"Yeah, there sure is, Kate. We're at war. The United States is finally going to war."

"Oh, my Lord. No," Laura said, her face turning pale and her hand clutching her heart as if it would break.

Kate took her arm and led her to a chair. Jack wiped his boots and went to help. "Is there any whiskey in the house?" he asked.

Kate went to the cupboard and brought back a small glass of cognac. "This is the best I can do," she said.

Laura sipped and some of the color came back to her face. "Please, Jack, pour a glass for yourself and sit. Tell me what you know. Mel will be in shortly."

He did as she asked and waited for Mel to come in. "Thought this would happen a couple of years ago, when the Lusitania went down," he said. "Surprised it took as long as it did."

"I'm so glad I have daughters, not sons," Kate responded in a daze.

Laura looked at her with something close to antipathy. "I have sons. One is your husband."

"Oh, my God," Kate whispered, regret and fear filling her eyes. "I'm so sorry! I wasn't thinking. He couldn't go. He wouldn't," she stammered. "War is for young men. No!"

Kate ran to the door and grabbed her coat, running to the barn as she put it on, Wolf by her side. She was talking as she went, begging him not to go.

"You wouldn't go, would you? You can't. You have a family. Responsibilities," she said as she burst through the door. He was leaning comfortably into the side of a heifer.

"What are you going on about? What's happened?" he asked, turning to look at her.

"Jack came. He said we're at war. Today. You won't go, will you?"

"Whoa, Kate. Sit. Let me finish with Pearl and ask Becca to wrap it up. Okay?"

Kate nodded and sunk onto a pile of fresh straw. She put her head in her hands and felt tears seep between her fingers. She didn't try to stem the flow, but let them fall. Wolf whimpered, his head on her shoulder, and Kate looked at him. "I'm okay," she told him and nuzzled his face with hers.

Her first thoughts had been selfish ones; for her children and herself, but close on its heels came all the men in her life. Her brother, Willie; his son, Rob; Jack; Rachel's Charlie; Mel's brothers and nephews; and . . . Mel. It just couldn't happen. It couldn't!

He came back and picked Kate up by the shoulders. "Let's go to the house, okay?"

Kate went along with him, her feet moving one in front of the other. Jack looked up when they walked in, his eyes dark and forbidding, his thoughts unreadable.

"What's Kate talking about?" Mel asked. "Are we really at war?"

Jack nodded his head, saw Kate's white face and got up to splash cognac in a glass, giving her his chair.

Mel was silent, thoughtful for a moment, his hand resting in comfort on Kate's shoulder. "Well . . . I'm not surprised. What *is* surprising is that it took so long. It's been a long, long time coming."

"Boys are lining up to fight left and right," Jack said, handing the cognac to Kate. "There's already a recruiter in Big Rapids; supposed to be in Reed City next and Hersey by the end of the week."

Kate looked back and forth at Jack and her husband. "You're not thinking of signing up, are you? You're too old."

Jack grinned, a sad grin. "I'm not too old to give them what for," he said, "but most likely I'm not going. I think they have much better choices, and U.S. troops are currently all volunteers. I hear that's likely to change to consignment, though."

Mel stood immobile. Kate looked at her mother-in-law and went to her. "It's going to be alright," she said, bending to put her arms around her. "It will."

"You don't know that," Laura said. Her voice quivered, and fear turned to bitterness on her tongue.

"No, I don't," Kate responded, shaking her head but agreeing. "I don't know what will be." She gathered herself and stood tall, recovering from her initial, selfish break down. "But I do know each of us will do what we have to, and we'll get through this."

"We will, Kate," Mel said softly. "We always have," and his eyes said more.

Jack got up and hugged Laura. "Kate's right. We'll get through this, Mrs. Bronson."

Her hand trembled as she reached to hug Jack, and Kate saw her fragility, the blue veins in thin skin, courier of age. It slapped Kate hard with a message she would not soon forget. Laura was old. So was Ellen, her mother. This war may force them to bury their grandchildren, their children. No mother, no father should ever have to put children in the ground. Laura and Ellen had already buried loved ones. They understood more than others what death was. And so did Kate.

The first boys who signed up were Boyd and Billy Jackson; Joshua, the youngest Reeves boy; and Lenny Tate, Charlie's older brother -- Rachel's brother-in-law. In late

June, an army lieutenant came by with a wagon load of boys from nearby towns to pick up the Hersey recruits. The entire town came out to see them off. It was like the Fourth of July, a celebration with music and back slapping, well-wishing and a great deal of false bravado. Lemonade, coffee and a keg of beer had been set up in the fire hall where a pot luck table was loaded with food. Each woman had cooked a personal specialty, and the dish sat wrapped in towels to keep warm or cool. The new recruits coming in on the wagon got down to join the party and were welcomed as if they were sons of the town.

Rachel was there with Charlie, her face aglow with admiration for the young soldiers. She hugged and kissed Lenny, her protruding stomach making embrace difficult and causing ribald comments from spectators. She moved on to hug Joshua, the Jacksons and some of the boys from the wagon who accepted her admiration with red faces and tentative, half fearful glances toward Charlie.

Harley and Kat stood in the back of the crowd quietly watching. Kate, Mel and the girls joined them, with Jack and Ruthie, Willie, Mary and their children, Ellie and Rob.

Watching Hersey boys leave for war was hard on everyone. They had known these kids their entire lives, and it was strange to think of them becoming men fighting as soldiers in another country, far away from here. Ruthie had raised the young people of this town. She'd spent hours with them in the classroom every day, brought them home with her, cared for them, mothered them. Especially the Jackson and Tate boys who came from such large families. Ruthie thought they deserved special attention, and she gave it to them.

Jack had his arm around her shoulder and whispered in her ear. "You gonna be okay?" he asked.

She nodded to her husband, wide puffy eyes indicating she'd already made her peace with the events of this thorny day, and turned to Kate. "Rachel seems okay. Is she afraid for Charlie?"

"I'm sure she is," Kate said, "but you'd probably know better than I. She doesn't talk much to me anymore." It wasn't said with angst; the words were what they meant. She didn't know her daughter well. Moments passed and she added, "Thank you for being there for her. She needs you."

Ruthie glanced over to where Rachel was flirting with Lenny, hanging onto his arm as if he was her husband, not Charlie who was also staring at his brother in wide-eyed admiration. Ruthie didn't like what she was seeing, but didn't know how to interpret it or what could be done about it.

Kat saw her, too, looked down at her feet and then over at Harley. She rolled her eyes and wrinkled her nose. "Dumb," she said.

"Well, possibly, but you never know how you'll behave under certain circumstances."

"Really? Do you think that?" Kat responded.

Harley paused and slowly shook his head. "No, Kat, I don't. Not when it comes to you. I'm fairly certain how you'll respond to any given situation. I love that about you."

It came time to say goodbye, and the atmosphere ignited. Jealousy was clearly in the eyes of the young men and boys left behind, at least on this day. There was excitement in going to strange places, seeing the unknown, battling the enemy. There was pride in becoming a hero, facing fear and adversity, testing your mettle. All the glorious internal bolstering overshadowed the horror no one wanted to admit was possible.

But it was there in the eyes of the mothers and fathers, in the tears barely held in check, in the dampness clogging throats making words of goodbye nearly unmanageable. 'See you later alligator' and a quick, hard handshake was easier from fathers. Strained smiles and desperate hugs just before the frantic turn toward home was the only thing possible from the mothers.

"Can you come to the house for a bit?" Ruthie asked. "Jack said the elderberry wine is ready to drink if you want to try some, and Ellen made oatmeal cookies. Willie and Mary are coming. Rob and Ellie, too."

Harley said, "I wouldn't pass up a cookie, or a sip of moonshine to honor these boys if that happened to be on the menu. What do you say, Kat?"

Chapter Seven

Sammy

On the corner of Main and Division, Jack slowed his walk until he was next to Kate.

"Got a couple of questions for you," he said.

"Sure. What do you want to know? I am the fountain of all knowledge," she teased. "Just ask me."

"I thought you were the Queen of Everything," he mused, then paused and she looked at him, waiting. "Well," he began, stretching out the word like he didn't know what the next one was and hoping it would come to him.

"Yes," she said, stretching out her response. "Is there another word forthcoming?"

He nodded toward the dark, empty smith shop. "Do you still own the building?" he asked.

"Gosh. I haven't given it any thought. I guess I do. I know Mark made payments on it to Pa. I haven't been inside since Mark left it. Why?"

Jack stopped walking and told the others to go on. He held onto Kate's arm, looked at Mel fidgeting in the road, and told him to keep walking.

"Don't be messing around with my queen," Mel said with a frown, "or I'll have to flatten you."

"I run too fast, you big ogre. You couldn't catch me."

When Mel walked on, Jack asked if she minded if he looked inside.

Kate was curious, had wanted to see the inside of the smithy where Mark had worked and they had lived, but for years it had held too many painful memories. She thought now would be a good time, especially with Jack by her side.

"Alright. Let's go in, but why now, Jack? What do you want to see?"

"Well, I'm thinking I might be ready to set up a law practice again, and I'd need somewhere to do it. If we don't see sky from the inside of the building, this might be the place to hang my shingle."

He paused while they worked the door open. Jack banged on the hinges, scattering the rust. It hadn't been touched in years and they objected to movement. Critters scampered when the door finally jerked open, and the acrid smell of the cold forge, still strong after all the years unlit, assailed Kate's senses.

Dim light, filtered by dust and cobwebs, came in through the grime covered windows and revealed Mark's smith tools in the shadows, laying where they'd been tossed on his last day at work. Hammers, anvils and chisels sat covered in layers of dust, and Kate ran a finger down the length of a wooden handle. She visualized it in Mark's hand as he worked, flattening and shaping the red-hot metal into a wheel or a tool or a horse shoe.

"Maybe this wasn't a good idea," Jack said watching Kate turn back the clock. He knew she was recalling the past because he was remembering, too.

"It's okay, Jack. It really is." She walked to the back rooms where they had lived, where she had given birth to Rachel and Kat, before they'd been able to live full time at the cabin. The two small rooms were empty, but long ago enough furniture for a family of four had filled the tiny spaces. Kate breathed in memories and wondered why she hadn't come here before. There was love and life in these rooms.

She looked up at the ceiling and didn't see sky. "It seems like the roof has held up."

"It appears that way. Solid rafters and floor. No rain marks in the dust. That's a good sign."

"It will take a lot of elbow grease, but this could be a good law office," Kate said. "I'll help. I'd like something like this to do."

"Well, let's check with Ellen, see who owns this place first and go from there."

"When are you thinking of setting up practice?"

"My law books came in last week, and I'll need to pass the Michigan bar exam. We'll see if my brain still works."

Kate put her arm through his and toured the shop with her eyes, loving every dusty, filthy inch of the place. "I will adore having you here, Jack. In fact, if you want this place, it's yours. I'll deed it over to you today. Payment for all the laundry you helped me with all those years. The scrubbing and wringing and rinsing and hanging. It's something I can do for you instead of you always doing for me."

"No, you can't do that. I scrubbed and wrung because I wanted to."

"And I'll do this because I want to." She took her arm from his and placed tight fists on her hips, feet spread wide in a fighter's stance. "Don't sass me, Jack," she said, leaning forward to put her face in his. "And don't tell me what I can or can't do."

Wolf, who had waited at the door, came in and put his front paws on the back of Jack's shoulders. His nose nudged Jack's cheek, and he rolled his brown eye.

"I know," Jack whispered to him. "You're right. But she's a girl."

Jack grinned and held up a hand in surrender, but only acknowledged discussion. "We'll talk, okay? We'll talk about it."

"Get down, Wolf," Kate said. She took his arm again, and they went to the door. "I love you, Jack. You're a traitor, Wolf."

Only a few minutes later because the smith shop was a stone's throw from Jack's house, they walked in to hear Harley setting up for a mile-long toast. It had been a while, and he was feeling the need to command an audience.

"We were about to begin," he said, "so pour yourselves a glass of elderberry 'liquor of the gods' and let us toast."

All except Charlie knew Harley well and simultaneously groaned and laughed hearing his demand.

Mel put an arm around Kate and peered into her face. She smiled to let him know all was well and held out a stemmed glass to be filled. "Tell you later."

"I'd like to be home before dark," Kat said dryly. "Let him get started, please."

A murmur grew and Harley moved about, trying to regain the attention lost when Jack and Kate came in. He raised his glass and began again.

"Here's to our brave young boys leaving to protect us from infidels on far away shores and to the mothers who bore them." He lifted his glass toward Ellen and Mary. "And here's to the old boys -- I mean -- our more mature ones who will stay and keep us well fed and safe on these shores." He looked at Mel, Jack and Willie and then paused.

"Here, here," they said in unison and started to sip and talk.

Harley moved forward into the circle. "Excuse me. Can't a man take a breath?"

"Most men do," Jack teased. "Not sure about you."

Mel ran a hand through his hair and shook his head. "I don't believe you do, Harley. Not when there's an audience."

"I am offended. Truly affronted to think you don't want me to finish such an important toast, a perfect opportunity to mention all that is good in the world and in our illustrious family . . . for instance . . ."

Hearty laughter filled the room. Even Charlie found the situation humorous without benefit of the history of Harley and his toasts.

"Let him finish before he gets up on the table," Ellen said. He'd stood in the middle of the Hughes table before and she didn't know if this one would hold his hefty weight.

They settled down and Harley began again. "Here's to the newest generation in our presence and cradled in a beautiful young woman's womb." He raised his glass to Rachel and she blushed, but pride began to rise from her like an aura. For a moment, Rachel felt powerful and significant.

Harley saw and continued. "And here is to the creators of the fourth generation." He stopped, and everyone waited, poised for more of Harley's words of wisdom, breath bated, arms quivering, beginning to shake from being held in the air for minutes that grew longer with each one that passed.

When no further words followed, there was shouting and back clapping, hugging and sipping of elderberry liquor of the gods.

Rachel received the accolades royally and reveled in them. Kate felt the glow of her daughter's transitory happiness and felt the small twist of a knife in her heart, wanting to believe in this fleeting joy, but not trusting in it. She saw Charlie ebb away from Rachel as the family flowed toward her. His awkward retreat made it clear he wasn't able to deal with the situation, with the wonder of fatherhood . . . with fatherhood in any of its fear-provoking forms. He was a boy, and he would soon have to leave the glorious state of boyhood.

Rachel grabbed her abdomen, gave a shriek, and everyone involuntarily stepped back as if they had inadvertently hurt her or the baby. She shrieked again and doubled over. Kate knew that sound and reached her daughter in seconds.

"Get her a chair," she shouted.

Rachel sat, and calm descended. She was quiet then and looked at her mother with fear in her eyes.

"It's going to be fine, Rachel. Can you stand and walk now or do you want to just sit a bit?"

Ruthie held her hand and murmured to her. "Remember what we talked about, Rachel. Do you think this is the beginning?"

"I don't know," she said sharply. "How would I know? I've never done this before. It was a sharp pain that went from my belly to my back."

Harley was listening and quietly said he thought Rachel's time had come, thought she should prepare for childbirth. "Perhaps she could use the spare room?" he asked.

"Do you really think it's time?" Kate asked. He nodded as another yelp came from Rachel.

"Look at how she's dropped just since we've been here," he said. "You might want to send someone for Doc Cheston."

They sent Charlie for the doctor because he looked like he needed fresh air and something to do, and he was glad to go. When he was out the door, they half carried, half dragged Rachel to a bed. Kate helped her remove her clothes and put on one of Ruthie's nightdresses. She berated Kate and Ruthie for the pain she was in and demanded they give her something to ease it.

"We don't have anything for your pain, Rachel," Kate told her. "It will be gone soon and you'll have a beautiful baby in its place."

"I can't stand this! And I don't want a stupid baby . . . not now or ever!" she shouted, the contractions coming too quickly and lasting too long. She moaned and sweat began to bead on her brow as she braced in anticipation of the next one.

Kate bathed her face with a cool, wet cloth and whispered gently to her, trying to soothe the pain, ease it with a mother's voice. Ellen took the cloths from Kate, dipped them into a basin of cold water and wrung them out. She handed them back to Kate and watched her granddaughter's angry face. Ruthie paced back and forth, wrung her hands and ran to fetch things she thought Rachel might need.

"God, Kate, this can't be right," Ruthie said. "What can I do to help her?"

"Nothing right now, Ruthie," Ellen said. "It's part of the process. She is earlier than we expected though. Pray for this baby." She took Rachel's hand and looked sternly at her. "Your noise takes energy. It will help if you reserve your energy for birthing the child."

Rachel looked embarrassed for a moment, but the look quickly passed as another spasm took hold.

In the kitchen, the family passed glances back and forth, sat sipping their wine and talked in hushed, brief sentences as if conversation might interrupt the process of bringing a life into the world. Willie and Mary went to the door to wish Rachel well and then left with Ellie and Rob in tow, both wondering why any sane person would bear a child.

After an hour or so, Mel went to the door of the room to say he'd take Becca and Jeannie home, get the milking done and come back later. "I think it will be awhile, won't it?" he asked, squeezing Kate in a long embrace. He saw fear and anguish in her eyes, and it tormented him. He didn't want to leave her.

She hugged back, reluctant to let go of his strength, his quiet sense of command. She felt better when he was near, like the world would be okay if he was in it, by her side. "I know you need to go. Thanks for taking the girls. I love you."

"I love you, Grandma," he teased.

"Thanks. I needed that," she responded with a laugh. "See you later, Gramps."

Hours passed, and those left in the house took turns sitting with Rachel.

Doc Cheston examined her, and in his gruff manner said, "Well, you're having a baby, young lady. It's gonna hurt. Haven't seen one that didn't." He went to sit in the kitchen with Jack, Harley and Kat.

"I could do with a bit of Will's moonshine," he said, looking disdainfully at the wine in their glasses. "I'm betting there's still some of that heavenly brew around."

Jack rose with a grin. "Yes, Doc, there is. I'll give you a drop if you promise a healthy delivery of the babe."

"No one can do that, Mr. Bay, but I'll promise my best. She's a healthy young woman and should do well even if she is a bit early."

They sipped and talked. Kat sat next to Harley listening to their banter, but mostly listening to the horrible moaning coming from the bedroom. Time moved on snails' feet as she watched the clock on the mantle. It was ten, eleven, midnight. Doc Cheston left, saying he'd check back in the morning unless someone came for him first.

Mel came back and sat with them, leaving Becca and Jeannie at home with his mother. Two o'clock came, then five, and Mel left to do the morning milking, returning afterward. The sun rose, arced across the sky, and he left again to do the evening milking . . . returning yet again. Doc came and went throughout the day.

Sounds of child birthing grew fainter. Kat slipped into the room and leaned against the wall. She watched her mother, aunt and grandmother tend to Rachel as she tossed about in pain, too exhausted to yell anymore, too tired to shout angry recriminations . . . to do anything except beg for it to end.

Kat went back out to the kitchen and sat, thought about life coming and going as she had seen in the forest and as she'd heard about through John Crow. He'd talked about how the Cherokee women gave birth sitting up on birthing stools, or logs if there were no stools, with a strong friend at the mother's back holding her upright. She tapped Harley on the shoulder and nodded for him to follow her. In the hallway leading to the bedroom, she told him what she thought needed to be done for her sister. He nodded and they went to deliver a baby.

Harley quietly spoke to the others while Kat told Rachel she had to stand up and walk with her.

"I can't," she moaned, and turned her face to the wall.

"Yes. You can. You will." Kat grabbed Rachel's arm and forcefully pulled her to the edge of the bed. Between Kat and Harley, they lifted her, made her stand, and began moving her around the room.

She stumbled and groaned, cried and railed at them, but they walked, half carried her through the door into the living room and then the kitchen. They all took turns walking Rachel and when the pains were consistent, close and rhythmic, they sat her at the end of the bed, and Kat knelt behind her sister, held her back upright and whispered in her ear.

"Breathe with me, Rachel. Breathe when I do and hold it. Then let it out really slow. Like you're trying to whistle really long or blow out a hundred candles all with one breath."

Kat said, "I'd like Harley to examine her. You can leave the room if you want."

Ellen gave him a long, hard look and stepped aside. Kate and Ruthie stood next to their mother, no one was willing to leave, which was fine with him. He'd rather have them there.

He murmured comfort to Rachel and looked for the baby with his fingers. The exit was blocked, and he felt the pulsing of the womb, the baby trying to be born but butting into a solid wall.

Harley told Kat what he felt and what he thought needed to be done. She asked a couple of questions and said, "Turn the womb like you said. You have to."

He reached, pulled and twisted, closing his eyes and ears to Rachel's screams, until the womb opening was facing the vaginal opening, and when he was done, the contractions came hard and fast. The head pushed through in minutes and soon after, the newest Tate boy was born. But for most of the closest relatives, it would be the newest Hughes-Ramey child.

Ellen, who was standing against the closed door, moved forward to take the wet, screaming baby. She wrapped him in clean cloths and laid him on Rachel's stomach. She put a hand on Harley's arm, tears in her eyes.

"Thank you, Harley. So much. I can't begin to thank you enough . . . again. I'll take it from here."

Harley nodded and helped Kat from the bed. "Come on, girl. I think you've earned a sip of wine."

Kat nodded, her eyes alight with a fire Harley recognized as zeal, love for what she had helped to make happen, passion for what she was meant to do. She walked from the room in a trance, humming a wordless song in ethereal pleasure, a soft smile lighting her face.

Harley watched her, his hand through her arm, leading her to the kitchen where family needed to hear the good news. "You were wonderful, Kat," he said. "You have found your destiny."

"You did the work," she responded.

"You told me what to do. I was merely the mechanic."

When they got to the kitchen, three stark white faces stared at them. They'd heard the screams and the silence. That's all, and fear darkened their eyes.

"You have a boy, Charlie. A beautiful, little boy," Harley told them. Three faces lit with relief and happiness. Wine was poured, wine for all, including Kat, except for Harley who got a rare, reserved glass of Will's famous moonshine.

When they were finished in the birthing room, Ellen came out to invite the family in to see the first of the next generation. Jack and Mel stood inside the door, each holding his breath as long as possible, like normal breathing might taint the room and the baby. Their eyes were wide with wonder and fear of the tiny, fragile life. Not fear *for* it because they knew the child would live. It was fear *of* it, like it was a being for whom they had no understanding, or any ability to cope, and so . . . it was frightening. He, the tiny baby, was scary! They made a few appropriate comments and fled back to the safety of the kitchen. They poured two hefty glasses of Will's stuff, toasted to the unknown, to the child, and tossed it back.

When Rachel was resting with her baby, Kate and Ellen joined them in the kitchen. Harley proposed an unusually short toast. "Here's to Kat, who brought this child safely into the world."

"I didn't do that, Harley. You did."

"No, sweet girl. You made all the correct decisions about your sister. All at the right times. It was you."

He held up his glass, and the rest moved forward to touch theirs to his, and with a word of thanks, to hers. Kat tilted her head and sipped her elderberry wine, a contented glow on her face. Wolf whined and nudged her leg. She patted his head and murmured wolf words.

Kate came to stand next to her and said, "You were unbelievable, Kat. I'm in awe and don't have a clue where you learned what you just did." She looked at her daughter with new eyes and high regard. Then she grinned. "And I love you, but don't be trying to steal my Wolf."

"I won't. But can I send him out to find a brother for me?"

"Sure. I wouldn't mind spending a day at the cabin. Would you be okay with that?"

Kat looked at her mother in wonder. "Well, yeah. It's your place," she said.

"But it's your home, right now. So, I need to ask."

"Come and stay awhile, Ma. It would be nice."

Yesterday, Kate would not have thought to ask permission, but today it had changed. Kat was a young woman.

"Maybe when Rachel and the baby get settled, I'll do that."

Chapter Eight

Victory gardens multiplied and flourished. While most folks planted gardens, they had doubled their efforts for the soldiers, planting more and preserving their crops as the government asked them to do. Mel sowed every available field for the war effort. His yield helped to feed not only American troops, but the allied forces as well, and no field was left fallow.

Ellen taught Ruthie how to plant and care for a small vegetable patch next to her house; she hadn't gardened before and was eager to learn. She remembered bits and pieces from when she'd been forced to weed and hoe Ellen's garden as a girl, but didn't know more than the simple basics of pulling a dandelion and not the leek.

Kate planted hers outside the farmhouse kitchen window where she could watch it grow. A small one had always been there, but Kate doubled its size and planted food they could keep throughout the winter in cold storage or in neat rows of colorful, filled jars.

Kat and Harley managed to find room for vegetables alongside the herbs in Kate's old garden by the cabin. At least that's what Harley teased Kat about.

"You're gonna starve me," he told Kat, "unless you think I can live on herbs and tree bark. Do you know something I don't?"

"I'm going to make you well when you get sick. Unless I do, you won't need food."

They increased the plot to make room for a substantial variety of vegetables as well as all the herbs Kat needed for her salves, infusions, teas and tinctures. Dr. Crow brought plants they wouldn't find in the forest, like Echinacea, artichoke, California poppy and eucalyptus. Kat tended them with care.

Harley was looking forward to the canning season, Kat to drying her herbs.

John Crow came by weekly and spent time with her, sometimes at the table pouring over books with tattered, yellowed pages. He brought more each week and left them for her to study. She treated his books with reverence, never breaking a spine or bending a page. They were precious.

Sometimes they walked in the woods with Harley close by, learning from John Crow's words. He pointed to juniper, goldenseal and St. John's Wort, American cranesbill and evening primrose. Tenderly, he manipulated the plants, showed Kat what to use, and told her how to use it. He tucked leaves and roots in the leather sack hanging from his belt and said he'd talk about them later.

"I want to help in the preparation," he told them. "It takes time, and it will keep for a long while if it's done properly. Did you buy the alcohol for steeping?"

Harley didn't question the doctor's interest in Kat, but he did watch and smile, and he gained in knowledge, as well. John saw a unique light in Kat that compelled him to make the time and effort to train her. He didn't question or test her afterward, knowing what he told her on their walks and at the table would be remembered. She'd write it down if she felt the need or ask him about it. She'd not be cavalier about learning.

Frequently, John stayed for dinner and sometimes the night. Those were the best of times in Kat's mind. They'd pull another chair up in front of the fire and Kat would coax him for more history of the Cherokees. It was different listening to John Crow tell a tale.

He was soft spoken with a deep rumbling voice, monotone-like, but it transported you to the villages of his people. His stories teased you to reach out and feel the texture of long extinct lodge poles and buffalo hides. John encouraged you to hear forgotten war songs and the chants for healing Kat badly wanted to know. She breathed in John's presence to capture and hold it forever within her because she valued and trusted him, revered his earthy knowledge, his Indian medicine heritage. She wished she could speak Iroquois because John's Great Lakes' people had spoken that ancient language. She turned the word around on her tongue, *Iroquois,* to savor its essence. It tasted exquisite.

Since Samuel Tate's birth, the Hughes women had taken over Rachel's work at the Woodward house. Eldon was fretful with the change and missed Rachel, but he soon came to enjoy having Ruthie, Kate or Ellen in his house, catering to his various whims. Kate and Ruthie did the cleaning and laundry and left meals and companionship to Ellen. They got along, and she had more in common with him than the younger women.

Rachel spent the first week after Samuel's birth in bed, letting Ruthie or Ellen take care of him until he was hungry. They brought him to her, sat with her while she breast-fed, and took him from her to burp and change. At first, Ellen excused Rachel's lack of interest in her child as a consequence of exhaustion. She'd had a difficult and grueling delivery. One week went by and then two. When she saw no effort to get better, no interest in Samuel, Ellen stepped in.

"It's time you got out of bed and saw to your son, young lady," she told her one morning, drawing the curtains to let in the sun.

Rachel squinted, threw an arm over her eyes and moaned. "I can't. I'm too tired. I hurt."

"You'll not be able to walk at all if you don't get out of that bed and use your legs. Now get up."

Ellen's voice was stern and her look was unyielding. The harsh words were difficult to speak and uttering them made her sad, but she knew this girl needed to be pushed. She took Rachel's arm and gently pulled her to a sitting position then shifted her legs so her feet were on the floor.

"Now stand up," Ellen said, putting Rachel's arm on her own thin shoulder, ready to hold her up if she started to fall or fainted with the effort.

Rachel began to cry, tears rolled down her face, her wail reaching out to Ruthie and Jack who were in the kitchen drinking coffee and getting ready for the day. Jack raised his brows and looked at his wife, a question hanging in the air between them.

"Is Ellen thrashing Rachel?" he asked. "It certainly sounds like it."

"God, I better get in there. Ma has been really perturbed with Rachel the last couple of days."

"Because?" Jack asked.

"Well, she won't get out of bed and take care of Sammy. She doesn't seem to want him near. She feeds him and tells us to take him away. I'd better get in there."

Jack reached out a hand and placed it over Ruthie's, holding it there. "Wait. Stay here and let Ellen work her magic. She's right, you know. Rachel has been letting everyone do her work. It's time she stopped playing princess."

Ruthie nodded and stayed put, listening. A long time later, Rachel shuffled into the kitchen, holding onto Ellen for support. Jack quickly pulled a chair out for Rachel and one for Ellen who'd been half carrying her.

"Good to see you up and about," he said with a smile.

Sammy chose that time to wail, and Ruthie went to get him. When she placed him on Rachel's lap, Ellen spoke up.

"The next time your son cries, you will go get him. You hear me?"

Charlie came by briefly on the weekends, looked at Samuel and tried to hold conversations with Rachel and her family. It was painful to see and hear. Charlie had no idea how to be a husband or father, and even worse, he had no desire to be either.

Jack tried to talk with him on their trips back to camp, but it did little good. Charlie was a child who had sired a child and married one. Jack held out little hope he'd grow up in time to take care of his wife and baby.

Rachel took Samuel to visit Eldon who was instantly enamored, couldn't wait for them to come home -- as he put it. "It's long past time you came back, Rachel. Look at that boy! He's going to be a firecracker, and he needs old man Woodward to help him figure things out."

"Has it been okay with Charlie staying here while I've been at my aunt's?" Rachel asked him.

He waved a purple veined hand in the air. "Ah, that young scalawag. He came a few days ago and got his things. I haven't seen him since. Didn't he tell you?"

Rachel pursed her lips, thinking back to the last time she had seen Charlie. He'd been distant and vague. She had wondered about it, but didn't ask why. She didn't care what Charlie did. He could stay or go. She was where she wanted to be, and in a way, she'd be glad if Charlie didn't come back.

Rachel shrugged mentally and went with Eldon to choose a room for the nursery. A small yellow room near Rachel's was perfect, and Eldon insisted on purchasing nursery furniture for it.

"Pick it out of Nestor's catalog and have him order it," he told her. "But no sissy stuff. We got ourselves a real boy here."

It took two more weeks for Rachel to get her strength back, and when it came, she moved with her son back to Eldon Woodward's house. He was eager to have them. The nursery was finished, and soon they settled back into the routine they'd shared before the birth of Samuel, except Rachel no longer went to school, and she spent time each day taking care of a baby.

In August, a second wave of recruits left Hersey and included Kate's nephew, Rob, and her son-in-law, Charlie. Mary wouldn't have gone to the celebration, hated the very idea, but she wanted her son to know she was okay; she'd carry on as she always did, and she was supportive of him, if not the war.

She kept it together, her head and chin held high throughout the eating and drinking, throughout the back slapping and bragging from those who were staying home about what they'd do to the enemy if they were there . . . if they were young enough -- or old enough to fight. The ones who were going were quieter.

Her looks were blank; her unreadable thoughts were not, yet she was alright. She took deep, painful breaths when the wagon pulled into the street to pick up the boys . . . and, still, she was alright. But when Rob said, "I love you Mom. I'll be back," she was no longer alright. She tipped her head back to take a final, long look at her son as she hugged him. She memorized his face with its downy fuzz where a beard should be, and with tears streaming down her own she thought she would never be alright again. Ever. And she couldn't swallow, and she couldn't breathe, and she didn't want to.

Mary stepped briskly toward home and Willie raced off to catch her. Kate started to go after them both when John Nestor came out of the store, flagged Kate down and put a letter in her hand.

"It just came in. I knew you'd want it right away," he said, waiting for her to open it and share the contents.

Instant fear grabbed her as it did everyone since the war, but when she looked at the envelope, she saw it was from Mark's son, Jamie, and it was in his hand writing. He had to be alive to write it! She tore it open and her heart soared. He was coming to see them -- for a long while. He'd been injured, but was healing well and had been mustered out. He was no longer in the army!

Kate grabbed John around the neck and hugged, jumped up and down and hugged him again while people watched and wondered.

"Good news, huh?" he said. "I know it's from Mark's son. He's okay?"

"Oh, John, he is and he's coming here. I am so happy!"

Mel came up, seeing the commotion with his wife, and teased John about having a duel at dawn. Kate handed him Jamie's letter, and a wide smile broke over Mel's face.

"Sometimes a foul day turns fine."

"Yes, it does," John said. "It seems Jamie just brought the sunshine to our Kate."

"Ours, huh?" Mel asked, squinting as wickedly as he could with his gentle face.

"Yeah," he said, puffing out his chest and hiking up his pants as if readying for a brawl. "I loved her first," he bantered. "Probably best, too."

"Boys, don't fight. I can handle both of you," Kate told them, sunshine radiant on her face. Her blonde hair lifted in the breeze and caught the sun in its honey glow. Both men simultaneously thought how striking she was. John Nestor still saw her as the girl hiding behind the pickle barrel and stomping her foot when she was angry. Mel saw her as the beautiful woman he'd always cherished.

"At this moment, I can handle anything and anybody," she told them. She was already planning for Jamie's arrival, excited beyond belief. She couldn't wait, and nothing, absolutely nothing, could put a damper on her spirits. Mark's son was coming!

Ellen stood apart from the crowd and watched the awkward celebrations -- thinking quietly. A single moment could hold the promise of joy or the agony of deep unspoken sorrow; a son returns, another one leaves; one is unharmed, and the other is wounded . . . or worse. She rejoiced for Kate and grieved for Mary and other mothers and fathers who said goodbye today and added to their silent prayers.

The next day, Kate was consumed with fixing up rooms for Jamie; not a simple bedroom but one with a connecting door to a second room. Into this room, she moved a settee and a desk where he could write letters, a table with two chairs where he could sit and drink his morning coffee, or have visitors and share a cup of tea. She put in everything he could possibly need, things she was using to entice him to stay. His bedroom was done in browns and greens, had curtains to draw and shut out the light for naps while he recuperated. Rugs made the room warm and cozy. The fireplace was set to go with the strike of a match.

When Mel came in from the barn, Kate excitedly pulled him upstairs to view the rooms she had prepared. She made him close his eyes, and only then did she open the door and move him forward.

"Okay, you can open your eyes now," she told him, her voice bursting with pride and anticipation. "Well, what do you think?"

Mel walked slowly around the room, looking, touching the desk and table. He moved into the bedroom and turned slowly around to take in the pictures, the warm colors and carefully placed towels next to a wash basin.

"Well?" she said, her breath held, waiting for a word from him. She began to worry he didn't like it, that she'd done something wrong in preparing so carefully for Jamie's visit. She hadn't told Mel she was hoping Jamie would stay, would make his home here, and she worried. She should have talked with him. Should have explained what this meant to her. 'Jamie is Mark's son,' she told herself. 'Should I expect Mel to open his arms to him?'

"Damn," she said, and added the obligatory apology. "I didn't think . . . I should have talked with you first. I was just so excited."

Mel stopped turning in the middle of the room and took her in his arms. "Are you kidding me? I'd move in! It's beautiful," he said, in between kisses on her forehead. "You've made Jamie's rooms very comfortable, better than comfy. They look like you and are just as fine. He'll love them . . . and you're forgiven for cussing," he said, his eyes hooded, teasing.

"You're okay with it? You don't mind?"

"Now, why would I mind?" he asked, holding her back from him so he could look at her face.

"Well, because Jamie is Mark's son, and because . . . I don't know. This is your house, not mine. I don't know how to deal with that sometimes. I've only lived in my own place where stuff belonged to me, and I made the decisions."

Mel thought for a quiet moment, watching worry dart across her face. "I didn't think how this might be for you, Kate, how not living in your own house might make you feel. I just wanted to give you everything -- so you didn't need to fight for it. I wanted your life easy for once."

Kate put her head on his chest and stayed there to breathe in his scent, to draw on his strength. Down to his toes, through to his soul, Mel was a good man

"I know, Mel," she said quietly. "I really do."

He tilted her head up with one finger and lightly pressed his lips to hers. "Come on. Tell me about everything. I don't know where you found all this stuff, but it looks great, and Jamie will love it."

He came within the week, and for the next many days, Kate's feet didn't touch the ground, she was so happy. She cooked his favorite foods and insisted on taking him breakfast in bed.

"You're recovering from a terrible wound," she told him. "It's the least I can do."

He looked older, much older than when she'd last seen him. His hair was grayed at the temples, and lines creased his brow and eyes. He was only thirty-two, but he'd been through a lot, as a foster child in the home of a cruel man, in an orphanage for years, and finally fighting a war on foreign soil. He enlisted long before the United States became involved. He'd gone when France had been in dire need, and on their behalf, he'd been starved, frozen, and without hope. 'But he's here now, Mark. Your son is home, and I'll take care of him,' she promised.

Jamie limped around the farm trying to help, eagerly spending time with Becca and Jeannie who still worshipped him as an older brother. As far as Jeannie was concerned, Jamie hadn't changed at all. He was still the beautiful boy who held her on his lap and told her stories.

They went to visit Kat and Harley at the cabin, and Kate watched Jamie take it all in, knew he saw his father in every corner of the cabin.

"I did that too," Kate told him on his first day.

Jamie looked at her blankly, unclear about what she meant.

"Your father was everywhere, in the very air I breathed. It was difficult to be here where we spent our lives together and not have him here with us, but it was impossible to leave it, too."

Kate paused, looking at him. He resembled his father in many ways, but there were parts of him she was sure looked like Lorraine, his troubled mother. She didn't know how she felt about seeing Mark's first wife every day in Jamie. She wasn't a good woman. She noticed Kat and Harley had left the room and silently thanked them for their consideration.

For Jamie, she continued. "Then it got so I was okay being here; I grew accustomed to the ache. Sometimes I even liked the pain because I'd grown used to it, and then I knew he was still with me." Kate smiled, remembering.

"Do you still miss him?" Jamie asked.

"Every moment, but it's not so much a miss as it is an empty space, a hole. It has become such a part of me I don't even know it's there anymore until I stop and be quiet, let it touch me."

Jamie nodded, understanding what she said. "It was that way for me at the orphanage and at the bad foster homes. I kept him close as armor against my hating the people who claimed to be caring for me." He touched Kate's arm gently. "He loved you very much," he told Kate.

"I was going to say that to you. He did you know," she said quietly. "Not having you and your sister with him was a pain that eventually became the color of his eyes." Kate laughed, a bitter one but a laugh, nonetheless. "Can pain be a color?"

"I believe so," he said solemnly.

Kate asked if he knew where his sister, Flossie, was. He shook his head and said it was probably for the best. She'd had a different life than Jamie, was a different person.

They walked outside where Kat and Harley were puttering in the garden, and they all reminisced about when he'd last visited. Harley told him about the fun and funny times they'd had here. Snow fights and dirt fights, water fights and more water fights. Jamie laughed and looked younger than he had since he'd come.

Harley brought out the jug, and they had the required toast to the prodigal son's return. Jamie laughed again, even louder, remembering from his last visit how this rotund man, supposedly a hobo, loved to give extended, detailed, and unrelenting toasts to everyday events.

"Are you still toasting to . . . uh, getting up in the morning?" Jamie teased.

"Hmmm. You are your father's son. Run your hand through your hair for me and groan, then I'll know for sure."

On their way back to the farm, Jamie said, "You love that place, don't you?"

"I do. I always have."

"I'd love it, too. It's quiet. It's overrun with tranquility. I can see why Kat wants to live there."

"It's overrun with critters," she said, trying for humor. "But yes . . . it has an abundance of stillness and serenity."

"Kat has turned into a remarkable young woman," he said thoughtfully. "She is someone to be reckoned with."

"She's a child, a woman child," Kate said with a laugh, still trying for a joke, but it wasn't working, and she was aware of it.

"Well, she isn't a child, and you really *do* know that, so you're kidding, yes?" Jamie looked at her for confirmation, but Kate wasn't buying his words completely.

She didn't want Kat to be grown. Not yet. But Kat was an enigma; that much she did know, and Kate went back and forth in her thoughts concerning her. "She's the epitome of dichotomy," she said with a giggle and moved to the cadence of her words.

Chapter Nine

Fall 1917

The entire town of Hersey had been picking, canning, pickling, and preserving food in every way possible to keep it from spoiling. Ellen and Ruthie, Kat and Harley, Laura and Kate; in teams, the women -- and men in some cases -- stored so much food they'd be well fed for a long time.

The effort was frantic and frenzied, necessary for their sanity. They were doing something productive and positive, putting food on the table, filling bellies, contributing to life and sustenance. It compensated for living safely in Hersey while their friends, nephews, sons and grandsons were in bunkers or trenches, slogging through mud filled fields, ducking bullets, fighting dysentery or lying in foreign hospitals, even foreign graves.

In late October, they had a festival in the fire hall with pot luck food, music and dancing -- bringing folks together to forget that people they loved were missing, were in places they didn't even want to think about.

The band played all of the old music and the newer war tunes. Gordon Tilman, the white-haired guitarist who had entertained Hersey for seventy-five years, was not in attendance, having passed away during the summer. But more noticeable was the glaring absence of Lenny and Charlie Tate who were hopefully making music for the troops in France. Leo and Martha Tate, their parents, bravely took their regular places on the small platform and made music with their younger children.

It was an opportunity for Jamie to meet everyone in town, and Kate proudly took him around to introduce him, her arm possessively through his. Everyone had known Mark the smithy, and most found a story to tell. When he began to look dazed from reminiscing with strangers, Kate passed him on to Wolf and Harley who gave him shelter and moonshine outside by the buggy.

The atmosphere at the town dance was peculiar. The people were the same, but life had happened and changed them. They were quieter, more subdued. Or they were boisterous, laughing too loudly as if making up for their distress, filling emotional holes with noise.

Kate mentioned it to Mel, and he agreed. He felt it, too. "Maybe their minds are somewhere else," he said. Mel danced with Becca and Jeannie, who were having a good time regardless of what the rest were doing. Both were content; they were loved and knew it. Kate and Mel were dancing when they saw Rachel come in, looking radiant, dressed to kill and carrying a bundle filled with Samuel.

"I thought she wasn't coming. I would have sat with him if she wanted to come," Kate said. "This is no place for a baby."

Mel didn't respond. There wasn't an answer to most things Rachel did.

They walked off the dance floor and over to Rachel. Kate held her arms out to take the baby. "May I?" she asked.

"Sure. Be my guest," she said, quickly handing him over.

The appearance of Sammy drew an immediate crowd, with Ruthie, Laura and Ellen at the forefront vying to be next in line to hold him. At four months, he could already beguile, smiling and gurgling at all the right times, taking every opportunity to captivate his audience.

When Kate handed him off, she turned to speak with Rachel and found her already gone -- on the dance floor with a friend of the Jackson's from Big Rapids. Kate waited for the song to end, but Rachel stayed for the next several dances. Other young men were there to take the place of the last one, and Rachel was in her glory.

Mel saw Kate's frustration and volunteered to cut in and bring Rachel back, but Kate told him no. "Remember the dance when she got so mad at you over Charlie? I don't think cutting in would be good."

"Yes, I remember, and you might be right," he said with a wry grin. "The older the child, the bigger the issues."

Ellen pulled Kate aside, a frown on her face, and eyed Rachel while she talked. "What is that girl doing?" she asked. "She should be at home with her baby, not out kicking up her heels and flirting with other men."

"Well, she's young, Ma. She wants a little fun."

"Her husband is fighting a war. Is he out having fun?"

Silence captured the moment. Kate couldn't respond and didn't want to get into a conversation with her mother about Rachel. Not here, not now. She had concerns about her daughter, questions needing answers, but not tonight. They were watching Rachel dancing with the stranger again when they saw Jack amble out to them, tap the man on the shoulder, and elegantly reach a hand out to Rachel who smiled at her handsome uncle. She willingly left the other man's arms. They danced twice, and Jack led her back to her family and child.

When Kate could be close to Jack she whispered a quiet, "Thank you."

He smiled. "You're welcome. Magic Jack, always to the rescue."

"True," she answered. "You've rescued me many times."

"And it was always my pleasure."

"Have you had a chance to spend any time with Jamie?" Kate asked. "I know he'd love to pick your brain about his father."

"Not much, but I won't be going back to the Petoskey camp anymore, so I'll have more time."

Kate's face lit up. "You're going to do it? You're going to set up shop?"

He nodded. "In fact," he said, "I've thought about asking Jamie for his help. I'd pay him, of course. But it would be fitting for him to help clean up and renovate his father's old place. It'd be a little like when your father and Mark refurbished the blacksmith shop. What do you think?"

"That's a wonderful idea! I love it for you and him, and he needs something to do that's not too strenuous while he recovers. He needs to feel like he's earning his keep." Kate was excited about all of it. It was perfect; the arc was coming full circle, and it felt exactly right. She forgot about Rachel for the moment in her excitement for Jack and Jamie.

"I think I'll stroll on out to the buggy for a nip and a chat. Want to come?" Jack asked.

"I do. Let me grab Mel and tell my mother where we are."

Harley stood with his hands hanging on the red suspenders he'd become famous for. Verna was grinning at him, most likely for some outrageous thing he'd said, and Jamie was laughing outright.

"We obviously missed the joke," Jack said, around Wolf's wet hello, "but hopefully not the moonshine. How are you, Miss Verna?"

"I'm dandy, handsome. You?"

"Good," he answered and held his hand out to Jamie. "And good to see you, Jamie. I'm glad you're here."

Harley reached under the buggy seat and pulled out the well-worn jug. "To keep you warm on this nippy night," he said, handing it to Jack.

Jack knew better than to give it back to Harley and passed it to Verna who passed it to Mel. When he had tipped the jug, Mel looked at Kate, his eyes saying, 'want some?' and her eyes answered 'of course!'

He laughed. "My girl," he said with sincere, if oddly placed, admiration.

When Jamie sipped and thanked Harley for the smooth home brew, Harley said, "The recipe either belongs to your father or your father's father-in-law. I know, confusing. Mark spent a lot of time trying to replicate Will's famous brew. I'm not sure I can tell the difference between them to tell you the truth."

"I've never seen the bottom of a jug," Verna said. "It's a little like Jesus and the wine. It keeps on flowing. Does He keep filling this jug when we're not looking?"

"Good thing Ellen isn't here, Verna," Harley said, "you blasphemous woman!"

"I am not blasphemous, old man! I'm paying homage to His mysterious ways . . . and yours."

"Well, we're grateful for the filler of the jug," Mel said, "whoever he . . . or she is," turning to Kate and then to Verna with a tip of an imaginary hat.

Jack took this moment to tell the others his plans to hang out his legal shingle and where it would be. They were happy for him and volunteered help if it was needed.

"Well," he said, drawing it out a bit, "now that you mention help, I could use some, and I'd like to hire this young man." He tilted his head toward Jamie and waited.

"Me? To do what? I mean, I'm not much good yet; I sort of limp around . . ." He quit talking, not sure what to say.

"Think of it as therapy. It's grunt work. Sweeping, cleaning, moving stuff, generally things you'd want to hire someone else to do, but in this case that someone will be you," he finished with a wide grin. "I'll be right beside you, though, being the other someone else I'd like to hire to clean up your father's smithy mess."

Before long Ellen and Ruthie, along with baby Samuel, came out to find the rest of the family. Kate looked behind them for Rachel, faintly hoping she'd be following along but didn't see her.

"Where's Rachel?" she asked.

"I don't know," Ellen said sharply. "I haven't the least idea where she ran off to. Last I saw her, she was dancing, and then she wasn't anywhere to be seen."

Ellen's thoughts were clearly written on her face, and Kate's mirrored her mother's. In a way, she was miffed at the thought. What woman wants to be the image of their mother? But in this situation, they were of the same mind. They agreed.

She was embarrassed for her daughter and afraid for her at the same time. She raised her eyes to peer into the distance, to examine the dark corners for a glimpse of Rachel's lavender dress and listen in between the intermittent sounds of laughter to hear the familiar echo of Rachel's voice.

Mel came to Kate's side and put his arm around her, nuzzled her hair and whispered. "Want me to go look for her?"

Kate looked up at him, loving his gentle manner and tranquil strength. She leaned her head against his shoulder and stood silently, thinking. She'd like not to care where Rachel was, but complacency wasn't going to happen. She might as well face it.

"Damn." She stomped her foot, like a kid who'd been told 'no, no cookie before dinner.' "Oops, sorry," she added with a quick glance toward her mother, a roll of her eyes and a grin.

"No," she groaned, "I need to go." She smiled at him and leaned to whisper to her mother that she'd be back soon with Sammy's mother in tow.

"Come on, Wolf," she said and began the search. She walked up and down Main Street, looking. She went back into the hall and asked the young men she'd seen her dancing with. She checked with the Jacksons to see if the boy from Big Rapids was nearby. They hadn't seen him in a while. By then, she was growing worried and a bit more than frustrated.

Kate finally found Rachel behind the hall building. She was pressed up against an outside wall in a compromising embrace with the stranger. Her hair had fallen from its comb and her dress was around her thighs, his hand holding it there.

In the half-second she stood watching, Kate was stunned and then livid. He was forcing himself on Rachel! Then she heard her daughter giggle, teasing him, encouraging his behavior. The noise coming from her was not the sound of fear or despair. It was the voice of passion.

Kate stopped, her mind slowly taking it in, and she grew furious.

Wolf growled and Rachel pulled away and turned toward the sound. Kate held out a hand to stop the animal from charging and stepped forward, grabbed the man by the shoulder and spun him around. She jabbed a pointed finger into his chest and pushed until he backed up. She did it again and again until he had backed into a buggy parked behind him.

"You scoundrel!" she said, her voice quivering in anger. "You bastard! You good-for-nothing, irresponsible, reprobate. You should be ashamed of yourself."

He held his hands out, palms up, trying for an innocent expression, looked side to side for an escape from this raging woman but didn't see one. "We were just . . . come on . . ." he whined.

"I could see what you were just . . ." Kate said. Then she thought about Rachel and where the responsibility lay. "Get out of here. I don't want to see your face again. Ever."

Rachel was leaning against the wall, half-heartedly trying to put her long, dark curls back in the comb. Her eyes were partly closed and her smile indolent, but when Kate was done berating the young man and turned to her, Rachel's chin went up and her face grew stony.

"You had no right to do that, Mother!" she said, every word steeped in acid.

Kate stepped back -- as if she'd been sharply shoved. She didn't speak, because she couldn't think what it was she should say. What *could* she say to this woman-child? Would it matter even if she found words? She didn't know the right ones for Rachel and felt she never had.

Rachel preened, thrust her shoulders back, her chin out in defiance, then tilted her head to look at Kate, and bitterness flew from her eyes.

Mel came around the corner, saw the heightened confrontation in progress and stopped. "If you want me, I'll stay," he said, "but I think it best if I leave you two alone -- if you're alright." Kate answered his question with a nod and turned back to Rachel.

"He's always there, isn't he? The brave knight," she said, a snide lilt in her voice and a sneer on her lips. "Coming to the rescue . . . and you . . . you're the damsel in distress. Don't you ever get tired of playing the part? Don't you ever get tired of pretending to be such a good, virtuous, righteous woman?"

Kate was shocked by what her first born child was saying to her, the way she was saying it, the venom in her tone.

Sorrow filled Kate's words, "You don't mean any of that, Rachel. You're angry right now."

"I do mean it," she said, moving forward to stand inches from her mother. "I am sick to death of you and your righteous ways, this village and its small-town mentality and morality. I'm getting out of here. Tonight."

"You're not serious. Rachel please . . . think about what you're saying. How will you support yourself? What will you do? You can't take Sammy from his family to go off with strangers -- who knows where. You can't . . ."

"Oh," she interrupted. "I don't intend to. He has way too many mothers as it is. He doesn't need me."

"What do you mean?" Kate asked, truly at a loss.

"I mean, he can stay, but I am going."

Rachel spun around and ran into the darkness. Kate didn't know how long she stood there playing the words they had spoken over and over, the meanings intended, the hate spitting from Rachel's tongue. She was in a daze trying to figure out what was real and what wasn't when Jack turned the corner and saw her standing motionless in the middle of the alley.

He moved quietly to her and took her hand. He saw the tears trickling slowly down her face, and his heart broke for her once again.

"Aw, Kate girl," he crooned. "What happened?"

She shook her head, unable to talk.

He put one arm around her and snuggled her close to him, waiting.

"Sorry, Jack, about the crying," she said when she could finally put syllables together between hiccupping breaths. "And thanks for the shoulder."

"It's okay. My pleasure."

"You mean you enjoy it?" she asked, trying to make humor in a bad situation.

"Yes. I love seeing you with puffy eyes and a tear streaked face. It gives me great joy."

"You're a cad," she said with a miserable smile.

"Yes, I am. Always have been. I don't know what your sister sees in me."

Kate put her head on his shoulder and sighed. "I do, but I won't tell anyone else and spoil your rapscallion reputation." Her words were frivolous, but the tenor was heavy and hollow.

She had just lost Rachel. How does anyone survive such a loss? It's an ache too deep to abide. She looked around at the dark shadows, dreaded coming out of them, and despised what would follow.

"I don't know what happened just now. I think Rachel is running away, and I know she hates me," she said. "What did I do to her?"

When they walked around the building where the others were waiting, Sammy was in Ellen's arms, peacefully staring at the night lights.

Kate told them about Rachel, leaving out the parts she couldn't say, couldn't talk about and didn't want them to know. She sent Mel and the girls with the others while she and Ruthie took Sammy and the buggy to Eldon's house. The lights were on when they got there, and through the window she saw Eldon sitting at the kitchen table looking like he'd been kicked by an angry mule.

"What are you doing up this late? Are you alright?" Kate asked when he opened the door.

He nodded. "She's gone. A young man came by and she left. Took her clothes and without a by-your-leave, she ran off. Damned girl. I couldn't stop her."

"I'm so sorry, Eldon," Kate said, leading him back to the chair by the table. "Can I make you some tea?"

"No."

"I need to get some of Sammy's things, okay?"

He nodded again, and Kate was sure he was fighting tears. Her heart broke for him. He was an old man who'd been enthralled by a young woman and her baby. His happiness went out the door with Rachel.

Ruthie changed Sammy while Kate gathered diapers, bottles, sleepers and a couple of clothes changes. Eldon was holding his head in his hands when they said goodnight.

"I'll come back tomorrow," she said, trying to reassure him. "Try to get some sleep."

Wolf, who waited on the porch, leaped off and took his place on the front seat. "Get over, friend, and please don't wolf slobber the baby."

He put his nose on Sammy who giggled, clearly loving it. Wolf gave her a wounded look along with a single eye roll to finish the point. Kate laughed and wondered how he always knew exactly when and how to pick up her spirits.

Back at Jack and Ruthie's, she told them Rachel was gone and that Sammy was going to stay with his Grandma Kate for a while. She asked Mel to prepare the buggy with warm blankets, warmed a bottle of milk and fed Sammy before leaving. He was sleeping soundly when they went into the cool night air for the ride to the farm.

Becca and Jeannie soon fell asleep, too, cuddled in the back. Wolf snuggled up to Kate, warming both her and Sammy with his body. A fall moon lit the way, but it wasn't needed. Mel's mares knew the way home, and they wanted to be there as much as Mel and Kate did.

Wolf was enjoying the night sounds, alert as ever for marauding villains. He pretended desperados lurked at every corner so he could perk his ears forward, curl his lips back to show big teeth, and make like a fearsome wolf. Every now and then it was necessary to maintain his formidable standing in his own mind.

It was their second Christmas at the farm. They brought in a tree tall enough to reach the twelve-foot ceiling in Mel's parlor. It was the perfect pine, a glorious specimen from the cabin forest in what had become tradition. The whole family contributed to its discovery.

Kat and Harley hosted the tree cutting party, and, again, Kate was forced to look at her daughter with different eyes. She'd made a large pot of soup and it simmered in the hearth kettle Kate had used for so many wonderful years. The cabin was decorated with pine boughs she and Harley had cut and placed on the mantle. It smelled like Christmas, like family, like home.

"Don't take off your coats and hats," Harley yelled to them when they pulled in. "We're heading for the perfect tree!"

Kate laughed, helped her mother down and led her into the cabin. Ellen looked around at the woodland decorations, smelled the pine and the aromatic soup and smiled. It had been a while since Kate had seen contentment on her mother's beautiful face, but it was there now. She took Sammy while Ellen removed her coat, and Kate nodded to the chair Will had made sitting in front of a crackling fire, waiting.

"This would be hard to leave, Kate. I think I finally understand," she said as she sat and pushed her toes against the floor to rock back slowly. Kate put the sleeping Sammy back into her arms and asked if she needed anything before they left to find the treasured tree.

Ellen shook her head, a sweet smile of contentment on her face. "Sammy and I are more than fine. Go find your tree."

Mel's boots stomped at the door and he ushered his mother in. Kate pointed to the rocker next to Ellen, and Laura's face melted in pleasure. "Oh, I am not going to want to leave here," she said. "Please take your time finding a tree. You don't want to cut a bad one, you know."

Before the entire group left, Harley slipped into the cabin. He poured two tiny glasses of the blackberry cordial he and Kat had made, set them next to the ladies, smiled and left.

"I love you, Harley," he heard as he closed the door. He smiled and wondered if he'd heard those words or had made them up. He didn't care. It was a beautiful day.

Jamie was the only one present who had not participated in a family search for the perfect Christmas tree. Kat watched him carefully, concerned about his troubled breathing, was aware when he lagged behind, and deliberately slowed down the pace.

Kate finally saw what she was doing and tried to help. She was in awe of her daughter. She couldn't think of a word to better describe how she felt about Kat. Awe. She was in awe. 'Damn. How did Kat get so wise?'

"You gonna say sorry?" Mel asked, walking by her side and enjoying the rosy look of her cheeks. He wanted to pull her behind a tree and smother her red lips with his, but thought the rest wouldn't appreciate it much. The thought, however, warmed him and he couldn't wait to be alone with her.

"Why?"

"'Cause you swore, Jezebel."

"I didn't. I just thought it," she countered.

"Nope. You said it."

Kate stooped, scooped up a handful of snow in one fluid movement and tossed it in Mel's face. "Did not!" she yelled and ran, knowing what the results of her rash actions would be.

"Did too," he yelled back, and threw a handful of snow at her.

She threw, and then he did. He did again, and she did. Before seconds had passed, the entire group had chosen sides and was engaged in a snow fight of massive winter proportions.

Mel had both Jeannie and Becca on the ground and was looking at Kate, holding the girls in one hand each. "I'm gonna bury your girls," he said. Wolf stared at him, let his front teeth show in warning and then leaped in the air and loped away having the time of his life.

"Go ahead . . . if you can," she responded. "Wolf will come back."

Becca turned the corners of her mouth down, trying her best to look sad. Jeannie began fake sobs, "but I love you," she said in between giggles.

Mel threw himself sideways into the snow. "I give. You ladies don't play fair."

They leaped on top of him and smothered him in the fresh white stuff.

"You earned this," Becca said. She piled mounds of it on him, buried him in it, not quitting until she heard, "Uncle...Uncle..."

He stood up, holding one girl under each arm and grinning like he'd never been happier in his entire lifetime. Their squeals matched his face. He looked around him and saw the rest of the group in various stages of snow coverage.

Harley was a Sasquatch, and Ruthie wasn't much better. Willie and Mary hid behind a tree trying to avoid the war, and Jack strolled through the melee totally dry. Not a speck of snow was on him. He looked like he'd stepped from a fancy parlor high tea with not a hair out of place. Jamie was crawling through the snow behind Jack, ready to pounce.

"What's the matter with you?" Kate yelled, diverting Jack's attention. "Where's your snow?" She chattered and watched Jamie crawl closer. When he was near enough, he pulled on Jack's legs and down he went. Instantly he was covered. Every hand held snowballs, and they were all aimed at Jack. He lay there, taking the punishment. Then he stood, shook all over like Wolf, and grinned his sly grin, a warning, but to whom?

They found the most perfect tree, cut it and hauled it back. They stomped off the snow and brought the cold inside with them, along with laughter and stories to tell Ellen and Laura. Harley brought out the jug and newly made blackberry wine. He waited for appropriate quiet and raised the jug.

"Here's to Jamie's return and his new venture with Jack and to Jack's new adventure," he said, "and here's to Sammy's bold entry into the world and this family."

"Here, here," some said. Others knew better. Harley was long from finished. He gave them the raised eyebrow, the wide eye, and continued.

"And here's to our absent daughter. May she be wonderful wherever she might be and may she return soon, happy and hearty. Here's to Becca, the most wonderful farm maid ever; and to Jeannie, our animal tamer and caregiver, and to Kat."

Harley paused, tilted his head and looked intently at her. "This is from me to you, Kat. I marvel at your specialness. The light you have been hiding under the bushel is shining through no matter how you may try to hide it."

Harley raised the jug toward Kat and lifted it higher before he sipped. Kate was engaged by the look in his eyes. It was one she couldn't absorb and didn't understand, but she knew Harley had put young Kat in a singular place of high regard. Like Kate, he was spellbound by her.

Sammy interrupted with a howl of glee, and Harley passed the jug. But not to Sammy, yet.

Chapter Ten

Winter was gentle in the farm house where the cold wind couldn't reach its icy fingers, and no one worried about where the next meal would come from. The kitchen table became a favorite place for Mel and Kate, where she read or mended, and he worked on projects by lantern light. Becca and Jeannie did school work or read until bedtime and Laura watched, contentment written in the smooth lines of her face.

Sammy made the rounds of everyone's lap by reaching his fat little arms out to the next person, knowing he was welcome on each one. Sometimes he curled up against Wolf, his head snuggled on warm underbelly fur and napped. Wolf didn't hate it, and Sammy didn't seem to miss his mother. She hadn't made contact with anyone, and Kate was saddened and concerned, but didn't know what to do about it. Didn't know where to look for her or how to even begin.

Initially, she was sure Rachel would come home, finding freedom wasn't all she'd hoped. She'd miss her child, feel remorse for leaving him, shame for her behavior. But she hadn't, and as time went by, Kate realized she might never see Rachel again. Sammy wouldn't know his mother.

When Sammy and the girls went to sleep for the night, Laura usually followed, leaving her son time alone with Kate. They tried to be respectful and wait a bit before running off to their bedroom, still eagerly anticipating each other's touch, his breath still catching when he gently removed her dress and saw again her golden skin, her slender body.

Her eyes closed half way, absorbing the feel of his lips on her skin when he kissed her bare shoulders. They grew to know each other better even after so many years, and

91

with each day, with deeper understanding, their passion grew more intense, more tender, and more complete. Mel lifted her out of the dress crumpling at her feet and laid her on the bed. His heart beat heavily and a moan escaped his lips in symphony with Sammy's cry. "No . . ." he groaned. "Does he have a clock? How does he know?"

Kate turned to him and wrapped her arms around his back as he sat on the edge of the bed, his feet planted on the floor, his head in his hands. "I'll be back," she said. "Don't go anywhere."

She picked up the wailing Sammy, changed him and went to the kitchen to warm milk for a bottle. She sat in the rocker in front of the fire with her grandchild, her head resting against the back, rocking gently. She heard the soft shuffle of Mel's feet and saw him ruffling his sandy hair, running a roughened hand over his face.
"Want some company?" he asked.

"If it's yours and you want to wait here with me," she told him, a warm smile enticing him to stay.

"I would keep company with you anywhere, sweetheart."

Wolf looked up at Mel from his place in front of the hearth, rolled one eye and turned his face to the wall, groaning. Kate thought it was a sound of aversion, and she smiled. Wolf didn't care for the mushy stuff. Mel took the seat by her, and her breath caught as she felt his warm hand on her neck and his fingers run through her hair. She looked at her husband, his weathered, angular face, his strong shoulders and lean body. She thought for the millionth time how lucky she was to be loved by this man.

"Mmmm . . . And I with you," she said.

"Anywhere?" he teased.

"You got it. Anywhere."

"I'm a lucky man," he said with warm feeling.

"No, I'm a lucky woman."

"Don't argue with me woman."

"Don't call me woman," she said and rose, handing him the baby as she moved. "Here, feed Sammy. Want some tea?"

Mel chuckled. "I do, woman, with a bit of whiskey in it to take the edge off my pent-up energy."

"Don't lose your energy, Mel. The night is young."

"Hmmm. I am definitely a lucky man."

While Sammy finished his bottle, Mel played with a small hand wrapped around his fingers. He watched the baby clench and unclench his small hands, and Mel marveled; they were so tiny and yet so perfect. At the same time, Kate was heating water for tea and watching her husband, wondering how anyone so large and masculine could be so gentle, so perfect.

"It's hard to understand Rachel when you look at Sammy," he said quietly.

Kate nodded, knowing exactly what he meant, having thought the same thing since the day Rachel left. "I hurt for her, but I mostly hurt for the day she realizes what she's lost. I'd rather she never knew it."

They sipped their tea, and watched the fire draw flickering flame pictures. They didn't rock because their shoulders touched, and they wanted the connection and warmth. Kate put an arm over his shoulder and played with the brown curls hugging his neck. Her touch sent sweet shivers down his back and melted his eyes, turned them smoky and languid.

The winter of 1917 was one of growth, of love and passion, of learning each other and finding how the girls, Sammy and Jamie fit into the family picture. It hadn't been a real concern for Kate because she knew how much Mel cared for them all, but she was continually surprised by his attention to them, to their needs. If he had to go into town, he made sure he had either Becca or Jeannie with him. They loved their individual time alone with him, and Mel loved it too. They usually made an afternoon of it, stopping for ice cream at the diner for a special treat.

Farming took a lot of time; plowing and planting in the spring, cutting and threshing in the fall, cleaning the barns and feeding the animals every day of the year, and, of course, milking which Becca always wanted to do with him.

If it had to do with the cows, Becca was going to be there, and she had become a real help, better than any hired hand. She did it with love.

He spent time with Jeannie, too, when they were feeding the calves or cleaning the stalls. She liked doing both chores, and he made sure he was with her at least some of the time when she fed the chickens and piglets. Though he trusted her to do it right, he didn't think it would have been fair to drop it on her. The season progressed with ease and pleasure; the family, though smaller with Rachel and Kat absent, was settling in and happy.

After Jack started on his new office, Jamie spent most of his days there, sometimes staying at Jack and Ruthie's instead of coming back to the farm. Mel had given him the use of one of his mares until he could get one of his own. As Kate had thought, he got along famously with Jack, and Jamie was getting stronger and filling out. He looked so much like Mark in his natural elegance, the resemblance was sometimes startling.

On a warm spring-like day, Kate said, "Hey, who wants to take a drive into town, go see Grandma and Mr. Woodward?" Becca said no, she was gonna help Mel with the milking, but Jeannie and Wolf leaped to their feet, ready to go.

"Go get Sammy's snow suit, Jeannie. It'll be a chilly ride, especially coming home. Wouldn't you like to go with us, Laura?"

She shook her head. "You go on and have a good time. I'm happy in front of this fire."

They bundled Sammy while Mel hitched the buggy, and Wolf was waiting on the seat when they got outside. When they neared the smith shop, they saw the door standing wide open and heard the sounds of work going on.

"Let's stop," Kate said, and pulled up by the door.

Jack poked his head out and beamed when he saw them. "Hey! Look who's here," he yelled to Jamie, then added, "Come on in!" She handed Sammy to him and hopped down. Wolf ran in ahead of her, scouting the place, making sure it was safe, and Jeannie was right behind him.

"Hey, big boy," Jack said, peeking under the warm cap at Sammy's rosy face. He lifted him up and down a couple of times like he was weighing a sack of potatoes. "I think he's eating well. This boy's growing fast. He's gonna be a big bruiser like your brute of a husband," he teased.

"Don't be jealous and petty, Jack," Kate teased. "It doesn't become you."

"Well I'm going to take this young man in and show him around."

"Wow. I wouldn't know it was the same place," she said, walking through the door.

All the tools were gone, and the floor had been scrubbed nearly white. The front entry area had been paneled with pine boards on the walls, and a low counter separated the entry from what would be Jack's office. Jamie greeted Kate with smiles, glad to show off their handiwork.

"Come in, come and see how great it looks," he said. Kate looked around standing just inside the door. It didn't look anything like the smithy. The only similarity was the huge hearth at the back where Mark had heated the iron he had worked. Jack had wanted the forge kept the same. It was now the back wall of his office.

"This is where the chairs will be for people to wait when I'm too busy to tend to them right away," Jack said grinning with delight. "And this is where my desk will be, and we'll want a couple of rugs -- one here and one here -- after the floor gets finished, of course."

Kate nodded, looking around with pleasure. "You and Jamie have worked wonders. It's beautiful, and it doesn't even smell like a smithy anymore."

She wandered through to the back rooms where they had lived, where she had tipped off the chair she'd been perched on trying to put new curtains up to surprise Mark. Where she'd fallen on top of him, much to her chagrin and delight. She turned to see Jamie watching the many moods cross her face, and she described the incident to him.

Jack came through the door to the back rooms and added to the story. "Your grandma was always after your grandfather," he said to Sammy in a fake whisper. "Couldn't

95

keep her hands off him. She was a fallen woman. Probably still is."

Jamie raised an eyebrow. "Is that true?" he asked her.

"Yes. Pretty much," she said with a giggle. She sounded like a girl again. Jack put an arm around her shoulder, and they surveyed the rooms.

"Yes, Sammy my boy, this is where your grandma and grandpa lived for quite a few years in the winter time." He leaned to whisper in Sammy's ear. "This is where they made your mother. Right here," he said pointing.

"Will you quit filling that child's ear full of your nonsense?"

"It isn't nonsense. It's the gospel, and I'm hurt. Hey, what do you think about fixing these rooms up again? Maybe Jamie would like having his own place," he added.

"But I like having him with me out at the farm," Kate said wistfully. "It's nice having him there."

"I'm right here," Jamie said grinning. "Don't fight over me."

"And don't pout, Kate," Jack teased in retribution for Kate's earlier words. "If we do it, it won't happen right away, anyway."

Sammy wiggled and Jack put him on his feet, held his hand and let him walk around the rooms. It was like he was inspecting the space, seeing what kind of a place it could make for Uncle Jamie. "He approves," Jack said. "He likes it."

"Come on, Sammy. Let's go see Grandma Ellen and Aunt Ruthie. Let's leave these silly boys to do their boy things."

"We'll be right behind you," Jack said. "In fact, you might even see Harley and Kat if you scoot. They were heading there a bit ago."

Ellen and Ruthie met them at the door, and Ellen immediately took Sammy, removed his outer layer of clothes, and looked him over like she was inspecting him for signs of abuse. Kate and Ruthie watched and rolled their eyes a bit, doing sister talk without words.

"Well, he certainly looks healthy," Ellen finally said.

"What did you think, Mother, that I wouldn't feed him, keep him in the cellar, maybe beat him when no one was looking?" She knew she shouldn't but she couldn't help it. Ellen was easy to tease, and then Kate always felt bad for having done it. It was the devil in her making her do it, and she wasn't to blame. That's what she told herself and anyone else who gave her the evil eye for pulling her mother's leg.

"Well, I didn't mean . . . of course not . . . I . . . Never mind. Sammy looks wonderful."

"I know. Just ribbing you, Ma." Kate put her arm around her and squeezed, not too hard. She felt so fragile. "He's beautiful, isn't he."

"Yes, he is. It's a shame Rachel isn't here to see him grow."

Ellen never failed to bring up Rachel's name. It was like a chant with her, and Kate didn't want to hear it constantly. She thought about Rachel all the time. She didn't need to be reminded her daughter had abandoned her baby. Sammy was both motherless and fatherless. She was short in her reply and immediately felt bad.

"But she isn't, Mother, and Sammy is a happy boy."

"Would you like tea or coffee or perhaps a glass of wine?" Ruthie asked.

"Did Harley and Kat come by?" Kate asked.

"Haven't seen them, why?" Ruthie said.

"I stopped by the shop and Jack said they were heading this way."

"Hmmm. Nope . . . coffee, tea, wine?"

"I think tea, at least until I know for sure if Harley is stopping by. I'm sure we'll have a toast to something if he comes," Kate said with a laugh and a lighter mood.

Ellen joined them at the table and tried to drink her tea with a squirming Sammy on her lap. She finally gave up and let him get down. He made a game of walking around the table holding on from chair to chair. He'd obviously be walking unaided soon. She thought he was a marvel, exceptionally precocious. Surely no other child walked earlier or was sturdier on his feet than her Sammy; no one existed who was brighter or of sunnier disposition. Kate smiled and wondered if she sounded like an infatuated grandmother, too, when John Nestor or some other unwitting person asked about her grandson.

"Well, too bad," she said.

"Too bad what?" Ruthie asked.

Kate looked at her questioningly. "What do you *mean*, too bad what?"

"*You* said, 'Well, too bad,'" Ruthie told her sister, looking at her with raised eyebrows. "I think you're losing your mind. Winnie Wellington is going to give up her town loony position if you keep this up." She paused, thoughtfully, then slapped her leg. "Wait just a cotton-picking minute, you already swear like a sailor, so you're half way there."

Poor Mrs. Wellington lost her husband . . . literally . . . he disappeared one day, and the next day, she began the downhill slide toward crazy. She wore multiple layers of clothes, chewed incessantly, and swore constantly -- mostly about men who just wanted to screw, screw, screw. Everyone in town knew her, tolerated her, and against all odds, had various degrees of affection for her. She was unique.

"Harrumph," Kate growled. "Winnie, my eye. I think you hear things. Who's right, Ma? Did I say 'well, too bad' or did Ruthie make it up?"

"How would I know? I was busy with Sammy and you two quit fussing at each other, right now. Heavens, you'd think you were girls again."

Kate reached over and tapped Ruthie's arm. "Quit making stuff up," she said with a grin and watching her mother for a reaction.

"Ma, Kate touched me."

"Crybaby," Kate said. "Tattle tale."

Ruthie couldn't keep up the pretense and laughed out loud. She whispered to Kate, "Do you want to sing off key and see if we can make her howl?"

Kate nodded, and they sang in off key harmony which drove Ellen mad. She couldn't stand it, and the more she yelled at them, the louder they sang. Wolf joined in with a howl from the hounds of hell. They continued even after the door opened and Harley and Kat entered with Jack and Jamie trailing them.

"What is going on in here?" Harley asked, hearing the cacophony of discord and seeing the evil glee in Kate and Ruthie's expressions. Ellen had her hands over her ears by then and looked up thankfully, hoping they could stop her brat girls from making this horrible noise. It hurt her melodically sensitive ears!

Jamie looked around at the faces in different stages of angst and glee, clearly confused about what was going on. Jack came in, leaned back against the wall with his arms crossed, watching the show. Harley pulled on his suspenders and looked from Kate to Ruthie to Ellen, while Kat shook her head. She'd heard this before.

Finally, Harley thought their distinctive voices needed a conductor, so he moved forward and started waving his arms -- conductor-like, leading the discord. Jeannie decided to add her voice to the clamor, and finally Kat joined in, too. The noise was horrific with the most bizarre and, in its way beautiful, dissonance that could be made by human voices. According to Kate and Ruthie, the best had always been the worst sound you could possibly make. As girls, they practiced hard to make it as bad a tune as could ever be produced.

Harley brought the quartet to its pinnacle of sound and, with a flourish, brought the symphony to an end. He waved an arm toward the singers to indicate applause was called for and elaborately bowed himself.

Ellen stayed bent over, covering her ears. When she was brave enough, she peered up at her wayward daughters to see if they were going to begin singing again, which they'd done in the past. Seeing no mouths moving in song, she took her hands from her ears and welcomed Kat and Harley, with a smack on the back of Harley's head for his contribution to the music debacle.

"You're old enough to know better," she muttered with a loving scowl.

Kate sidled up to Ruthie. "Felt good, like a kid again."

"Yeah, it did. We need to sing more often. Now, do you want wine?"

"Yup. Earned it. Great concert," a satisfied, Cheshire cat look on her face, love for Ruthie in her eyes. 'Sisters are the best.'

Jack brought out the jug and Ruthie poured wine and made hot chocolate for the girls. It felt like a party. Jamie hadn't been to many of their family gatherings, and to him it was an amazing, novel experience, people who cared about each other, spending time with each other. The orphanage and foster homes had not been kind to him, nor had they given him warm, loving memories. He looked around, taking in the faces and smiles and comfortable closeness.

Harley watched them and said, "Raise your glasses to the beautiful Hughes girls because that's what they were a few minutes ago . . . girls. May they always remember to sing off key just because it feels good to do it. And here's to Kat and Jeannie for learning from their mother and aunt that a little discord is a beautiful thing."

They were about to drink to discord when the door opened and a white-faced Willie walked in. He stood in the opened doorway, still and silent, staring blankly at them. His mouth worked, but no sound came out. He looked dead standing there, body alive, face white, heart no longer pumping blood. Ellen got up from her chair and folded her son in her arms, whispered in his ear.

"What is it, Willie?"

"It's Rob. He's missing . . . in action." Tears filled his eyes, and he bent to put his face on his mother's shoulder. His shoulders shook and silent sobs racked him. Ellen held her son, knowing his pain, trying to take some of it for him, trying to share the horrible burden. When they moved apart, she said, "Mary. Does she know yet?"

"No. I couldn't. I just got . . . it just came . . . I didn't . . ."

Harley moved to give Willie the jug. "Take a nip," he told him, and added, "I'm sorry, Will."

He drank, then drank again, drawing deep on the second one. It calmed him a bit, and he sat when they led him to a chair and sat with him. He reached for the letter, pulled it from his shirt pocket and handed it to his mother.

Ellen slowly opened it, stared at the words, not reading or comprehending, yet. It was too ugly, too painful. If she didn't read the words, they wouldn't be true. She turned it over on the table and let her hands lay on the single page. She would look later, when she could face what was written there.

Right now, her son needed her attention, her love and care. He was a full-grown man with a child who was a full-grown man in the service of this country, and he was missing in action . . . whatever missing meant.

How can you lose a soldier? she thought. It's ludicrous. You can't just go missing.

Harley watched her face reflecting all the thoughts marching through her brain. His heart had broken for her when Will died, and it did again as he saw Ellen's mind find some new hell to ponder. He poured moonshine into a glass and placed it in front of her. He moved behind her, put his hands on her shoulders and whispered in her ear. She took a gulp of the home brew and gave him a weak smile.

She breathed deeply, her back stiffened, her narrow shoulders thrust back, and her face grew stonily determined around the soft, tearful features. This is what mothers do. They try to bear the burdens of their young, to absorb their sorrows, insulate them from grief. They support their children in their losses as long as their own shoulders can bear the weight. Ellen found new strength in her son's mourning, and she would continue to find power as long as her slender bones held her upright, as long as her faith gave her strength to stand, to hold them when they needed it and to soak up their tears in the thin cotton of the shoulders of her dress.

Harley held the jug up once again and toasted, "To Robbie's eyes, his grandfather's twinkling blue-gray eyes . . . sparkling and cajoling eyes. They got him into trouble, but they got him out of it, too." He paused for a moment, thinking, and looked around the room with purpose. 'I'm not done; I'm pondering,' his look told them.

Then he finished. "If our Robbie is missing as the authorities say, it's because he wants to be somewhere other than where they think he should be. So here is to Robbie's warm bed this night, hot breakfast in the morning, and bit of fun in between. He'll be back doing his service to America before we know it, and he'll no longer be missing." He made a show of his sip and passed the jug on.

After Willie held the jug in his hands and took a long swig, he rose saying he had to go to Mary. It was evident he didn't want to, dreaded the conversation he must have with her more than any hateful thing in his life. Kat watched her uncle, hesitated only briefly. "I'll go with you," she said. "I have some herbs. They might help Aunt Mary get through the night and over the next few days. She'll sleep better."

Willie's eyebrows rose in question, but Harley took his arm and told him Kat could do what she said. "Believe in your young niece. She's becoming a doctor of the highest order."

They left, giving Willie a ride in the buggy. He stared off to the side of the road as if seeing something in the growing darkness. But he wasn't seeing anything except his son as a child, as a young man, and finally as a soldier going off to war.

Mary met them at the door, her expression saying more than any words could do. She knew. Whether it was the fact her husband came home with Harley and Kat, or the face he wore, his eyes; she knew and she crumpled. Fortunately, Willie was close enough to keep her from falling to the ground. He held her and spoke soothingly. "He's only missing, Mary. He'll be found."

Kat moved into their small kitchen and put water in the tea kettle and set it to boil. She took two cups from the cupboard and carefully measured a variety of herbs she took from a small bag she'd brought with her. When the whistle blew, she poured the hot water into the cups and waited for the herbs to steep. She took the cups to her aunt and uncle who hovered together on the sofa.

"Drink this," she told them.

"What is it?" Willie asked skeptically.

Kat smiled warmly at him, knowing she was still a girl to him, not a doctor, and she knew it too. She wasn't a doctor yet, but she would be, and right now she was the best he had.

"Would you like me to get Doc Cheston, Uncle Willie?" she asked, sincerely. "I'm sure he'd come if we asked."

He shook his head and sipped the tea Kat had made. "No. Let's sit a while."

It wasn't long before they relaxed and were able to talk. Kat and Harley stayed as long as they were needed, as long as Willie and Mary wanted to talk, and then they took their leave. On the way home, Harley patted Kat's blanket covered leg. "You're something, Miss Kat. You're surely something."

"And you, Mr. Benton," she said and snuggled against his shoulder like a little girl ready to nap on the way back to the cabin.

Chapter Eleven

Summer 1918

Kate walked to the barn, strolling slowly, turning to look at the flower beds burning with a flood of color, reaching for sun and soaking it up, much like Kate was. She ambled, taking her time and enjoying the warm, balmy morning. Her face was turned to catch the heat of the sun's rays; her body was alive with joy. Kate's world was beautiful.

Sammy turned one in June. He took his first tentative steps and was a happy child, sturdy, handsome and precocious. Kate was having fun with him, especially since she didn't have to work as hard as she had when her girls were young, or leave him to go off to the camp or the diner. It was a peace she hadn't known before, and each day, Kate recognized what a treasure it was.

Jamie was healing from his wounds and enjoyed working with Jack in making the old smithy into an office fit for a top-notch attorney. He was beginning to smile again and charmed everyone he met, as his dad had done.

Becca was blossoming as a herdsman; she was coming to know Mel's heifers better than even he did. And he knew his cows . . . he loved them. But, so did she. They gently pressed into her when she was near, and a soft, velvet nose nuzzled her when they came in for milking. They spoke to her with their lowing, and she responded with murmurs and cow-talk.

And Jeannie believed the world existed for her pleasure. She loved the animals, was enamored with Sammy, was kind to everyone and was sure the world and everyone in it felt the same. Jeannie didn't have hidden fears that plagued most people at least some of the time.

She knew she was cute, intelligent, and loved by all. Unbridled confidence was her gift, and it brought a sparkle to her eyes. They captivated anyone who gazed too long. Those who did were under her spell.

Except for nagging concern over Rachel who hadn't been heard from and Robbie who was still missing in action, Kate's days moved on easy, drifting clouds of near perfection.

She was tossing corn to the chickens with Jeannie, and they were chattering away when she heard a shout and saw Becca running from the milk parlor.

"Oh, God! Ma! Come quick," she said. "Hurry!"

Becca's face was white, her eyes wide and frozen in fear. Kate dropped her grain bucket and raced to the barn. Inside, she saw Mel on the floor next to his milk stool, an overturned bucket, and milk spreading out over the straw littered floor around him. He was moving and mumbling, trying unsuccessfully to lift his head when she reached him.

"Becca, get the cow out of here, please," Kate said, afraid the animal, who was shuffling around in anxiety, would step on him.

She knelt next to him in the milky straw, lifted his head and placed it on her lap, looking for wounds, a reason why he should be on the floor. "What's wrong? What happened?"

Mel blinked his eyes and ran a hand over his face trying to come out of a daze, but his mind was foggy, and his arm was so heavy it fell from his face to his chest. He had never felt so weak, so hot. He mumbled to her, and she put her face close to his mouth to listen but couldn't understand his muffled words.

Kate felt intense heat coming through his shirt and knew he was sick. He hadn't been hurt; he was burning up with fever.

"Becca, run to the house and get Jamie. Fast, please. And take Jeannie with you."

Kate looked around for something to wipe the sweat beading on his brow and running into his eyes, but nothing was near and she didn't want to leave him to go look. She took the end of her skirt and dabbed at his face, whispering words of encouragement. She kissed his face and felt the high temperature on her lips, on her face even though it wasn't touching his skin.

"You'll be fine, Mel. Please, be fine. Jamie will be here in a minute, and we'll get you in the house."

He groaned, hearing her voice but not understanding where he was or what was happening.

Between the two of them, they half carried, half dragged Mel into the house and to the couch. They rested a moment as Mel lay sprawled, then lifted him again, and moved him to a bed. After Jamie helped her with his clothes, she sent him to the cabin to get Harley and Kat.

"Tell them what you've seen; he's burning up and incoherent; he fainted or fell or . . . something." Her eyes started to fill, and she stomped her foot, squared her shoulders.

"Tell them to bring whatever herbs they need and to get here fast. Take one of Mel's mares."

"Jeannie, find Mel's mother. She's probably lying down in her room. Tell her Mel is sick. And then will you finish up the chores? Becca, too?"

Kate was bathing him in cool cloths when Laura came in.

"What happened?" she asked.

"I don't know. I sent for Harley and Kat."

"What about Doc Cheston? Shouldn't we get him out here?" Laura asked. She didn't like leaving it to someone who wasn't a doctor.

"We can do that. Jamie can go when he gets back with Kat and Harley," Kate murmured. She didn't care how many people it took, how many they needed to call on.

Mel began moving fitfully on the bed, tossing around, trying to get up and falling back, thrashing about. Kate tried to hold him down, tried talking to him, but he either didn't hear or couldn't understand.

"Help me, please! Hold him down," she yelled to her mother-in-law. "He's going to hurt himself."

Laura pushed down on an arm, but she was nothing against Mel's strength. Finally, Kate lifted her long skirt and climbed on top of him. She straddled his waist and lay down on his chest. She pulled his arms around her back, and he stopped tossing and began to embrace her. She stayed there holding him, and he her, for a long while. When she felt him grow calm, she got up. Her shirtfront was dark with perspiration where she had lain against his bare chest. She'd felt the fever come through her clothes to heat her skin, and she was frightened. She was more than that; she was terrified.

They were sponging him with cold water when they heard hooves pound into the yard and feet slamming the floor and racing into the house.

Harley and Kat burst into the room, and John Crow followed more gravely. When Kate saw him, she breathed a sigh of relief. "I'm so glad to see you," she told him and moved to put her arms around him. "Help him, please."

John went to Mel and stood still, looking at him much like he had when Jeannie's leg was broken. Kate had wanted to scream at him . . . 'Do something!' Since then, she had come to understand his ways, come to respect his unusual knowledge, methods, and intuition.

Jeannie stood pressed against the wall, silent in her fear. Laura hovered near the bed, watching intently. She didn't know this strange looking man, didn't know if he was a doctor or what he was. She hadn't been introduced and didn't want to interrupt. But she wasn't leaving her son.

John would have liked them all to leave. He needed calm and positive energy, a clear path to knowing and healing. Having negative interference made his work more difficult. He'd like Kat to be present, possibly Harley because he was Kat's guide, but the rest -- even Kate -- no.

John dismissed them from his mind and put himself in a place alone with the patient. He heard no one else and saw no one else. He put his hand on Mel's forehead, then his chest and his stomach. He pinched Mel's fingers and watched as the skin changed colors. He looked at Mel's eyes and his tongue and throat. All the while, Mel submitted calmly to the examination. He asked him to roll over on his side, and he did so. John pressed his hands to Mel's lower back and worked his fingers in and up his spine to his neck where he pushed in around his jaw line.

He told Mel he could lie back again and turned to Kat. "Borage flower and cinnamon to bring down the fever," he said to her. "In my bag. Two teaspoons in one cup of boiling water." When she brought the tea, he said, "Make sure he drinks it all. One cup every other hour. Also, steep willow bark with wintergreen, for pain and inflammation. One cup every four hours." He took Kate's arm and walked her out of the room.

"What is it?" she demanded as they walked, not wanting to leave Mel but being propelled by John's firm hand. "What's wrong with him?"

"Have you heard of the influenza outbreak?" he asked.

"Of what? What influenza? I don't know of any outbreak." She thought she was babbling, but anxiety was in charge of her tongue, and she couldn't stop.

Once in the kitchen, he pushed her into a chair. His eyes were hooded, his mind carefully assessing what to say, what to keep.

"He has influenza. They call it Spanish flu and it's serious, Kate. Not simply because your husband's sick, but because everyone who is in contact with him could become ill. People die from this Spanish flu."

"You are surely incorrect!" she said in disbelief, angry he would suggest such a thing was possible. "He is a strong, healthy man. He couldn't die from a little flu bug."

John sat quietly, carefully choosing the words he had to say. "There have been outbreaks all over the world, starting in the close confines of military quarters and places much like our logging camps where men live and work in near proximity to each other. Many have died, but many live, also."

Wolf rose majestically and put his front paws on John's shoulders. He placed his nose on John's cheek, and left it there, waiting. Wolf didn't like the furious anger he felt in the room and might have to hurt someone he respected for

Kate. He held perfectly still, waiting to understand the situation.

Several moments of silence followed as John's words began to seep in, to become a horrible reality. Visions she would never share flashed through her brain, images her heart and soul fought against with every ounce of strength she had. 'He will not die! He will not!'

Wolf finally left John alone, sensing no harm, and came to put his head in Kate's lap. She silently stroked him, and a long, drawn out breath preceded her words. "Okay, what do we do? How is it treated?" she said in a whisper; the truth and gravity of his words had sunk in.

As she waited for his response, she thought of those who had come into contact with Mel. Becca ... Jeannie. She turned to look around the room when she realized she hadn't seen Becca since she had sent her to find Jamie.

Kate leaped to her feet and called to Jeannie. "Where's Becca, Jeannie? Where is your sister?"

"I don't know, Ma. I haven't seen her."

"Well, get Jamie or Harley and go look for her, please?"

When they left to look for Becca, Kate and John went back to the room where Mel lay. Laura, her face whiter than the cloth she held in her hand, was bathing her son's body, trying to bring down the fierce heat consuming him. No sooner did she rinse the cloth in cool water and place it on him than it was heated by his skin, and she repeated the process.

It didn't matter to her how long it took, how many hours she needed to stand by his bed and bathe his burning skin; she would do it forever if forever was necessary. If it meant he would recover from the illness that had taken over his body, if it meant he would have health again, she would give her own and be content. More, she would praise the Lord for her good fortune.

Kate took one glance at her mother-in-law's face and stopped. She remembered seeing the same hollow, poignant eyes just recently. *'Where?'* she asked herself, turning away. Deep sorrow had been the only thing holding them in their sockets. If not for the sorrow, they might have fallen out, leaving empty holes. They haunted her.

"Mary," she whispered. They were Mary's eyes when her son left to fight in this God forsaken war. She'd worn dead eyes when she turned toward home. Kate looked back at Laura. "I need to go see Mary," Kate said.

John nodded, understanding intuitively the connection between Mel's illness and Kate's need to see her sister-in-law.

Harley came quietly into the room much later and asked Kate to come out. He was perspiring heavily and his breathing was rapid. "We've looked everywhere we can think of. We can't find Becca."

Kate moved out to the hallway to talk. "Harley, she's out there somewhere. She's the one who found Mel and called out to me. She got Jamie for me to help carry Mel in the house. She's here. Find her, please."

Kate was beginning to fall apart. Harley saw and gently pushed her into the kitchen and poured her a small glass of Will's moonshine.

"Sit and drink this," he said, handing it to her, and tipped the jug to his lips for a sip of his own.

"Who is Becca closest to?" Harley asked. "Jeannie? Kat?"

Kate shook her head. "Neither really. She spends most of her time with Mel. Him or his cows. Did you look in all the barns?"

"Yes, we went through them twice, calling to her."

"I don't understand. Why would she disappear?"

Harley was quiet, thinking about Becca. She'd been only six when her father died. She had dealt with it as they all had, quietly and with grim determination. But when Mel brought them to the farm, Becca had fallen in love with it all: the animals, the feeding and milking, the scent and spirit of the whole farm experience. To her, people didn't farm to earn a living; it was a way of life, a loved one. She would jump out of bed and race through breakfast to get to the good part of her day outside, the farm chores. She adored

Mel, loved her life and him because he was the farm. Becca was happy.

Harley didn't know what she had seen when they brought Mel inside or what she had heard as John Crow explained Mel's condition. He was concerned Becca was terrified of losing another father.

"I don't understand," Kate repeated. "There aren't many places she could be. Why can't you find her?"

"She may not want to be found, Kate," he said, and then thought about the hay mow and the ladder going up to the top. "I have an idea. I might know where she is. Wait here," he said and got up to leave. When Kate started to protest, he stopped her. "Mel will be taken care of. He has people with him. And I'll go find our girl. Sit there and wait; drink your medicine," he added with an attempt at a grin.

Kate put her head in her hand and did as he said. She sipped her medicine and waited. She sat painfully still, stayed put while unbelievable, hateful events whirled and eddied around her. She had no control over anything anymore, and she didn't like how it felt. She liked organization, a map of the future showing what would happen if she put one foot in front of the other and moved forward. This wasn't right at all, this dust storm of life she could do nothing about.

Outside, Harley told Jeannie where he thought Becca might be. She nodded, a bright smile lighting her eyes. "You're right, Harley. I didn't think of that, but why didn't she answer us when we called?"

"Well, maybe she was asleep. What I want you to do if she doesn't answer us this time is to climb that rickety old ladder and see if she's there. Okay?"

Jeannie nodded and when they got near, they both began calling her name. As he expected, Becca didn't answer, and Jeannie looked confused.

"Scoot up the ladder, Copper Top. See if your sister is playing hide and seek."

Harley knew Becca was there before Jeannie got to the loft. He heard, "Go away. Leave me alone." Jeannie turned around to look at Harley, hurt pouring from her eyes. "Mom needs you, Becca," Jeannie told her. "She sent us to get you."

"Well, I'm going to stay here until Kat and Harley go back to the cabin. Then I'm going with them."

"Why? You love the farm. Why would you do that?" Jeannie said, wanting to cry and growing more upset by the moment. Everyone was moving away, just when they had a huge place for them all to stay -- together.

"Come down, Jeannie." Harley said. "Let me go up and talk with your sister, okay?"

When Jeannie was on the floor once more, Harley asked her to run in and tell her mother Becca was fine, just sleeping in the hay mow.

"But that's not true, Harley."

"Well, this time a fib is best. Say she was sleeping, okay? Anyway, she might have been sleeping earlier, before we woke her up yelling her name. We'll be in momentarily."

"Are you gonna climb up there?" she asked when he put a foot tentatively on the first shaky rung of the ladder. Her face scrunched up, and it was clear she was doubtful about his success in getting to the top.

He nodded. "Sure, no problem. Go on in and do what I asked, okay?"

He maneuvered his rotund body slowly and carefully up the ladder, leaned over the top rung, hung there, and then rolled into the hay onto his back. He lay there, thanking God for strong ladders and soft hay. He opened his eyes to see Becca staring into his face, six inches from his nose.

"Are you okay?" she asked, her eyes wide and worried.

"I'm fine. You?"

"I'm okay. Why?"

"Well . . . you're hiding up here and not answering when we're calling your name and worrying about you. That's kinda' why I wondered."

"I didn't want to talk to anyone."

"I understand not wanting to talk, Becca. Do you want to tell me why you don't want to talk?"

She shook her head and her long, nearly silver, blond hair swung back and forth. It covered her face as she wanted it to. She didn't want Harley to see the dirt smeared tear tracks on it. She didn't want him to see the fear on her face. It was so strong inside her she could smell it on her skin. It had been curling and boiling in her since she saw Mel fall from his milk stool. People who got sick died. Maybe not today, but tomorrow or the next day, sick people died. He would die, too, and she wouldn't stay here to see it this time. She couldn't. She'd move back to the cabin and be with Kat and Harley. That's what she'd do. Tonight.

"It's nice up here," Harley said. "Warm and cozy."

Becca nodded. She loved the hay mow. But she loved everything about this farm.

"Do you feed this stuff to the cows?"

She nodded again. "Grain, too."

"I hear them mooing. Is that what you call it?" he asked.

"Mel calls it lowing. They low when they need to be milked."

Harley nodded this time and waited awhile, then asked, "Do they low when they need to be fed, too?"

When she nodded again, Harley said, "There's a lot of nodding going on here. Does that mean we agree on most things?"

Becca gave half a laugh, and Harley thought he was making headway. "You're afraid for Mel, aren't you, Becca?" he asked gently.

She looked down, hiding again, and shook her head. When he didn't respond, she peered up at him.

"Let's agree to be truthful, okay?" he said. "I'm going to be truthful with you. Mel is very sick. He has influenza. He feels terrible, and sometimes it's serious, but Mel is a strong, young man. He will most likely beat this. Do you believe me?"

Becca thought for a moment, then nodded again. He held out his arms, and she fell into them, tears finally washing away the dirt streaks. He murmured to her, held her, and rocked her as if she was a baby, and she let him.

"Are you ready to go down?" he asked when he no longer felt her shuddering and trembling.

"I have to finish milking and feed the calves. Jeannie needs to feed the chickens. Maybe Jamie could come help me clean the stalls and throw hay for the herd?"

Becca was back, and Harley smiled. "Don't fall climbing down," she warned as he tentatively maneuvered his feet back on the ladder.

"I won't. Stop in to see your mother before you finish chores, okay?" he asked.

Girl of few words and much like her sister, Kat, she nodded one more time and, after she climbed down, ran to see her mother. Relief flooded through Kate when she saw Becca.

"I am so happy to see you. Were you really asleep all this time?"

Becca was still for a moment or two, looked in her mother's eyes and couldn't lie. She slowly shook her head. She wanted to explain, but now was not the time.

"I'm gonna finish up the milking," she said. "So, I gotta go."

"I understand, Becca. We'll talk later."

"I need Jamie and Jeannie to help with the chores. Will you send them out?" When Kate said she would, Becca gave her mother a quick wave of her hand and flew out the door.

Kate sat unmoving, her hands covering her face. She didn't want to see Mel the way he was, so helpless, so unlike himself. But if she turned her head away for one moment, she felt something horrible would happen. She'd lose him. She didn't want to go back in his room, and she couldn't stay away.

She was terrified of what she would find. Her heart beat madly, and until she peeked in and saw him moving around battling the fever demons, she couldn't breathe. As senseless as it was, she felt like her presence in the room, her vital strength, would sustain him.

She sat holding his hand and talked to him. Hearing the words out loud felt like she was discussing things with him, and it clarified what she had to do.

She moved to his side, put her hand on his chest, and leaned down to whisper in his ear. "I love you, and I'll be back in a few minutes, but right now I need to make arrangements, need to plan some things so you can get well. Don't go anywhere." She tried to tease, but it didn't work, ". . . please;" she choked out, unable to stop her eyes from filling with tears there wasn't time to shed. She turned to Mel's mother, "I'll be back as soon as I can, Laura."

"Harley, John, Kat, can I see you in the kitchen, please? I need Jamie, Jeannie and Becca, too, before they finish the chores. Will someone go get them for me?"

When they were all gathered, she heard Sammy waking up from his nap and howling for attention. "Hang on. Jeannie, please change Sammy and bring him to the kitchen."

Kate talked while she fixed his bottle. "We need to make some changes. I can't feed Sammy. I've been too close to Mel, so whoever hasn't touched him can give Sammy his bottle while we talk. Kat or Jeannie, maybe?" She paused and took a deep breath. "Will you explain the contagion, John?"

John did, and he also emphasized the seriousness of Spanish influenza. When he was finished, Kate outlined what she believed was the best plan for keeping everyone safe. Mel needed to be moved upstairs where she and Laura would stay for the duration of his illness. They were both needed to care for Mel. Becca and Jamie would stay downstairs, take care of the farm and fix food for the upstairs people.

"I am really sorry," Kate told them. "I hate to do this to you, but I don't know another way for everyone to stay healthy."

Becca spoke up. "I don't mind doing the work, Ma. It's what I do anyway -- well, except for the cooking thing, but I'll have Jamie's help," she said with a bit of a grin and nudge on his arm.

"It's what we have to do," Jamie said. "Besides, it's not forever."

A hush hung in the air while thoughts were processed. Until when, then? Until Mel got better? Until what? No one wanted to think beyond the moment, beyond taking care of today.

John spoke up, breaking into the black void of silence. "Recovery times vary depending on the length of the fever and the depth of congestion in the chest. Anywhere from three days to three weeks. Of course, beating the influenza and getting back on your feet are two different things."

They all nodded, were glad to have some concrete knowledge to help guide them.

"You'll have to let Jack know you won't be in for a while," Kate said, looking at Jamie.

John spoke up again. "I have to go into town anyway. I'll let him know. You'll want your sister and mother to know, too."

"Kat," Kate said, "I'm giving you some serious responsibility. I need you and Harley to take Jeannie and Sammy back with you. I'd rather they weren't in the house. Do you understand what I'm asking?"

"That's not a problem," Kat and Harley both said at the same time.

"I'll put them to work," Kat said with a soft smile.

"I don't do work," Jeannie piped in as she walked into the room carrying Sammy. "But I can take care of this little guy."

Kate stood, pushed up the sleeves of her shirtdress like she was preparing for battle. "And you do that well, Jeannie. That's why Sammy loves you so much. Would you mind feeding him? Kat, pull down the blankets on Jamie's bed, please. John and Jamie, we'll need four to carry Mel up the stairs. Do you think Harley and I can manage it with your help?"

They nodded, and all of them set about making Mel comfortable upstairs.

There was a flurry of activity. Kate packed up things for Sammy and Jeannie's stay at the cabin. Jamie and Becca moved their stuff downstairs. Everyone had a job to do and took Kate's direction, eager to step in where needed.

And there was quiet. The hours became days of waiting and praying. Kate tried to stay positive and strong for Mel's mother when she really wanted to lay her head down on Mel and sob, beg him to get well, tell him how much she needed him.

Laura and Kate took turns by his bedside, alternately bathing his skin with cool cloths when he was burning up and covering him when he shook with chills. They kept water hot in a pot hanging in the fireplace in Jamie's sitting room, and used it to make the willow bark and wintergreen teas. The soothing drinks helped make him comfortable. They doubled the dose of borage flower and cinnamon trying to reduce the fever.

Food was left at the bottom of the stairs. Kate picked up the tray without making contact with either Becca or Jamie, and left the covered tray at the bottom when they were done. It was a huge load for young Becca, and Kate silently thanked God for sending Jamie to her in time to help them.

Chapter Twelve

Spanish influenza

They had come to a manufactured way of life, artificial but comfortable, predictable. Laura, Kate and Mel lived upstairs and battled the illness. Becca and Jamie lived downstairs and did all the farm work and meal preparation. They were all tired, especially upstairs where they were on constant watch and lived with continuous, debilitating fear that if they left the room, Mel would die. So they stayed with him, leaving only when absolutely necessary, resting rarely. But they went on.

Kate worried about Mel's mother. She grew older and frailer by the day, but she wouldn't rest when Kate tried to send her away to her room. She shook her head, puckered her thin lips and furrowed her brow. She wouldn't discuss it and wouldn't outright refuse. She simply didn't move from his bedside.

"What will I do if you get sick?" Kate asked her one day when Laura looked like she might collapse from exhaustion. "What will Mel do?" She knew it was rotten to use her sick son against her, but she was worried. Laura needed sleep. She couldn't continue without rest.

Tears filled Laura's eyes. She knew Kate was right, but knowing didn't make it any easier for her to leave his side. Kate hugged her. "It's okay. Why don't I bring a footstool in, and you can rest in the rocker right by his bed? Will that be okay?" she asked.

She tucked a blanket around her, put a pillow behind her head and her feet on the footstool, turned the light down low, and pulled the window shade. She sat in the second rocker and watched them both. Mel's breathing was steady for the moment, and she had close to an hour before making the next batch of tea. She talked to whoever would listen, whoever was out there, about how much she wanted this man to get well, how she needed him. "He's a very important person," she whispered. "We all need him."

She was making tea in the sitting area when she heard the outside door open and John call her name. She went to the stairs and beckoned for him to come up, her finger across her lips to suggest quiet. They talked for a time in another room, trying not to disturb either Mel or his mother who had gone to sleep in the chair. When they heard stirring in Mel's bedroom, John went in. He repeated the process he'd done when Mel first got sick, and shook his head when he listened to his chest.

"He's becoming radically congested. We need to elevate his torso, keep his lungs above the lower body. A board lifting the head of the mattress would work better than many pillows that would sag. We don't want him hunched over so his lungs struggle for space or fill with fluid. He needs to sit as upright as possible and move around . . . as soon as he can, get his body working whether it wants to or not." Kate nodded and called down to Jamie, told him what they needed and where he could find it, and left Laura and Mel to rest again.

They were sitting at the table in Jamie's rooms, now turned into a sitting room for Laura and Kate. John told her Mel's condition was undetermined; he was still at risk. The fever needed to abate, and it wasn't. He was coughing, but no frothy blood was coming up which was a good thing. She knew bloody sputum sometimes indicated the worst was inevitable, but no one would say the words. No one would allow the unthinkable to be made concrete with a whispered word. It couldn't be spoken. It couldn't happen.

John spelled out once more what they must do to contain the virus, and he kept checking with everyone to make sure his precautions were taken seriously. "And that means no contact at all, Kate, but I believe contact with the ill person's fluids are the most dangerous," he emphasized. "You must wash thoroughly after touching him, and Becca and Jamie need to use gloves to wash dishes."

"Becca says they are. I ask constantly."

"Good. And the dishes need to be submerged in hot, soapy water, as hot as she can stand, and washed thoroughly," he said.

Kate smiled at his concern. "Yes, Papa. We're all minding."

"Sorry," he said. "It's just . . . important. I don't mean to harp."

"I know that, John. I appreciate your *harping*."

He'd brought more masks with him and laid them on the table. "Are you and Mrs. Bronson using these?"

"We are, John. But how can you come up here, touch Mel and not fear getting the virus?" Kate asked him.

"I've had it. I survived because I'm too stubborn to let anything happen to me if I don't want it to," he said with a grin, "and now I'm immune. I worry about you, Kate."

"Well, I worry about Becca being in this house, and Jamie."

"As long as they stay away from him, they should be safe," he told her. "But it does have a long arm, Kate, and we really don't know how far it extends."

"*Should be safe* isn't very comforting, John. How is everyone at the cabin? Are they holding up?"

John smiled as a graphic memory flooded his mind. They were doing more than alright. They were happy. Sammy was walking all over and getting into everything. Jeannie was mother, sister, aunt and playmate all rolled into one. Kat was matriarch in her realm, the queen bee who quietly set about having things done her way and succeeded without having to demand it. Harley, too, was happy, guiding and guarding. Yes, they were concerned about everyone at the farm, especially Mel, but they were content, too.

"I need to find a wolf for Kat," he said, to himself.

Kate looked quizzically at him. "You need a wolf? Is that what you said?"

"Yes, Kat wants her own wolf, so I must find one for her."

Kate looked long at John Crow, wonderingly. "Hmmm," she murmured.

"I have so little contact with everyone that I feel out of control," she said. "You see more of the people in *this* house than I do, and I live here. Damn, I sound like a whiner. Sorry," she added automatically. "Is Becca okay? Is Jamie still healing? What's going on in town? Is anyone else sick?"

He laughed at her stream of questions and told her the truth, after a long, deep breath, about why he had come. "Many in town are sick, a great many. A makeshift hospital has been set up in the fire hall."

Kate was stunned. "Many people sick? How many? And they made a hospital in the firehouse?" she parroted because she didn't know how not to. Mel had helped to make the fire department a reality so many years ago when fires raged through the area. Back when he was young and strong, not sick and fighting death.

"People are filling in, doing what they can to care for the sick. They're nursing, changing linens, doing whatever they can for those who are ill -- some who are dying -- and then going home to tend their own sick."

"Have you seen Ruthie? Ma? Are they alright? What about Jack, and Willie and Mary?"

"They're fine," he said, and went on to describe the ravages of the Spanish flu on the people of Hersey.

Nestor's store had temporarily closed, so had the diner, and neither of the churches had a sermon in the last week. Both pastors had passed away; they'd been the first to come into close contact with the infected and deceased. He shook his head in sorrow, but he didn't tell Kate everything. She didn't need to know the supply of coffins had dwindled and finding enough strong, healthy people to dig graves was becoming difficult. There would be time for more disclosure later . . . when it was necessary for her to know.

"We're trying to quarantine effectively, to keep the contaminated away from the uninfected, other than the hospital workers, but it's hard to know who's been exposed and who hasn't," he told her. "We have to rely on them to volunteer for quarantine. That's all we can do."

Kate nodded and tried to visualize the picture he was painting. She couldn't. It was too horrific.

"Because there's no doctor here, and Big Rapids has two, I've been helping out in Hersey," he said, "and staying at the cabin. We've rigged up a place to decontaminate out in the horse shed. That's where I change and rinse my clothes in a tub of disinfecting water, then hang them outside. Kat, too."

Kate's head snapped back. She gave John a hard stare. "What do you mean, Kat, too? What does she have to do with this?"

John figured on this reaction, had considered he might evade it with a lie of omission, but he couldn't. He respected Kate too much.

He sat in stony silence for as long as she would allow. He was trying unsuccessfully to think of a way to smooth his words, but there wasn't one. Kate determined an end to his silence.

"Just what the hell do you mean, John Crow?" Each word struck like a hammer meeting stone. "What do you mean by Kat, too?" she repeated, and now she knew why John, who was normally so reticent, had been loquacious. He was nervous trying to decide what to say and what to leave out.

"Tell me Kat is *not* tending sick and dying people in a makeshift hospital!" Kate snapped at him.

John's handsome, stoic face settled into an attitude of peaceful repose. It was the only place he could go when two principles warred. He knew Kat would not be separated from the sick. She was meant to use her knowledge, as much as Kate was meant to protect her child with the ferocity of a mother bear for her cub. Neither would be changed. And neither should be changed. He understood.

"Kat is a healer. The people of Hersey, your friends and neighbors, need her. She goes daily to the hospital to heal them. She was born to care for the sick, Kate."

"That's crazy! What about her? What about Sammy? She could get sick and give it to Sammy! And Jeannie!" Kate got up to leave, to go to the cabin and her children, fix things. She would see her daughter and stop this insanity. Still sitting, John reached out and grasped her arm. Wolf was between them in an instant, his mouth around John's forearm, not biting down, but definitely giving him a stern warning of what he could expect.

"Get your hand off me!" she hissed at him. "I thought you were a friend, you were special. You're nothing but . . . I don't know what you are, but you need to get away from my daughter. Leave us alone."

Kate finally sat in the chair indicated when the gentle but insistent hold on her arm and his black, pleading eyes forced her to comply.

"Please tell Wolf to let go," he said quietly.

She delayed a moment, then called Wolf to her. He obeyed, but stayed by her side, alert and watching.

"You wouldn't say these things if you saw what's happening in town. You would help the sick and dying people who have no one else to tend them. Come with me to town. You'll see, and I know you, Kate. You would not shirk this responsibility for your daughter."

Kate was still angry and wouldn't give him the satisfaction of agreeing with him. She sat in stony silence mulling over everything he'd said. Was it as bad as he'd said? Were that many people sick? Many had already died? It wasn't possible.

My God . . . her mother, Ruthie and Jack, Willie and Mary. They lived in town, in the middle of it. "Just tell me honestly, please. Is any of my family sick?"

"No. Not at the moment. Ruthie closed the school in an effort to make the children stay home and safe. She knows the only way to stop the spread of this killer is to contain it, let it die by not giving it any new victims."

He didn't tell Kate her sister and Jack were also taking shifts in the hospital. Spreading news of their activities would be up to them. He'd done what he knew he must in telling her about her daughter.

She rubbed her face with both hands trying to wipe away the horror, to go back to when Mel was well and strong, when the house had sounds of laughter, and the front door banged open and shut with people coming and going.

"How can life change so damned fast?" she asked. "Never mind. I already know the answer. *Death* is how. Isn't that odd? Death transforms life, alters everything without a by-your-leave. It doesn't consider those left in its wake, how many lives are turned upside down. Where is God? It's wrong!"

Kate's words were angry and directed at John, but he knew it wasn't him she was mad at. When she was finished, she sat immobile, watching him watch her.

Finally, he said, "Do you want to ride into town with me? See for yourself?"

"How can I do that? I'm needed here."

"Mrs. Bronson will be fine here for a couple of hours. Jamie is here, and Becca. We can ask them to stay close by until we get back."

"I don't know," she said, unwilling to accept kindness from him when she was still angry. She was frustrated and wanted to take it out on somebody. On him.

Her hands lay on the table clenched tightly together, and he covered them with his, the long brown fingers in stark contrast to the white of Kate's and concealing hers almost completely.

His eyes were heavily lidded, sleepy, like he was peering backwards into his mind in order to better see hers. "I know you are troubled, Kate. I understand. Cuss again, and let it go." Then he smiled at her.

She stood so abruptly the chair tipped over backward with a clatter, and she added to the din by stomping her foot and pounding her fist on the table.

"You don't know anything, damn it! And you can stop smiling at me. Now! Stop it!" she said and emphasized it with two more foot stomps bringing Laura rushing into the room.

"What's going on? What's the matter?" Her eyes were wide with fear and her hand was a fist over her heart.

"We were just talking, Mrs. Bronson," John explained. "That's all. But now you're here, would you mind terribly if I took Kate into town for a couple of hours? Would you be okay? We'd let Jamie know to stay close by in case you needed anything."

"Pretty loud talking," she said, obvious distrust in her eyes. "But it would be fine if Kate needs to go for a bit. I can take care of things here."

"I didn't say I wanted to go, John. I don't want to leave Mel."

"If you're sure, but when he is well enough, you should see for yourself."

"I will," she said, not unkindly, but with an added hint of frost, "I'm not done with you, yet."

He didn't respond to her threat. He nodded once indicating he understood and left.

Kate called for Jamie to bring up the planks he had cut to fit Mel's bed. They attached them to the wall at the head of the bed, sliding the ends underneath the mattress. It was a difficult process. When it was done, Mel's head and chest were raised about twelve inches higher than his body, and Kate believed his coughing abated momentarily, just slightly, or maybe it was belief based on desire. Kate reminded Jamie to scrub thoroughly with soap as soon as he went downstairs, and she did her best to settle her husband comfortably.

Mel's temperature spiked after Jamie left, and he began coughing again. Laura bathed his forehead, and Kate made more hot tea to try to relieve the congestion, this time out of the asafetida John Crow had left. She worried about the congestion in his chest that was determined to keep him ill. But she had to smile when she opened the packet of asafetida. It did smell, like John said. "No wonder they called it *asa fetid a*!"

"My God," she said, as she stirred it into the hot water. "How will he ever drink this stuff?" She smiled again thinking John probably gave her this smelly stuff as punishment for getting angry with him. When she took it into his room, Laura looked up, her nose wrinkled, her eyebrows raised.

"What is that stuff? It's horrid!"

"Asafetida. It's supposed to clear the congestion in his chest, help him cough. It's an expectorant, according to the witch doctor -- and the eastern cultures," she added trying not to be so petty in her irritation.

Laura stared, trying not to breathe.

"I didn't mean that -- about the witch doctor. I'm just . . . nothing. Why don't you pinch his nose and I'll hold the cup? He needs to drink as much as he can."

They put a cloth under Mel's chin to catch the spillage and got as much down him as they could. They sat again and waited.

Two days later, his fever broke, and he ceased thrashing around incoherently. He still coughed incessantly and was too weak to get up, even to take the few steps to sit in a chair while they changed the soiled bed linens.

In another two days, they celebrated his graduation to sitting up in bed. He could take meals upright, even spoon his own food. It was a mark of how much better he was when Kate began to tease him about being a lazy lay-about wanting everyone to wait on him -- even spoon feed him, for crying out loud.

For the first time in weeks, Kate breathed easier, could look at him without a catch in her own chest and a lump in her throat. He would make it. She didn't say it out loud. She wouldn't even say it to herself under her breath, but she allowed it to flicker in her thoughts momentarily every once in a while. Her smile came more easily and she slept in a bed for the first time in weeks. Laura, too, finally got some needed rest.

The day after Mel was able to move from his bed to the chair in his room, Kate finally decided to make the trip into town and stop out at the cabin to see Harley, Jeannie and Sammy . . . from a distance. She didn't hold out any hope Kat would be there, but she'd more than likely see her in town. She made arrangements with Jamie and Becca to be available and nearby in case Laura needed them, scrubbed herself from head to toe, and stepped into the buggy Jamie had hitched up for her.

"Come on, Wolf," she called. He leaped on the seat, and if wolves can grin, it was on his face. It had been a long time since they had gone traveling together, and he was ready.

The sun was shining, the leaves were glorious flames shifting on the ground and drifting from the trees. She didn't remember them so vibrant before. When had it changed? The world was alive with color! She breathed in the scent of fresh air, marveled at its fragrance, and realized it had been a long time since she'd smelled the outdoors. She had missed it.

"Look at this, Wolf. It's unbelievable."

Wolf obediently glanced around. It looked like it always had, he thought, but he wasn't going to burst her bubble. She was happy again, and so was he.

She clicked gently to the mare, sat back to enjoy her freedom and immediately scolded herself for thinking of freedom while Mel was still restricted to his room, still weak. No one knew for sure how long contagion might exist in his body, plus he had no desire to move from his room. His lethargy was Kate's biggest concern at the moment. She believed he was truly recovering from the flu, but he made little effort to build his strength.

John told her it might be a long time for complete recovery, if he ever reached the full strength he'd had before.

"We were lucky, Kate," he'd said. "Instead of taking the weak, the old and young, this flu kills the strongest, people who are in their prime like Mel. It's different from any other influenza in that regard. And it sometimes takes them within twenty-four hours. It's that deadly."

"It's alright if he needs the quiet of his room and rest, as long as he feels well. That's all I want right now," she'd told John. But it did worry her. It wasn't the Mel she knew.

It wasn't who he had been his entire life. She tried to shake worrisome thoughts and enjoy the day.

She pulled into the cabin clearing, Wolf jumped down, and Harley came outside with Sammy in his arms and Jeannie by his side. He was grinning from ear-to-ear. Jeannie flew toward her mother, but Kate stopped her from getting too close.

"Jeannie," Kate pleaded, "I would love nothing better than to hug you and smother you with kisses, but for a while I think I'll have to be happy just looking at you. Sammy, too."

"But . . . John said Mel was getting better. The flu was gone," Jeannie said, her words more questions than statements.

"True, but I don't want to take any chances infecting you or Sammy -- or Harley. But I'll bet that old coot has already had the Spanish flu and is immune because he's lived forever and done everything," she teased.

"Back in the seventies, or was it the sixties," he said with a grin. "In California." He stretched out the 'i' and 'a' just for fun. "What are you up to, just out and about? Enjoying this beautiful day?"

"I needed to see you all. I've missed you so much. And I need to see family in town and what's going on there."

"It's ugly in town. I haven't been there in a while, but from what I hear, it's not a pretty sight to see," Harley told her.

Kate eventually got down from the buggy and went to sit in the chair by the door where she had spent hundreds of hours, maybe thousands, many in the middle of long, dark nights. Harley moved the second chair a couple more feet away from Kate and sat holding Sammy. In moments, Sammy struggled against Harley's arms and tried to get down.

"Please don't let him near me," Kate said. "I would die if I infected him, and I just don't know."

Jeannie took Sammy's hand and walked him away. "Show Grandma how good you walk and run now, Sammy. Come with Aunt Jeannie."

Kate watched and a rosy glow spread across her face. "What a joy, this fourth generation is," she said to Harley who watched too, his expression holding the same admiration.

"Tis true," he said. "Tis true."

"I want him back with me so badly, but I'm afraid." She watched Sammy's antics, and a smile oozed from her eyes to her mouth, lighting her face with a youthful flush. "I'd have to just look at him from afar, and it wouldn't be fair to saddle Becca or Jamie. They have so much to take care of now."

Harley rocked and observed as Jeannie chased her nephew around the clearing, his shrieks and giggles startling in the quiet of the forest. Sammy's chubby legs moved quickly, and he fell down quickly, too, but was up again just as fast. He dove into a pile of red and orange leaves all raked and ready for the garden, and Jeannie dove in after him.

Kate saw their shared love and wondered how they had come to be in this place with a twelve-year-old acting mother to her nephew, a philosophical hobo standing guard and guiding them, a sixteen-year-old girl functioning as a doctor for the sick and dying of Hersey, a Cherokee shaman channeling her, and all of them living in her cabin. Well . . . what she thought of as her cabin even though she didn't own it and didn't live there. It was still hers.

She peered around the open door to see if the owner's clothes still hung on a hook by the door. Kate knew it was more than silly after all this time, but she always felt better if his clothes were where he'd left them, and were cleaned and pressed.

Harley saw, knew what she was looking for and said, "We've taken care of them. We've washed them, hung them out to dry and put them back. Just like you did. Who knows? He may just show up some day."

Kate thanked him and smiled. "I appreciate that."

"Everything here is good, Kate. In fact, we're quite content." He didn't want to say they were happy. Tales of too much happiness would be adding insult to injury, a slap in the face. But they were.

"I'm afraid I got angry at John the other day. I snapped at him."

Harley didn't respond, but his eyes sparkled and he tried not to grin. He would have known she'd be mad without being told. "Bet you stomped your foot, too," he said finally.

Harley's knowledge piqued Kate. "John told you! He didn't need to, the rat."

"No, he didn't tell me. I know you, and I can visualize what happened when he told you about Kat."

"He had no right to take her into town to be around all the sick people. No right at all," she sputtered. "She's a child, not a doctor or nurse!"

"She's sixteen, Kate. Hardly a child . . . if she ever was one. Personally, I think she was born old. She has something . . . spiritual or . . . other worldly knowledge." Harley fumbled for words to describe what he saw in Kat and floundered.

Kate had to smile because Harley was never without words. They normally spewed from him like molten rock from an active volcano.

"She has an inner peace one only achieves from having lived long. That's what I mean, I guess."

"Well, he still had no right."

"Kate, she would have gone without him. She doesn't need John to know her own mind. And John is not only there for the sick; he's there for her, to keep her safe. He watches over her like a guardian angel, or a hawk." He laughed at his incongruous metaphors. "He is dedicated to her and unwavering about her safety."

Kate gazed into the forest, watched squirrels scamper about with acorns sticking out of their mouths, looking for places to bury them for the winter. She thought about the many families of raccoons she had seen make homes at the edge of the forest over the years, about how Wolf had followed her back after her longtime friend, her dog, Bug, had died. She'd spent time afterwards in the woods beating a tree in anger and howling with rage and sorrow. Wolf had howled right along with her. When she left, he followed her back to the clearing and waited. Those thoughts led her to something John had said.

"Did you know Kat wants a wolf of her own?"

Harley nodded. "She's said it a few times."

"John said he had to find one for her."

Harley nodded again, and something in his face brought Kate up short, and she didn't like what she was feeling. Left out. Ignorant. In the dark.

"Is there something going on I should know about, Harley?"

"Nothing is *going on*," he said. "Nothing at all. I see something in John's face when he's near Kat or when he looks at her. That's all. I suspect even he doesn't realize it's there or understand what it is. John is entirely noble and decent. Toes to nose," he added with a self-satisfied little grin.

"What do you mean -- when he looks at her? If he touches Kat, I will certainly do murder. You know that! He shouldn't even be living here! There are other places he can stay, I'm sure. Besides, he's old, and he's . . . I don't know." The breath and starch went out of her, and she dropped her face into her hands, elbows on her knees. "Damn, damn, damn it all," she whispered.

Harley knew Kate, and knew, too, she would sputter, stomp and rant. Eventually, she'd calm down and make sense of what she'd heard. So, he waited. He crossed his skinny legs and tipped back and forth in the rocker, pushing with the toe of one foot. He could wait. He had all day and then some.

He gazed at Jeannie and Sammy playing in the leaves and turned his face to the sun to catch a few of its rays on his face. He glanced at Kate who still sat with her face in her hands, but he saw an eye peeking through her fingers and smiled.

She'll never grow old because she'll never grow up, he thought with a silent laugh and was glad. Other people would be rocking-chair old if they'd gone through what she had, but Kate managed to stay young. She looked like a girl. Slender and tanned from the summer. Hair so light a blonde it was white honey. 'Where is the gray?' he wondered. 'Same place mine is,' he mused, answering his own question.

"I know you're peeking," he said out loud. "I see your beautiful eyeball through your fingers."

She straightened. Rolled her eyes much like Wolf and sighed deeply. "Why does everything go so off kilter? Why can't I do anything about it? Why?"

"What are you afraid of, besides the obvious Spanish flu?" he asked.

"I don't know. I guess I just don't want my girls to grow up and leave me. One already did. Well, two actually. I don't like it. They're not old enough."

"I understand, but you can't control it and you know it. Who could control *you*?"

"Smarty pants. Nobody."

"Well, there you go!" Harley paused and then added, "She's dedicated, and she's good, you know. She is definitely something else."

"That's what John said. It's hard for a mother to envision her child being *something else*, especially when she's so young."

Harley laughed again. "We've gone over her age. Want to do it again?"

"Don't laugh at me! Damn it! Sorry."

"Kate, you're not going to like what you see in town. Be prepared. A lot of people are ill and many have died."

She didn't respond to his words; she put them in a place where she could deal with them later, on her own, maybe on the ride to town.

"I'd better go so I can get back to Mel."

She said goodbye to Jeannie and Sammy and climbed into the buggy. Wolf was waiting for her.

On the way, she tried to prepare herself for what she might find. She'd been isolated for a long while, but it was still hard to imagine much had changed since she'd been there last. She talked it over with Wolf, and he listened ... better than most people, but when his mind drifted and was captured by a deer grazing perilously close to the road, he couldn't help but turn to look at it. He was a wolf, after all.

"I'm talking to you, Wolf. Pay attention."

'Sorry,' his look said, but the brown eye rolled while the blue one stared at her. He looked maniacal, a crazy wolf.

She tugged on the reins trying to slow Kitty and the buggy as they crept down Main Street, taking in dramatic changes in familiar places, past Nestor's store bearing a closed sign on the door, past the smith shop, which looked empty, too. She turned down Division and up to Jack and Ruthie's house, threw the reins around the post and opened the door as she knocked.

"Ruthie? Ma?" she yelled. "Jack?"

Only silence greeted her. She looked around the kitchen, did a cursory glance into the parlor while she called again and left.

"Nobody home," she told Wolf. "Let's try the infamous firehouse hospital."

She parked down from Nestor's and walked past the diner and Sadie's toward the firehouse. The closer she got, the louder the noise vibrated from its open doors. Moans were constant, and the voices ranged in tenor from male to female to child. She heard fear in the pleas. Voices groaned in pain, some were harsh in unbridled anger, some weak, and all needed something, attention, water, their mother, their Lord. Their wants were critical, life sustaining, and their combined anguish found a home in her heart. These people, her neighbors and friends, were sick and in need.

As she neared the fire hall, she heard strong voices giving and taking orders, others talking softly to patients. Soothing voices. Firm voices. She recognized Kat's, smiled and peeked around the open door. She jerked back, horrified.

She saw three long rows of cots, the full length of the fire hall, forty, maybe fifty beds with people in them. Some coughed, deep racking coughs bringing up vile spew. Several lay still with glazed unseeing eyes. Some tossed, wrenched back and forth, fighting with the small blankets covering them. All were in various stages of this venomous illness, and Kate was aghast, stunned.

She took a sustaining breath and peered in once more, looking for Kat. She finally spotted her. She was giving instructions to several women about brewing the herbal teas used to help bring down fever. She pointed to the different packets to make sure the women brewed the right ones for specific patients.

Kate watched, hardly recognizing her daughter. She appeared so self-assured, sounded so knowledgeable. Kat turned to two men who were awaiting their instructions. She pointed to a male patient who was thrashing about on a narrow cot. His face was florid, his mouth frothy.

"Nathaniel's fever is dangerously high. Lift him into the cool water tub at the far end outside the hall. Pour water over him slowly for ten minutes. Stay with him and don't let him slide under. It has disinfectant and wintergreen in it that will cling to his skin and help keep him cooler when he comes out. Understand?" They nodded and walked off to carry out her orders.

John moved over to Kat and leaned down to say something to her. Kat smiled softly as she looked up at him, and Kate's heart thudded in her breast. The girl was in love . . . Kate wondered if John knew. Hell, she wondered if Kat knew. Kat looked up and saw her mother in the doorway. She smiled and walked over to her.

"You come to help?" she asked. "We can use every available able hand."

"Not yet," Kate said. "I can't leave Mel too long. When he's better, I will."

She wanted to talk with her daughter about what she'd seen, about her work here at the hospital, about her desire to heal people. Heck, about everything, but it wasn't the right time. Not now. Kate was growing to dislike herself more every minute. How could she have been so selfish about Kat helping the sick? She must apologize to John. Another day. A lump the size of a mountain lodged in her throat and she struggled to say anything.

"I just wanted to see you, make sure you're okay. Tell you I love you."

"You okay, Ma?" Kat was concerned. Her mother sounded strange, but she looked healthy.

"I'm fine. I was looking for Ruthie and Grandma, Jack, too. Do you know where they might be?"

"Grandma is probably at Mr. Woodward's house. She's staying there for awhile. And Uncle Jack just left here with Aunt Ruthie. They put in shifts here and at the school where we put the overflow. They were heading home. I don't know how you missed them."

"I'll try again." Kate shuffled her feet like an awkward boy. "Kat, I want you to know how proud I am of you. Please . . . please take care of yourself."

"I am, Ma. John makes sure I take all the precautions. I mean to the extreme."

"Okay, well . . . I'll go now. Tell John Crow I understand. Would you do that, please."

"Understand what?" Kat asked, turning to head back into the hall and the people who were depending on her.

"He'll know."

Chapter Thirteen

Fall, 1918

Not a single family was spared the ruthless, grasping fingers of the Spanish flu. Many of them grieved a loss, and their sobs were left in the cemetery along with the bodies of loved ones who held their hearts. The tears had to be left behind, too. There was work to do, disease to battle, and a war to fight. There was no time to grieve save the middle of the night when it didn't interfere with labors or undermine strength, the cornerstones of their lives.

The deceased were interred quickly to restrict contamination as much as possible. They were wrapped in their blankets and put into the ground, buried with nothing between them and the earth. They were closer to God, their loved ones said to make the notion acceptable, and the idea had to work for them because that was all they had. Wooden boxes to lie in, their homes for eternity, were long gone. Used up. Caskets had been buried with the lucky few who had died first.

All of Hersey watched the virus ravage their mate, or their parent, or their sibling or child. They knew the frustration of a spiking fever they couldn't stem or control. The sick needed strength for the fight to survive, and their coughing sapped the little they had left. Caregivers felt the stab of fear every time they entered a sick room to bring broth to a child, cool the brow of a wife or husband. They suffered their own nausea as they carefully checked cough spittle color and waited for it to turn red . . . or black.

They prayed they wouldn't sicken because they couldn't. They were needed to nurse the sick. And they wept in relief when the fever left and the coughing abated. They looked around in church when laypeople offered a service and noted the empty spaces. So many were gone. They wept again for their neighbor's pain. They thanked God for their own reprieve; they hadn't suffered loss today.

Those who survived were in the long process of recovering. As Mel grew stronger and could move around the house with ease, Kate kept her promise to Kat and spent a few hours each day at the hospital. She began to understand Kat's desire to heal the sick. It was more than a yearning. It was part of her psyche, her soul. She was a healer. She'd been born to become a healer and had no choice in the matter.

Kate took instructions from her daughter when she was at the hospital, or from John, depending on the section of the hall she was working. At first, she was assigned to bathing faces, and bodies if necessary, with cool water.

"I use a different cloth each time, right?" she asked Kat who nodded, her eyes on a patient two cots down who looked about to throw himself off the cot and onto the floor in his thrashing around. "And just keep doing it?"

"That's it, Ma. About ten minutes each for those I named. We're trying to keep their fevers down, and they're the ones with spiking temps. We can't let it get past a hundred and four." She walked off to tend the tossing man.

The ailing women were kept at the back half of the hospital, the men at the front, so the genders were divided. But the division meant little. There was nothing to separate them, like a wall. A string of blankets had been hung between the two areas, but it hadn't been used for a long time. It was in the way as workers moved quickly back and forth between cots, and John and Kat needed to be able to see what was going on the whole length of the hall.

Kate did what she was told. Once or twice she nodded to John as he flew past her to tend to a patient, but she hadn't talked with him since he'd felt her wrath over Kat. She would. She intended to. Soon.

She felt her neck muscles tighten and knot up as she bent over her third patient. Her arms began to tire, and she scolded herself.

"You're a tenderfoot, Kate," she said. The man she was helping answered.

"A pretty tenderfoot, you are," he croaked in a raspy whisper.

"Mr. Talbot, I thought you were too sick to flirt."

"Never, lass. And you call me Sean." His voice was terribly weak, but Kate could see the Irish shine still aglow in his eyes, and she prayed those eyes would not close forever. She gave renewed energy to her work, and the aches disappeared.

"Come back later, lassie," he whispered when she rose to tend another.

"I'll be back, Mr. Talbot . . . Sean."

She tossed her used rag in the barrel of things to be washed and disinfected, got a clean cloth and went to bathe another man she'd been assigned, a younger one. She sat next to him, running the wet cloth over his face and chest. He was much younger than Sean Talbot, looked to be in his thirties. He looked strong but emaciated, if the juxtaposition was possible. His skin was both red and gray at the same time. He didn't respond to her administrations. The only movement he made was when a cough cruelly racked his body.

John Crow came over with a large square of wood he shoved under two legs of the cot at the man's head to elevate him as he'd done with Mel.

"Don't let him cough the legs off the wood," he said.

"I won't. I'll try," she said. And she would, but she felt so incompetent, so out of her element. She was amazed at what John and Kat were able to accomplish, and they still needed more helpers. 'Who washes all these cloths?' she mused. 'Who cuts them into these squares? And where did they come from in the first place?' Her thoughts rambled on and on as she bathed the poor man in front of her. Then it registered.

"I know you. You're one of the Jackson boys," she whispered.

His eyes opened, and he stared at Kate's face. He was too weak to talk. He blinked twice and closed his eyes again.

She spent another ten minutes cooling his body and repeated the process with another agonizingly sick person. She talked to a few others who needed reassurance and went to find Kat for further instructions.

When she returned, she glanced at the Jackson man. He was motionless, not coughing, eyelids stilled, and Kate stood staring, begging him to breathe again.

But he didn't.

Her eyes filled and she closed them, not wanting to see anymore. "No more . . . no more dying," she begged. She felt hands on her arms, coming from behind, and heard John's voice.

"Move down the aisle, Kate. Outside."

She opened her eyes and tears made quick tracks down her cheeks. She walked woodenly with John right behind her. Once outside, John pushed her into a chair and stood in front of her.

"I'm sorry that had to happen."

"So am I, John. I've know the Jacksons since they were children."

He didn't respond. Just patted her arm gently.

"They stayed at our house until their new one was built after their old one burned during the drought." She paused, staring, and her words were wooden. "I don't remember which one, which year that was."

"Kate," he said finally. "I have to go back in there. I need to take care of Andrew."

She nodded. "So, it was Andy," she whispered. "I didn't know which one he was. I wish I had known. Go do your work, John. I'll be in shortly."

Nestor's general store opened again after being closed during the worst of the flu epidemic. John Nestor had been a victim and had survived; his wife had been a victim and had not. John finally gained strength enough to work a few hours each day.

One church held services. They were generic, deliberately unspecific to any denomination, and the sermons were given by laity, not an ordained pastor, but they were necessary now more than ever and appreciated.

Harmon Stewart had finally been sent by the Grand Rapids diocese, and the townspeople were happy to have the doors of the Congregational Church open again and its bell ringing in the tall, white steeple, ordained reverend or not. He was in training so he would eventually have the title, but they called him pastor anyway because he earned it by his presence and his words of faith.

Fewer people were coming down with the flu, and the hospital began to empty. Sighs of relief could be heard if you stood still and silent on Main Street, listening. A chill breeze carried the exhaled breath of relief, like air had been held for too long and was finally released. Tentative smiles replaced the wide eyes of constant fear as people began to allow hope to grow.

John told Kate she wouldn't be needed anymore, and she was grateful. While she hadn't visibly fallen apart over the death of Andy Jackson, inside she had crumbled. She contained the grief, swallowed it so it wouldn't show, so she could continue to do her job and help the living. They needed it desperately.

She saw others die, and the worst of it was the indignity of their passing, not in their own beds with family cherishing them, but coughing up an ugly mess in a fire hall with an unfamiliar person tending to their needs.

"I don't know how you do it," she told her daughter one day as she was leaving for home. "You're here all day, day after day, sometimes at night. How do you keep from screaming or sobbing? You look so calm, so serene."

"I cry, inside, where it's safe."

"You're my hero, Kat," she told her and meant it over and over.

Kat shushed her mother and told her to go home while she could, but before she had hitched the mare, joyful shouts and raucous laughter made her pause and look in the direction of the saloon.

People were pouring out of Sadie's Saloon, hugging each other, dancing in the street with mugs of beer raised high and spilling sticky brew down their arms. They didn't care about the loss of their beer. They danced with whoever was nearest and kissed their cheeks with exuberance, sometimes their lips.

"What's happened? Why the glee?" Kate shouted. Others came out of the hospital and watched their friends and neighbors acting like crazy fools and not caring how foolish they looked. Leo Tate ran over to Kate, picked her up and swung her around. Her feet flew off the ground as he turned in circles, and she was dizzy when he finally set her back on her feet. Kate tried to smooth her dress back down, but Leo was busy kissing her cheek and trying to hug her.

"You crazy man! What is going on?" she demanded.

"It's over!" he shouted, his grizzled face lit in a huge grin. "It's done. A treaty was signed on November eleventh!"

"You're sure?" Kate asked, unbelieving of good news after the wretched time they had all recently lived through.

"Posi-damn-tively! Telegraph came. It's done!"

"Oh my God, Leo! That is such wonderful news!"

It was her turn to hoot and holler, and she did. She followed the noise making with hugs and kisses for Leo, for anyone and everyone else she saw. For the first time, she wasn't thinking about contaminating them. She couldn't at the moment. She would remember later, but the war was over! Verna came out of the saloon and joined in the impromptu festivity. She brought a jug with her and shared with anyone who wanted it.

John and Kat came out and stood by the door of the hospital. When they heard the news, John grabbed Kat and picked her up in a huge bear hug. When he realized what he'd done, he set her down carefully and began to apologize. Kat poked him in the ribs and smiled.

"Knock it off. It's alright," she said, and the blush on her cheeks spoke loudly.

They walked over to Kate who'd witnessed their hug. She didn't mention it, and they stood quietly apart and watched the revelry.

"This is good," John said. "We've needed something good for quite a while."

Kate nodded. "It is. I wonder how long before our boys will be home."

"With over a million men in Europe, it's going to take awhile," he said. "Plus, they'll want to leave troops there for rebuilding and insurance."

"What happens with the missing in action, John? Does Robbie get left behind somewhere?"

"I can't answer that, Kate. He may be in a hospital or prison camp, and word hasn't gotten to the right people. We'll have to wait and see."

John Nestor came out of the store to see what the ruckus was, saw Kate and moved in her direction. He used a cane to walk since he'd been sick, and he moved slowly. Kate saw him and met him half way. She gave him a long hug and kissed his cheek.

"Can you believe it John? It's over."

"The war?" he asked incredulously. "Is that what all this is about?"

Kate nodded, and John's face lit up.

"My God, my God. That surely is a good thing."

"It is," she said, "and there have been no new cases of flu in the last several days. I think we've beaten it. The world is a much better place today."

John threw his cane up into the air, caught it, and tossed it across the street. "Let somebody have it who needs it," he said with a laugh. "I can get where I want to be without help! It is a good day."

He hugged Kate again and then joined the large group of revelers who had congregated in the middle of Main Street. Numbers grew by the minute, and servers from the saloon were taking orders and delivering drinks in the street.

Kate went back to the hospital to find Kat and John. "I'm going. I can't wait to tell Mel. I think we're due for a celebration. What do you say? A party at the farm? Would it be safe to do now?"

"As long as no one comes down with it between now and then, I think so," Kat told her.

"Precautions still need to be taken . . . thorough washing, decontaminating after leaving here. I don't trust it," John added.

"We can do that, and I agree. How about Saturday for supper?"

They agreed and Kate left, thoughts jumping from here to there and back again. Jeannie and Sammy could come home. Mel was gaining strength so Jamie might be able to go back to work with Jack. He hadn't been needed lately at the hospital due to the decline in patients and was working on the smithy again. Kate hummed as she drove; she was weightless, buoyant, her face glowed with happiness. It felt wonderful. All she needed to be content was for Rachel to come home.

Kate was still exhilarated after she decontaminated and went in to tell Mel about the war treaty and the victory celebration on Saturday. He hugged her a long, long time, whispering words of praise for her hard work and determination over the last few weeks, and not a few words of love.

"'Twas nothing, kind sir. I live to serve," she teased, and then grew serious. "Do you think we can bring Jeannie and Sammy home? I think you're safe. You can't spread the flu now, right?" she asked.

Mel saw the pleading in her eyes. It had been horrible for her sending Jeannie and Sammy away. Hard to spend day and night nursing him, and harder still watching friends and neighbors die.

"You've earned a break or two, Kate. I'd say they could. Do you want to ask John, first?"

She nodded agreement, but wanted to go get them today. However, the day was too good to waste being unhappy.

"How about if I go get Jamie, Becca and your mother and we have an early celebration right now?"

"Sure thing, sweet girl. You go get the barn kids, and I'll round up Ma."

He had the cognac poured and hot chocolate heating when they came in from the barn. Becca and Jamie were nagging her for the reason they were celebrating, but she wouldn't share the news.

"Not yet. Wait til we're all here and ready."

"Good Lord, I think Harley has rubbed off on you, Kate," Mel teased. "You can't just tell them, can you?"

"Don't hurry me! You can't rush a good toast. Okay," she said with joy bubbling from her face and spilling into her voice, her eyes beginning to water, "raise your glasses to the end of World War I. A treaty was signed. We are no longer at war!"

There was a lot of noise. Jamie was slapping his leg and hugging Becca which was hard to do because she was jumping up and down. Laura was audibly crying, and Mel put his arms around her. He'd like to cry, too, but couldn't. He was the man of the house. Jamie hugged Kate, and Becca hugged Mel, and everybody hugged everybody. Kate stood back watching and loving.

When they wound down Kate told them the plans for a victory celebration. "What do you say?"

Saturday dawned beautiful and cold. But the sun soon warmed the earth and fooled Michigan into thinking winter had come and gone. Kate watched the buggy roll down the driveway with pent up anticipation evident in the dancing of her feet. Harley, Jeannie and Sammy showed up at three saying they wanted to help with all the preparations and climbed eagerly down from the buggy.

Wolf greeted Harley with a nose on his cheek, saying, 'Hey, where you been, old man?'

"I've missed you, too, Wolf," Harley told him and meant it.

Sammy ran to Kate and threw his chubby bundled up arms around her legs. Kate picked him up and nuzzled her face into his sweet-smelling cheeks.

"I've missed you, Sammy. So much!"

Kate peered around Sammy's head looking for Kat. She wasn't with them, and Kate was disappointed and concerned.

"Where's your sister, Jeannie? Why isn't she with you?"

"She went to the hospital with John early. They'll come later."

Kate nodded, understanding but not liking.

"Well, come in. I am happy to see all of you!"

Kate was bubbling, so eager to have everyone all together, she couldn't concentrate on what needed to be done. She removed Sammy's outer wear, hung it on hooks near the door, and smiled thinking how good it was to have him near. Harley hung his, too, but Jeannie wanted to check on the chickens and calves, so she raced outside to find Jamie who was in the barn making sure chores were done so he was free for the festivities.

"Where's Mel?" Harley asked.

"Resting. He wants to be bright eyed for the party."

"Is he doing okay, Kate?"

"He's getting better."

Harley moved to where Kate was stirring a large pot on the stove. He took the spoon from her. "I can stir. You can sit before the rest of the tribe comes."

Kate sat and watched him. She loved this odd man so much. It was rare she stopped to think about his place in the family. He wasn't related. They didn't know who he was or where he came from, but Harley was loved. His knowledge was revered, and his heart was constant. And he loved them all.

"How about you, Kate? You doing alright?"

"I'm great. Ready to get my kids home, though."

"I'm sure of that. Jeannie will be happy, too," he said.

Mel came into the kitchen and gave Harley a bear hug. Kate noted the open show of affection. Most men wouldn't hug another man, but Mel -- big tough Mel, the man who looked like he'd punch your arm or pound your back in friendliness -- hugged everyone he loved. It was one of his many charming qualities.

"Good Lord, man," Harley said. "We need to fatten you up. You're a scarecrow! You're skin and bones!"

"Well, I've been trying out this new diet. It's called Spanish flu. It must be working."

"Time to try the *eat everything in sight* diet. Look at me. I've been on that diet for years, and it works," he said, rubbing his rotund belly.

"Yeah, well I'm trying," Mel responded. He knew he looked like hell. He was gaunt and pasty colored. The robust man Kate had married was a memory, and Mel was concerned he would never get his strength back, the muscled physique he had taken for granted since boyhood.

"You look wonderful," Kate piped in, "you handsome devil." But she knew he didn't. He looked frail . . . fragile and feeble. Kate was worried. It seemed to be taking an unreasonably long time for him to regain his strength. He chafed at the enforced inactivity, grew morose over it, and sat staring at the wall. She was fresh out of ways to keep him occupied and content.

"Look at him. He has freshly combed hair, and he smells wonderful," she said kissing his neck. "What more could a woman want?"

"A man who didn't have to take naps like a baby?" Mel asked.

"Hey, hey!" Harley said. "Never disparage a good nap. There's nothing in this world, or maybe even in the next one, quite like a good nap. Restores the soul, replenishes the mind, and just plain feels damn good!" He stirred the pot, watching, worried, and drawing conclusions. He'd have to talk to John about it. Soon.

At five, Ruthie and Jack drove down the drive. Kat and John followed and brought Ellen and Verna with them. The saint and the sinner, Harley had dubbed them, or the barmaid and the missionary. But he was the only one who could get away with the nicknames.

They came in with a gust of real Michigan late fall weather. It had turned cold with the setting of the sun, and they chafed their hands and blew on their fingers.

Everyone made a dash to touch Mel, prove he was well with their fingers and hands. It had been a long time since they'd seen him. They'd kept up with news of his progress, but no one had seen the outcome in person. Comments about his weight followed their greetings. They tried not to show concern for him, but apprehension was written in their eyes.

"Good to see you up and about, Mel," Jack told him.

"You can't believe how good it feels to be back among the living. I thought for awhile I'd be laid up all winter."

"Winter won't be long," Jack said. "I feel it in the air. Snow by morning."

"Leaves say early winter and a hard one," John added.

Jack tilted his head toward him and raised a playful eyebrow. "Really? Leaves speak? And what do the acorns say? And the chipmunks, my good Cherokee friend."

John drew into himself as only he could do. It was daunting if you weren't used to it. He grew taller, more imposing. He knew it, too, and used the transforming ability to intimidate people when he felt like it.

"You would do well . . . my pale companion . . . to listen to the chipmunks. They have uncommon intelligence. More than you could appreciate," he said with a stress on *you*, somber eyes, and a fierce but calm demeanor. If you didn't know him, you would swear he was angry. But he laughed, slapped Jack's back heartily and asked if it was time for a toast. He shook Mel's hand and murmured well wishes, looking him over as he did.

Ellen batted a hand at both Jack and John, moving them out of the way and grumbling good naturedly. Kate noted she treated John with familiarity, and wondered how her mother had gotten to know John so well. She received him as part of the family. As they moved into the room, removed outerwear and finished the greetings, Kate thought about what she'd seen. She was alert, watching and wondering.

"Supper will be ready in one hour," Kate told them. "But I believe we have some toasts to make. Good to see you, Verna," she added. "Is Sadie's settling down now? It was sure crazy the other day."

"Yeah, it's okay. Kind of nice to have it busy again. It's been like a morgue around there." She paused in the silence following her words. "Ouch, sorry. Really sorry. Rotten thing to say." She was almost embarrassed by her thoughtless remark, and Kate helped her out of it.

"It's toast time, Verna. You want to start?"

"I'm liking the toast idea, and it's good to see you, too. Where's the jug?"

Kate nodded toward the end of the counter. Verna grabbed the well-worn jug and pulled the cork.

"I'm just testing," she told the group, "to make sure it's palatable for this very special occasion." She poured some into her glass and drank, everyone watching and waiting for the pronouncement.

"Well?" they asked in unison.

"Not sure. Let me test again."

Harley snapped his red suspenders and moved to her side.

"Woman, you're trying my patience. You know I am the toast master and do all the testing around here."

"You're right about one thing," she told him with the Verna sparkle back in her blue eyes. When she smiled, her cheeks bunched up and her eyes squinted. They were squinting now at Harley. "I am trying your patience out. Seeing how much you have." She poured and sipped again.

"Okay, I think it's fine." She handed Harley the jug and told him he could make his toast secure in the knowledge the moonshine wasn't contaminated.

"Gather round, friends and family," he said expansively, in charge once again and commanding the troops. "Make a circle. Where's the cognac and hot chocolate?"

"Right behind you," Kate told him. "Come get your drinks, please." She had Sammy on her hip and was holding a cup so he could toast, too.

Harley waited until everyone was back to the circle and settled before beginning his toast, not wanting anyone to miss even a small portion of his eloquence. He looked around the circle of family and friends slowly, nodding to each person.

"Harley," Mel said, drawing out his name in warning. "Do you want me standing upright or collapsing on the floor? If you do . . ."

"Right. My apologies. Raise your glasses to wellness, to beating the demon influenza, to you, Mel. You are a mighty warrior to have won your battle. May you forever be the strong beast you were born to be," he said, poured the moonshine into a glass and passed the jug before he sipped.

"Here, here," they said in unison, and those who had beverage in their glasses drank. Those who didn't, waited for the jug to be passed so they could splash some in theirs. It was a concession to the virus. No one wanted to take chances by sipping from the jug. They were afraid of spreading the flu as much as getting it, and all heartily agreed to the change in toast protocol.

"Now," Harley shouted over the noise of their chatter. "Raise your glasses to the real reason we are gathered this fine day. Not that your toast wasn't first and foremost in everyone's heart, Mel," he added, forestalling a furor over his error. Laughter followed his words, along with good natured ribbing.

"Thanks, Harley. It's good to know my health is at least somewhere on your toastability list," Mel teased.

"Not at all, Mel. Not at all. Remember, it was my first toast." He tried again. "Raise your glasses, please, to the end of World War I, to the treaty, to bringing our young men home. Here, here."

Shouts followed Harley's words. More hugs and back slaps followed the draining of their glasses. Their lively chatter resonated with joy and the promise of a good day today and even better tomorrows. Their life-filled voices negated the problems of yesterday. It wasn't that sorrows hadn't occurred, but that they were of the past and ceased to hold power. Harley moved around the circle refilling the small glasses of moonshine and cognac. When he was done, he cleared his throat and began again.

"Here's to our warriors, those men whose lives were spent in their quest to keep us safe. Bless you and thank you for paying the ultimate price for our freedom and safety."

"Here, here," they said over and over, adamant in their praise of the soldiers and their sacrifices.

"I have one more toast," Harley said, holding his glass high. "A special toast and prayer for the men who are missing in action. May they be found and returned to the loving arms of their families." He spoke through the watering eyes and the lump growing in his throat. His emotions matched every heart in the room. It was a quiet toast, but heartfelt. He was silent for a moment, the thought of Robbie uppermost in his mind and in the minds of the others who hoped and prayed for his return.

"Is there any news?" Verna asked, breaking the silence. Ruthie shook her head.

"How is Mary?" Laura asked. "And Willie?"

"Just going from day to day," Ruthie told them. "That's why they aren't here. I worry about her. About Willie, too. Maybe if they knew. If he had died, and they knew it."

"It would be devastating, but easier in a way," Laura said. She knew how odd 'better off dead' sounded. How could anything be worse than devastating? But wondering about a child was the worst punishment, the worst torture any parent could live through. The pain of it was reflected in her eyes. It was in the eyes of every parent in the room. Still, they could hope, and hope was something.

There were murmurs of agreement, understanding. Sammy chose that moment to wail, wanting down from Kate's arms. She stood him on his feet, and he ran around to each person in the circle. "Up," he demanded. As soon as he was picked up, he demanded to be down again. It was a blessing. He lightened the mood, and it was needed.

"Okay, I need Ruthie, Laura and Ma in the kitchen. Everybody else, get out," Kate ordered.

The family took the golden opportunity to catch up with their favorites. Jeannie dragged Becca outside so she could check on what she thought of as *her* chickens. She petted all the calves and fed them grain specially made for the young ones.

Kat and Verna sat together, catching up on each other's news. Verna held Kat's work at the hospital and her knowledge of herbal remedies in high regard. But she had always been impressed with the young woman. Kat thought similarly about Verna. It had been a mutual feeling for them since the beginning. When Harley brought Verna home to the Hughes house one Christmas day, she found her family, and later her surrogate child in Kat.

Jack and Jamie filled Mel in on the work they had completed on the smithy building. Mel asked questions and tried to visualize the conversion from smithy to attorney's office.

John watched Mel and tried to figure out why he was still so frail. Under the guise of paying attention to the conversation, he watched and listened as Mel talked. His voice was soft, without its normal heartiness. Every now and then he coughed and John heard his lungs work too hard in the effort to intake and expel air. He wished he could see inside Mel's lungs, know if they had been scarred or harmed in some unknown manner. If so, was it a permanent or temporary condition? It sounded like they were not working as they should, were laboring to provide enough air for normal speech. It was a vicious cycle. He needed plenty of breath to recover his strength and feel well, but he needed health in order to reclaim deep breathing.

Kate called them to dinner, and John's fixation on Mel's health was temporarily dismissed. Roast chicken, mashed potatoes with gravy, buttery squash, bread pudding and sweet potato pie were lined on the buffet. It was a feast. And it felt so good to Kate to be able to provide it for her family, and not worry and wonder if she would be out of food come spring because of this wonderful dinner. She beamed at the bounty before them.

She heard "Look at this food." And "God I'm hungry. Let me at it." And "Wow, you women have done yourselves proud." Kate loved every comment and found the face that uttered it so she could smile and acknowledge their praise.

"Fill your plate and find a seat, everyone. It'll be a tight squeeze, but I think we'll all fit at the table."

"Sure we'll fit," Laura said. "We've done it before. Had fifteen around this table when all the kids were here. Well the kids and their kids." She looked proud . . . and proprietary. Kate noticed and tried to back off and give Laura some room at the helm. She had earned the right.

"Where do you want everyone?" Kate asked her in acknowledgment.

"Well, Mel here, at the head. Then I don't know. It's a free-for-all," she said, grinning and loving the moment.

"Why don't you sit at the other end, Laura? That's where you should be."

"Well . . . if you think . . ."

It was a noisy suppertime. And it was wonderful. Laughter. Good natured bickering. Poking some fun and huge amounts of affection. It ended too soon. When the meal was over and talk of home began, John cornered Mel privately.

"I'd like to examine you," he said.

"What do you want to see?" Mel joked. "You're looking at pretty much all I've got."

"After Jack and Ruthie and their charges go, can I listen to your chest upstairs where it's quiet?"

"Sure, but why?" Mel asked, confused. He was over the flu and recovering. What else was there to see?

When John listened to Mel's breathing and tapped on his chest, his concern grew. There was a lot of noise in the cavity that shouldn't be there.

"You need warm sun and dry air, Mel. The congestion in your lungs isn't going away like it should."

"And where do you think I should get this wonderful warm, dry air, Doc?"

"Someplace warm and dry?" he said with a sardonic grin. "Do you want me to spell out the states answering your needs?"

"Well, I'm going to have to get well right here. I can't just up and leave like a vagabond. I'm not Harley. I have responsibilities right here." His thoughts went back to when Kate's first husband was ill. They were traveling to South Carolina for the warmth because Doc Cheston said Mark needed it, but they had to stop in Tennessee when his condition became grave. Kate and her four little girls had endured unspeakable horror. Broke and without hope, they'd had to depend on Red Cross for train fare to get home, and they watched Mark die on the way. It had been too late for warm air to do him any good. Telling Kate they needed to go south for his own health was the last thing he would do -- ever.

"I recommend warm, dry air, Mel," John repeated.

"That isn't gonna happen, John. Take my word for it. And I'd appreciate it if you kept that bit of wisdom to yourself." He looked at John directly in the eyes, his face relaying the immediacy of his message. "I mean that."

"If that's what you want. However, in lieu of traveling, find a southern exposure window and spend some time in it. Stay warm, do some light exercise -- light -- to get the congestion moving. Stay away from the barn and the hay. Your lungs don't need the dust right now. I'll be back in a week."

"Kate's gonna ask you about this. What will you say?"

"What I just told you. Warm south window. No barn. Light exercise. No more."

Mel nodded. "Thanks."

Chapter Fourteen

The second wave

Mel's exercise was playing with Sammy. He was the horse and Sammy the cowboy. He galloped from room to room, sometimes on his feet holding onto Sammy's legs and sometimes on all fours with his rider spurring him on and slapping his backside. Sammy shot bad men who always died on the first shot, and they always deserved it. After all, he wore the white cowboy hat Harley had given him.

Mel was totally enamored with Sammy and would do anything the child asked. Kate frequently told Mel he was spoiling him. But it didn't register. How could playing with him, kissing his wounds and caring about him not be a good thing? It was a novel experience for Mel. He spent December making a wooden rocking horse, one Sammy could ride all day if he felt like it. And Mel wouldn't wear out trotting around the house with Sammy on his back.

He didn't stay away from the barn totally, but conceded to wearing a mask like the ones Kat and John wore tending the sick, and he bundled up to stay warm. Sometimes he'd stand immobile, entranced watching Becca and Jamie milk. The two worked together like they'd been doing it forever, like they were entwined in their thoughts and movements, and it cut milking time in half. He missed the hours spent with his heifers, leaning against their warm sides, breathing in the musty smell of their hides. He wanted to be back there, and he was determined to. Soon, regardless of what John said.

Harley began coming to the house twice a week to continue lessons for Jeannie and Becca, and Kat came with him when she wasn't tending the few sick who still needed care.

Most often, Kat went with John Crow when he was called on, and she eagerly listened each time he diagnosed or gave remedies to patients who looked at him with something close to worship. Kat wondered about the reverence, but knew she felt something akin to veneration of him and didn't want to dissect the feelings.

Not all of his patients had the flu virus, so Kat learned about other illnesses and wounds as he tended them with her by his side. He brought another baby into the world, and Kat saw how much trouble a breech birth could cause. He let Kat handle what he thought she was prepared for which both terrified and exhilarated her.

John continued to live at the cabin with Kat and Harley. It was accepted now, and no one thought it strange or inappropriate. They went about their days much like any Hersey family did. They ate breakfast, performed the chores that meant survival, and cared for the people with whom they spent their days and nights. Harley made their meals while Kat and John tended to the ailments of others who needed them.

They were paid for their services mostly with goods. One day Harley came home with two loaves of bread, two long stalks of Brussel sprouts, a head of cabbage and a chicken he called Dulcebella, vowing no one would ever relieve her of her head. When Kat and John asked about his bounty, he went to the cupboard for the jug.

"Really?" Kat asked. "Do we need a sip first?"

Harley nodded and poured three.

"Remember the chili plant you asked me to get from the cellar and drop at the Westbrook's for Emily's rheumatism? Well, I did." Harley took a sip from his glass, and seemed in no hurry to explain further.

"Uh-huh . . . And?" Kat prodded with an exaggerated eye roll.

"Well, after I gave Emily her chili plant, she asked me if we ate Brussel sprouts, and I said yes, so she gave me four stalks because they had more than they could use, and I left after having a couple of really good molasses cookies and milk."

"Okay. What about the bread?" John asked.

"I knew their neighbors, the LaTours, had cabbage, and I wanted one, so I stopped in, asked if they'd like some Brussel sprouts, and they did, so I gave them two of the Brussel stalks, and she gave me a cabbage and some loaves of bread. That's all. That's how it was. Simple."

Kat said, "Well, that makes sense."

John looked at her, shook his head in wonderment. "It does?"

"Sure." But then she said, "Wait . . . Dulcebella. What about her?"

"Oh, well, she not for stewing, you know," he repeated and reinforced it with a hard stare.

"Of course not," John said, looking up at the ceiling. "Not Dulcebella."

"Well, further on down the road I see old man Eaves running around the yard, chasing her with a hatchet in his hand. He was yelling obscenities, and she was squawking and screaming something fierce. When I pulled up, he had her by the tail feathers and she looked at me. Raised those beady little eyes and begged me for help. You know how it is."

Harley searched both of them for understanding. Waited for approbation.

"Sure. We know," Kat said. "So, what did you do?"

"I traded him. Dulcebella for a loaf of bread. Nothing else I could do. She's our chicken now."

"She's your chicken, Harley. All yours," Kat told him, a grin wanting badly to spread on her lips.

They had a tree cutting party at the cabin . . . like they used to before Spanish Influenza, a lifetime ago . . . or yesterday.

As they drove down the long lane to the clearing, her thoughts were mixed. Kate had lived at the cabin for so long, she felt like it was still hers when, in reality, it belonged to who ever lived there at the moment. It wasn't hers any more than it was Kat's or John's or Harley's. She had no right to claim it, but it didn't feel like anybody else's. It felt like hers. Down to her bones.

Sammy bounced up and down on the seat next to Jeannie and Wolf glared at him.

"It's alright, Wolf. He's just excited."

Sammy babbled something, and Wolf turned to look at him. Kate laughed. "I think you just spoke Wolf, Sammy. I speak it, too."

"Do you think Sammy recognizes the lane from his stay here?" Mel asked. "He sure acts like he knows it."

"I'd think so. Babies and animals know a lot more than we give them credit for. I wish your mother had come with us. She'd enjoy being here."

Mel was quiet, wondering whether to tell Kate what he thought or leave it be. He decided Kate should know and be prepared.

"I don't think she's feeling well," he told her. "She won't talk about it, but I can tell."

Kate's eyes widened and she looked at her husband. "But that's terrible. We should have stayed home with her."

"I tried to tell her we would stay home. We could do this on another day. She wouldn't have any of it."

Kate thought back to the last time she'd really noticed Laura – looked at her closely. She remembered seeing her flushed face the day before and thinking it was heat from the stove. Laura had been doing her weekly bread baking, and the kitchen was warm from the oven, so Kate had dismissed it as normal. Now she wondered.

It had become a practice since the epidemic to search for signs of illness in the faces of the people she cared about. Everyone did it. It was routine. Were they feverish? Were they eating well? Were their eyes bright and clear?

Kate was silent in remembrance and grew nervous, frightened the Spanish flu had returned.

"You don't think . . . she couldn't have . . ." Kate couldn't say the words. The idea was too horrible.

"No. Don't even suggest she might have the flu. She'll be fine."

But she wasn't. Laura was on the floor when they returned from the tree party. Kate helped settle her upstairs, grabbed some of Sammy and Jeannie's things and sent them with Jamie and Becca back to the cabin.

"You'll need to continue the chores," she told them. "I'm sorry Jamie. I was hoping you could get back to work with Jack. You must be sorry you came, huh?" she said with a smile, hoping he wasn't unhappy.

"Never, Kate. You're my family." Her eyes watered because he looked so much like Mark when he smiled back at her.

Kate spent the next hours disinfecting the kitchen. She scrubbed anything Laura might have touched, boiled towels and aprons, and then scoured the table, the counter, the floor. Becca and Jamie returned, and she sent them to their rooms until the kitchen was spotless, sterilized. She was exhausted when it was finished, and only then did she climb the stairs to see how Mel was doing with his mother. Her children were safe. That much she believed, and that was all she knew how to do.

He was sitting hunched over next to his mother's bed. Kate stopped in the doorway and watched. She loved him, well or sick, frail or brawny, but it was the times he was tender like this, taking care of the people he cared about, when she loved him the most. She moved into the room and put her hand on his shoulder. She massaged the muscles running up the back of his neck and he tilted his head to look at her.

"That feels wonderful. You have an hour to stop."

"How is she? Have you given her any of the teas John left?"

"Yes, one to bring down fever and the one to sleep -- at different times. You shouldn't mix them, right?"

"Right. But thirty minutes to an hour apart is okay."

They were quiet watching Laura breathe. Both feared the worst. She was no longer young. She was worn out and thin from taking care of Mel. Would she have the strength to beat this harsh master?

"Maybe it's not the Spanish flu," Kate said. "Maybe she has a regular old bug and will be better tomorrow."

"I can't pretend, Kate. It is. I know it well. She has it, the damned killer... I wish it was human. I could deal with it then."

Kate wrapped her arms around him from behind, nestled her face next to his, her chin on his shoulder. She could feel the lean bones through his shirt. He had been a large, healthy man, in his prime when it struck him, and look what it had done. How could Laura fight it?

"Why don't you go get a few hours sleep? Let me keep watch with her. When you've rested, we'll switch."

He picked up his mother's hand and held it, gently rubbed the back with its prominent veins; reddened, arthritic knuckles and browned age spots. Her hand was the embodiment of her age. Her hair, too. It was wiry and silver gray, but still thick and curly. Mel didn't see the signs of her aging. He saw the mother who chased him until she caught him when he needed a swat. He saw the woman who climbed trees with him and helped him hide from his brothers and sisters. He saw the brave, grieving wife who buried her husband way, way too early. He saw his champion, his friend of more than several decades.

He wouldn't sleep, yet.

"You go on to bed, Kate. I'll stay here a while and wake you when I'm ready for sleep."

"Well, maybe in a bit. Would you like some tea or coffee? I could stand a cup of tea."

He nodded and she went into the upstairs sitting room, her mind roaming. She hadn't even asked Jamie how it went when they took Jeannie and Sammy back to the shelter of the cabin and Harley. The people in this house would go back to quarantine in the morning. Poor Becca and Jamie would again be in charge of meals, clean up, and all the chores. It felt like they'd been living like this for years.

She pulled a chair next to Mel and sat with one hand on his leg, the other holding her tea. She leaned against him, soaking up and giving warmth.

"I love you, Mel. We'll get through this."

"I love you, too, Kate. We will. What would I do without you?"

"Ditto."

Toward morning, Kate went to sleep for awhile and was roused by Becca calling up the stairs to pick up their breakfast. She retrieved the tray and took it into Laura's room. Mel was swabbing Laura's forehead, and she was tossing frantically back and forth. The fever had risen during the brief time Kate had been sleeping.

"How long since she's had any yarrow tea?"

"She can have more now," he said, handing her a face mask. "Wear it, please. Want to make tea?"

"Becca sent some hot water in the tea pot, so it's ready. I just have to add the herbs. Why don't you eat some breakfast and let me do this."

"I am hungry," he said, a withered grimace holding her gaze. He began to eat and watched Kate move about the room tending to his mother.

She raised Laura's back and slid a thick pillow behind her. Laura was aware enough to know something was expected of her, but not enough to be able to do it. She flailed and bobbed, her movements a trial, an energy expending effort that accomplished nothing but a rise in temperature.

"I have some tea for you, Laura. Will you drink some for me? Please?"

Laura nodded but turned her head when Kate brought the cup to her lips.

"Laura, you need to drink some. Please."

She nodded again, then turned her head.

"You must take some tea, Laura," Kate told her growing frustrated. "It will help you get better. Please try."

She repeated the process without success, and Kate was becoming concerned. If they couldn't keep liquids in her, she'd never beat this. The fever had to come down, and they couldn't let her become dehydrated.

"Let me try, Kate," Mel said.

He sat behind his mother's head, holding her against him. He put the cup to her lips and tipped it. Some went down the front of her onto the towel, but a little went in. He kept repeating the process until the cup was empty.

"This isn't good," he said. "We need to talk with John. He might have some ideas about getting the tea into her."

"I'll call for Jamie to go get him if you'll go rest for a while."

"I will."

"Promise?"

"Promise," he said, wrapping Kate in his arms and holding her tight. "You know where to find me."

John came with Kat who put on the mask Kate handed her without a fuss. They did with Laura what John had done with Mel when he first was sick. He looked over the entire body, pinched fingers and fingernails. Thumped the abdomen, the chest and the back. Pressed his fingers into the flesh at various places and listened to the breathing and the chest. He asked Kat to repeat what he'd done. When she was finished, he questioned her with his eyes and she nodded, then spoke.

"It's Spanish flu. She desperately needs hydration. Her fingers and fingernails don't respond to pressure as they should. Her chest is fluttery like blowing bubbles under water. She should be elevated so her lungs don't collect fluids. Don't give her any decongesting herbs -- better to have an expectorant for when she begins coughing. You must get the fever down. If it gets any higher, give her a cool water bath. Cool cloths until then."

"How will she get fluids if she won't drink them?" John asked of Kat.

Kat paused, thinking of a solution, and John waited as if time was of no consequence. "Well, when we had sick critters or baby critters, we used an eyedropper. Pushed it in their mouths and squeezed the end. They either drank or drowned."

John had to laugh. Even Mel laughed at the incongruity of the healer drowning the patient. But the words were so

Kat like, no gray -- just black and white. Drink or drown. Sorry.

John nodded again, pleased at her creativity in a tough situation. "Do you have any eyedroppers?" he asked.

"I have some large ones we use with the calves when they can't be with their mothers," Mel said.

"That'll work. Have Becca or Jamie sterilize a couple and send them up."

"How about you two?" Kate asked. "Would you like some tea, food, anything?"

"Tea would be great," John said.

Kat said to make it two.

They had their tea in the room still equipped to be a makeshift parlor left over from Mel's illness. Kate sipped her drink and looked at her daughter, still struggling to accept the changes in Kat, the transformation from child to young woman . . . and trying to understand the complexity of her feelings about it all.

When they were finished, John asked Kat and Kate to look in on Laura while he had a chat with Mel. When they left, Mel read John's immobile face, and what it said wasn't good.

"I fear for your mother," John said.

"I do as well, but I beat this. Why not her?"

"I don't know if she has the strength to recover. Or the desire."

Mel moved unconsciously back a step and straightened, poised for a fight. He couldn't have said why, but he wanted to punch John. Flatten him.

"What do you mean, no desire to get well? Why wouldn't she want to get better?"

John was thoughtful and still, not serene but accepting, and Mel grew anxious.

"What do you mean?" he repeated, louder this time and enunciating his words. "And how can you tell what her desires are by pinching her fingers or whatever the hell else it is that you do?"

He was growing belligerent and aggravated, but John knew it wasn't anger at him. It was his fear causing the distress. Mel had his hand on his hips and his chin was jutted out like a fighter ready for a brawl.

"You had many reasons to survive, Mel, though there were times I wondered if you would. Others who had this flu as badly as you didn't live. Who knows why one does and one does not? However, I do understand this much about illness. Your mother has lived her life and is happy knowing you're loved and happy. She may feel it's time to leave you."

"What makes you say that?" Mel asked, still irritated.

"She isn't fighting to live. She's fighting those who want to help her live."

"So, what are you telling me? Don't help her? Don't fight for her when she doesn't want to drink her tea?"

John took a long, deep breath through his nose and let it out slowly through his mouth. Then he did it again. His shoulders relaxed and the stern lines in his face disappeared.

"A long time ago, my grandfather on my mother's side was my guide. He was a healer, what some would call a medicine man. I loved him. He loved his wife, and he loved his daughter who was my mother."

"Are you going to tell me a story, John? Now?"

John smiled and went on. "His daughter, my mother, died when I was five. His wife, my grandmother, died when I was fifteen. He finished raising me, and when I was twenty, he left."

"Where did he go? Why?"

"He went into the woods. He was ill and didn't want to fight the illness. I was content, had learned what I could from him. He had taught me what he knew and was ready to leave me behind, be with his wife and daughter. He told me he was eager to be where he wanted to be, with them. He had no more reason to stay."

"Well, that's a nice story, but it has nothing to do with my mother," Mel said. "She isn't Cherokee, and she knows we want her here, with us." While his temper had been calmed, he was still annoyed.

John sat wordlessly. He waited for Mel to melt the words into ideas and the ideas into his reality, his current circumstance.

"Well, I can see she might not see a lot of reason for hanging around, but I don't want to lose her. I want her here, with all of us."

He was uncomfortable with the conversation, with the whole idea of wanting to die. Or, if the issue wasn't *wanting* to die, then it was *not wanting* to make much of an effort to live. It was confusing. Even the words were confusing. Any way you looked at it, it was about not caring one way or another whether you lived or died. And then you absolutely died because the Spanish flu ran roughshod over people who didn't care. He couldn't let one of them be his mother.

When John and Kat left, they promised to check back the next day. Kate reminded them to disinfect before going in to the cabin. They both said they would, and everyone knew they would have taken their regular precautions without a reminder. It was ingrained in them. It was what kept Kat healthy, as well as all the people in the cabin.

Hour after hour, Mel sat with his mother's head resting against him while he filled the eyedropper and slowly squeezed herbal tea into her mouth, drop after drop. She would swallow if it was in her mouth, but she still wouldn't make an effort to sip from the cup. He continued to sit with her when the tea was gone, bathing her forehead with damp cloths and smoothing her hair from her brow. He talked with her, softly, his words caressing the air around her, urging her to care.

"Remember that year we had snow up to the window sills, Ma? Boy, did we shovel. And I don't care what I said then, you beat me to the end of the walkway. I fibbed. You remember that, don't you?" Mel watched her face, looking for a sign she heard him. None came, but he continued to talk, continued to urge her to live.

"Did I ever tell you how much I admire you, Ma? How much I love your strength? You've been the rock that held this family together. I couldn't have done it without you."

Every once in a while, he'd lay his head back against the wall behind him and close his eyes. He could have been asleep. He could have been talking to the Lord. If his mother wasn't listening, maybe the Lord would hear his words.

Kate's heart broke. Mel's face was drawn and pale, his anguish fathoms deep. And there was nothing she could do but touch him tenderly, try to get him to rest. She heard a commotion in the yard and went to the window.

She saw Jack leap from the buggy, bend and reach back to lift something out of the second seat. He straightened with a limp bundle in his arms. Kat followed him to the door, and Kate knew. She flew down the stairs and had it open before they got there.

"Upstairs," she commanded. "Take her up to the second bedroom."

Kate yanked the covers back, and Jack laid a flushed, ravaged Ruthie on the bed.

"My God, Jack. How long has she been sick? She was alright when we were at the cabin."

"She felt sickly on the way home. By the time we got there, she was burning up. I'm sorry to barge in like this, but I can't care for her by myself. She's not going to the hospital and be alone with all those sick people!"

"Of course not. It's alright. This is where she needs to be," Kate said, busying herself to keep from falling apart. "Let me just get some things from Mel's mother's room."

Kat, coming through the door, said, "I've brought towels, cool and hot water, and the tea herbs." She set about making the tea and handed a wet towel to Jack. "It's all over the village again," she said. "I left John to deal with it, so I'll have to get back. I wanted to see Aunt Ruthie settled here first."

"Of course," Kate told her, "and thank you, Kat, for coming with them."

Kat turned to Jack. "You'll be staying?"

He nodded, his face looking much like Mel's, and Kate felt tears gather once again.

"I'll be taking the buggy then," she said, hugged her mother and uncle, and left. "Don't forget your masks," she threw out as she went through the door.

Jack lifted Ruthie as Kate held the cup. She sipped some and turned her face away.

"How long since she's had something for fever?"

"Just before we left. Kat gave her jasmine tea with anise for both the fever and cough. She left some here, plus some stuff she said was really smelly, but works."

"Yeah, it is. I gave some to Mel. It stinks. Asafetida. Let's try to get some more down her and then let her rest."

Jack lifted her again, so gently it looked like he was afraid she would break. He couldn't lose her. Ruthie couldn't die.

"Drink, Ruthie," Kate pleaded. "You need to drink."

Kate stood by her sister, rubbing her hand and praying to a God she wasn't sure of any longer. But that didn't stop her. She'd pray to a rock if she thought it might help Ruthie.

"Have you slept at all, Jack?"

He shook his head.

"Can you?"

"Not now. Later."

Kate put the cup down and turned away from Jack. "I need to check on Laura and Mel," she said, her voice thick and trembling. "I'll be one door down. Yell if you need me. I'll hear you."

Kate bypassed Laura and Mel and ran to their sitting room to be alone. She shut the door quietly and leaned her forehead against it, tears running down her contorted face. She tried to silence the wail building inside her chest and to stifle aching sobs. Her fists pounded silently on the door as she railed against the Spanish flu, against seeing people you cherished ravaged by fever, against watching death break the hearts of the living. Their pain was overwhelming. It was destructive, devastating.

When her eyes quit burning with salty tears and she could keep her composure, she splashed cool water on her face, dried it, and straightened her shoulders. When she walked into Laura's room, she was ready to be strong again.

"Go lay down for a bit, Mel. I'll be here with her."

He wouldn't go, but Kate managed to move him to the rocking chair where Laura had slept when she stood guard over him. She put his feet on the nearby footstool and covered him.

"If you want to shut your eyes, I'll be here," she told him. "Would you like a cup of coffee or tea?"

"Not right now. Maybe in a bit."

Chapter Fifteen

Kate moved back and forth between the rooms, making tea, bringing refreshments to Jack and Mel, bathing the brows of the sick, and helping them take their tea potions. She slept for a few hours and then insisted on relieving them for a brief time.

"You'll sicken, Jack. And then what will we do?"

"I know. I'll go. Call me if Ruthie wakes and needs me."

"Of course I will."

Mel refused to leave his mother, but slept briefly in the chair. Jack slept until six in the morning, three whole hours, and came back ready to take over again. Kate left him to check on Laura and Mel.

She knew before she entered something had changed. Mel sat by the bed holding his mother's hand and talking to her much like he had earlier. He was bent over, his forehead pressed into the side of the mattress. When he heard Kate, he raised his head, and the look on his face was peaceful, but his eyes were bottomless pits of anguish. Kate went to his side and touched Laura's face. It was no longer burning up with fever. It was cool to the touch, and Kate couldn't hear Laura's raspy breathing. There wasn't any.

Kate knelt and wrapped her arms around him and leaned her head on his shoulder. He spoke to Kate about her, about how she had taken over after her husband had died so young. How she had helped Mel, the oldest of her children, run the farm. How her quiet determination influenced his own behavior, how much he admired her, how grateful he was. He finally put his mother's hand on her chest and closed her eyes. He got up and went outside.

Kate straightened the bed around Laura and picked up the room. She didn't know what to do. She felt hollow. When the room was done, she combed Laura's hair and went to her room to find a pretty dress for her to wear. She'd want to look pretty. She passed by Ruthie's room. She had to. She didn't want to tell Jack Laura had died. He didn't need to know at the moment.

Kate picked out a delicate blue print she knew Laura liked and took it back to her room. She washed and dressed Laura and opened the window to let the fresh air blow into the room and bring the clean scent of winter. When she was done, she sat in the rocker and talked with Laura herself. It seemed to be the thing to do.

There were things she could have said to her mother-in-law when she was alive. But she hadn't, and now Laura would have to know Kate's heart from above. The time for talking was over, but Kate had the need to say a couple more things.

"I love your son, Laura. We have that in common. And it's big. I am so happy to have him in my life. How lucky I am . . . thank you for making him who he is. There is none better. None. Thank you for that . . . for him."

Kate looked in on Ruthie and then went to look for Mel. Kate saw he'd taken his horse, but that's all she knew until she found Becca and Jamie in the milk parlor.

"He went to the cabin to see Harley," Becca said, her head pressed into the cow in front of her.

"Do you know why he wanted Harley?" Kate asked.

She looked up with tearful eyes, and Kate understood.

"Did Mel tell you about his mother?"

Becca nodded and continued milking. Kate wanted to go to her, kneel down and put her arms around her daughter. But she couldn't, couldn't be near her, couldn't touch her. All she could do was talk from a distance of a few feet that might as well be miles.

"It's alright to cry, Becca. It's always sad to lose someone we care about."

"Is Mel gonna die, too?" Becca asked through wide eyes filled with tears.

"No. He's better now."

"No he isn't, Ma. He looks terrible. He's skinny and pale and he breathes hard."

"But he is better, Becca. It's just taking a while for him to recover completely. It took a lot out of him. We have to make sure he gets a lot of rest and doesn't worry."

"Are you sure?"

"Yes, I am, and you need to trust that I am telling you the truth. Do you want me to do the milking for you tonight?"

Becca laughed and tilted her head toward her mother. "We want to actually get milk out of them, Ma." Kate was glad to hear the sound. It had become rare.

Kate smiled and wondered at how good it felt. "Okay. I'll leave you to your work. I love you, Becca."

When Kate went back upstairs, she brought the bottle of cognac and three glasses with her. Ruthie was sleeping, so she beckoned to Jack to follow her. She poured two glasses, handed one to Jack and invited him to sit.

"I need to tell you something, Jack, but you're not to misunderstand what it means because it doesn't have anything to do with Ruthie. Okay?"

"What, Kate? Just say it." He ran a hand through his hair and down over his drawn face. He looked tired and drained of life.

"Laura passed away. John said she had no desire to get better. That's what I mean by saying it doesn't have anything to do with Ruthie. So, don't think it does."

"Where's Mel?" Jack asked.

"Becca said he went to see Harley. I don't know why."

"He wants a beautiful resting place for his mother. There aren't any left."

"Oh. You're probably right. I hadn't thought of a coffin for her. Harley will make a beautiful one for Laura. It's fitting." Kate sipped at the cognac and felt it slide smoothly down to her stomach. She relaxed for the first time in -- she didn't know how many hours or days. Was it days?

"Do you need help with preparations?" he asked.

Kate knew what he meant, and she shook her head. "It's done."

They finished their drink and went back into Ruthie's room. She'd awakened and was burning with fever.

"I'm going to fill the bathtub with cool water. Carry her down in a few minutes," Kate told him.

Ruthie screamed and thrashed when he put her in. She continued to moan and yell as they poured the water over her.

"God, I can't stand this, Kate," Jack said with tears threatening his eyes. "She's miserable. This can't be good for her."

"It's what I was told to do. Now do it, damn it!"

Jack held her in the water, soaked himself to his waist and further. Kate poured the water. Ruthie's hair was soaked. Her nightdress was up around her waist and falling off her shoulders. She'd stopped screaming but kept up a quiet moan that tore your heart out. She finally slumped against Jack's arm and lay limply in the water.

"Ruthie!" Jack yelled, panic setting in. "Ruthie!" he yelled again, shaking her.

"Stop, Jack! She's alright. I can see her heart beating. She's just exhausted. Two more minutes and we can get her out of the water."

Jack breathed deeply, closed his eyes and prayed. 'Don't take her. Please don't take her.' Kate was making the same prayer. 'This is my sister, Lord. My sister. Hear me!' It wasn't as much a plea as it was a demand. She was beyond asking. Now she was telling -- demanding her sister's life be spared.

It was time, and Jack was ready to take Ruthie from the water, but Kate stopped him.

"Let's get her out of this wet nightgown first. I have a blanket we can wrap her in. She'll be more comfortable."

He carried Ruthie back to the bedroom, her body shivering and her teeth chattering loudly. They dressed her in one of Kate's gowns, covered her with blankets and gave her some hot anise tea. She slept immediately.

Kate took the footstool from Laura's room and put it under Jack's feet, wrapped him in a blanket and gave him another small glass of cognac. He drank it, and his head nodded in sleep. Kate sat and watched them both.

Sometime later, she heard the sound of Mel's horse in the yard and tiptoed quietly out of the room and met him outside. She told him what they'd done with Ruthie and asked him about his trip to the cabin.

Jack had been right. He'd asked Harley to make a coffin for his mother. Of course, he'd agreed and would bring it when it was done.

"I told Jack about Laura. He's pretty scared. Me, too."

Mel took her in his arms and held her for a long time.

"I'm so sorry, Kate. Ruthie is a strong woman though. I'll pray for her."

"Come on up. I have a glass of cognac waiting upstairs. Then, a nap for you. Did you tell your brothers and sisters?"

He nodded and told her telegrams were sent.

"I bathed and dressed her, Mel. I hope that was okay. I needed to do something for her, make her look pretty."

"Of course, it's fine. It's good of you, and I'm grateful. Not a fun duty."

"It was alright. We had a conversation."

"Excuse me?" Mel said, confusion written clearly on his face. "You had a conversation?"

"Yes, and we're in agreement. You are unique and wonderful," Kate told him, looking up at his face, much thinner than it was, but still handsome and alive with warm and loving eyes.

He looked in on his mother and told Kate she did indeed look pretty . . . and contented. She looked at peace and ready to meet her husband.

"Thank you, Kate. It means a lot to me, and to her."

Mel slept awhile and then convinced Jack to take a nap in a real bed. Between the three of them, Ruthie had around the clock care. Two days later, her fever broke and the coughing began. They elevated the head of her bed. They knew what to do. It had become routine. Get the fever down; elevate the bed; change to an expectorant herbal tea; watch for signs of blood.

Laura hadn't made it to the coughing stage, and as Mel watched Ruthie become ravaged with coughing, he was content with his mother's death. She hadn't had to go through this. Mel remembered too well the painful, racking cough and the debilitating exhaustion it caused.

Jack sat on the bed next to Ruthie and held her propped up against him. He smoothed limp, damp hair away from her face and held the cloth for her to spit into after each cough. He felt the spasms grip each time they seized her chest, and he wondered how long she could survive this stage of the illness.

He looked as disheveled and ragged as Ruthie. His black hair was greasy, lay like a stringy cap on his head and fell down over his eyes. The crisp white shirt he'd become famous for was wrinkled and stained. He was a mess, inside and out, and he didn't care.

Kate came into the room and stood beside Jack with her arms around him. She stayed there for many silent minutes holding him while he held her sister.

"There's some hot soup in the parlor." They called it a 'parlor' to feel better about needing it, so it might feel like a place they'd enjoy rather than a sick room escape.

Ruthie coughed all night long, and Kate was growing more and more afraid her sister wouldn't survive. She needed rest to recover, to give her body time to fight the virus, but the constancy of racking coughs wouldn't allow her a moment's respite. Jack was growing morose. He barely responded to Kate when she talked to him and refused to leave Ruthie for even a short break.

"We need something stronger, Jack. Something that will force her to sleep for a while," Kate said just as the sun was rising and coloring the chintz curtains orange. "I'm going to send Mel for John. Are you okay with John looking at her?"

Jack nodded and dipped the eyedropper into the cup of tepid tea. He put it between Ruthie's lips and squeezed the rubber tip, and the liquid ran down her chin and onto the wet towel on her chest catching the drips. Kate automatically removed the wet one and put a dry towel in its place. Her moves were mechanical, too, much like Jack's.

She was tired, more than tired, but couldn't rest when she lay down. Her mind wouldn't quit. It became a random collection of pictures -- of her and Ruthie when they were children, of Ruthie in a white wedding gown, of Ruthie throwing snowballs, of Ruthie making curtains with all the women in the family and Kate's daughters. Tears slid from the corners of her eyes, and she didn't bother to wipe them away. She was too tired.

Mel brought John back with him, and they watched as John examined Ruthie. His process didn't seem strange anymore. They'd seen it too many times. But it was difficult with Ruthie because she couldn't stop coughing long enough to lie still. When he was finished, he gave Kate a small brown bottle of laudanum.

"This will help her sleep. Don't give her more than thirty drops and not more than once every three to four hours. She needs to cough, to clear her lungs, and this will suppress the coughing. After she sleeps, if you can get her up and moving, do it."

Kate nodded to John, her eyes glazed, her mouth forming a smile without the help of her eyes.

"It looks to me like both you and Jack could use some of this. Are you alright, Kate? Are you sleeping at all?"

"Sure. I'm fine. Jack needs to sleep, though. He hasn't left Ruthie's side in a long time."

"The doctor is ordering ten drops for both you and Jack in a cup of chamomile tea. Bring a second bed in here if you need to. Mel can sit with Ruthie for a few hours by himself."

"That's what I told them both," Mel said. "They won't mind me."

"Let's get a bed in here, then. Come on Mel."

Minutes later, another bed was set up, and Jack was in it with a cup of laudanum laced tea. Mel tucked Kate in her own bed with her own cup of tea. They were out for several hours. Ruthie was, too, and Mel had time to sit and think while he kept vigil at Ruthie's bedside as he'd promised. He rocked in the quiet room to the sound of Jack's soft snore and Ruthie's rhythmic struggle for breath.

He thought of his mother lying in the next room with no breath at all. She was pain free, and for her peace, Mel was glad. "I already miss you, Ma," he whispered. It was strange to think she wouldn't be cooking breakfast in the morning as she'd done his entire life. The world, his world, had changed and he wasn't sure how much of it was truly different because he was out of touch.

He felt isolated, remote.

It was a strange reality, a microcosm of the world here on his farm where nothing existed outside of the boundaries of his acreage. Except it did. He didn't know if he had the strength to deal with it again. He didn't know if he had the desire. This may be enough. If he never left the farm again, it might be fine. Maybe enough to fulfill him, but it was a lonely feeling.

Mel's thoughts wandered. He didn't fight their directions, but let them take him where they would, and it was peaceful . . . even good.

Kate woke first. She was groggy and had to battle her way from sleep to wakefulness through a dense fog of angst. Once fully aware, she was instantly afraid, terrified something had happened to Ruthie while she was asleep. She ran into the room, skidded on her stocking clad feet and stood at the end of the bed watching for movement of Ruthie's chest, something to let her know her sudden fear was unfounded. Satisfied with the regular movement of her sister's breathing, she turned Mel's way, smiled and climbed on his lap. She put an arm around his back and laid her head on his chest, listening to his raspy intake and expulsion of air. Was there ever a time she had not listened for the sounds of troubled breathing? Would she ever again?

"This feels nice," she said. "But maybe you should sleep for awhile, and I'll take over here. It's about time for her to wake up and take some more tea."

"I'm happy right here," he whispered into her hair. "This is more than nice. It's good medicine. I miss you."

"I've missed you, too. And I'm so happy you are feeling better. You are, aren't you?" she asked, tilting her head to watch his face. "Feeling better," she added.

Mel nodded and squeezed her tight against him. The move made him cough, and he tried to stifle it for her sake.

She watched his efforts and worry etched her face.

"You should be resting, Mel. Really you should."

Ruthie woke and Kate went to make tea for her. She dumped the herbs into the cup, poured in the hot water and looked hard at her husband. He rubbed at his face and eyes as if he could wipe away the lines of distress. He was ashen colored and wasn't eating enough to fill out his long frame.

Kate turned her head so she didn't have to look any longer. She couldn't deal with it, not now. Ruthie needed her most at the moment, and right now she could only take on one thing at a time.

She was spooning tea into Ruthie's mouth rather than letting her sip from the cup. Too much of the precious liquid was lost down her front the other way. She'd taken about half when Kate heard noise in the yard and Mel rose to look out the window.

"Who is it?" Kate asked.

"It looks like Willie."

"Really? I wasn't expecting him, were you? Wonder what's happening?"

Mel shook his head and watched as Willie leaped out, leaned back into the buggy, and came out with a large bundle. It was a limp Mary he cradled in his arms. Mel couldn't know it because he hadn't been there, but the scene was a repeat of what Jack had done just a few days ago, and in a minute, he heard Willie's boot kicking the door. Mel's eyes closed and pain settled in over his face. 'Not another one. How many more?' he groaned to himself.

"What is it?" Kate demanded when she saw the anguish on Mel's face. But she heard Willie's feet pounding up the stairs and saw her brother's white face in the doorway. Mel didn't need to answer.

Another room was turned into a sickroom for Mary. Kate made another pot of tea with the same herbs she'd used with Mel and then his mother and Ruthie. She was becoming confused about the past and the patients she had tended, given what and when. The longer time she spent, the more confused she became.

Kate removed Mary's damp clothing and began sponging her fever ravished body. She shooed the men from the room and exposed Mary's naked form to the cool sponging and the even more cooling air. She was burning up, her face scarlet and her body white. The wet cloth grew warm in an instant against her hot skin. Kate continued to rinse it in the basin of cool water and drag it dripping over Mary's body. When she finished sponging and had given her a cupful of yarrow tea through the eyedropper, she called for Mel.

"I need help. Mary needs the cooling bath. Will you fill the tub for me?"

"Of course."

"Come on, Mary. Fight this. You can do it," Kate whispered after Mel left. She begged her, badgered her, threatened, and when all else failed, bribed her with the return of her son.

"What will Robbie do when he comes home and you're not here to greet him?" Kate asked through a choked voice. "He's gonna need you, Mary. Fight, damn it! Fight!"

She didn't hear his step as Mel walked slowly up the stairs. When he came into the room, Kate's face was pushed into the side of the bed, and her shoulders were heaving with sobs. Mel pulled her to a standing position and put his arms around her. He held her quietly for a long time while she sobbed. Too tired to stop. Too tired to continue. Just too tired.

"Come on, girl. We have to take Mary down to the bath. Just follow me. Okay? All you have to do right now is follow."

Kate nodded. He scooped up the silent, unclothed Mary, not even seeing her naked form, and carried her downstairs to the bath. He carefully placed her in the tub and held her upright while Kate began pouring the cool water over her. Mary screamed, incoherent words came from her mouth, words Kate was surprised her sister-in-law knew. She thrashed in the bath water, drenching both Mel and Kate until Kate slipped and landed on her bottom. She screeched as she landed and Mel worked to keep Mary upright with one hand and help his wife with the other.

Jack, just outside the room, heard Kate's shriek and leaped through the doorway trying impossibly to catch Kate as she fell. They both landed in a wet heap by the bath with Mel hanging onto Mary and helplessly watching. Kate laughed. Jack laughed.

Mel half grinned and half scowled. He was holding a sick woman, a naked, sick woman, and he was watching his wife floundering around in water with another man. Was that funny?

Kate tried to stop laughing, but couldn't. As she giggled, Jack couldn't help but follow suit. He was exhausted, sick with worry, but laughing felt good. They rolled on the floor and hung onto each other. Their shouts filled the house of sickness and sorrow bringing Willie downstairs and Jamie and Becca into the house.

"What's going on?" Willie shouted. "What's the matter?"

Jamie echoed the questions as he threw open the front door and strode into the kitchen.

"Nothing. Nothing . . . really," Mel soothed. "They just fell down, and it was funny."

Kate and Jack sat upright on the drenched floor and choked out apologies while trying to stop giggling. They leaned against each other, their shoulders still shaking with attempts to suffocate embarrassed laughter.

"I'm really sorry," Kate said through hiccups and tears. "It's not funny. It's just . . . I don't know . . . it's just, not funny. I fell and Jack . . ."

She couldn't finish because there was no explanation other than that they needed to laugh while they cried. They'd seen the horror and carnage left by illness, felt the anguish of loss, suffered through too damn much feeling, and she couldn't say what was in her mind. No one could because Willie's wife sat in cold bath water burning up with fever, incoherent and possibly dying. And there was nothing they could do because they didn't know how to fix her. They didn't know how to make her well, and it felt like their efforts were minuscule, absurd weapons against a mammoth monster. They were failing . . . and dying minute by minute themselves.

When they recovered, they tried not to be discomfited at their silliness. They tried not to recognize Mary's nakedness. Mel covered Mary with a towel and Kate again began to pour cool water over the feverish woman. She wasn't recognizable as their Mary. She wouldn't even know herself. She was flesh and bone fighting for life, for breath, and like an animal she was in a primordial battle. Her breath labored. She gasped as the cool water splashed against her skin.

Finally, Jack lifted her from the water and placed her into Willie's arms, waiting with a blanket to cover his wife. It didn't register that they had seen her nakedness, or that she had been incoherent and babbling. It didn't matter. His only thought was Mary needed to get well. To come back to him. He needed her, loved her.

Chapter Sixteen

It was long past dark when John Crow and Kat drove down the road to the cabin. It was fortunate the mare knew her way because they were both more tired than either of them would admit, and thanks to Kitty, neither had to drive or pay attention. They sat with their heads against the back of the seat, their eyes closed. Brief words passed between them -- about the patients they'd treated during the day, about those who would come in the next day, about those who had passed. But silence was preferred. It was sweet and comfortable. They prized quiet and togetherness. It was better than talk.

They were wrapped snuggly in several blankets, warm under layers of tightly woven wool. Only their faces were exposed to the winter cold, and they didn't care. It felt good. Toasty inside the cocoon, a chill wind bit their cheeks, especially where snowflakes landed. When the buggy came to a stop, neither moved. The cold, dark night was a healing force. One they needed and wanted to embrace for awhile longer. John finally moved. "We need to cleanse, Kat. I'm so sorry."

"I know. I'm coming." She threw back the blankets and leaped from the buggy. Together they unhitched Kitty and put her away for the night.

"Beat you to the tub," Kat yelled as she ran to where they'd installed a disinfecting area to safeguard Jeannie, Sammy and Harley.

John smiled at her youthful exuberance. It was at odds with her serious nature when she was tending to her patients. At odds with her behavior at most times. Kat was an old soul, and he may have known her before -- he wasn't sure. Wasn't even convinced he believed in some of the things his grandfather had told him. What he knew with certainty was that Kat was unusual, distinctive, and he needed to guard her, care for her. The world was a better place with her in it.

He folded the blankets and put them away, safe from the weather so they'd have dry ones in the morning, and went to join Kat in the shed. When he opened the door, steam escaped, and he quickly entered and shut the door. He smiled, recognizing Harley's handiwork. He had anticipated their arrival and had the bath filled with hot water. Well, warm water. It was difficult to keep water hot in the cold shed where they decontaminated before going into the cabin.

Kat removed her hospital shoes and trousers, then her shirt. She didn't even nod to John, just accepted his presence as a natural part of events. Still in her camisole and pantaloons, she stepped into the bath water and ducked her head under.

"Did you add the vinegar and jasmine?" he asked when she came up out of the water for air.

"I did. Can't you smell it? I'm going to be pickled soon with so many vinegar baths. I'm becoming a jasmine dill pickle."

John smiled again. She amused him. Her intelligence and irreverent tongue added to her attractiveness. He looked away from the bath, anywhere else to give Kat privacy, though she'd made it clear she didn't care.

"I don't have anything new, John Crow. I'm not unique," she'd said with a cocky grin the first time they'd used the shed to decontaminate, and he'd voiced concern.

That's where you're wrong, little one. You are more wrong than you know, he'd thought. But he hadn't said the words, and she'd readied herself for the bath, and he'd looked away, regardless of her indifference over his presence.

He believed she saw him as an old man. Twenty-six had to be ancient to her at seventeen, and he felt prehistoric at times, but not near Kat. She made him feel like a young man, a callow youth, awkward, entranced by the woman-child-old soul who was Kat. She confused him, but she didn't know her impact. She was unconcerned about the correctness of the situation and left propriety, if there was any, to him. He held the blanket high between them, as always, before she stepped out of the water, and wrapped her in it to dry and don her cabin clothes. She always left before he used the bath water.

Kat was in a high-necked nightgown and serving up bowls of Harley's barley soup when John came in. Harley was leaning against the cupboard listening to Kat's tales and asking questions. The room was warm with a full fire in the hearth. It invited him to sit, leave the soup for later and feed his soul with orange and red flames crackling and begging to be watched, to be heard.

"Are you ready to eat, John?" Kat asked.

"Actually, I'd rather sit for a minute if you don't mind," he replied, seating himself in one of the rockers near the hearth. "This fire feels too good to leave."

"Not a problem. It's here when you're ready."

Harley sat next to him and they rocked in peaceful silence. Jeannie joined them, having put Sammy to bed and glad to see them home.

"How is everyone?" she asked, tentative and hopeful she wouldn't hear about more friends and family who had sickened or worse, about those who had succumbed to the illness and were awaiting burial.

Jeannie sat at the table with Kat while she ate her dinner and talked of her day with Sammy and Harley. Kat watched her sister recount events and knew Jeannie was no longer the little girl she'd been a few months before. Those days were long, long past. She'd been taken from her own mother and forced to become one to her young nephew. Though Harley was here taking care of them, it was Jeannie who had become mother to Sammy. It was she to whom he turned when he was hurt or sad. It was Jeannie who played games with him and read to him. She wouldn't have had it any other way. Well, she'd have liked for Rachel to come home and mother her own child, but a mothering Rachel no longer seemed a reality for her, not even likely. It was a dream she didn't believe in. Sammy didn't cry for her any longer. He had even stopped crying for Kate and Mel. Perhaps the shuffle back and forth between homes and people had become a way of life. Not something to cry about.

"Did Harley give you your lessons today?" Kat asked.

"Sure. He always does. He's a harsh taskmaster!" she said loudly for his benefit.

Harley smiled. "Only for my favorite carrot top kid," he teased.

"I'm not a kid, Harley. I keep telling you that and you're not listening. I think you're getting hard of hearing -- and senile."

"What? I can't hear you," he said and turned to Kat. "Copper Top is so smart, she's gonna be teaching me, soon."

"I'm going to college someday, so you better make sure I'm ready, Harley. I'm going to be a nurse or maybe a teacher, like Ma and Aunt Ruthie."

"You can do anything you choose, Jeannie. Anything," Harley told her, pride a glow on his face and a fire in his eyes.

John watched the interchange and pondered about Harley -- the hobo -- as the family called him, among many other names and never unkindly. Harley reminded him of the Shaman in his own Cherokee tribe. He was wise and spiritual, too, but everyone expected wisdom of a Shaman. He was supposed to be a sage, perceptive and erudite, was marked so by birth and generations of ancestral knowledge. Harley wasn't a Shaman, as far as they knew. But was he born with his knowledge?

"How about being a lawyer like your Uncle Jack?" Harley asked.

"I could be that. Are we going to get a Christmas tree?"

"I hadn't thought about it, Jeannie," Kat began, and paused in thought. Her little sister needed Christmas. She'd taken on the responsibilities of a mother, but she wasn't nearly old enough to be one. She was a little girl, a twelve-year-old little girl. And Sammy . . . he needed Christmas, too.

"Of course we are," she said more brightly than she felt. "You and Sammy and John and Harley will make a party of it."

"What about you?"

"And me. Of course. You can't have a party without me." Kat looked at John for confirmation of her words, her eyes wide in a plea for help.

John nodded and Kat went on. "Day after tomorrow. It'll be late, but when we get home we'll pack up Sammy and some refreshments and head to the woods."

"Can we ask Ma and Mel and Jack and Ruthie?" Jeannie's face said she knew better but wanted it to be, hoped it could be, like it was before, with the whole family trudging into the woods, having snowball fights, making angels in perfect, untouched snow.

"Not this year, baby girl. I'm sorry." Kat put her hand on her sister's and left it there. She swallowed, choking back her sorrow for the child Jeannie couldn't be. "Next year we will. I won't promise, but if I am alive and walking on two feet -- well maybe even limping along on one," she teased, "we will go to the woods as a family. You know I'll hop if I have to. You can count on me, Jeannie."

"I do, and I'll hold you to it. I'm not a baby, either."

"I know. That was a term of endearment, silly."

"You don't do endearment. Stop it. You sound silly, silly."

No one heard him riding into the clearing, and they were startled when his fist pounded on the door. It opened and Willie strode in with a gust of cold air. He stomped his feet and slapped his gloved hands together, looking around at the faces staring at him. Kat was the first to see her uncle was holding it together with the thin twine of shattered stamina. His eyes were glossy and his lips alternately pursed and grimaced. Kat rose and tried to push him gently back out the door. Willie didn't grasp what she was doing and shoved to try to get around her.

"Stop, Uncle Willie! You must stop!" she commanded.

He stared at Kat with blank eyes, uncomprehending.

Light in the Forest

"John, Uncle Willie needs to leave or decontaminate. Will you take him to the shed? I'll bring clothes and a glass of whiskey."

He nodded, grasped Willie's arm and forcefully led him out the door. The water left in the tub was tepid, but Willie didn't notice or complain when John had him strip and get in. Kat came to the door with clothes and whiskey and left them there. Willie looked dazed when he came back in. He stood still, unsure what he was doing at the cabin, knowing there was a reason but unable to come up with what it was.

"Have you eaten, Uncle Willie?" Kat asked.

He shook his head and stayed where he was. Kat looked to John and Harley for help. Harley pulled himself from his chair and went to Willie, grasped his arm and led him to the rocker.

"Your Pa made this chair," he said. "A fine job, too. Kate has loved it for years. Kat, perhaps you'd find the jug and pour us a glass?"

Willie sat, tried to stand again, and Harley pushed him back into the chair and left his hand on his shoulder, a kindly restraint. Kat poured small glasses of her grandpa's moonshine and passed them around. Willie drank and began to babble, growing more agitated as he spoke. They understood. Mary had died. Spanish flu, the cruel thief, had brutally robbed them of another loved one.

John Crow turned toward the tormented man, placed his hand on Willie's and began to speak. He talked of meadows and streams, sun on fields of wheat, tamarack trees as the moon kissed their tops and slid over to gloss the river in silver. He spoke of the Milky Way shining the way to God's house where there were glorious mornings and peaceful nights, how His home is filled with mothers and fathers, daughters and sons.

"Rob," Willie whispered, and settled back in his chair. "She'll be with Rob. That will make her happy. I should be happy for her. I'm not! God no, I'm not! What the hell? I need my son. I need her," he moaned, his face old, his eyes blank. John continued the soothing chant, and before long, Willie's eyes closed and John sat back.

185

"Let's move him to your room, Kat. He won't wake, and his soul will heal in sleep. Morning will be soon enough to face the reality of his loss."

Kat pulled the quilt over her uncle and turned to Harley. "I think he came for a casket."

He nodded, put on his outdoor clothes and left, his thoughts on the woman he had helped to bear two children, the pregnant young woman riding side saddle to the smith shop christening and giving birth instead. He shook his head and tried to ban the memories -- for the moment. He'd give them proper recognition later, when there was time.

In the morning, John woke him gently, brought him from the controlled trance he had induced. Willie was rested and tormented. He drank Harley's coffee but refused the pancakes and eggs. Kat and John had hitched the wagon to Kitty and loaded Mary's casket.

"We'll take it on our way to town, Uncle Willie. Will you be right behind us?"

He nodded and they left.

Two pine caskets lay on the snow in the cold December sun. They held Laura Bronson and Mary Hughes. Nearby, headstones inscribed with the names of other Bronsons stood as stark reminders of our transience. The dates told stories of dogged determination, dreams fulfilled and dreams cut short, loves and loss. Beloved wife, husband, daughter, son; adored mother, revered father . . .

According to the dates etched into stone, some had reached maturity and beyond, lived full lives and were finally taken by old age. Others had succumbed early, leaving heartbreak following brief journeys, cut short by the jagged edged sword of early demise. In this time of sickness, the small Bronson cemetery on Mel's farm could be a frightening place, yet it was strangely comforting to note other generations had lived and died, grieved and lived again.

No minister presided over the double funeral. He had died. Pastors continued to be the first to succumb because they were at the bedsides of the sick and dying. None were left nearby to send the deceased on to their final homes.

They chose to lay Mary at Mel's family cemetery even though she wasn't a Bronson. It was easier and safer than going into Hersey. Harley spoke and said a prayer as they lay Mary and Laura in their graves. Kate held her brother's hand while Harley talked of Mary, her love for family, her beautiful smile, her adoration of Willie, always, from the first moment to the last.

"I was blessed by her faith in me," Harley said. "Mary gave me the greatest gift of all when she let me help her bring Robbie into this world. She blessed us by letting us give without questioning, by receiving our gifts with a hearty smile. She made us better people."

When Willie's knees buckled, Kate held him up, and she caught Mel's eyes to say, 'I'm needed here, or I'd be holding you.' He nodded, understood.

Mel's brothers and sisters each threw a handful of soil on Laura's casket and left as soon as the first shovel full of dirt was tossed in. Spanish flu was still a threat, and it didn't respect grief and loss. There would be no gathering after the funeral, no sharing of food and stories to ease the pain of their mother's death. Disease might be shared instead, so parting was quick and distant, a wave and good wishes for a better time.

"Stay here for a few days," she urged Willie when it was over and the few people there quietly dispersed. "You need some rest and people around, Willie."

After checking on Ruthie and Jack, she poured a hefty glass of whiskey and handed it to him. He didn't have the energy to disagree. He drank, and Kate tucked him into bed like a child.

We should all be together, eating and drinking, talking about Mary and Laura, helping each other to feel better -- or crying, Kate thought. Anything except this isolation, this deathlike quiet. Harley should be toasting Mary and telling about Laura's great cookies. When she found Mel, sitting with his head in his hands, she told him her thoughts.

"It's the separation, Mel. Look at us! We're all split up! It's Christmas time, and we can't even celebrate together. We can't sit at a dinner table with people in our own house! Hell! We can't even be at a funeral together! I'm so damned sick of it!"

Mel got up, got the jug of moonshine and poured her a small glass. "I'm not even close to the erudite Harley, but here goes." He raised the jug high into the air. "Here's to Mary who gave our brother, Willie, love and children, who gave us her smile when she probably wanted to yell at us for acting like fools, Mary who was a peaceful, sweet soul."

He poured from the jug and nudged Kate to sip at her glass, and raised it again.

"Here's to my mother, Laura, who gave me life, who stood by my side every day of my life with quiet fortitude. She taught me how to love absolutely, tenderly, and resolutely. I pray she knows how much I loved her." Mel sipped from his glass and wiped the tears from Kate's face with his lips.

"We'll get through this, Kate."

"We're gonna have Christmas, damn it all!" Kat muttered and handed Jeannie a plate to dry.

"Of course we are, and it will be a good one. Did you think we wouldn't?" Harley said with surprise in his voice.

"You swear just like Ma," Jeannie said. "Only she says sorry, afterwards."

"Well, I'm not sorry, and I'll bet she really isn't either. Why don't you let John dry and you go get Sammy into some warm clothes? We're gonna go get a Christmas tree," she said, her voice painted in determination with a colorful grim edge.

Kat, John, Jeannie, Sammy and Harley trudged into the forest and found a tree. They decorated it with popcorn strings and colored paper cutouts. Harley put brightly wrapped presents under it, surprising them all.

Christmas day was deafeningly quiet in the cabin, but Harley told Sammy and Jeannie made up stories to while away the time until Kat and John came home. They were going to make a short day at the hospital. They promised. Jeannie recalled other holiday tales from Harley and wondered about the boy angel once again. Can boys really be angels?

They were fairly successful in their effort to forget other holidays when the family was all together. It smelled like pine boughs from the green sprigs on the hearth and the tree in the corner, and like spicy pumpkin from Harley's pies cooling on the table.

After decontaminating, Kat and John walked into a warm, fragrant room to find Harley in front of the fire holding Sammy on one leg and Jeannie on the other. Even at twelve, she wasn't too big to snuggle for a Christmas story.

Kate and Wolf rode out on Christmas day and sat in the buggy outside the cabin, talked with them from a distance, said "I love you. Merry Christmas."

What a horrible joke, she thought. There's no merry anything, no angels, no joy, no peace on earth. Water froze in her eyes before it could become a tear and roll down her cheek. She gave a sardonic snort at the idea.

"Finally!" she spouted to Wolf. "I know how to stop tears from falling -- after all this time. Just let them freeze!" She turned her mare toward home.

When she got there, she was greeted by the holiday aroma of their own pumpkin pie and roast beef. Jamie had been at the stove, and he greeted her wearing an apron and a grin. "There's a surprise waiting for you upstairs," he said. "You're going to like this Christmas gift."

"What is it, Jamie? Are you going to make me guess?"

"Not telling you. Go on up and see for yourself."

She did, and he was right. It was the best gift anyone could give her. Ruthie was waiting for her at the table in the sitting area. She was sitting up, drinking a cup of tea.

Kate stood still, shock keeping her from moving, afraid if she tried to touch her sister, she would find it was a mirage or hallucination.

"Well, aren't you going to say anything?" Ruthie asked.

"Oh, my God ... This is wonderful. I'm so happy, I don't know what to say. I was terrified, Ruthie, so afraid I was going to lose you. Should you be up? Are you tired? Do you need help getting back to bed? Why are you sitting here all alone?"

"Whoa," Ruthie said weakly. "Slow down, girl. I need to sit up. That's what John said."

She rested a moment; talking tired her out. Just breathing tired her. She took a slow breath and began again.

"I'm sitting alone drinking tea Jack made -- hot tea laced with honey, for my chest and whiskey – medicinal, of course."

Kate nodded and sat, then got up and fixed a cup of her own tea and whiskey. "Where's Jack? And Mel, where is he hiding? We should be having a party."

"They'll be back. And we will have one. A damn big party."

"Ruthie, you never swear."

"It's a new day, Kate. A brand, new day."

"I'm so happy . . . you can't begin to know. And it's Christmas! You getting well is the absolute best, most unbelievably wonderful present in the world."

"That's a lot of adjectives."

They heard boots on the stairs along with rustling and laughter. Jack and Mel barged through the door dragging a thin, scraggly evergreen and bucket of sand. They put the tree in the bucket and the bucket in the corner, then stood back to admire their handiwork.

"What do you think?" Jack said. "A few strings of popcorn ought to do it?"

"Sure. It's a great tree. The most beautiful I've ever seen," Ruthie said.

Kate couldn't hold it in any longer and burst out with an unladylike guffaw. "You're kidding, right? Most beautiful? That is the scrawniest, sickliest, ickiest best Christmas tree in the world. I love it."

She put her arms around Mel and held him close. Then Jack and Ruthie, again.

"You're passing out a lot of hugs, girl," Jack said. "Not that I'm complaining."

"I'm gonna be hugging everyone everyday for as long as I live, so get used to it."

"Everyone?" Mel asked.

"Yup, even strangers."

"Winnie Wellington?"

Kate nodded. "Even her. Everyone, I tell you. No one is safe from me. I'm now and forever more a human hug machine. My arms are like the rollers on my wash machine, squeezing everybody they touch."

"Hmmmm . . . Agatha?"

"I'll work on it. Merry Christmas," she said, putting her arms around them again.

Chapter Seventeen

Spring 1919

"You must take only one of every three plants," John told her, "to be sure there will be more Cat Tail next year."

"But look at all this. There's hundreds here," Kat told him as she plucked one from the marsh and put it in her bag. "We could never take them all. And is it cattail or Cat Tail?"

"Well, maybe we couldn't take all of them, but what if many came?" he asked, and added, "Cherokees call it Cat Tail."

They had taken the afternoon to search for spring herbs, to refill their supplies and to teach Kat. The sun was warm on their shoulders and it felt good to be away from the hospital. With spring had come a lessening of Spanish flu. Nearly all patients were in recovery and would be going home soon. Everyone prayed there would be no new cases, and John and Kat were determined to enjoy the stolen hours in the forest.

"So, is that a Cherokee custom? Taking one of three?"

He nodded and moved further down the marsh edge.

"What other customs do you know?" Kat asked, interested because Cherokee traditions were important to John, and if they were to him, well . . . they were to her.

"There are many, Kat. Do you mean about the healing arts?"

"That and others. Any you want to share."

"Well, we're to ask permission from the plant before taking it."

"Really?" Kat asked tilting her blonde head to stare up at John. "You wouldn't kid me about plant approval, would you? Make me talk to the plant just for fun?"

"No, no kidding here."

"Do I wait for an answer?"

He laughed, a deep rumbling sound, music to her ear and making a melody sing in her heart.

"No, you ask out of respect. That's all."

"May I take you home with me, Cat Tail?" Kat murmured, quiet enough so she didn't feel ridiculous and loud enough for John to hear and know she was accommodating his customs.

"How was that?" she asked.

"Fine."

John's smile was affectionate, and Kat grew warm under his gaze, his approval. She nodded, and moved on with a hint of rose on her cheeks, her rubber boots sucking with every step and making each stride forward a feat of strength. With each step, she expected to do a face plant in the swampy ground. *That would be just perfect*, she thought. A face full of muck would really impress John.

"Did you ask? I didn't hear you," Kat said.

"I praised them silently."

Thankfully, they left the marsh for higher ground where they found blackberry, sumac and yarrow.

"Steep the blackberry root as a tea for swollen joints," he explained as he pulled the root from the ground, careful to leave others undisturbed in the moist earth. "Shake the dirt off and set it in the sun to dry." He placed it in her hand, and Kat thanked it silently as John had done.

"This is Sumac. The leaves can be mixed with tobacco and smoked. Later on, it will bear fruits, or bobs. Steeped in cool water it makes a flavorful drink and can be used for sore throats and diarrhea. It can even be ground and used as a spice. If we find Staghorn Sumac, we'll be fortunate. Staghorn is a powerful antioxidant."

"Wait! Wait a minute, John. I need a minute. Let's stop and sit. Let me digest this, look at it all again and get it settled in my foggy, little brain."

They sat on a nearby log. Kat pulled the plants from her bag and spread them on the ground.

"There is nothing foggy about your brain, Kat; you are a wonder," John said.

Kat held her breath.

"We have blackberry root, yarrow, Cat Tail and sumac," she repeated, looking at their bounty spread on the ground, hiding her face from John. "Sumac - antioxidant or smoke the leaves," she repeated, memorizing their properties as John had told her.

"Yarrow stops bleeding. Grind stems, leaves and flowers into a salve and apply it to wounds," he said, picking it from her pile, cupping it in his hands and holding it out to her.

Kat tried to take it from him and he enveloped her small hand in both his, closing it around the precious yarrow. "Never be without yarrow. This plant, with its tiny white flowers, is sometimes called Soldier's Wound Wort and can mean the difference between saving and losing your patient. It's also good for colds and fevers. Brew it as a tea."

She looked up at his strong, grave face. Hers was as intent and staring into eyes so brown as to be black. She wanted to brush the shiny, black hair from his forehead, touch it, feel its silk, let it fall between her fingers. She heard a sharp intake of breath and didn't know if it was his or hers. She did know she could no longer *take* a breath and would surely die if she couldn't breathe soon.

"Stops bleeding. Colds and fevers. Yarrow," she finally whispered, then added, "Tell me more of you, John."

"What would you like to know?"

"Did you never marry?"

"I took venison to a woman's house," he said solemnly as he dropped her hand, stood and looked deep into the woods, "and she brought corn to mine."

Kat stood, too, and stared, wondering what this might have to do with her question. "And that means . . . what?"

"We were promised. The gifts are customary and meaningful."

"What's the significance of corn and venison?"

"The exchange of corn and meat is part of the wedding ceremony. They're vows to provide for one another, much like your own vows to love, honor, cherish."

Kat nodded and made a vow of her own. She would bring corn to John . . . soon, even if he didn't bring her venison first.

Spring began to wear summer weather like a flannel shawl on a chilly night, thawing bones and calming worries. The temporary hospital emptied as patients recovered to the point where contagion wasn't an issue, making it safe for families to care for them at home. When the fire hall was emptied completely, John and Kat, along with enlisted help from friends and family, organized a village-wide decontamination.

They weren't sure how Spanish flu was spread, just knew it did . . . in epidemic proportions, and they were determined to do everything possible to prevent a fourth outbreak. Tom Reeves and two of the Jackson boys drove wagons from house to house collecting anything the sick may have come into contact with.

They washed blankets and clothes in boiling tubs of lye soap and burned pillows and mattresses. Anything that couldn't be disinfected was thrown onto the huge bon fire at the back of the hall. It was hard for poor families to burn their belongings, but it was necessary. Jack and Kate were in charge of the fire, controlling it and the people with humor and rakes. Ruthie was ordered to stay home. She still coughed periodically and smoke increased the spasms.

The firehouse floors and walls were scrubbed with more lye soap in hot water and rinsed with the fire truck hose. Harley, John and Kat pushed mops, and Mel ran the hose with John Nestor's help. They limited workers to those who had already been infected and survived or had at least been in close proximity to Spanish flu patients and yet remained healthy. And they wore masks.

The decontamination became a celebration and people gathered to give a hand or watch. It was a battle cry of victory over the virus, a valiant fist raised against adversity and death. Jugs came out, but they weren't passed around. If you wanted a drink, and all were welcome to one, you needed to provide your own glass. They were scared.

Three separate waves of illness had taken a toll. It levied a fee on survivors as heavy as the payment made by those who had lost their lives. Dying wasn't the worst thing that could happen to people, and those left behind could tell the story. Over half a million people in America had died. They didn't trust it not to return, didn't trust they'd be spared again, and along with their grief, they carried guilt for surviving, for living. Merciless irony claimed they were the lucky ones; they lived to bury their loved ones.

It was late when the fire began to turn to embers. The sun had set and most spectators had long since gone to their homes. Kate leaned on her rake, her face a blackened smudge around sparkling blue eyes.

"This is good," she said to Jack who was poking at embers in the dying fire.

He nodded and sent sparks flying into the dark sky with a hefty jab at a black, smoldering mass near his feet.

"You're gonna set yourself on fire, Jack." He didn't respond, so Kate peered sideways at him. He was far, far away.

"Kate to Jack," she said. "Where are you?" She tapped him with a fist on his shoulder.

"Knock, knock, Jack."

"I'm here, Katie girl. Just thinking how lucky I am. Why me?"

Kate pondered. "How odd. Most people ask the why me question when something bad happens. You ask when it's something good. You're strange, Jack."

He raised his eyebrows but didn't have any words to add, just "Yup."

"I would say in answer to your theoretical question, why not you? You above many others should reap rewards for your goodness."

"I'm not so good, Kate."

She linked her arm through his and rested her head on his shoulder, watched the embers rhythmically spark and die, like fireflies on their way to heaven, and thought about the man by her side. He had been good to her, good to her girls and Mark. More than good. She trusted Jack as she did no other except her husband.

"When you even begin to think you aren't so good, come ask me, and I'll tell you. Jack Bay, you are a good, good man. Don't ever doubt it."

They were quiet, listening to the voices in the fire hall as the inside workers were finishing up their work. Two men strolled out of the dark, around the corner of the hall, and up to the dying fire. They stood still then came tentatively closer. One was thin to the point of skeletal and dressed in a tattered uniform. The other was stout and in civilian clothes.

"Aunt Kate?" a timid voice asked. "Is that you?"

"I'm Kate, but did you say Aunt?" she answered. She walked nearer as he removed his cap and recognized him with a gasp.

"Oh, my God," she cried and wrapped her arms around him. "Robbie! You're alive . . . I don't . . . somebody get Willie!" she screamed.

In seconds, Harley, Kat, and John were outside pumping Robbie's hand, slapping his back and checking his face to be sure it was really him and not an apparition. Mel ran to get Willie. Harley brought the jug, some cups and poured liberally.

"No toasts," Kat told him. "Let the poor man drink and tell us where he's been. No, wait for your pa. For the telling, not the drink."

"Pardon us for ignoring you," Kate said to the other man. "I'm Kate Hughes. I mean Kate Bronson. Haven't been Hughes in forever. Sorry. I'm so excited." She shook his hand.

"Clayton Flats," the stranger said.

"How do you know Robbie?" Jack asked. "Army?"

"Sort of," Clayton said and didn't elaborate.

"Well, we're really happy to see both of you. We never heard from Robbie or his unit. You can imagine what we thought."

Willie rounded the corner of the fire hall and threw himself at his son, sobbing and repeating his name. When he ran out of words, he stepped back and patted Robbie's face, held it like a fragile vase.

"You can't know how happy you've made me, Son. You just don't know how much . . . Oh, God . . . You don't know."

Willie crumpled, shoulders sagging, tongue unable to say the words, happiness and horror battling. He couldn't tell Robbie his mother had died while he was off waging war, killing Germans, watching brothers die. The world was off kilter. He didn't know if he wanted to be part of it anymore.

Mel took Robbie's arm and moved him away from the group, told him the terrible news, and saw emotion waver in his eyes. But when he looked at Mel, his eyes were dry. He nodded, said thanks.

"A lot has happened here," Mel said.

"A lot happened everywhere. Pa doesn't look good," Robbie said, watching Willie stand alone by what was left of the fire.

"He struggled when Mary died. He loved your mother so much and thought . . . well, he thought you'd been killed. We all did when the war department couldn't find you. Glad that wasn't the case."

"Nope. I'm not dead."

"What happened? Where have you been all this time?"

Robbie kicked at the ground and looked around at his family. He was silent, and Mel could see the gears in his brain clanging and banging. He guessed Robbie had a story he wasn't eager to tell, and Mel would let it lie. He didn't want to poke a sleeping bear, and Robbie's tale might be better left in hibernation.

"Well," he said patting Robbie's shoulder and moving them toward the others, "we're glad you're home."

Verna joined them when her shift at Sadie's was over, and Harley toasted to the prodigal son's return, a surprisingly short toast given his usual oration, but a toast nonetheless. His gaze shifted back and forth from Clayton to Robbie, and while he didn't come right out and say it, he was uncomfortable. About what? He didn't know.

He waddled over to Clayton and looked up at the tall boy, peered into eyes shaded by a cap and the night.

"I was on the road for a spell before settling down here. You, too?" he asked.

"A spell," Clayton said, repeating Harley's terms.

"Yup, I rode the rails, stopped whenever I wanted and just loved talking to folks in different towns. I expect freedom feels good after the Army. Where you from?"

"Here and there."

"Well, you're no more than a boy now. You move around with your family?"

"Some."

"What'd your father do for work?" asked Harley, picking at the chinks of the boy's armor.

"Lumber. Any camps around here?"

"Not anymore."

"Where're they now?"

"Why? Looking for work?"

"No, my pa,"

"Try north," Harley said. "You lose track of each other because of the war?"

Clayton shook his head. He was done answering questions, had learned what he wanted to know.

Harley gave it up, but only for the moment. There was something worrisome about the boy.

Mel hosed down the fire so no stubborn embers would burn down the town, shook Robbie's hand, and gave Willie a one-armed shoulder hug.

"You bunking in with Robbie and Willie tonight?" he asked Clayton who chewed his lip and nodded. "Then I'll say goodnight."

Harley watched the exchange and was pensive as he hitched the mare to the buggy for the ride back to the cabin. Little hairs pricked the back of his neck, and he didn't like not knowing why.

On the way home with John and Kat, he asked them what they thought about Clayton. John listened to Harley describe what he saw in the young man and his uneasiness -- without any real reason for it.

"I don't know," Harley said. "Don't trust him and don't know why. What was your impression, John?"

"Uya walked the ground tonight," John said solemnly.

"Could you explain a little, Doc?" Harley asked.

"Uya is the evil earth spirit who fights right and light."

Kat nodded. She'd been uncomfortable near Clayton, too. She didn't like him -- at all, but she knew why. She saw who he was and wondered why no one sent him away. He was malevolent, wicked.

"He's not a good man," Kat said. "Clearly."

"Did you see evil, Kat?" John asked.

"Of course. It was standing right there."

"Perhaps it wasn't right there for everyone, Kat."

"What are you talking about? That's silly."

"Kalona Ayeliski is invisible except to medicine men -- or medicine women."

"John . . . don't talk crazy."

"You wanted to know my culture. Here it is."

Chagrined, she said, "What are Kalona Ay . . . what you said?"

"In Cherokee mythology, Kalona Ayeliski spirits roam the earth to prey on people, torment them until they die, and then they eat their hearts. Only medicine men -- or women can stop them. As you obviously are."

"Didn't you see evil?" she asked.

"Yes."

"Harley, you did too," Kat said, trepidation tightening her words, a shiver tensing her shoulders. She looked into the dark night, beyond the trees, for Kalona Ayeliski and shuddered.

"I didn't see it," Harley said. "Just felt something. And we are here together where no harm can come to us. Kalona is mythology. Remember that."

"John?" she said, wanting confirmation.

"It's true, Kat. It's mythology -- almost always," he added with a grin.

"Hmmm . . ." Kat hummed. "I don't know."

Mel and Kate's conversation driving home from cleansing Hersey of the Spanish flu virus was of a different nature.

"We can never be certain. Life isn't like that, Mel. If I was any more sure, I'd be absolutely positive. Tomorrow! Please say it's safe, Mel," she begged.

"I want them home, too, Kate, but first let's do the same kind of cleaning at home that we did in town today."

Kate bounced on the seat, eagerness making it too difficult to sit still. "Okay, fine. Then the day after, right?"

Kate and Mel scrubbed, and burned, and exhausted themselves getting ready for Kate's youngest daughter and grandson to come home. They kept Becca and Jamie out of the way of possible contamination, only allowing them to tend to the fire and the farm chores. And they were ready.

Sammy and Jeannie jabbered all the way back to the farm, bounced around the rumble seat, excited to be going home. Wolf rode imperially next to Kate. He wouldn't be left behind when they went to get them.

"Kat's gonna miss us," Jeannie said. "I know she will. Harley, too."

"Well, Harley will be coming often for lessons, so don't think you're skipping school," Kate said.

"He could come and live with us at Mel's house. There's lots of room. He always lives with us, Ma." And from her perspective, he always had. She'd been five when Harley had come to live at the cabin to care for the girls when Kate was delivering laundry to the camps.

A sick, perverted lumberjack had changed their way of life, leered at Rachel at the camp, found where they lived, and forced his way into the cabin. Bug and Poochie stopped him with their teeth, caused him to bleed and beg for release. Kate threatened him with an iron skillet, and he left. Later, the same man assaulted Kate, tried to rape her as she was coming from the camp. The most painful of his horrible deeds was that he killed Bug, her beloved canine protector, her red Water Bug, to get to Kate.

Jack visited the man, and he hadn't been seen in the area again. Until then, the woods had been safe for Kate and the girls; it had felt peaceful and serene. Not so afterwards. Harley came to live and had been with them ever since. To Jeannie, having no Harley around was a lifetime ago.

Chapter Eighteen

Clayton Flats needed a partner. One who wasn't squeamish. He'd never worked alone and had made do with Rob in France, but Rob wasn't his pa. Too particular when it came to doing what needed to be done. He'd made up his mind to find Dugan Flats.

Dugan had been lumberjacking the last Clayton knew. He couldn't imagine his pa working so hard, though. Lumbering was a lot of effort, and hard labor wasn't like him at all.

Talk was trees were gone except for in Michigan's Upper Peninsula, so north is where he'd look next. Clayton said his goodbyes and hopped the train north. It crossed the Straits of Mackinac by rail car ferry, and he grabbed his pack and rolled off just before it stopped at the depot north of the Straits. He ambled to the platform looking for conversation.

"Any lumber work near here?" he asked walking up to a portly man waiting by his luggage.

"Not around here, anymore. Trees are gone. Three hundred-year-old pines, eight feet across, chopped down in the blink of an eye. Damn butchers . . . taking trees that aren't even theirs to take."

"I didn't ask for a history lesson," Clayton said, his surly voice left behind as he strode away from the man, thinking he'd get quicker help elsewhere, before the train left. He asked again and found the camps had moved further north, possibly as far as Marquette. A direction was all he needed. When the train left, he was on it.

Once there, it didn't take long to find where the camps were. His bedroll on his shoulder, he started walking. Hearing the axes, he unrolled his pack and took out the picture. Dugan wouldn't have given his real name, so asking for him would never work. The picture was his best bet, his only one.

He tried to put on a pleasant face, but it wasn't natural to Clayton. He didn't have a pleasant nature, so faking it looked exactly like what it was -- phony.

"Howdy," he said strolling up to the cook tent and speaking to a man sipping coffee.

"Howdy back," the cook said. The coffee drinker nodded.

"Been here long?" Clayton asked, trying for some casual conversation.

"Not too," coffee drinker said.

"My name's Clayton. I'm looking for a man. Lumberjack last I knew." He didn't want to claim him as his father. You never knew what Dugan had been into, and he didn't want to hang onto fugitive shirttails unless he had to.

"Eli," coffee drinker said with another nod. "You a lawman?"

Clayton couldn't help but smirk, though he tried to stifle it. "Nope, just looking for a friend." He took the crinkled, faded picture from his pocket. "This is old, taken maybe fifteen years ago. Seen him around?"

Both men shook their heads at the picture and stared, like they might recognize him if they looked long enough.

"Where's the next camp, Eli?"

"That'd be Landmark. Keller's camp," he said. "Head west on the only road there is. You'll find it."

Clayton strode off, hoping it wasn't too far and they'd share a meal. A man's gotta eat.

Matt Keller's camp turned out to be only a few miles down the road, if you could call it a road. It was a dragged path made by the loggers. It didn't matter. Clayton didn't care.

He'd find Dugan, get him out of there, and they'd make some real money.

Matt saw him walking into the camp and thought he most likely wanted work. He could use another man. Michigan's Upper Peninsula was short on people and long on trees.

He stuck out his hand, and Clayton took it.

"Looking for work?" Matt asked.

"Nope. Looking for a man." He dug out the picture, and Matt looked at it, knew immediately who it was.

He'd worked for Matt back in Hersey. Well, he tried to look like he worked. He accomplished little and was an irritant to everyone around him. He recalled Kate having some words with him once. Something about him leering at one of her daughters.

"What's his name?" Matt asked.

"Dugan Flats."

Matt stalled for time, thinking. He hadn't known him by that name, and Dugan Flats, or whatever his name was, had disappeared. Was at work one day and gone the next. Didn't clear out his bedroll or clothes; didn't even pick up his pay.

Matt had always wondered about the man, thought he had probably wandered off and gotten himself into trouble. It followed him. Or he made it. He wasn't real likeable, and you didn't want to stand downwind of him. Matt was relieved he'd gone away.

"He looks familiar, but I don't know," Matt said.

"Mind if I talk to your men?" Clayton asked. He'd do it anyway, but it might save trouble if he got permission.

Matt gave it up. He'd find out from the men. "He could be someone who worked for Landmark at the Hersey camp a number of years back."

"Where'd he go from there?" Clayton asked. "Different camp?"

Matt shook his head. "Don't know. He just up and left."

"He have any friends here who might know more?"

Another shake of the head. "The man I'm thinking of wasn't real popular. Got himself into trouble a lot, and I heard he did at all the camps. Kept getting booted out of one after another."

Clayton kicked at the ground. "That man is my pa," he grunted belligerently, "and I want to find him."

"Sorry. Just telling you what I know. If you want to ask around, see what the other men remember, feel free. Just stay clear of trees they're dropping."

"I'll do that," Clayton said.

"I wish you luck," Matt said, thinking he'd need it. No good would come from this man, much like his father. Both walked through life wrapped in a black, angry cloud.

Several men glanced at the picture and said they didn't know him. Never saw him before. Clayton was beginning to think Keller had been wrong about recognizing Dugan when one of the lumberjacks poked at the picture with a short, grimy forefinger and guffawed.

"Old Hank!" he bellowed. "What's up with Hank?"

"That's what I'm trying to find out. Do you know where he went when he left Landmark?"

"Hell, no. We were supposed to hit Sadie's Saloon after work, and he never showed. Bastard just didn't show. He sure liked the ladies."

"Explain," Clayton demanded.

"Why, he liked women, all of 'em. Young, old, fat, skinny . . ."

"Not about the females, idiot. About Dugan . . . Hank not showing up at the saloon. Did he show for work next day?"

"Nope. Never saw him again. I always thought it was strange. That Ramey woman said she'd kill him if he looked at her girl again. I heard her say it. I was picking up my clothes, and she pointed her finger right in his face and snarled at him. Gave him a real tongue lashing. He'd always do that, you know. Look at girls. Couldn't help hisself. Maybe she did. Kill him, I mean."

"What Ramey woman?"

"Pretty little Kate. Did our wash for us, and all the boys were in love with her, or . . . you know. She had pretty little daughters, too."

"She from Hersey?"

"Lives out in the woods near there. Tell the truth, old Hank talked a lot about paying her a visit. I think he might've done just that, and I think that big red dog a hers gave him a greetin'. One night, he sure was in pain. Moanin' and groanin' and washin' blood in the river. Swore he wasn't done with her. Well . . ."

"Anybody else hang with Hank?"

"Nope, just me. Nobody else liked him much. Me? I just didn't care about nothing but getting a glass of whiskey, and he'd do that with me."

Clayton started to walk off. He stopped when the lumberjack called after him.

"Ya' know, if he messed with Kate, Jack woulda' had something to say about it. He was always nearby when she was at camp. He protected her something awful."

"Jack who?"

"Don't know. Just Jack. That's the way it is at these camps. Best not to know."

Clayton nodded and left. He was heading back to Hersey. Somebody there knew Dugan. *Funny how things work out,* he thought. He'd find his pa yet. He was a bastard, but blood ran thick.

Chapter Nineteen

Dot

An empty automobile was sitting in front of the house when they got back with Jeannie and Sammy.

"What is that doing there?" Jeannie asked with hope filled eyes. "Is it yours, Mel?"

He laughed. "Don't I just wish, and I have no idea why it's here."

They bounded out of the buggy and ran inside to see Jamie, Becca, a stranger and Rachel sitting at the table drinking coffee. Rachel held a toddler on her lap.

Kate froze, her eyes round saucers, her mouth an open circle with no sound coming out. Jeannie ran headlong to her sister and wrapped her arms around both Rachel and the baby.

"I'm so happy to see you. Who is this?"

"This is Dorothy," she said, looking at Kate, waiting for her mother to get over her shock. Waiting for a sense of her reception. Would her mother turn her out?

Kate took a deep breath and went to hug her daughter. "You look wonderful, Rachel. And Dorothy is beautiful. Say hello to Sammy."

She pulled Sammy out from behind her where he'd been hiding and led him by the hand to see his mother.

"Say hello to . . . Rachel, Sammy. Jeannie's sister."

Silence filled the room, an uncomfortable, cold hush. Kate turned to the stranger and held out her hand. He looked like a fashion model from one of Nestor's catalogs, dressed in narrow, beige trousers, a dark shirt with a light beige tie. A jaunty newsboy cap lay on the table in front of him. He had blond hair, neatly combed to the side and he was clean shaven except for the thin line of a mustache. He didn't look like Hersey men.

"I'm Kate, Rachel's mother. You must be the owner of that beautiful auto out front."

"Raymond Battle," he said, stood and shook Kate's hand, then Mel's and Jeannie's. Sammy wouldn't, but Raymond tried. "Yes, it's mine. Want a ride, sport?" he asked Sammy.

Kate wondered if Raymond knew Rachel was Sammy's mother. Had her daughter told him about having a baby, about leaving him with her family?

Wolf lowered his head, moved toward the stranger, then stood to see better. He nosed the man's cheek, nosed it again and rumbled disapproval.

"Down, Wolf," Kate said. "Sorry," she added with a chuckle. Wolf sniffed Raymond's leg before lying down to watch the show.

Another long silence stretched, twined like a suffocating vine around the room, tangled with unspoken thoughts and words, pictures of the past.

"Well, I think this homecoming calls for a sip of something stronger than coffee. Anyone else?" Mel asked, and didn't wait for an answer. "Becca, will you find some lemonade, please? I'll get the cordial."

Sammy climbed on Jeannie's lap and stared at the strangers. Dorothy stared at Sammy. Sammy stared back. Mel poured and toasted to coming home and the newest child.

"Well . . . we're not exactly coming home, Mel, to stay, that is," Rachel said awkwardly. "We're on our way to Atlantic City to ride the trolleys. Not just that. Raymond has business there, so we thought we'd make a vacation of it."

"How nice. I'm sure Atlantic City is lovely," Kate said. "You'll stay the night here first, won't you? We have plenty of room and haven't seen you in a long time. Have never seen little Dorothy."

"Why don't we all go sit on the porch for a bit and let Kate and Rachel have some time by themselves, huh?" Mel asked. He grabbed the bottle of cordial, picked up his glass

and nodded to Raymond to do the same. Jamie, Becca and
Jeannie followed with Sammy trailing. Mel came back in
briefly and poured another for Kate. *She was going to need
it,* he thought.

"I've missed you, Rachel," Kate said when they'd gone.
"Really, really missed you. How have you been? Where
have you been? I have so many questions."

"I've been a lot of places. Just go where friends go
usually."

Kate nodded, unable to ask the real questions. "Your
little girl looks like you. She's beautiful. I don't see
Raymond at all."

"Ray isn't her father, Ma."

"Charlie?"

Rachel shook her head. Kate lowered hers and rubbed
hard at her knotted neck. She twisted her head sideways,
stretching the tight muscles in her shoulders and rubbed
harder. Tried not to judge, to be hurt or angry.

"Who is Dorothy's father?"

"Do we have to go into that right now?"

"Oh, Rachel," Kate whispered. "Help me understand.
What can I do to help you?"

"You can take Dorothy while we go on our vacation.
That's all. Will you do that?"

"And what then? Where do you live, Rachel? How do
you live? Are you still married to Charlie?"

"Are you just going to ask questions?"

Kate took a long, deep breath and knew if she didn't
stop she'd lose her granddaughter. Love collided with
frustration, and the ashes of conflict still glowed with
embers of a need to mother and mold.

"No, Sweetie. I'm not," Kate said gently and tenderly. "I
love you, and I would love to care for Dorothy while you're
away. I hope you have a lovely time. Will you stay long
enough to see Kat before you go?"

"Where is she?"

"She lives at the cabin with Harley."

"We'll stay the night, and Ray will drive me over to see
Kat after dinner. Is that okay?"

"It's fine. Let's go get this baby's things and get her settled. May I?" she asked, holding her arms out to Dorothy who came willingly into her grandma's arms.

With the baby on her lap, Kate rocked automatically, and the toddler snuggled. "Dorothy," she cooed, "little Dot, that's you. You're no bigger than a minute." The Dot looked up, and Will's eyes danced in her face. Kate grinned and fell in love.

"What about Sammy, Rachel?"

"What about him? Isn't he happy with you all?"

"You're his mother," Kate said gently, as tolerantly as possible. "Will you be taking him with you when you come back?"

"He doesn't even know me, Mother, but sure. Next time I come, though."

Kate nodded, knowing with harsh certainty Rachel wouldn't be back to get Sammy. It occurred to her she was not planning to come back for Dot either, but she pushed the thought away, wouldn't believe it. When Rachel put Dorothy in her mother's arms, had it been for the first and last time? Kate tried to shake the notion, but it stuck there, a monotonous melody playing over and over in her mind no matter how hard she tried to drown out the tune.

At the cabin, Kat welcomed them with cool reserve. John and Harley watched Rachel dance around her sister, flip her bobbed hair and run her fingers through its glossy black strands.

"It's nice, Rachel. Is that what you want me to say? Probably easy to take care of. I like that."

"No. I wasn't looking for compliments . . . Why are you out here in the boonies? Don't you hate it?"

"No. I love it. It's home," Kat said. "Where is yours?"

"Oh, the city."

"Just any city or a particular one?"

"Different ones. Don't you want to hold Dorothy, your niece?"

Kat shook her head and Harley stepped in.

"I would like to hold our baby girl." He held out his arms and Dot went eagerly, snuggling into the big belly like she'd been there all her life.

"I think she knows you Harley," Kat said.

"Let's go for a walk, Dot. How about you, John? Ray?" He stood and moved toward the door. The others followed.

As soon as they left, Rachel turned on Kat.

"What's he doing here? Does he live here with you?"

"Who? John or Harley?"

"John."

"Yes, John lives here most of the time. He's teaching me the practice of herbal medicine."

"You?" Rachel sputtered. "Why would you do that?"

"Because it's what I was meant to do. Why do you do what you do?"

Rachel's mouth opened, momentarily stayed a wide circle and then closed.

"You know he's Indian, don't you?" she said as a matter of information.

Kat's head tilted and her eyes widened. "Really? An Indian?"

"Well . . . I can't believe you're living in this cabin with an old man and him," she said nodding towards the door. "Do you go out? Date any suitable boys?"

"No."

"Hmmmm . . ." Rachel found nothing to say. She fidgeted, squirmed on her chair, and tried to see the little sister of her memories. She felt judged by the woman across the table from her and didn't know if it was Kat eyes or her own conscience working on her.

Kat finally spoke, relented under her sister's obvious discomfort.

"John and I ran a hospital in the fire hall for Spanish flu victims in and around Hersey. I've delivered babies, cared for dying people, set broken bones and collected my own pharmaceutical herbs. I am learning to be a doctor through John. I'm a woman of medicine, a medicine woman in Cherokee language,"

"My God, Kat. I don't know you anymore."

"No, you don't. You dropped your baby off and ran. Sammy has lived here with Jeannie, Harley and me -- and John most of the time. Jeannie has been his mother because I've been caring for sick people, and Ma has too. Sammy and Jeannie were safer here. Mel's house had sick people in it. Your Aunt Ruthie, Mrs. Bronson, Aunt Mary and Mel. Mrs. Bronson and Aunt Mary are dead. Did you know that?" She let her words sink in. Watched Rachel's face for signs of compassion.

Kat read uncertainty, confusion, and eagerness to leave, flee the harsh reality of what she'd left behind in the first place. Kat knew her sister wasn't coming back for Dorothy. She was dropping her off on her way to a permanent vacation from her children.

"Don't make any more babies, Rachel. You're a terrible mother. I told Harley several years ago you would be, and I haven't changed my mind."

Rachel's eyes filled, and tears rolled down her cheeks. She was beautiful in her distress. A raven-haired damsel. *All she needs to do*, Kat thought, *is put her hand to her heart, tilt her head back and sigh, 'Oh, woe is me.'*

"Why are you being mean to me?" Rachel asked, hurt by Kat's disdain.

"Because I know you're leaving Dot, too. You're not coming back for her. Just like Sammy. You're too much a coward to say so. At least have the courage to own up to it."

"I can't help it. I just can't be a mother. You don't know, Kat. Babies are . . . they make you old. I'm not. I'm young, and I want things, and I can't get them with babies. Men don't want women with children."

"Then stop making babies. Now go home and tell Ma."

"I can't tell her, just come out and say it. She'll know anyway when I don't come back. And I can't look at her face and say it. She'll hate me."

"You know better than that, Rachel. Ma loves you. I don't know why."

"Besides, it's mostly her fault anyway."

Kat rocked back, stunned. Even for Rachel, blaming her mother for her own sins was blatantly, masterfully stretching reality. She stared at her sister and wondered where this woman had come from. Did they have the same parents? The same upbringing?

Rachel bit her lip, looked at her fingers knotting together, plucking the white lace at her cuffs.

"Exactly how is it Ma's fault you bore a child, ran off, bore another, and are getting ready to leave that one, too?"

"We were always poor, and she was so wrapped up in Mel," Rachel stammered. "She didn't have time for us. She was always working."

"What a bad woman."

"You don't understand," Rachel moaned.

"No. I don't, but it's alright. Like I said, you're a terrible mother, so leave them with us. Just don't make more."

"You wait, Kat. You're going to have babies, then you'll know -- probably with that John person."

"I hope so," Kat said, further shocking her sister.

"He's old, Kat. And he's Indian."

"Yes. He's Cherokee, and he's a beautiful person."

"You are strange, Kat."

"Thank you."

Rachel and Raymond left in the morning saying they'd be back in a week, and Kate knew they wouldn't. They fixed a nursery upstairs next to Kate and Mel's room, and Sammy and his sister settled in. Kat rode over to see her mother and told her some of the conversation she'd had with Rachel.

"I know, Kat, and thank you for sharing with me. I think I knew first thing that Rachel was dropping Dot off for good. I don't understand her. Don't know what I did to her that made her this way."

"You didn't do anything, Ma. Rachel just wants everything, and she doesn't want to wait for it or work for it."

Kate nodded sadly and tucked the blanket around Dot who they were putting down for a nap. Damp auburn curls clung to pale cheeks, and her thumb found its way to a cherub mouth. Her great grandfather's blue eyes were hidden behind closed lids, and Dot drifted easily and comfortably into dreamland. She was home.

One long week went by, and Kate kept hoping. She stared down the driveway listening and watching for the automobile, waiting to see Rachel's beautiful smile, hands held out for her child. She knew it wouldn't happen. Rachel wasn't coming back, but she couldn't stop watching, hoping.

Two weeks later she had a family dinner. Harley delivered invitations, and on Saturday the house was filled. Jack and Ruthie brought Ellen and the ancient Eldon Woodward.

Ellen had been living at Eldon's, taking care of him since Rachel left. She'd grown fond of the old man and pampered him in ways he'd always wanted. It worked for them both. He loved to be mothered and she loved mothering. He needed her, and she wanted to be needed. It was a matched set.

In her more mischievous moods, Kate wanted to ask if there was more than caretaking in the relationship, but she didn't. One didn't snoop in Ellen's privacy. Other people's, but not Ellen's.

Harley brought Verna, and John came with Kat. Willie and Rob came late, but were there. Seventeen people gathered, sixteen to pay homage to the newest member. When all were ready with favored drinks, Harley lifted his.

"Here's to Dot, to Dorothy . . ."

"Oh, my God," Kate gasped. "I don't know her last name!"

Tears came, and she got mad and stomped her foot. "Damn! Damn!"

"It doesn't matter, Kate," Harley said with a grin at Kate's outburst. "She's our beautiful Dot. Let's welcome her properly."

He began again. "Here's to Dorothy, our little Dot. She is the newest of many in the beautiful line of Hughes and Ramey girls. She will be treasured in our hearts and held safely in our arms."

Harley's eyes roamed the faces turned toward him and raised his glass to each. "Amen," he heard from many.

"I missed out on birthing this one, but I intend to be here for any others."

"Are you going to be done soon?" Verna asked. "Or should I take a seat?"

"Hold on to your pretty britches, sweetheart. I'm nearly there. Here's to you, little Dot. We love you and always will."

Harley sipped from his glass, set it down and picked up Dot. He raised her high into the air, and she giggled -- a low pitched gurgling sound that delighted them all. Then she grabbed his beard and pulled, opened her mouth in a wet kiss. Harley was in love.

Willie hung onto Rob, sat next to him, followed him when he went into the kitchen, and followed him back. He watched him, tracked his voice, and would have held onto his shirt tail if he could. It was worrisome, unhealthy, and Kate spoke to Ruthie about it when she showed her the new nursery.

"Has this been going on since Rob got home? With Willie, I mean. Do you see them often?"

"Not a lot, but some, and yes, Willie seems desperate to keep Rob near. I'm afraid for our brother, Kate. He hasn't begun to heal from Mary's death."

"Is he keeping up at the mill?"

"From what I hear, no. Tom Reeves has picked up some of Willie's slack, but Tom's old, nearly Ma's age."

Kate smoothed the already neat quilt on Dot's crib and moved a small crocheted teddy bear to the corner.

"Maybe Rob will step in soon. He's been home long enough and he needs to work. Why not at the mill? Something's strange, though, Ruthie. I can't put my finger on it, but Rob isn't the same person as when he left."

"War does things, Kate. And who knows what Rob saw?"

"Life does things, and just plain living, trying to live. Nothing stays the same for long, and it gets harder and harder to keep up."

Kate was thinking about Sammy and Dot, raising two more children when she felt like a failure with her first child. She didn't understand her second daughter, but admired her. Didn't fear for Kat . . . much, although she didn't care for John being constantly nearby. Becca was a rock, and Jeannie was, well . . . Jeannie. She had her critters and was happy.

But being both mother and father, providing for her daughters, had been hard. More than hard. Now . . . here were Sammy and Dot, and Kate was afraid.

"I used to think if I worked hard enough everything would come out alright. I don't think that anymore. I can't control life because it has the reins on me, jerking me right and left like an old mule without a gee or a haw." Kate chuckled. "Funny, aren't I? And I'm old! That's not funny!"

Ruthie grinned and put her arms around her sister. "You've been everyone's rock, Kate, nonstop. You didn't even have a proper honeymoon before we all descended on you when we were sick. Give yourself a break. Remember, you're bat lady. You know where to fly and how to fly there, even if you are old."

"Sure I do, brat. Let's go downstairs and get a little tipsy."

"I always knew you were the bad sister. You've had the family fooled for years."

Chapter Twenty

Clayton

He took his time getting from the camp to Mackinac, hitching rides when he could, and walking when none were available. He lifted money from small family stores when he needed to and slept in barns for a couple of hours each night. It wouldn't pay to be seen in daylight after holding a gun to a couple of heads when they didn't want to open the money drawer.

He didn't care how long it took to get back to Hersey. He wanted to think about his next moves. His pa had disappeared, it seemed, was probably dead unless someone in Hersey knew differently.

He had to be. He was there one day and not the next. Clayton didn't waste too much time wondering about the circumstances. Knowing Dugan, nothing would surprise him. His pa was always getting himself into scrapes. Trouble came looking for him if he couldn't find any on his own. He bet the trouble had been this Kate woman he'd been told about, and Dugan had gone looking for it. Once his pa set his mind on having a woman, nobody stopped him. Father and son were the same in this regard; perverse, indifferent, and cruel. The difference was Clayton had a better sense of how to get himself out of trouble.

He had a plan; stop in to see Rob first, make sure of a bed, and then call on pretty little Kate, the washer woman, if she was still around. Clayton hopped the train south from Mackinac City. He had a feeling Hersey could be an easy gold mine.

Rob was glad to see him, anything to break up the boredom and his father's stifling grasp. He pulled out the whiskey bottle and set it on the table, grabbed two glasses and filled them.

"Tell me everything," he said to Clayton. "Where you been? Did you find him?"

Clayton shook his head and fingered his beard. You could hear the rasp of dirty fingers grating against stubble.

"I been around Michigan. Upper Peninsula is pretty but damn poor. Had to find a little money the hard way."

"Don't be talking about that around here," Rob whispered and looked around to see if his pa was near.

"You know any Kate's around town?"

"Just my Aunt Kate."

"That's right. I remember her. So," he drawled, "she was a washer woman?"

Rob nodded. "Why?"

"I just wondered. Isn't her name Bronson?"

"Now it is. She used to be a Ramey like her girls. And before that, she was Kate Hughes like me and my pa. Why are you so interested in my Aunt Kate?"

Clayton poured another full glass and drank half before answering. His eyes narrowed as he wondered how much to tell his buddy. Rob had been in on a few jobs, so he had a background that gave Clayton a hold on him, but he wasn't sure how strong that hold was now that he was back in the sweet arms of his family.

"No reason. Somebody mentioned her and her girls, so I just wondered. Let's ditch this place and head on down to Sadie's."

"I don't know. Pa's not doing too well, so maybe I should stay here with him."

"You gotta be a nurse maid now?" Clayton mocked.

"No. Course not. I'll just go tell him we're going."

Clayton's eyes rolled in scorn behind Rob's back. He'd been able to control the boy since the day they'd met, and he'd used Rob's weaknesses for gain.

Rob didn't have the backbone for military service in war time. He was terrified, flinched with every sound, cowered when a blast came close, curled up in the trench when men were piling out to chase after the enemy. Tears rolled down his face, and he couldn't help it. The rest of his unit knew and ignored him, scorned him. Stepped over and on him when they pitched themselves headfirst out of the trench. Rob didn't know what to do and who to turn to. He hated them, and he hated himself. Feeling alone was the worst. Clayton pulled Rob out of the trench after one horrific battle. Said, "Come on. Let's get out of here. I've had enough."

Rob was catatonic and went where he was told. He was reported missing in action. In reality, he was scouring the country side of France, looting and worse, going where and when Clayton told him to.

Back in Hersey, Clayton bided his time, slept late and drank. Rob was happy Clayton had returned, and Willie would have welcomed anyone who brought his son back. Sadie's embraced both Clayton and Rob as soldiers of war, and her girls were happy to entertain them providing their coins kept sliding between their breasts. When the back door of Nestor's was jimmied one night and cash came up missing, no one suspected two of Hersey's heroes.

Clayton waited for the right time and knew it when he saw Mel Bronson in town without Kate. He borrowed Willie's mare and rode to the farm.

Kate was in the kitchen when she saw him in the doorway, and her heart stopped. She saw another man's face and was unrealistically terrified. She tried to smile and knew it was a lame attempt.

"Can I come in?" he asked.

Kate looked around her like an excuse might be hanging in the air. There wasn't one. Wolf got up to stand next to her.

"Sure. Clayton, isn't it?" She peered over his shoulder hoping to see Rob. "Are you alone? Isn't Rob with you?"

"No. I'm alone. I wanted to talk with you."

"I'm just about to feed the baby, so . . ." Kate didn't know why this man disturbed her, but he did. She fumbled with the nipple of the bottle and dropped it. He bent to pick it up, and they bumped shoulders. She flinched like she'd been burned. Wolf positioned himself in front of Kate.

Clayton hid his smile. She was afraid of him. It was amusing when women feared him. The dog, too.

"Here you are," he said, handing her the nipple and deliberately brushing her arm. "Do you want to get the baby now?"

Kate shook her head. *Not on your life*, she thought, but said, "No, I was just getting ready. Have a seat Mr. . . ."

"Flats. Clayton Flats."

"What is it you wanted to see me about?"

Clayton pulled the picture from his shirt pocket and laid it in front of her, watching her face as he spoke. "Have you seen this man?"

Kate tried not to flinch, tried to keep her face still, but she wanted to throw up. She felt him tearing at her dress, saw him kill her dog, Bug, felt his mouth on her bare breasts. She seethed with hatred, loathing, terror and grief. She gripped her hands to keep them from trembling, felt her eyes grow dry as she stared without blinking.

"No," she finally whispered. "Why? Should I know him?"

Clayton studied her. She was lying and afraid. She knew him. Her lie was obvious. It was in her eyes, her hands.

"He worked at the lumber camp near here, one you did washing for. Thought you might have seen him around there."

"I didn't do wash for all the men. I really should go feed Dot, if you don't mind." Kate got up and went to the door, but Clayton didn't follow.

"I would like it if you looked again, just to be sure," he crooned, his hand under his chin, the forefinger running back and forth over his wide, thick lips.

When Kate looked at him, she understood he knew. Maybe he didn't know everything, but he knew enough. It was in the lazy slouch he'd perfected, the unflinching stare, the flare of his nostrils as if he'd sniffed out her secret, smelled her fear. She walked back to the table, looked down briefly and shook her head.

"I don't know him, Mr. Flats. I'm sorry. Now, if you would please leave, I'd like to tend to my baby."

"That's your daughter's baby, isn't it? Rachel's?" Wolf stood on his hind legs and growled close to Clayton's ear.

Kate stepped back. "That's none of your business, sir." She went to the door and opened it. "Please leave now."

"I will as soon as your dog gets down."

"Down, Wolf."

Clayton strolled to the door and turned back. "Thank you for your hospitality. Nice dog."

Kate bit her tongue. "Certainly, and don't call him dog. He doesn't like it."

She watched him ride down the drive and collapsed, her head in her hands, tears stinging her eyes. Who was Clayton? Who was the man in the picture besides her rapist? What now? Becca and Jeannie bounced in the door yelling, "Who was here? We were in the barn and just saw him leaving."

"No one. I mean, Rob's friend, Clayton, just stopped by on his way . . . somewhere."

Becca looked sideways at her mother. "Are you alright, Ma?"

"Of course. Jeannie, will you go get Dot? It's time for her bottle."

Jeannie skipped out, and Becca pulled out a chair. "You're fibbing, Ma. Why? What's wrong?"

"Nothing, Becca. Really. I just don't like him. He upsets me, and I don't really know why," she lied. When Jeannie came back in with Dot, Kate elaborated.

"Clayton Flats, that's his name, is someone I'd like you girls to avoid."

They looked intently at their mother. This was unusual.

"Why?" they asked together.

"Because . . . God," she said, frustrated she didn't know how to explain without saying what she could never tell.

"Because I looked under his skin, and I didn't like what I saw. Remember what we talked about?"

Four eyes widened in understanding.

"Really bad under there?" Becca asked.

"I think so. Please stay away from him. Okay?"

"I don't like him," Jeannie added.

Kate laughed and handed Jeannie the bottle. Dot was oblivious and happy. "Me either."

Kate walked, needed space to think, and found herself on the way to the cabin. It and the surrounding woods had always been her place of solace. White pines, oaks and leafy poplars with their dusky shadows healed her, freed her mind. Wolf rubbed her leg with each stride, and she chastised him. "You're gonna trip me, Wolf. Why are you so glued to my leg?"

Wolf looked up at her, swung his head to each side of the road and back again. He was vigilant and ignored her rebuke.

She laughed when she tripped over him and went back to reflecting. She wished she could tell how much Clayton knew. But how could he know anything? No one but Jack and Mel did. Maybe Harley, just because he knew everything. God, she couldn't say anything to Jack. He'd turn himself in or confront him or ... but shouldn't she warn him? "I just don't know," she groaned.

Mel, too. He'd fight and lose against Clayton, a younger, stronger man, especially in his weakened condition. Kate argued with herself until the cabin stood in front of her. Harley met her at the door, a towel in one hand and an apron over his protruding belly. His smile faded when he saw Kate's face.

"Welcome, Kate" he said, motioning her inside. "Kat and John are in the woods collecting herbs, and you're just in time to stir the jam while I get the jars out of the water."

Wolf went to his rug in front of the hearth like he'd never been gone from it, and Kate stirred while Harley expertly pulled glass containers out of a pot of boiling water and turned them upside down on a white cloth. They worked without words until bright red jam filled the jars. Kate ladled wax over the tops, and Harley wiped down the sides and edges.

"Beautiful, isn't it?" he asked stepping back to admire his work. "A bit of Christmas in October." Harley poured water into the pot, put the sticky utensils in to soak, and waited.

"Something up, Kate? You look a bit lost. Want to talk?"

Kate shook her head and looked around the room. She missed it. This was home though Mel's house was grand and lovely. It wasn't this. She looked at Wolf in front of the hearth and wondered if he felt it too.

"I'm thinking I'd like a spot of shine to celebrate a job well done. You?"

"Sure, Harley. Can we sit outside for a bit?"

Harley grabbed two glasses and the jug, remembering the hundreds of times they'd done this same thing together. Well, it seemed like hundreds. Morning and night, under the sun, and when the moon flowed over the tree tops to shine on raccoons scampering near the clearing. How many times did they count owl hoots and bat shadows as they skittered from tree to tree?

"Girls okay?" he asked.

"They're great."

"Sammy? I miss him."

"You need to come more often. And we need to turn one of the upstairs bedrooms into a schoolroom."

"Want me to move in? Help take care of your babies?" he asked. "Kat doesn't need me to teach her any more. She's beyond me, and John has taken over her training."

"She needs you here, Harley. You can't, well . . . leave. I'd love it, but . . ." Kate fumbled around the words she couldn't say, her tongue tangling with her brain.

"I mean . . . of course you can live where you want. You've always been able to do that, but I'm grateful you choose to live with us."

Harley nodded and murmured noncommittal words of solace.

She paused. Too much thought. What if Clayton came here like the man in the picture had done and John was out seeing a patient? Who knows what he would do? Kat couldn't be alone here. She sipped her drink and let her head lay against the back of the chair. Moments later she bolted upright. What about John and Kat living together without Harley here? That would never do.

"Harley, once again, I'm asking for your help. John and Kat can't live alone together."

Propriety would have to be her reason, not Clayton, and it was a real one. *It wasn't appropriate,* she thought. God, she sounded like her mother. I've turned into Ellen! And I'd have lived with Mark, and everyone be damned, even if we hadn't been married. I told him that.

"You're shaking your head, Kate," he said, handing her the glass of moonshine she'd put on the ground. "What's going on in there?"

"I've turned into my mother," she said with a smile. "Never thought I'd say that."

"Nothing wrong in becoming your mother, Kate. Ellen is quite a woman and you know it. Anything else?"

Kate took a deep breath and made a decision. Harley needed to know about Clayton. He couldn't be there for Kat if he was kept in the dark.

On an expulsion of held air, she blurted it out in a single breath. "Clayton Flats visited me at the farm. He's an evil man. I don't like him or trust him. I'm sure he waited until he knew Mel was gone. He showed me a picture of the man who came here years ago, the man who leered at Rachel, scared us and he . . . was the reason you came to live us."

Harley chewed the inside of his lip. "Are you sure it was him?"

"Positive."

"Is the man in the picture his father? He said he was looking for his pa the night we met him."

"I'd forgotten. Oh my God, it probably is."

"Well, Kate, there's nothing that says the son is like the father," Harley said, although deep down he knew Clayton was a vile man. It was in the foul atmosphere surrounding him.

She hadn't felt a speck of ease since Clayton visited her at the farm, brought visions with him she thought long vanquished and conquered. Harley patted her hand, and she felt better. It always worked. It was comical. He soothed, and she'd be comforted. Kate sucked in his reassurance like air.

Harley lifted his glass. "Here's to us, Kate." He drank and sat back in his chair, turned his face to the sky. "Warmth feels nice. Won't be with us for long. Early winter coming."

Kate did the same, and they rocked silently in the chairs her father had made. She felt his arms once again.

"I think that's the shortest toast you've ever made, Harley." Kate saw a sweet smile spread like warm sunshine over his face.

It was a week before Kate made the decision to talk with Jack. She finally decided he couldn't protect himself without all the information she had. She and Wolf went to his office near the end of his work day.

Jamie was in the outer office reading a law book. He'd taken to learning law like a drowning man to a raft. A book was always in his hands or nearby.

"Can I come in?" Kate asked when Jamie looked up. A wide smile lit his face, Mark's smile.

"You can come in any time, day or night, Kate." He got up from his chair to hug her and ask about the girls. He was especially close to Becca who had been his mentor and sidekick all the months they'd run the farm during the flu outbreaks. "She still bossing the bossies around and taking charge?" he teased.

"Yes, but Mel likes to think it's still his farm, so don't tell him. Is Jack busy?"

"Probably taking a nap at his desk. Let me check."

He knocked and Jack yelled, "Door's open."

His eyes lit when they landed on Kate, and she got her second bear hug in five minutes.

"So glad to see you, but I'm guessing this isn't just because you love me and miss me."

"Yes, it is. Mostly. But I do want to talk with you."

He asked Jamie to close the door and motioned Kate to a brown leather couch. "Sit. What's on your mind?"

She had practiced what she would say to Jack so it would be perfect, but when she looked into her brain, it was empty. Nothing was there, no words, nothing, not even any pictures. She twisted her fingers and pulled her bottom lip between her teeth.

Jack waited. He'd seen Kate struggle before and knew she'd get there eventually. "Want a coffee, tea?"

"Sure, that'd be nice."

"Which?"

"Which what?"

"Drink."

"Yes. That'd be nice."

He laughed. He loved this girl. Woman. *But she still looks like a girl,* he thought. Still trim. Still beautiful. Skin unlined and fresh. He smiled at her confusion. It was Kate, every syllable.

As she struggled with words, he began to worry and poured her a brandy. Handing it to her, he said again, "What's on your mind, Kate?"

"Remember the man who . . . the one you . . . who isn't here anymore? Well, I think Clayton Flats is his son, and he's asking questions, and I thought you should know, but I don't, really don't want you to do anything about it. Just be aware -- who he is and all."

Jack sat back, stretched his long legs out in front of him and drummed his fingers on the arm of the sofa. It was a staccato rhythm, repeating its down stroke with emphasis, a primitive sound that heard in the jungle would have invited and incited warfare. Kate wondered if war was in Jack's mind.

"Jack?" she said, breaking into the finger drumming.

He turned to her on a long sigh. "Well, I always figured the day would come."

"Please don't do anything. He'll leave soon, I'm sure. Hersey's too small for him."

"What do you think I'll do, Kate? Hurt him? Tell him? You know me better than that."

"No!" she blurted. "No, it's you I'm worried about! I don't want *you* to get hurt. Ever. That's why I told you, so you wouldn't be hurt by him. He's not a nice man. He isn't," she insisted, her eyes glistening with fear and mirroring memory.

Jack put an arm on the back of the sofa and pulled her close. She rested her head on his shoulder, and they sat unmoving for a long while. They shared much, cared even more. "Thank you, Kate. I will be aware and safe."

"You won't . . . tell . . . anything, will you?"

"There is nothing to tell. A bad man was here once and is now gone. That's all."

Chapter Twenty-one

Kate was nervous, jumped at every sound, and Mel noticed. She tried to calm herself, but it was hard. She believed Clayton wasn't finished and couldn't stop thinking about what he might do.

She was at peace only when she was rocking Dot and watching Sammy sleep. They were near and safe. She worried constantly but didn't know what she worried about. She didn't think he would hurt her family. How could he?

"Are you okay, Katie girl?" Mel asked.

"Sure. Just thinking about making a real schoolroom up here. Won't that be nice?"

"Is a new classroom what put the frown on your face?" He came up behind her and rubbed her shoulders. She leaned her head back and smiled up at him. "That's better. You're beautiful, Kate."

"Do you need spectacles, Mel?"

"Yes, but they wouldn't help. I'm blind with love."

"I love you, too, Mel. I always have."

"I know," he murmured, bending to put his lips against her hair.

"Do you?" she asked, never sure.

"Yes. I always knew you always loved me. I mean I know you always loved me. Are you trying to make me do a tongue twister?" he asked with a grin.

"Will you?"

"There are no thistles in my fields as I am a successful thistle sifter. There. Good enough?"

"Better than that. You're great."

"I know."

Jack rode out to the farm a few days after Kate came to his office and found a moment to chat with her alone.

"Has he been back?" he asked.

She shook her head. "Any news from town?"

"No. Pretty quiet."

After Jack's visit, Kate began to settle down, to think she'd made more of Clayton's visit than it was worth.

They turned a bedroom into a classroom, with real desks and a chalkboard on one wall. A map of the world covered another, and a third had a peg board on which Harley could hang his students' work. Jeannie was delighted.

"It looks like Big Rapids, like the school there. Can I put my lunch in my desk?"

"Well, lunch is usually down in the kitchen, but I suppose we can fix you up with a bag lunch," Kate told her.

Becca and Jeannie did their chores and went to school twice a week with Harley, three days each week with Kate. Sammy went for a couple of hours in the mornings only. He was too young for school, but he enjoyed it and was learning to read already.

The sumac had turned a brilliant fire red, then brown, and was ready to be harvested. Kat and John walked deep into the woods to the swamp and cut the tops of the sumac stalks. They moved to higher ground, laid the stalks on a sheet, and went to gather blackberry, Pull Out a Sticker, Yellow Dock and Wild Rose roots. The long tap roots ground into powders made healing salves and disinfectants, soothing teas, and diuretics.

They worked with little conversation, both naturally content with the sounds of the forest. John helped Kat occasionally, pointed out a stalk or dried blossom with medicinal properties, and described its preparation and use. Once in a while, he held her hand as she learned to strip bark and usable leaves from their mother stalk.

Kat couldn't breathe when she felt his hand on hers and a drumming sounded in her ears. She tried to concentrate on the procedure she was learning to do, but her eyes strayed to his face, his wide cheek bones, strong jaw, and full lips. She felt her hand shake and tore her attention back to the stalk they were carefully stripping.

John made an effort to keep his distance. Kat was his student, a medicine woman, and he would not defile her with his primal needs. She was above others. She was . . . he couldn't put it into words except to say she was Selu, goddess, medicine woman, to be treasured and revered.

Back at the cabin, they took their goods from individual muslin bags and began the drying process. They carefully wiped off any moisture and laid the stalks, roots, and blossom heads in drying frames to sit in the sun curing for several weeks. Kat stood back and surveyed their work with satisfaction and glanced at John.

"You're a natural. You did well, Selu."

"Are you calling me names?"

"Yes, I am."

"All right. Just wondered."

They didn't know a pair of eyes watched from the cover of trees. Were unaware those eyes had watched before. He waited until they went inside before sprinting back through the woods the way he had come. He knew he hadn't been spotted and didn't want to alert them to his presence just yet. He knew what he was waiting for, and the time would come and be exactly right.

Early one morning, John went to town to tend to a man who had fallen from his roof. Kat was making salves, and the process couldn't be stopped, so she stayed. It didn't sound like something he needed help with, and John wanted to go on to Big Rapids to see a few patients there.

She ground the stalks and leaves to a fine powder, mixed them with binder to become salves, spooned the mixtures into stone jars, and sealed them with melted wax just like Harley and her mother did with jams and jellies. Kat smiled. She preferred putting up medicines rather than food. Was she odd? Probably, but she didn't care. All was as it should be.

"I'm going out to check the drying frames, Harley. Do you need anything from the storage cellar?"

Harley had become house chef and was growing adept at his trade, trying out new dishes, using some of the roots, herbs and spices John and Kat brought from the woods.

"Carrots, if you wouldn't mind bringing me four or five."

Kat nodded, grabbed her jacket, and was out the door. When she came out of the shelter with a fistful of carrots, a hand went over her mouth, and she was dragged into the horse shed. She kicked and twisted, but Clayton was strong and large. She was no match.

Inside, Clayton whispered in her ear. "Scream and I'll squeeze til you can't. Understand?"

Kat nodded, or tried to nod, and Clayton took it as affirmation and slowly released her mouth but kept his other arm tightly around her neck.

The mare shuffled, bumped against the wall and Clayton grumbled. "Calm that mare."

"What the hell are you doing?" she growled as soon as she drew breath.

Clayton smiled. He liked spunk. Almost as much as he enjoyed fear. "Nothing bad, little girl. Just want you to answer some questions."

"Couldn't you have come to the door like a normal person?"

"Nope, and you're not going to tell anyone I was here, either."

"You're crazy. Of course, I'm going to tell. You're here, aren't you?"

He squeezed tighter, and Kat couldn't breathe again. "No one," Clayton repeated. "Do you understand? You have sisters. Pretty little things." He let her breathe a little.

"What do you want? Just ask your questions and get out of here."

He pulled out the picture and stuck it in front of her face. "Recognize this man?"

"Of course. You didn't have to half kill me to ask that. I'd never forget his ugly face."

"How?" Clayton snarled.

"That miserable excuse for a man tried to push his way into the cabin once. Bug and Poochie thought to have him for dinner, and he left trailing blood. Never saw him again."

"You sure he left and you didn't bury him in the woods somewhere?"

"Killing him might have been best for the world, but no, we didn't. Against better judgment, we let him live. What's he to you?"

"That miserable excuse is my pa, and you're kinda mouthy for a girl whose neck is squeezed in the crook of my arm."

"Well, if I'm not back inside in a few minutes, and if Harley sees you with your arm around my neck, you'll probably die instead of your wretched father. How does that settle?"

Clayton slowly released her. "I'm going, but you're gonna wait here a few minutes before going in. I meant what I said about telling . . . and about your sisters. I know where they are."

He loped off. Kat leaned against the wall trying to still the shaking. She'd managed bravado when she needed it, but now her knees went watery and wanted to buckle. She held onto the door frame for a moment longer while her knees stopped knocking; her heart slowed down, but her mind screamed obscenities.

She needed to get to the farm, tell them who Clayton was, her Ma and Mel especially. Clayton was dangerous. He was evil.

She went inside and gave Harley his carrots, still in her closed fist, with a strangled laugh. He looked at the twisted carrots, her white face and was instantly afraid. Kat wasn't easily shaken, and her look said she was now.

"Clayton was here. He's crazy! Evil! Showed me a picture of the man Bug and Poochie bit years ago. The one who tried to force his way in here. It's his . . ."

The door crashed open and Clayton barged in swinging a log at Harley. It connected with a thud, and Harley dropped to the floor. He struggled to sit, and Clayton's boot connected with his head. He fell back, stilled.

Kat screamed, flew at Clayton's back, leaped on like he was a mule. He shook her off, and she landed on the floor next to Harley.

"I told you not to tell, didn't I?" he screamed.

He reached down, grabbed Kat's arm and yanked her up.

"Now, I got myself some pretty company and a sweet little hidey-hole all set for us. Just a little earlier than planned. Didn't know which sister I wanted, but you'll do just fine."

He tugged her out the door, and she resisted.

"I'll drag you if I have to," Clayton said with cool calm. "Don't make it harder on yourself, or me. I get irritated easy."

"You vile piece of donkey shit! I will see you in chains," she said, twisting and jerking to get away. "I need to help Harley. He's hurt."

Clayton had her arm in a firm grip and pulled her away from the cabin and into the woods. "Your concern is touching," he sneered. "You can spend your love on me, little Kat. You'll like it better. I ain't no old man."

Kat swung at him with her free hand. Clayton ducked, then pulled her against him. Hard against his chest. He was a foot taller and twice as wide. Brute force wasn't going to work for her. She saw that.

"Sweetie, this can go easy or hard. Which do you want? And there's a gun in my pocket. Want to see it?" he said in an intimate whisper.

Cold crept from her toes upward to sit like a block of ice in her stomach. She was afraid, and she didn't like fear. It made her mad.

"I can walk," she growled, pulling against his grip on her arm. "I won't run, so let go."

"No. You won't run. Remember what I said about your sisters. I'm sure they're alone right now, taking care of baby Dot and Sammy. That littlest one, Jeannie I think her name is, would be a sweet companion. Easy to please."

The block of ice turned to water and ran through her veins, up to her brain and froze there. He knew so much, too much. And he was obviously unstable, mentally deranged.

It was hard to combat a sick mind. She knew normal ways wouldn't work. She couldn't talk sense to him, plead for decency or kindness. He had no morality or goodness to work on, and common sense means a shared wisdom, a view of the world both of them understand. She didn't comprehend his and knew with certainty he couldn't begin to fathom hers.

"Where are we going?" Kat asked.

"A little place I found where we'll be cozy and warm."

"Ma and John know every inch of these woods. They'll find us."

"Glad to know that," he smirked. "Thanks for helping. I think you're kinda sweet on me. Just like your mama and my pa. Makes us related sorta."

Kat was breathing hard trying to keep up with Clayton's long stride and told him to slow down. He pulled her up against his side and half carried her with his arm around her middle. He knew where he was going and covered ground fast. He toted her like a sack of potatoes down the river for a long stretch before crossing to the other side. She was soaked and freezing when he put her down, but he grabbed her again to make sure she kept up with him. She wasn't sure how much time had gone by when he dropped her arm and she fell to the ground.

Clayton was breathing hard by this time. The terrain hadn't been easy, and both were scraped and scratched by branches and briars, their clothes wet, tattered and torn. Kat's hair had come loose, was tangled, and full of twigs. She worked to cover her breasts where buttons had been lost and her shirt gaped, not looking at Clayton, not wanting to see if he was looking at her.

He was. He stared, leaned against the trunk of a huge oak and reveled in the power he held. He ran his hand down over the bulge in the front of his pants and took a deep breath.

She was alarmed as he moved his hand once more, and the bulge grew. Kat tried to ignore him, contain her fear, but he knew she'd noticed, and he gloated. He could bide his time. He could do whatever the hell he wanted. *Thanks a lot papa,* he thought, and his thick lips spread in a cruel grin. Saliva squeezed out at the corners.

Harley didn't show up for school. Kate waited, thinking he was late and would stroll in soon, but when an hour had gone by, she called Jeannie in to stay with Dot and Sammy and told Mel she was riding out to the cabin. She called to Wolf and was gone.

When she got to the clearing, her heart stopped. The door hung open and no one greeted her. She leaped from her horse and ran screaming Kat's name, but no one answered. Just inside the doorway, she froze. Harley lay motionless on the floor, bleeding. Kate kneeled and put her ear to his chest, listening for a heartbeat, a breath of air. She picked up his hand and put her fingers against his wrist. A rhythm answered back, faint, but there.

Harley stirred as Kate was stopping the bleeding on the back of his head. She pressed a cloth to the wound and pushed him down when he tried to rise. A low growl came from Wolf who circled the room once and went outside the cabin.

"Just lay there, Harley. You're hurt. Don't move."

He groaned and lay back.

"Hold this towel to your head, Harley, while I get something to prop you up with." She got a couple of pillows and pulled him slightly upright. She held the towel to his head again and waited for him to rouse enough to answer some questions.

"Did you fall?" she asked.

"Hell no, I didn't fall. Why would I fall?"

"Well, I don't know. Then what happened?"

Harley closed his eyes. He didn't want to tell her. Twice now, he had let Kate down. Once when he'd let Jeannie get hit by a car, and now ... Kat. Tears seeped out of the corners of his closed lids, and Kate knew it wasn't pain from his wound.

Fear clutched her. "What happened, Harley?"

"I'm not sure," he whispered. "Kat and I were . . ."

"Where's Kat?" she cried out, interrupting.

"I . . . I don't know. Kat went to the cellar for carrots and came back talking about Clayton being here, showing her a picture, and next thing, the door crashed open and my head exploded."

"Clayton!" An instant vision came to mind, his father killing Bug, and she called to Wolf, needing him nearby and safe.

"I tried to get up, Kate. I tried to help Kat, but everything went black."

"It wasn't your fault, Harley." She paused, thinking. Got up, stomped around the room, back and forth from the open door to Harley. She looked outside, like he might still be lurking close by, and around the room for answers that should be there but weren't.

"That son of a bitch," she said. "I knew he was vile. I'll kill him if he hurts her. I swear I will kill him."

"I know, Kate. I would happily kill him."

"Did you hear anything before he walked in the door? Horse hooves? A buggy?"

Harley shook his head weakly. "Nothing."

"How did he get here? And leave dragging Kat? I'm sure she didn't go willingly."

"I don't know, Kate. I don't know anything."

He tried to sit up and struggled. Leaned back against the cupboards, holding the towel to his head while Kate paced.

"Where's John? Why wasn't he here? You need a doctor."

"I'll be fine, Kate, but we do need John. He'll know what to do."

"Why John?"

"He knows these woods better than anyone. He's covered every inch with Kat. If Clayton's on foot, John will find him."

"You're right. Where is he?"

"Big Rapids. He went to check on some patients he still sees."

"Should I go for him?"

"You'd never find him. He'll be back in the morning. Help me up, please."

Kate cleaned and patched Harley's head the best she knew how, got the horse she'd abandoned in the clearing, and left Harley resting to go find Mel.

"Here's our cozy love nest, Sweetheart."

"You ass," she retorted, but curiosity got the better of her, and she looked where he pointed. "Where? I see nothing but brush."

"That's the point. It's all anyone will see. No one will find our sweet hideaway."

"Sure," she said, and rolled her eyes to let him know she wasn't impressed.

Clayton pulled a dead tree aside, its branches still thick and providing the perfect cover. Part of a shack came into view. What was left of the roof tilted precariously to one side, making it more of a lean-to than anything resembling a house. The other half was held up by new wooden posts. Clayton had been planning for a while.

"Will you go without a fight, or do you want me to carry you in?" he asked.

Kat didn't give him the satisfaction of a look, just got wearily to her feet and went in. She held her arms tight across her chest and shivered. It was filthy with nests, spider webs, and skeletons of critters past. The floor was dirt, and the whole thing smelled of mildew and rot.

"You really think I'm going to stay here?" she asked.

"I know you are. Have a seat."

"I'm cold. Can I make a fire?" she asked, hoping he wouldn't think about the smoke, a beacon for rescuers.

"No fire," he said and handed her a ragged blanket. He jiggled it in front of her. "If it's not to your liking, I can keep you warm." A smirk followed his raised eyebrows. He ran a hand over her back, and she shuddered.

"I think you like me, girl. I felt you shiver."

"That was a shudder, ass. Know the difference?"

"You need to quit calling me that," he said, sulking like a boy who'd been called names all his life.

"Hurt your little feelings?" she chided, and knew she was walking a tightrope. She wanted him to dislike her enough to keep his distance, not enough to hit her.

"Shut up!" he barked. "Just shut up! I'm going outside. You stay put."

"What am I supposed to do in here?"

"I don't know. Clean it up."

While he was gone, she tried to clean enough to stand being inside the place without throwing up. It was hard to clean without water. A broom was in the corner, though, and some rags on a shelf. She knocked the webs off the walls and ceiling, and dusted the two chairs and table, swept the trash up off the dirt floor. It was the best she could do. She wandered into the back room and stumbled backwards when she saw a mattress on the floor. It looked like it had been brought in recently because it wasn't covered in dust and webs. Her stomach churned. She thought she would finally throw up and headed to the sink.

Only bile came to her throat when she gagged and gagged, but it became clear to Kat she had to make plans to escape, soon. How? She was no match for his strength. Would he tie her at night? Or worse? God, no! The thought of being touched by him brought the bile back to her mouth, and she cringed. She'd kill him first.

Right, Kat . . . with your fingernails?

She had no idea where they were but thought it was about four fast, walking, half running hours east of Hersey. She'd watched the sun, what she could see of it through the canopy of the trees. If she managed to get away, she'd just start walking west. No problem. Finding her way home wasn't her biggest worry. Getting away was.

Kat sat again and waited, thinking. When Clayton came in, she had questions.

"Can you tell me your plans? How long will we be here?"

"Just tonight," he told her. "That's all."

"Then what?"

"Then your stupid stepfather will give me money and a horse, and I'll be gone."

"So, you're letting me go then?"

"Sure."

"They'll come after you, you know. You'll never get away with it."

"They can't prove it was me. The old man never saw me. And you won't say anything, right?" he asked, a leer on his face.

Kat thought about it and didn't believe he'd ever let her go. She could identify him. She was as good as dead.

"Are we going to eat today?" Kat asked. She had an idea.

Clayton didn't answer, but shook his head. He hadn't planned on taking anyone today and wasn't prepared.

Kat made a decision. Come nightfall, she would be gone . . . or dead. At least, that was the plan. The gone part. She didn't want to think about the possibility of being dead, but she couldn't hope for a rescue. Not by Clayton's timeline.

She would be nice to him. She would be idiotically sweet, and she would cook for him. Given her knowledge of root vegetables in the forest, she would make a wonderful meal for him, a special meal.

She told him what she wanted to do. He was skeptical, but pleased, and thought it would be alright as long as he went with her to collect the food.

"I know of some roots like sweet potatoes and herbs to put with them that will make your mouth water. Sound good?"

She knew what she wanted, jimson weed, what John called Devil's Snare. If she couldn't find jimson, then pokeweed or nightshade would do. They'd all be tall enough to spot easily and were plentiful. The roots would also look like edible sumac. She'd combine enough tasty herbs to make it palatable, like mint, and be careful not to mix them up and put the jimson or pokeweed on her own plate.   Jimson caused hallucinations, and reactions to pokeweed root could be violent; both could be fatal.

Kat was nervous. Could she do this? Make a poison supper? What if she killed him? Well, dead was surely his intention for her, so . . .

Chapter Twenty-two

Kat

Kate helped the girls finish chores and told them briefly what had occurred, trying to leave the anxiety out of her voice, not wanting to scare them more than circumstance made necessary. When they had gathered their things and loaded it all in the buggy, Jeannie saw the rifle Mel had given to Kate.

"What's that for?" she asked, her eyes wide with the fear Kate had hoped to suppress.

"It's just a precaution, Sweetie. That's all. I'm sure we won't need to use it."

Jeannie nodded, but the look on her face didn't reassure Kate that she was convinced. Wolf stood guard by the buggy. For once, he refused to ride, but stayed on the ground, watchful and alert.

All the way back to the cabin, both Becca and Jeannie bombarded Kate with questions, so she explained in more detail and emphasized how much they were helping by caring for Dot and Sammy.

"Uncle Jack and Mel will find Kat, girls. Please be sure of that, okay? And we all will take care of each other. Harley, too."

In town, Mel found Jamie and Jack. They stopped by to ask Rob some pointed questions about his friend, Clayton, couldn't find him and left. They decided not to waste time getting the Reed City sheriff. It would take too long, and he was lousy at his job, anyway, preferring to earn his pay at the saloon.

They were frustrated. Scared. They didn't know what they were doing either, and their uncertainty was expressed in the rein ends they flapped against their horses, spurring them on. They rode like the devil was on their trail. Horse hooves kicked up dirt, nostrils flared, sweat glistened. Anger and fear transferred from thighs to horse, and it came out in a frantic race down the dirt road.

Jack balled up his fists, anger firing his eyes. "I should have taken care of him when he came."

"What are you talking about? Taken care of Clayton? Why?" Mel shouted.

"Kate didn't tell you," he shouted back, a statement more than a question.

Mel pulled back on the reins, and they slowed to ride three abreast.

"Tell me what?" Mel asked.

"Clayton went to see her. Wanted her to look at a picture."

"What the hell for?"

Jack rolled his eyes toward Jamie, letting Mel know it wasn't for Jamie's ears. "Guess he thought the man in the picture might be someone she knew at the lumber camp when she was doing wash for them."

Mel rode silently for a bit, his big mare dwarfing the other two. Like Mel himself. Jack waited and knew when he understood. Mel's head and shoulders drooped; defeat settled on him like a shroud. The rapist . . . He was the man in the picture.

"This way," she said. "The ground looks a little swampy, like it would grow great sumac. Their roots are great. You're gonna love them."

Clayton mumbled something she didn't understand, but she didn't care and moved toward what she hoped was jimson. Once there, she was sure. Black, dry berries clustered and hung from the stalks like grapes on a vine. She pulled the berries and seed pods and dumped them into her skirt. She'd made it into a bag by holding up the hem. Her calves showed, but she couldn't care. Not now. She pulled at a stalk trying to dislodge the root, but it wouldn't budge.

"Will you help me, Clayton? You're a lot stronger," she said, filling him with flattery he couldn't distinguish from lies.

He puffed up his chest and pulled out two roots she knew were enough to kill an elephant. She must be careful. She didn't want him dead, just incapacitated, rolling around the floor in happy, hallucinogenic delirium.

She asked for help again when they found sumac. Sumac could be safely eaten, she knew, like a potato, and hoped she remembered her lessons correctly.

She tried to visualize the notes she had written in her journal. She recalled aspects of the herbs by picturing her written words, seeing the details on the page.

Kat snorted, a harsh kind of laugh when she thought about the lie of her memory. Once Jeannie asked how she could remember everything, all the herbs and their mixtures. "I'm an imposter," Kat told her, "a phony. I look it up in my mind. I don't remember it at all."

"Hey!" Clayton shouted, poking her with a long sumac stalk. "We have four. Isn't that enough?"

"Plenty."

"If you can cook good, maybe I'll take you with me," he told her as they trudged back to the shack. "How'd you like that?"

"Maybe. Where are you going?"

"South. Don't know how far. I want to be warm. I hate cold and snow. You'll like it." He stared at Kat as they walked. "I think you got used to me a bit."

Kat stumbled at his words. *God, Kat, be careful*, she warned herself. You still have to get through the rest of the day and supper.

Clayton grabbed her arm to steady her and gave her a knowing, sensual look, curdling her stomach. "Maybe when we get back to the shack, huh?" He pulled her closer, and Kat held jimson stalks between them, a toxic barrier. "You'll like what I got for you."

"I'm sure, but I need to work on our supper, because *you'll* like that. You want a nice meal, don't you?" she asked, tilting her head in what she supposed was coquettish flirtation.

Kat didn't know how to flirt, had never done it or ever wanted to. She was direct, straight-forward, and candid with wide-eyed honesty. She didn't appreciate the fine art of eyelash batting.

She needed to stretch out the preparations for supper because Clayton would never let her light a fire until it was dark or close to it. She asked for water to clean the roots, and he brought her a bucket full. Washing them took up some time, but she worried he would interrupt her work at any moment. She couldn't look his way, didn't want to meet his eyes for fear he'd take it as an invitation.

While she was removing the skin from the roots with his pocket knife, Clayton came up behind her and she tensed. He put his hands on her shoulders and rubbed them.

"You need to relax," he whispered in her ear, continuing to rub. She tried, but her back was so stiff it felt like it would crack if she bent or turned.

His huge hands moved lower, covered her breasts, and her breath stopped. She clenched the pocket knife until her knuckles turned white and wondered if she could spin and plunge it into his heart. How deep would it go? Would it even reach his heart? Could she turn fast enough, before he stopped her? Knocked her to the floor? Killed her with his bare hands?

His hand slipped into her open shirt where the buttons had been ripped off, and he cupped her bare breast.

God, help me, her tortured soul begged, *Please,* but her lips said, "I'm busy, Clayton. Wait til after supper and you won't be disappointed."

He pinched her nipple, and she flinched. "Nice," he said before turning away, licking saliva from his lips, confident his charm had worked on her. He would have Kat tonight. And she would be compliant, even eager. He'd seen to that. She was more than amenable; she was ready.

Kate asked Becca and Jeannie to look after Dot and Sammy upstairs as Jack, Mel, Jamie and Harley began discussing the best plan for getting Kat back. They were sketching out a map of the woods, and Kate moved the journal Kat was working with before she went to the cellar, before Clayton broke in. Between its pages a note stuck out.

I no what you did. If you want kat alive pay up you owe me $5000 and a horse. Leave it *at the old sugar shack* tomorrow. *Don't try to find her and don't wait after you leave it cuz I'll know and she'll die.*

Kate fell into a chair when she saw it. It brought everything home, made it clear, and fear for Kat's safety was a raging flood in her brain. *God, don't let him do to her what his father did to me,* she begged.

They were all stunned, petrified with shock, and stepped back from their planning. This changed things.

"What now?" Mel asked.

Harley went to the cupboard. "I'd like a bit of whiskey. Anybody else?"

They all grunted and sat like statues, not looking at each other, waiting for someone to come up with a plan, waiting for a miracle to happen. It was a joke, right? A pathetic, sick joke?

Five minutes later, they agreed to get the money and a horse. That was the only thing they agreed on.

Jack wanted to head into the woods immediately and find him. Beat the shit out of him once and for all. Mel sat with his chin firmly planted on his fisted hand, eyes narrowed, deep in thought. Jamie's experience of war saw Kat's abduction as a battle. It took a strategic plan to win, or Kat would be the loser.

Kate went light headed at the vision in her mind. "That isn't going to happen. Never!" she whispered. She sat tall in her chair, her head held high. Scum like that couldn't be allowed to win.

"If we have enough men," Jamie said, "we flank the woods on three sides and move in. We have a couple of men waiting for when he comes out on the fourth side. He has to come out, cuz we'll be loud and moving him in that direction. It works in battle and this is war."

"What about Kat? Is he going to just drag her along or let her go when he knows he's beaten?" Mel rubbed his face, stubble a harsh rasp that felt appropriate.

"I know every inch of these woods. I've worked it for years and I'm a fox, light footed. He won't even know I'm there, and I'll find him. I'll bring her back," Jack offered.

"And if he hears you, knows you're close on his trail? What then?" Kate asked. "We have to think first about Kat's safety."

"I want to find him alive and beat him until he isn't, but I don't think that's the safest way . . . for Kat," Mel said. "I think we need to do what he asked, at least for now. But it's up to Kate."

"What do you think?" he said, turning to her, and his heart broke at the sight of her white, drawn face. He put his arm around her shoulders and whispered. "We'll find her, Kate. I promise you, we'll find her."

Kate's head whirled around to face him. "You can't promise! Don't promise something you have no control over!" She buried her face in her hands. "I'm sorry," she whispered.

"It's alright. I'll get the money together and a horse."

Kate threw her arms around him. "Oh, Mel, I'm so sorry. Thank you. Thank you. I will never be able to thank you enough."

"It's nothing, Kate. You, your girls are worth twenty times that, an infinite number of times. You must know it."

"I love you," she whispered in his neck.

They decided they would leave for the sugar shack first thing in the morning, since Clayton hadn't been clear about the *when*. As he was also vague about the *who*, they decided Jack and Mel would both make the delivery. A little security should Clayton's plan include killing the delivery boy.

No one felt like eating. It was just something you did, something you had to do even if your stomach was upside down and your heart was sore. Food was the eternal answer to questions no one wanted to ponder, even if it stuck in your throat and laid like lead in your belly.

They were cleaning up when they heard John's mare race up the path to the clearing. He left his horse in the yard and ran toward the cabin, feeling a chill wind chase him. Kate met him outside, saw his distress, and wondered if he knew.

When he saw her face, he grabbed her shoulders.

"What is it?" he demanded, towering over Kate, his fierce eyes blazing.

"Kat's . . . missing. She's been taken," Kate said as straightforward as possible.

John blanched, went still and quiet. The only sound was his slow breath.

"We'll get her back, John. He wants money and a horse. He can have it."

When John remained silent, Kate continued. "We leave it at the old sugar shack tomorrow. Come in and get some dinner."

Kate walked toward the cabin, and when she turned back to speak to John, he wasn't there.

Kate and Jack stayed with Harley while the rest went back to the farm after John disappeared. Becca began the milking, and Jeannie put Sammy and Dot to bed for the night.

"I don't know how much more these girls can be put through," Mel said while they rubbed down the mares. "They've seen a lot. Way too damned much."

"They're tough. They're ma has taught them well. And their pa when he was alive," Jamie said. When Mel didn't respond, Jamie added. "No disrespect to you, Mel. You're part of them, too."

"I know. None taken. Mark was a good man, a good pa. I wish you could have been here, too, Jamie."

They were quiet for a time, content with their own thoughts and the rasp of brushes on horse hide. Mel didn't want to go into the house right away and stretched out the care of his mare until she was dry and glistening. He was

248

happier in the barn, easier with the sweet smell of cows and horses, the tangy odor of molasses corn feed, the sound of chickens settling in. He knew what to expect here with the familiar animals. He didn't have to think what was right. He knew. No complex, unanswered questions to figure out, just simple work.

"Seems like Kate can't catch a break. If it's not one thing, it's another. Doesn't seem right," he said to Jamie, his voice a murmur on the night air.

"She has you, Mel. That's a pretty good break."

"Yeah, and I brought her Spanish flu and a husband too weak to run his own farm without help. Big break."

Jamie couldn't answer. Didn't know what to say.

Mel looked in on Becca, still milking the cows. He tried to reassure her, let her know Kat would be okay.

"Know it, Becca, have faith in it," he soothed, his large hand dwarfing her slender shoulder. "I won't let anything happen to Kat."

But he lied. He didn't mean to, but he didn't know if he could help Kat. Didn't know what to do or how to do it. No one did. They were all guessing, and it was a twisting knife of self-doubt.

He looked around his barn, taking in the known smells and sounds. This stuff he knew. It was familiar and comforting.

"You're my rock, Becca. Thank you for taking good care of my girls."

"I thought Jeannie and I were your girls," she said with a welcome grin.

"You are," he said with an answering smile and a final pat. "I meant my bovine ladies." He left her and Jamie to put the farm to bed for the night.

Jeannie was sitting on the porch. Mel sat with her. They were quiet for a long time.

"Bring Kat home," Jeannie said, tears flooding her eyes. Her lips quivered, and she swallowed hard trying to stem the flood before the dam burst.

"We will, Jeannie. Don't you ever doubt it. Kat will be back safe and sound. I promise."

His arms went around her, and she pressed her face in his chest. He absently caressed her back and murmured soothing sounds until her sobs quieted.

"I'm sorry," she muttered in the folds of his shirt. "I can take care of Dot and Sammy. Really. You go find Kat."

"I know it, Jeannie. I know you can. You are something else, and I love you."

Jeannie took a deep breath, relaxed and snuggled into Mel. He held her close, thinking again they'd been through way too much.

The hardest part was waiting, and pacing the floor which was what Kate had to do. Sit in the cabin, worry and wait. She tended Harley's wound, wishing John had stayed long enough to see to it. She wasn't sure if she should keep him awake, make him walk around, or let him sleep. She bound his head tightly, talked to him, and watched him closely as he stared into the fire.

What a mess. She needed to be everywhere at once. She was worried about Harley, terrified for Kat. Thought she should be with Becca and Jeannie but couldn't leave the cabin in case . . . in case what? Kat would be returned or find a way to escape and come home? Maybe . . . maybe what? She didn't know. Not knowing was a hot, heavy rock in her gut. Nausea rose to her throat, and she swallowed it back.

She wasn't sure of anything and she hated it. Inactivity was killing her, and she paced the floor, stared at Harley, and paced. There must be something she should be doing . . . something! Not doing anything was the worst kind of punishment.

Kate was glad for Jack's company. He got up from his chair next to Harley and pulled Kate into it.

"Sit," he commanded, and went to the shelf where the jug was kept. He splashed a liberal amount in three glasses and brought them over.

"Drink it, Kate. Harley, sip yours slowly. Don't know what it will do to your lumpy head."

Harley nodded and continued to stare into the fire.

Jack watched them both from a seat on the hearth by Wolf and waited. Kate sipped, leaned her head against the chair back and rocked, the toe of one foot barely touching the floor. She heard the silence, heard tangible words that weren't spoken, only thought. She looked around the room, up into the corner where she imagined Mark hovered, their guardian, their angel. The spiritual essence of Mark was so concrete as to be touchable.

'Are you there, Mark?' she wondered. 'Go to Kat. Go to your daughter; wrap your arms around her if you can.'

Harley was still. Jack bided his time and sipped his own drink, watching, assessing.

"You going to talk soon, Harley?" he asked.

He turned his face to Jack and slowly lifted his drink to sip. Then he turned to Kate and pain clouded his eyes, an ache that burned in Jack's belly. He knew that face, that feeling. He'd seen it in the mirror a long time ago. It was the look of failure.

"What do you suppose Clayton would have done if Kate had been here with Kat instead of you, Harley?" he asked.

Harley shrugged, and Kate's eyes moved from the flames to Jack. She visualized various scenes. Saw herself on the floor bleeding. Saw Clayton dragging both of them away. She wished for that. At least then, with the two of them, they'd have a better chance. Could fight him easier.

"He might have taken two of the Ramey women, or one might be dead while he kidnapped the other. What do you think, Kate? That about how you see it?"

Kate nodded. Knew it was the truth. It was exactly what he would have done. Kill her or take them both.

Harley raised a hand and rubbed his face, squeezed his eyes with a thumb and forefinger.

"I guess you think you should be impervious to human frailties. Is that, right?" Jack said, pushing Harley, trying to bring him out of his torpor.

Harley squeezed his lips together, jaw muscles quivering, his eyes stagnant ponds of sorrow. Kate saw and put her hand on his.

"Rock with me, Harley. We've done this so many times. Rock with me . . . please? I need you."

"Kate might be dead if she'd been here instead of you, Harley. Face that reality. You'd be dead, but your head is too hard. Remember how Kate would have looked on the floor instead of you any time you get to feeling bad."

Harley gave a slight nod and squeezed Kate's hand.

It wasn't long before Harley lifted his glass. "Here's to Kat," he said. "She's smarter than all of us. She'll find a way to get herself out of this, and John will know where she is or how to find her. Bless them both," he said, and tilted his glass. "I'm going to sleep now. Don't worry about me. I mean it, Kate."

Harley went to his bed, and Jack took his chair. They spent the night there, waiting.

As soon as dusk began, Kat laid the wood for a fire. "Is it safe now?" she asked. "Food is ready to be cooked. Do you like your potatoes mashed?"

She was nervous, worse than nervous, terrified. Would this work? Would she kill him? Herself? Would it have no affect at all, leaving her vulnerable, at his mercy until he decided to use her, take her, or kill her?

"Sounds good. Hurry, cuz I'm hungry," he said, grinning, and wrapped an arm around her, fondled her in places she'd never thought to be touched. *She'd kill herself first,* she thought, but knew better. She wouldn't die for him, but he might for her.

She fixed his plate and handed it across the table. Her hand trembled and he noticed.

"What's wrong?" he asked.

"Just a little tired. That's all."

"We'll be in bed soon. I think you can't wait. That's what it is," he said, a meaningful smirk spreading over his broad face. He was content to linger for the moment knowing she was now a willing partner. She didn't realize what a good time he had in store for her.

He ate, moved the food around in his mouth with his tongue and frowned.

252

"Don't you like it?" she pouted. "I really wanted to make something special for you."

"It's different," he said, and began shoveling it in, not bothering to chew.

Kat took her time. Chewed each mouthful carefully, stretching out the meal as long as possible.

"Where are you from, Clayton? Do you have family who miss you?" she asked, trying to distract him from his goal.

"Nowhere near here," he said on a mouthful of mashed root. "Tastes funny."

"It's the herbs. You're not used to fresh herbs, but they're good for you. It's called tansy. Makes you virile," she said with a forced smile. She didn't know where the thought came from, couldn't even remember what tansy was or what it was for, but it seemed to encourage his eating.

"I know I'd miss my family if they weren't around."

"I told you about my family. It's just my pa and me, or it was. And he and your ma had a bit of fun together from what I understand. I think your Uncle Jack did something to him when he did your ma," Clayton said, sitting back in his chair and tilting his head. "He liked your sister, Rachel, too. He was good with the ladies."

Kat flinched and instantly thought back to the day her ma had come home in tatters, the day Bug died. Jack had brought them both home, and her ma had gone to the woods to beat a tree. Hate brewed in her heart.

"Don't you be jealous of Rachel, now." He raised his eyebrows like he was trying to open his eyes wider and Kat saw the beginnings of what she'd been waiting for. His pupils were huge and didn't change when he moved his head toward the candle on the table. They stayed dilated.

Hold on Kat. Just hang on. It's working. She moved her food around the plate some more and batted her eyelashes again. She tipped her head down, thinking a shy maiden might do that, and peered up at him. She saw one of his fingers lift, an involuntary jerk upwards, and her heart soared. Minutes later, his foot twitched, and a tremor began in his right shoulder. When his facial muscles convulsed, he leaped from his chair screaming.

"You bitch! You fuckin' bitch!" He stumbled to his jacket and fumbled with it, trying to remove what Kat remembered was his gun.

She jumped on him, and he tumbled to the floor with her riding his back. He rolled over, twisted, and sprawled on top of her. She struggled to take a breath, bucked and jerked, tried to dislodge him, but he was heavy, and she was losing strength fast. She heard his chuckle, and knew it was over. She'd lost. He moved off her, and she saw the barrel of a gun in her face.

Chapter Twenty-three

Mel and Jack were kicking up road dirt. Three mares snorted in the morning air. One had a bag of money. They took the road east as far as they could before heading into the woods to the sugar shack.

"You think there might be more than one of these shacks around?" Mel asked, growing more nervous as they neared the site.

"I've been all over these woods when I jacked for Landmark. Where we're headed is the only abandoned one."

Mel quieted, listening for sounds they weren't making.

"Do you think he's waiting for us?" Mel whispered.

"He'd be a fool. It'd be a good way to die."

"He is a fool. I hope he's waiting," Mel said, a knife edge cutting his words.

Jack nodded. Mel hadn't killed a man, wasn't the kind who could kill and sleep. His sort would take a life if it was needed, but for them it didn't end when the heart quit. It never ended.

Jack hoped Clayton would wait to pick up his horse and money. Leave Kat and be gone because Mel might see fit to end Clayton's life, and Jack would have to fight him for the pleasure.

It was quiet when they found the place. They tied their horses a good distance away and walked closer, stopping periodically to listen and watch for movement. A partridge flew up in front of them, its wings frantically flapping, making noise enough for a covey of peacocks, and startled them both.

When breath returned, they looked at each other, gave a nervous laugh, and moved toward the shack.

"Thought we were goners for a minute," Jack said with a sheepish chuckle. "Damn bird. Should've shot it for dinner."

"Yeah, sounded like he had an army with him. Almost drew my gun."

"You brought a gun?" Jack asked.

"Course, didn't you?"

"Well, sure, but . . . never mind."

The shack was covered with vines, and the roof touched the ground on one side. It obviously hadn't been used in years. A syrup trough sat outside and was rusted through. They peered inside a broken window and saw a couple of small kegs and a stool, nothing else except cobwebs, dust and vines creeping in through the open window and door. Whoever worked for maple sugar in these woods had roughed it for sure.

"Let's go," Jack said, and tied the horse to a nearby tree.

"We're gonna leave? What about Kat?"

Jack shifted his feet, kicked at the ground, considered their options. "I don't like it, but I think we have to. That's what Clayton demanded, and it's what Kate wanted." He paused in thought. "It's probably our safest bet. Kat's best chance at coming out of this alive."

When Mel didn't respond, Jack continued. "We'll watch for him just off the road. He'll probably come out of the woods that way. It's the easiest. Actually, it's the only sensible way. And he doesn't know these woods well enough, I'm thinking, to try escaping into the forest. Once you're off this hill, it goes into swamp on two sides, Hersey's on the west, and we're south. He'd be a fool to try to go through the swamp. He'd circle around and die trying to get out. It doesn't make sense he wouldn't come out this way."

They picked up their horses, retraced their steps back to the road. It was far enough they couldn't be heard from the shack. They moved into the trees on the far side of the road where they wouldn't be seen when Clayton came out.

The first hour, they sat on their mounts just in the woods, in the cover of scrub and ready to rush from the trees and ambush Clayton. They were alert, nerves on edge, waiting. The sun grew higher in the sky. Every minute felt an hour long. They dismounted to kneel in the brush closer to the road and worried.

"Don't know if this was the right choice," Jack whispered, fearful he'd sealed Kat's fate. He should've gone along with Mel, waited right there for Clayton at the shack, demanded Kat with a gun barrel pointed at Clayton's head.

"Can't second guess, friend." Mel stood, peered out of brush cover, and squatted again.

"What now?" Jack asked.

"I think we head back to the sugar shack, see if he's been there, then go on back to the cabin. Maybe he left her at the shack or, hell, maybe she's already home. Maybe, we just missed him, maybe he went through the swamp or something . . . Damn! I don't know," he groaned and wiped his face with a shaking hand.

Back at the sugar shack, their hopes were dashed to find he'd already been there. It looked like two sets of feet had come and gone, along with the horse. He'd taken her with him.

"Don't know what we're doing here. We need to be out there," Jack said pointing to the woods, "and we need help. Fast. Let's go."

Kate came running out with Harley not far behind when they burst into the clearing. Her face fell when she saw they were alone. She rubbed her forehead and pushed a hand through her hair.

Mel slid from the mare, grabbed her shoulders and pulled her into his arms.

"She'll be back, Kate. We'll get her back. I promise. You've got to believe that."

Kate pulled away, her eyes throwing sparks. "What do you mean, you promise? How can you say that? You can't promise anything because you don't know. Not where she is or how she is. Don't promise me anything." She babbled until she ran down, fear and anger bitter on her tongue.

"What happened?" she mumbled. "Didn't he come for the horse?"

Jack spoke up and explained. Took the blame for not waiting where they'd left the horse and money. "We didn't even hear him. I was afraid to wait too close, Kate. Afraid he'd do what he promised."

"We went back before we came here. The horse and money are gone. Looks like he still has her," Mel said, his anguished words a harsh whisper.

Kate began shaking, tried to pull herself away from Mel's hand on her shoulder. She didn't want to be touched. There was no comfort. She wanted her daughter!

"We'll find her, Kate," Jack consoled.

She turned her back and strode off toward the woods.

"What are you doing, Kate?" Mel shouted at her erect back. Her head was thrown back and her stride determined.

"Finding my daughter!"

"Wait! You can't . . . come back! We need more men to search. We're heading to get them now. We'll comb the woods. Come on, Kate."

She turned and threw herself to her knees, hands over her face. Harsh sobs racked her shoulders. Both men raced to her, knelt by her side.

"Come in the cabin, Kate. We'll figure it out. Please?" Mel begged. He felt responsible. Jack, too. They'd let Clayton walk away with Kat. Neither wanted to consider other options. That horror was unthinkable.

Inside, Harley waited with small glasses of whiskey. He pulled out a chair for Kate, said, "Sit," and handed her a glass. "Drink."

Harley took over. "We need to use the sugar shack as the point from which we begin our search. We'll cut the area like a pie and divide the slices between us. Mel, your horse is the fastest here. Ride for help. Get Jamie, Rob, anyone who can walk, but don't dally to find more. Get back here, pronto. We'll wait for you, but hurry. Agreed?" Harley asked. "Anyone have a better plan or difference of opinion?"

"Nope," Mel said, kissed Kate and left. His colossal horse ate up the ground.

When he had gone, Harley drew a map of the area, put the shack in the center and a circle around it. He figured the distance Clayton could ride and calculated time, then cut it into slices and named each slice with a person.

Kate added landmarks she remembered. She knew the woods both near and far, and Jack, too, from his years working in them.

They didn't hear her come in the open door, they were so engrossed with their map. She had to speak twice to get their attention.

"Hello . . . Hello . . . anybody miss me? Ma?"

Kate's mouth was a perfect circle. She closed it, sat back in her chair and stared at her daughter. Took in the details of her disheveled appearance in one searching glance.

"Have you been gone?" Harley said and got up, wrapped his arms around her, and squeezed until Kat squeaked, "Can't breathe . . . Harley, can't breathe."

Jack led Kat to a chair, poured a small glass from the jug still on the table, and handed it to her. "You okay?"

Kat nodded and looked at her mother who was frozen, still searching Kat for . . . she didn't know what. To see if she was okay, to see if . . . Kate didn't want to think it. Never mind. Kat was back. That's all. And it was everything.

"Aren't you going to say anything, Ma? Welcome me home?"

Kate's eyes filled and she laughed. Tears ran down her cheeks, and she laughed some more. She put two hands on either side of Kat's face and caressed it, ran her hands over it, murmuring and laughing unintelligible sounds no one tried to interpret.

"Ma, I can't see," Kat said. "Can you move your hands?"

Kate laughed louder. "God, I love you, daughter! We have so much to talk about."

"Yes, we do," Kat said, remembering what Clayton had said about his pa. "Where's John?" she asked, looking around the room as if he might be sitting in one of the rockers or loitering nearby.

"Don't know," Jack said. "He came back earlier than expected from Big Rapids, found you missing, and left. He hasn't been back since."

"Hmm," she hummed.

"Pretty sure he's combing the woods for you, and he'll be back," Harley said, patting Kat's hand.

Kate roused herself from the stupor claiming her since Kat walked through the door. "Let's get you cleaned up, Kat, then you can fill us in. Jack, start some water heating, please. Harley, will you drag the bathing tub to Kat's room?"

Mel rode in when Kat was soaking in lavender water, relishing it, washing away the filth of Clayton's touch. She'd been soiled. She felt contaminated and stained, but she'd get over it. She'd done what she had to, let him touch her because it was necessary, and she felt no remorse. Dirt can be washed away. Dead can't.

Mel had brought Jamie, Rob, Willie and several men from town to help with the search. When he heard she was home, he whooped and looked for her.

"Where is she? Want to give that girl a hug!" he yelled, his smile wide and his heart light, released from the pain of thinking they had done the wrong thing, and she'd paid for their mistake, would be lost to them forever.

"Not now. She's bathing!" Kate said, with a slap on his arm and a hug for good measure. "I'm sorry, Mel. I was awful."

"Yes, you were," he said with a hug. "But I still love you."

They celebrated with the jug. *It sounds like a party,* Kat thought. She listened as she luxuriated in the warm, scented water. It was a welcome sound, more than welcome. She sunk lower and allowed her thoughts to follow John.

Where are you my spirit other? Are you looking for me?

When Kat was dried and dressed, she joined the party.

"How'd you get away, Kat?" Rob asked. He knew his old army buddy and was sure he wouldn't have let her go, not willingly. He'd use her. He'd seen Clayton use a lot of women, whether they wanted his attentions or not. He claimed they liked it. Women were just lying when they said they didn't. All women lied.

"Maybe now isn't the time?" Kate said. "You don't need to talk about it."

But when Kat looked around at the eager faces, eyes dancing with curiosity, she let go of the desire to wrap her arms around the experience and keep it to herself. Not to treasure, but to bury, carry it to a grave. A pauper's grave with weeds for decoration and a wooden cross that falls to the ground and rots. Soon, the corpse of her time with Clayton would turn to dust and ash, forgotten.

"I'll tell you this much. I cooked a meal for him, and he hallucinated, twitched, and fell to the floor. I tied him up and left. That's pretty much it."

"You cooked for him? What? Poison mushrooms?" Rob asked.

"Good idea . . . but no, jimson and sumac."

Harley smiled a broad, proud grin. He knew exactly what the jimson weed had done, and his heart swelled. He pictured the entire scene.

"How much jimson?" he asked.

"Just a little of the root and berry seeds to commemorate the occasion. With a lot of dried mint for flavor."

"So, you wanted to give him a party, not kill him."

"Of course. I'm not a murderer," she said, but knew she would have killed him if she'd had to, without a backward look, without remorse.

Other faces in the room bounced back and forth between Harley and Kat, not understanding, brows furrowed.

"Are we missing something?" Kate asked.

Kat indicated Harley with a hand, palm up, like she was introducing him to speak, which she was. She was done.

Harley tilted a splash of whiskey into his glass, cleared his throat and began.

"Jimson weed has been used for many years as a hallucinogenic by certain Native Americans, by others as well. It has been smoked quite happily without fatal results, ingested, too. Some used it to communicate with ancestors, some to recover from an illness, some just for the fun of it. It can incapacitate. It can kill. It's wise to use it sparingly . . . which Kat has apparently done."

"Maybe you did kill him. Maybe he died after you left," Rob said, and his face wore an expression Kat couldn't define. Was he glad? Sad? Did he miss his friend?

"Unfortunately, he's still alive," she said.

Harley cleared his throat and raised his glass. "Here's to you, my girl. Well done. John would be, will be, proud."

Kat lifted her glass to her lips and took a small sip of whiskey, swallowed it and the lump in her throat. Where was he?

"I need to go, Kat, as much as I want to stay. Becca and Jeannie will be so worried. I love you . . . so damned much. Sorry." She hung onto Kat's arm, needing to feel her daughter's flesh, wanting to stay and make sure she really was safe. Never let go again.

"I know, Ma. Go. Harley is with me, and we'll be fine. And John will likely be back soon."

Rob's job was to tell the rest of Hersey Kat was back and doing well.

"Probably won't tell them how you got away. They'll think you're a witch," he said grinning. "I know it, but they don't need to."

"You're right, Rob. Let it be our secret." She wasn't sure about her cousin. He was guarded, secretive, his eyes didn't settle on a person, but flitted about. Kat was uncomfortable around him and glad to see him leave.

Mel drew Kat aside. "Honey, I'm pretty sure Clayton got away. The horse was gone when we went back to look. We thought he had you with him cause it looked like there were two people. Did he have another man with him?"

"No. It was just him. And no way would he get loose by himself. He was really hogtied."

"The only other explanation is somebody else found the horse and took it. But that's a stretch."

"I'll take you to him. Show you where we were."

"Are you sure you don't want to wait? Get a little rest? Maybe start in the morning?"

"If he's escaped, then we need to know. Now," Kat said, concern for her family overcoming fatigue.

Mel, Jamie, Jack, John Nestor and a couple of men from town rode with Kat. She was taking them back to the shack where he'd kept her prisoner, where she'd poisoned him. Where she feared she would either kill him or die herself.

She took quiet breaths, recalling the nightmare of last night, of Clayton's gun in her face.

"Thought you'd outsmart me, little girl? Not a chance," he said, his words slurring around a tongue that no longer worked.

"No, Clayton, I know better," she said biding time, waiting, hoping for more of the jimson to work. *"I was just afraid for you. Didn't know what was wrong. Thought you might hurt yourself. Are you alright?"*

"I'm not only alright, but I'm getting better by the minute." He reached with his free hand and ripped the rest of her shirt open. *"That's the cure,"* he said, saliva dripping from his mouth.

Kat watched his eyes, waited for the hallucinations. She let his filthy hand maul her breasts, let him paw her like an animal, laid there and died while the foul creature touched her. When he put his mouth on her, she was beyond retching, beyond feeling. If the jimson didn't work soon, she didn't know what she would do.

She would not lay with him. That was a certainty. The knife was still on the table, and Kat calculated the number of steps it would take for her to reach it. She would kill him.

Kat was within moments of leaping for it when she felt his body spasm. His head came up and his eyes rolled back until the orbs were nearly all white. On his face was intense pleasure, rapture.

Kat shoved him, jumped up, shredded her shirt into strips and tied them together. Hoping he didn't wake while she was kneeled half naked in front of him, she rolled him over and tied his hands behind his back. She pushed and pulled until he was against the table leg, and she tied him to it. With strips of his shirt, she tied his legs, bent them at the knees and wrapped the end around the table leg, too. He was hogtied.

She stood up to survey her work and was light headed; her knees almost buckled. She grabbed his jacket and gun and ran. And ran. She tripped and stumbled in the dark, fell to her knees and got up. Branches slashed her face, her body, and she didn't care. She ran further.

When she was positive he wasn't behind her, she stopped and sat, rested her back against a tree trunk. She leaned over and retched, deep heaving retches from the bottom of her stomach, from her soul. She took cleansing breaths and looked around.

It was probably around ten. The moon hadn't risen yet, and the woods were black. She listened for sounds of water and didn't hear any.

Kat curled up in a thatch of heavy brush growing at the base of a low limbed willow. She was exhausted and no longer knew which way to go. She wrapped up in Clayton's huge coat and covered herself with dry leaves. She lay listening to night sounds and was content.

"Thank you, John. You saved me tonight; your lessons saved me." A deep breath later she was asleep and slept soundly until the sound of an insistent woodpecker woke her, the sun peeking at her through the tree canopy.

Kat was brought back from her memories by the sight of the shack . . . where she wondered if she might die, where death might have been a preference.

Mel watched Kat, wondered how she'd respond to seeing Clayton again. Jack was praying he'd still be there, a trussed duck waiting to be turned in to the sheriff. They all listened, waited to hear movement from inside. The door hung open. No sound, not even the skittering of mice met them as they entered. The place was empty.

Kat was stunned! Even though they told her the horse was gone, she hadn't really accepted it was Clayton who'd taken it. It couldn't be! But it must have been him. What other answer was there?

She took it all in. There was no sign of the ropes she'd made from her shirt. Why had he taken those? How had he gotten free? She knew the ties were solid. Knew it! Had he really managed to recover from the jimson, loosen the ties, walk off and collect his horse and money?

When she was over the initial shock, she looked around . . . at the sink where she cleaned their dinner, where he touched her, where she fought the urge to plunge his own knife into his black, rotten heart. She breathed deeply, forcing clean air into her lungs.

"That monster is loose now. Out there where he can prey on other people," she hissed.

Jack fought the urge to hit something, anything. He was worried, knew Clayton didn't want other women. He wanted Kate or Kat, or any of the Ramey girls. He thought he was owed. But Jack couldn't say that, couldn't explain why. He had to pretend the man was gone and wouldn't be back and said so.

"We'll alert the sheriff's office, let it be known he's out there and dangerous."

They rode to the sugar shack, hoping to find clues that might lead them to Clayton. If they found any, they'd track him, find him, bring him to justice.

They all agreed there'd been two people at the site. John Nestor got down on one knee and poked at the prints left in the soft ground. "There were definitely two. Look at the different size tracks."

"That's what it looked like to us," Jack said. "We assumed he'd taken Kat with him." He swallowed and drew a deep breath and looked at Kat. "Damned glad he didn't."

The tracks were confusing. How could there be two if one set wasn't Kat's?

"Maybe he had an accomplice," Nestor said. "Did he hang with anybody in town except Rob? I never saw him with anyone else. Except Sadie's girls."

"Doesn't mean he didn't have a pal keeping out of sight. Maybe that's the way they plan their jobs," Tate said.

The rest shook their heads, not knowing Clayton well enough to guess who he knew or didn't. Clayton was too new in town. He could have brought someone with him or met up with him later. But wouldn't he have asked for two horses then? No one had an answer to the puzzle.

Kat stood motionless trying to feel the events that had taken place here. Tried to see Jack and Mel leaving the horse. Tried to envision Clayton getting on it and riding away. She couldn't.

It didn't feel right, and she didn't think it had happened that way. She didn't know it -- she just felt it. She was certain Clayton wouldn't have been able to untie himself. Those knots were tight! He couldn't walk away on his own, not in his hallucinogenic state, especially not so early in the day. It didn't fit, and it troubled her. In her world, facts had to fit. She suspected he had help out of there . . . maybe Rob, but he'd been at the cabin, not wandering around the woods with his buddy Clayton. No. Not Rob.

She was bothered by the unknown. If an answer was available, she wanted to know it. If one didn't exist, she was okay with its absence, but in this case, there was an answer. She just didn't know it.

Kat left the others and walked over to the ram shackled structure. The shack was dilapidated and covered in grime. She looked inside through the broken window and saw a spider hanging from a cobweb, a gentle breeze causing it to move back and forth. She watched as the spider went about its spinning, admired its elegance, and appreciated the artistry. For a moment, she felt joy in the simplicity of its beauty. Then . . . Clayton!

She began to turn away when something caught her eye. Something the breeze had found. It looked like . . . yes! It was a piece of her torn shirt on an old barrel!

"Mel? Uncle Jack . . ."

Chapter Twenty-four

John

John loped through the night, through the same dark hours Kat was making dinner for Clayton. His footsteps made no more sound than the stealthy wolves appearing and disappearing like apparitions. He spotted one on the crest of a hill watching him, and John remembered his promise to find a wolf pup for Kat.

"I will, Kat. As soon as this is done. I will," he told the night. It took only moments for his eyes to adjust to the early dusk, and he crisscrossed until he found their trail. When complete darkness fell, he lay down beneath a willow and rested until the moon rose, then started again.

It was painstaking work in the moonlight. He was afraid he'd miss a mark and waste time backtracking. When a broken branch caught his eye, he'd stop, check it carefully to be sure it was human and not animal damage before he moved on. It had been a long time since he'd tracked in the woods. If not for the reason of this trek, he would have enjoyed the night.

He lost them at the river and spent hours picking up the trail again, cursing the river his people revered, cherished. If the man hurt Kat, he would have to avenge. He didn't want to take a life; he was a healer, but in this case, he would, without shame. His heart ached, his mind in turmoil, and he tried to still it, to clear his thoughts of everything except their tracks. He'd succeed for awhile, but again her visage would return and he'd mentally falter.

He sat at last, where the forest cleared and the moon's yellow glow lit the ground. He crossed his legs in Cherokee fashion and called on his grandfather.

"I'm a healer, Grandfather, but I want to kill a man. My blood boils with hatred and will only be stilled with his death. My mind is a maze of thoughts. Help me put my hatred aside, so I can do what I need to do. Kat is a healer, a medicine woman. I need to find her. She's needed by many, by me."

He sat motionless, and the yellow-white orb moved further across the sky. Dark began to shade the moonlit earth, and still John waited, immobile. When he rose, his heart was comforted. He knew his medicine woman was in charge, and she would be well. John resumed his search.

In the dark of early morning, John saw the shack and knew immediately it was Clayton's lair. He tracked by moonlight and saw their footprints going in, coming out, and going in again. There was no smoke from the rickety chimney, no sound from the shack. He squatted to watch and wait. Birds awoke, flew off for breakfast, and late geese flew overhead, heading south. He couldn't see them under the cover of the forest canopy, but their honking echoed in the sky.

When a brief time went by and no one stirred in the shack, John slipped around to come up behind, through the brush. He stepped quietly, slowly, like the woodland specter he'd been taught to be as a youth. When he was close enough, he peered between the logs through the cracks where mud chinking was missing. His eyes roamed the room, grew accustomed to the dim light, and finally landed on the trussed man lying prone on the floor next to the table. Clayton.

He looked again, trying unsuccessfully to spot Kat. He let minutes go by, waiting for a second person to appear, listening for the sound of another body. Nothing. He slipped back around to the front door and shoved it with his foot. It swung open, and Clayton lurched forward on his side, pulling the table with him and screaming obscenities. John walked over and pushed him down with a foot on his chest.

"Where's Kat?" he asked, his voice so deathly quiet it made Clayton shudder in fear.

"I don't know."

"Think about it."

"I don't know," he repeated.

"What do you know?"

Clayton fumbled around for words, words that would save him from this man. He was afraid, and he didn't know why. But he was.

"We, uh, we were eating," he stammered, "and . . . I got all jerky and saw crazy things. When I woke up, I was tied to the table, and she was gone."

John smiled. Clayton wasn't comforted by it. It unnerved him.

"She poisoned you. You're lucky she didn't want you dead. If she had, you would be," he said, untying his legs.

"What are you going to do? I didn't hurt her," he whined. "You taking me to the sheriff?"

"No, I'm setting you free," John said.

Clayton wished he'd speak up. That low, calm voice, the steely eyes were creepy. He didn't trust the man. "Free?" he croaked, his voice breaking. "Why?"

"Let's go. You'll see."

While Mel and Jack were waiting for Clayton to appear on the road, John was marching him the back way to the sugar shack. As promised, the horse was there, and no one waited in ambush. John was glad. He didn't want to explain where he was taking Clayton or why.

He took the money out of the saddlebag and stowed it in the shack at the bottom of a barrel, covered with dusty burlap bags, out of sight. He put Clayton on the horse, held onto the reins and started walking. It would look like Clayton had picked up the horse as planned, but he wouldn't take the road for a quick getaway. He'd go north, in the opposite direction, where John led the way through the swamp. When they came to a road, a long while later, he climbed behind Clayton to make quicker time. He knew it would be a long ride.

Day after day, they travelled north, eating jerky from John's pack and drinking from streams. At night, John tied his feet, untied his hands to allow him to eat, and retied them to his feet and attached him to a tree until morning. It was growing colder. This far north, winter was closer. They hadn't seen houses or people in days, no farms, no signs of civilization, nothing.

"Where are we going?" Clayton bellowed, growing more antagonistic by the days and the degrees of falling temperature. He whined and roared alternately, confused about which would gain him release. "Tell me where," he demanded. "You can't just kidnap me you arrogant heathen!"

"Really?" John asked.

"That family owes me! I know Jack did something to my pa."

"I'll remember to thank him."

They traveled eighteen hours a day for fourteen days, north to Lake Superior and west to the end of the Great Lake, then north again until John wanted to stop. Thick crusted snow covered the ground. Few birds flew, but signs of bear, wolves, elk and moose were plentiful if you knew how to look.

He pulled Clayton down from the horse, climbed up and looked out at the frozen landscape. White glared off the snow and sky alike. It was hard to tell where one began and the other ended. John stared at a tiny dark speck in the sky. *A buzzard cleaning up carrion,* he thought. Appropriate.

Clayton squinted, trying not to believe what was slowly sinking in. "You can't leave me here? I'll die!"

"Maybe," John said, threw the bedroll on the ground next to a pocket knife, the one he'd taken from the hidden shack, and turned the horse, riding away slowly.

"You can't do this!" Clayton thundered, running after him. "You can't!" He stumbled in the snow. "You son of a bitch! I'll find you! You haven't seen the last of Clayton Flats!" he screamed, a high-pitched squeal that pierced the frigid air.

John stopped and turned in the saddle. "*This*," he said in deathly quiet, his eyes glistening black coals, "*is* my last sight of Clayton Flats."

He spoke in sorrow as the horse trotted south. "You should have considered your fate before you took my medicine woman."

Chapter Twenty-five

Maize and mayhem

Kat kept busy. Went into the woods, gathered late herbs, and prepared them for the drying frames. She tucked a knife in her boot, just in case.

At night, she had dreams. Clayton was coming to get her, and she couldn't run. Her legs wouldn't work. As hard as she tried, it felt like running through deep water, through slush. She woke herself trying to get away. Sweat dampened her bed and tears her face.

She didn't know where John was, and she couldn't concentrate on anything else. He came to her, in spirit, and his silent voice comforted her. He was coming. He was safe. That's what he told her, but . . .

During the day, she kept her sorrow at bay, stayed busy, but her eyes searched out every noise, hoping the sound was John returning, and fearing it could be Clayton.

December was closing in. The days were long, though shortened by the coming of winter sun. She spent them in the forest doing work John had trained her to do. She filled frame after frame with leaves, seeds and roots. She even dried a tray of jimson weed. Thought it could be useful in small amounts to alleviate pain when setting bones or stitching up wounds.

Besides, she thought, *you never know.*

Kate brought Jeannie and Becca to visit, and Sammy and Dot. They made a day of it, playing games with Sammy, taking turns holding Dot. It didn't cheer her. She wasn't a game playing kind of girl, but she went along with it because it seemed to cheer her mother.

"He'll be back, Kat," was all Kate could say. She had nothing else to offer. "Will you come for Thanksgiving?"

"You come here. I'll cook," Kat said. She didn't want to leave and miss him. She knew he'd be back if he could. And that was the concern . . . the 'if he could' part. She sensed him, though, and knew he felt her.

Kat's nights were even longer, and she spent many of them sitting outside wrapped in a quilt watching the moon and the raccoons, just like her mother had done when she lived at the cabin.

Harley joined her when he thought she wanted company. It was cold, and his blanket was wrapped around him, too. Only his curly head poked through, his nose and cheeks rosy in the moon's glow.

"You warm enough?" he asked.

Kat said she was fine and watched a night bird loop over the clearing.

"Nighthawk," Harley said. "Hear its 'peent, peent?'"

"I didn't notice what it was saying."

"That's how you know the difference between him and a bat. Nighthawks say 'peent' and bats don't."

When she didn't answer, Harley went quiet and waited.

Before long, Kat said, "Where is he, Harley?"

"I don't know. He'll be back, though. If it's at all possible, he'll be back."

"What does *if it's at all possible* mean?"

Kat's words were a mere whisper on night air, sliding off her tongue to take wing in the forest. She would go with them, search for John Crow, take him corn, and make him see her . . . as a woman.

There was no answer to her question. Well, there was, but not one Harley would give. He patted her hand and watched the nighthawk search for a mate. Soar high and dive straight downward in an aerobatic maneuver designed to impress his lady bird.

"John is capable, Kat, more so than any man I know," was all he could say.

Kat took a basket full of small muslin bags and headed to an area of the woods she had yet to harvest. Different herbs were only ready in late fall, and she was prepared to spend the day. It was warm for November; the sun was beginning to burn off morning fog, and the forest was busy with critters doing exactly what she was . . . gathering for the coming of winter.

She hummed a tune and decided to walk far and work backwards. She would make a mental note of what she passed and needed to stop for on the return trip.

Squirrels ran part way up tree trunks and turned to wait and watch as she walked near, making pretend lunges to scare her away.

"Foolish critters. You know I'm harmless," she told them, and they chattered at her back.

She wanted roots from black gum bark, hummingbird blossom, and greenbrier, or as John called it, *Pull Out a Sticker*. She smiled when she said it out loud and saw his face as she spoke. She smiled again, broader as the face in her mind grew larger.

"Pull out a sticker," she sang, turning it into a tune. "Pull out a sticker, a sticker you shall pull." The face in her mind stayed put, watched, didn't fade like the apparition it was. She whirled around to get away from it. "Go away!" she cried. "Leave me alone!"

"If that's what you wish," he said. "But I have something for you before I go." He moved toward Kat, and she knew. He was real, not an imaginary vision. A wish. It was John!

Kat dropped her basket and flew at him. Leaped into the air and wrapped her arms and legs around him. He steadied himself and hung on, buried his face in Kat's neck and murmured. "Selu, my Selu, I've missed you. I was so afraid."

"You're here," she whispered in his neck. "It is really you. I've dreamed of this."

"I, too. Many, many nights and days."

He kissed her softly, cherishing her lips with his, and then her eyes and brow, her cheeks and neck. His breath faltered, and his heart pounded in his chest. She tilted her head back to make more room for his lips, and her groan of pleasure nearly undid him. He shut his eyes and tried to still his growing fervor.

"Kat," he whispered, his voice harsh with passion. "I have a gift for you."

"You are my gift, John. Don't leave me, ever again. Don't let go."

"Never," he murmured, his lips moving over her skin. "You'll see." He set her down, slowly, not wanting to let go but needing to, and went to the horse he'd left nearby. He pulled a hide wrapped package from the saddle bag and handed it to her.

Kat looked up at him, eyes wide with hope. "Please tell me this is venison," she said.

John's face was immobile, and Kat was fearful of her own hope, her want of him too great. She held her breath and stared at him; firm, tan skin stretched over high, wide cheek bones, deep set black eyes, long ebony hair tied behind his neck. She loved him madly, totally, constantly. She couldn't remember not loving him. Surely, she hadn't been alive then. He possessed her, mind and soul. Her reputation for rational thought was based on a lie and flew away on wings of beloved, irrational passion.

"Wait," she said in a rushed whisper. Excitement bubbled from her lips. She flew to her basket. In one of the small muslin bags was a single ear of corn she'd been carrying since her escape from Clayton. She lifted the bag and went to stand in front of John, handed it to him reverently.

"I've been carrying this poor thing a long, long time . . . forever. You first."

When he peered in the bag, his face split in a smile that freed her heart, and she peeked under the hide wrapping to find a ham of venison.

"Love me, John," she said, moving toward him, her voice strong, indomitable. "We're married, now."

"Not in the eyes of your people," he said, with half a laugh, backing away, his hands spread out in defense of her determination.

"In my eyes, we are," Kat said, went to him and stood on her toes to kiss him, properly, as a wife. She touched his face, ran her hands over his broad chest and back. Felt his muscles quiver under her hands and reveled in her power. He loved her.

John, stood still, groaned and let his hands roam, to the curve of her waist and hips, to the swell of her breasts at her sides.

Kat stepped back and began to unbutton her shirt.

"Kat," he warned, but she continued.

"You love me," she said. "Say so."

"I do."

"You gave me venison. I gave you corn."

"Yes."

"Well?"

John took a deep breath. "Yes . . . yes. Wait." He retrieved his pack and spread a blanket on the ground.

When he placed her on it, she was as pure as the day she'd been born, without clothes to hinder their pleasure, without fear to stifle her passion, without inhibition to restrict their joy. He was a statue of perfection, a quiet god in the forest with Selu, his goddess.

"You are flawless, my Kat. So beautiful." He lay next to her and began to love her. She sucked in a deep, long breath when his lips tasted her cool skin. He teased with his tongue and gazed at her beauty. She stretched, arched to him, unashamed of her pleasure, her fiery senses, let her thoughts free and focused only on sensation, his touch.

Kat rose on one arm to look at him, take delight in his smooth splendor, his lean waist and broad chest. She touched him with pure ecstasy, as if he'd been designed for her alone.

"I don't know why you love this Cherokee, Selu, but I'm so happy you do."

"You were mine from the day you were born, John."

"But you weren't even a sparkle then, Kat. How could that be?" he said, a slow smile lighting his eyes, turning the black to deep, sun-lit brown, and twirling a length of her blonde, silky hair on his finger. He let it slide across his lips and kissed her as it fell.

"That doesn't matter. You're Kanati, the other side of my soul. You had to wait for me," she said with half lowered lids and a matching smile, loving these moments, the beginning of their lives together.

"What do you know of Kanati?"

"All I need to know. Kanati is you, and I am Selu."

They went home as dusk began to cool the sun in its slide over the horizon. Harley met them at the door, his eyes full of mischief and delight.

"Dinner's ready," he said. "But how about a sip in celebration?" When Harley went to retrieve the jug, Kat looked at the table set for three. Did he know John was with her? How would he have known?

Harley poured and began, "Here's to the return of Doc John, belatedly to Kat's return, and to their union." He heard gasps, saw Kat's growing blush, and continued. "Here's to the horse that showed up here about mid-day, riderless. Here's to the autumn forest, a good time for a walk."

Kat looked at John. John looked at Kat. Both had forgotten about the horse, had walked home without giving it a second thought.

"Here's to you both. I couldn't be happier." Harley drank deeply. John and Kat gulped theirs and then burst out laughing.

"Okay, Harley. Did you really take a long walk today?" Kat asked.

"My little secret," he said, his eyes squinting in laughter. "Let's eat."

They pulled a third chair in front of the hearth, and the three of them watched the flames. Kat touched John frequently as if to reassure herself he was there next to her. He did the same.

"Wait til you see what I've done while you were gone," she told him. "I've got tons of dried roots and leaves. I made some salves from my journal directions and stored the rest. We were waiting for you."

"You're good, Kat. Shall we start processing them tomorrow?"

Kat nodded, and Harley watched, wondered where they would go from here. He left them and went to his bed.

John lifted her hand, stared at it like he hadn't seen it before. He caressed her palm with one finger. "How did you get away, Kat? You haven't told me."

She told him about collecting the plants and herbs in preparation for a 'special' dinner.

"You helped," she said. "I knew I couldn't overpower Clayton. He's big and strong -- and stupid," she added with a laugh. "So, I fixed him a wonderful meal of jimson weed and sumac."

"Dangerous," he murmured. "How much did you give him?"

"That was the tricky part, getting the right amount and keeping his meal separate from mine. I didn't want to kill him, just incapacitate him. It worked."

John nodded, pride spilling from his eyes. "You could have died, Kat. Quite easily."

She nodded. "I know. I was afraid. I was more afraid of Clayton than the jimson, though."

John was thoughtful. He didn't want to pry. She was a private woman. But she needed to know she could talk about it, share it with him, lessen the burden of bad memories by dividing them between the two of them. He turned to her. "Did he hurt you?"

Kat's eyes grew dark in memory, and she shivered, felt Clayton's cruel hands on her breasts. "I teased him," she said, and followed her words with a false laugh.

"You don't have to talk, Kat."

"No, I think I do. Then it will be done. Gone. I will never have to think about him again."

"I needed to keep him away from me until I could feed him the jimson," she said, much more matter-of-factly than she felt.

"How did you make him leave you alone?"

"I flirted! I, Kat Ramey flirted! It was hard. It was disgusting! I didn't know what to do or how to do it."

"So . . . how did you do it? Show me."

Kat laughed a little and batted her eyelashes. She tilted her head down and looked up at him through her fluttering lashes. When she grew still, John watched memories cloud her eyes.

"He touched me, and I let him. I gagged and hid it so he wouldn't know. I kept promising. When supper was over, I would be his. I let him think I was a little eager, but just shy."

Moments went by in stillness.

"Once, I had his pocket knife in my hand, cleaning the jimson, and I wanted to shove it into his heart, drive it in again and again and again. I wanted him to die. I was hateful!"

Kat was silent, reliving the nightmare of those moments. "I was afraid, John. I hated the fear. But I was afraid I might die if I tried to kill him, that he'd take the knife and kill me in his anger."

"Come here, Kat. Let me hold you."

When she was in John's arms, the horror of those days faded, melted away in his warmth. Kat told him more, and they laughed. She described Clayton's hallucinogenic antics, how furious he was when he figured out what she'd done, how she'd ripped up her own shirt to tie him and had stolen his jacket to cover her nakedness.

"He was flopping around on the floor, and I was afraid to get close enough to rip up his shirt until I had tied his hands with mine, and his pupils were huge! I did think he might die."

"He would have deserved it," John said quietly.

"Your turn," she said, rubbing her cheek against his, nipping his ear with her teeth. "How did you come by the horse meant for him? Where have you been all this time?"

John nuzzled his face in Kat's hair, turned her to face him on his lap.

John told her about the bad feeling he had in Big Rapids, how he raced to the cabin to find she'd been taken, Kate telling him a horse and money would be left at the sugar shack. About tracking them.

"I must have gotten to the place where he kept you prisoner soon after you left, perhaps only hours later. He was still hallucinating, but was as angry as a hungry bear in spring. I untied his feet and made him walk to the sugar shack. He cursed all the way . . . mostly about you, you flirt."

Kat batted an eye and said, "Go on."

"I found the money, covered it with dusty old burlap sacks and stuffed it in a small barrel. A stranger wouldn't find it, but easy enough to find if you were looking. I thought a clue might help with that."

Kat laughed, hard. "I thought you left it to keep me from going crazy trying to figure how Clayton got loose. He was hogtied good, and those knots were tight."

"Yes, they were."

"What happened next?"

"Mostly I made him walk while I rode. He cursed me the whole time."

"Where? How far?"

"North to Lake Superior, west to where the lake ends, then north again. I told him I would set him free. He didn't believe me. I did. In snow country, with wolves and bears for company. There weren't any people for many miles. I gave him back the knife you wanted to plunge into his chest and my bedroll, which was more than he deserved."

Kat was deathly silent picturing it. Clayton standing alone on frozen tundra. Her breath was shallow, the memories harsh and frightening.

"Will he die?" she whispered.

"That's up to him. He has a chance. His choices will determine his fate. It's more than he gave you."

Kat settled against his chest, quiet, letting go of pain and fear, holding close the serenity that was her husband.

"I wanted to kill him. I would have preferred to kill him for hurting you," John said.

"I know."

Chapter Twenty-six

The next morning, he left before they were awake. Kat had always wanted a wolf companion like Kate's, and now John wanted one for her, as well. Clayton wouldn't have stood a chance with Wolf guarding. Wouldn't have gotten close enough to grab her. On his search for Kat, he'd seen a wolf den inhabited by a late breeding juvenile. It was providence. He saw she'd had five and would be, if not happy to give up one, at least better equipped to keep four alive rather than five in the coming winter. He'd help her out with meat left by the den, in thanks, if Kat could raise one for her.

He neared the den before dawn and was in a tree where he could watch when the female left to hunt. He waited until she was far enough away she wouldn't hear the whines of her pups when he reached in for one. He'd like a male, a big male. He felt around in the den until he found the one he wanted. He knew they were five or six weeks old because the mother left them for lengthy periods of time which meant they were in the weaning process and could leave her. When John pulled him out, he tried to be brave and pulled back his lips to show fearsome baby teeth, threatening John the best he knew how. He was fat and healthy, his yip strong.

John stuffed him in his shirt and strode quickly away in case the mother had heard and was loping her way back. The pup was asleep, snuggled against his stomach when he reached the cabin and Kat raced out to greet him. She threw herself against him, and John had all he could do to hold her away so she wouldn't crush her gift. Her face registered hurt at his rebuff, and John smiled knowing it would change momentarily.

"What's wrong?" she asked. "No morning hug? Hmmm…. Not liking this."

"Patience, Selu. I have a surprise." He pulled his shirt from the waistband of his pants, carefully holding the bulge. Kat watched, even more confused.

"A surprise in your shirt? Well, I do like your manly chest," she teased, then quickly looked around to see if Harley was lurking about. He'd made it clear he couldn't be trusted not to show up at inopportune times. Kat's croon when she saw the furry wolf pup was everything he'd hoped for. She nuzzled it, kissed it, nuzzled again and then kissed John. The cub snuggled in like it had been born to her.

"I need to ride into town," John said. "Want to go visit your mother and sisters?"

"If I can take Waya."

"You named him already? How did you know the Cherokee word for wolf?" he asked. "Are you in my head again?"

"A while ago, when I mentioned wanting a wolf, you called it a waya. So, that's him … Waya. And yes, I'm in your head always. I'll see if Harley wants to come."

Kate ran out when she heard them, Sammy following close behind. "John! It's so good to see you. How have you been? *Where* have you been? And what is that?" Kate cried. "It's fuzzy and cute and cuddly!"

"My very own wolf, a present from John," Kat told her.

"I love him," Kate said, and Sammy tried to pull him out of Kat's hands. She held him out for a kiss, and Waya came away with a Sammy wet spot on his head.

Harley left to find the girls while they introduced Waya to Wolf, carefully, not knowing how the older animal would respond to the presence of another wolf. He pushed him with his nose until Waya rolled and yipped sharply, then stood and pulled his lips back in a toothy warning. Wolf sat back on his haunches and stared. Waya got up, walked to Wolf and yipped again, took a piece of Wolf's belly fur in his mouth, shook it and growled.

Kat started to grab him, laughing at his boldness, but John asked her to wait. "I think Wolf can handle it. He's had little critters crawling on him nearly all his life."

Wolf pushed the pup again, and the process repeated until Waya got tired, curled between Wolf's legs, and went to sleep. Wolf rolled his brown eye and lay down, curled around the pup.

John left them to run his errands. In town, he found Jack at his office. Jamie was at the desk and waved him toward the back. He went in and closed the door.

Jack welcomed him heartily, motioned him to a chair and gave him a cup of coffee. "I know this isn't a simple social visit, so what's on your mind?"

"No. You're right."

"I'm glad to see you here, home, I mean. I worried something had happened," Jack said.

"I'm well. I've been on a journey. I left Clayton far to the north, in frozen country. It'll be up to him if he survives. I doubt he will, as it should be. I told Kat and want to ask your advice. I'm not sure who should be told about Clayton. It wasn't the lawful thing to do, but it was right. He should have to fight for his life as he made Kat do. So, who should be informed?"

Jack thought about it, was glad John had asked, and had not kept the knowledge to himself.

"Kate should be told. I know she worries, feels somehow responsible, and looks behind her constantly."

John nodded, knowing from Clayton's ranting Kate suffered from another in the Flats lineage long ago.

"Mel, too. I know he still looks for that face wherever he goes. Do you want me to let them know?"

John nodded. "Thanks. And Rob, his friend?"

Jack shook his head. "I think not. Not right now."

John went to the door and stopped, turned back, something obviously on his mind. He wasn't sure he should say anything, had battled with the decision. He came back to Jack and held out his hand. Jack took it wondering what this was about.

"I want to acknowledge your courage many years ago," John said. "Clayton talked, and I made assumptions. I don't want or need to know anything, but it was you he talked about, and I respect you. I tell you so you can know brotherhood and comfort. I believe you acted with honor."

Jack was quiet as John talked. He didn't agree or disagree, admit or deny, but he felt a weight lift. He'd known years ago what had to be done. For him, in his heart, there hadn't been a choice. It felt good to have a friendly hand on his shoulder, the hand of a wise man, and affirmation.

When John left, he went to his second meeting of the day. He found Ellen and Eldon at the table drinking coffee.

"Can I speak with you, privately?" John asked her.

Ellen was curious why Doctor John would seek her out and settled Eldon in the parlor to wait for them.

"Have a seat, John. What can I do for you?"

"It is customary to bring you a leg of venison, Mrs. Hughes, to ask for your granddaughter, Kat. However, I have given it to Kat already, and she has given me corn."

Ellen's eyes widened in confusion. It crossed her mind John might be a little mad. What on earth was he going on about venison and corn and Kat? Why would she want him to bring her meat? She stared. Her mouth opened to respond, but she couldn't think of anything to say, so she closed it.

"I accepted Kat's corn and she my venison," he said, trying to clear up her obvious confusion. When that didn't work, he tried another tack.

"I have high regard for Kat. She is Selu to me. I thought for a long time I was too old for her, or she too young, but she insists I am what she wants."

It finally came through to Ellen. He wants to marry Kat!

"Oh! I see!" Ellen said, a twinkle lighting her eyes. "Well, I don't know . . ." she teased. "Without venison, it's a poor request you make."

John nodded, "I realize that, now. I apologize and will find another leg of meat."

He started to rise, and Ellen burst out in a sweet giggle. "Oh, sit down. I'm pulling your leg -- there's your leg of meat," she said, loving her little joke and laughing.

John blushed and sat. Ellen patted his hand, everybody's grandmother at that moment.

"I'm sorry to tease, John. I was just so confused by what you were saying, I couldn't help it. When it finally came through -- well, you know the rest. Why are you coming to me?" she asked.

"You're the clan mother. It's your right to grant permission. I understand in your culture, I would ask Kat's father, but can't. So, I'm asking you."

"Does Kate know?"

"She will later today."

Ellen nodded and watched the beautiful man sitting with her. Even in his nervousness, he didn't fidget. He was outwardly still, serene. Black eyes looked into hers without flickering, hesitating. His bearing was regal. She admired his straight back and thought about when she tried to teach her girls to stand like a string was attached to their heads pulling them to the sky. Kate had hated it. *Not the string thing again....* she'd groan.

"And Kat, what does she say? Does she love you?"

"She says yes."

"And you?"

"I say yes."

"No, John. I meant, do you love her? More than life? Would you follow her around the nation if needed? Does she give you butterflies?"

John watched the older woman, grandmother to his bride, and wondered if she'd followed her husband where he wanted to go, whenever he wanted, had gotten butterflies in her stomach, and knew without asking she had. He would like to have known her when she was first in love and wearing it on her sleeve as he knew she would have done. She was still attractive in a stately, assured way, and he envisioned Ellen as a glowing bride, blushing and eager. The Hughes family made beautiful women.

"I do. I would. And the most striking butterflies come to me when Kat is near."

Ellen smiled, an open, beatific smile, and reached her hand to him. "I think you and our unusual Kat were born to wed. You most certainly have my blessing, but I'm not sure it counts for much with my daughter."

A burst of air escaped his chest, air he hadn't realized he'd been holding. "Thank you. Thank you."

Ellen laughed, a hearty laugh, from her belly. "You were nervous," she said. "I wouldn't have thought it."

He gave her a sheepish grin. "I was. I wouldn't have believed it, either."

"Go, talk to your new mother-in-law. She's scarier than I." She walked John to the door where he stopped, bent down to kiss Ellen's cheek. She put her fingers where his lips had brushed and blushed. "Welcome to the family, John Crow. I like you. Kat is a lucky woman."

"I'm a lucky man, Mrs. Hughes."

"Ellen, John."

He rode slowly back to the farm, enjoying the cold air, the sounds of autumn, the waning color of the trees. Fall smells assaulted his senses, and he inhaled deeply, grateful to the earth for sharing its bounty and scents. A chipmunk darted into the road, and he pulled on the reins to slow the buggy. Once across, it stopped and sat up, its cheeks puffed with acorns or seeds it would bury for the coming winter.

John watched, spent minutes thinking about his future with Kat, asking himself questions, and trying his best to answer them. Where would they live? Would they open a clinic in Hersey? Work from the cabin? Whose cabin was it? Kate's? No one knew. He had many questions and no answers.

"One step at a time, John. It's the best we can ever do. Maybe you should build a cabin. Your own. Yours and Kat's. Your beautiful, intelligent, passionate Kat."

Kate met him in the yard. "Kat said you'd want to speak with me, but she wouldn't say why."

"I do, Kate. Do you want to go in? Sit?"

"This sounds serious," she said with a nervous giggle. "Is everything alright?"

"Everything is fine."

When they were at the table, John laid it out. He'd just been through this, so he felt like he'd practiced, and now it would be easy. It wasn't entirely painless, but it was easier than the first time. At least now he knew better than to lead with venison and corn.

"Kat and I want to marry. I have the blessing of Ellen, and now I ask yours as is custom with my people."

Kate knew they had strong feelings for one another, but she wasn't prepared for this. She took her time, looking for words. Her mind fashioned Kat as a little girl in dirty, torn trousers, not a woman thinking of marriage.

"I will make her happy, Kate," he added, prodding.

Kate nodded. "Yes, I know you will try and that Kat thinks she loves you, John, but she's too young to know."

"Kat was never young," he said with a slow smile.

Silence hung in the kitchen, a heavy, grave hush that filled them as John struggled to understand her opposition.

"Do you have an objection to me?" he asked.

She shook her head. "No. I think you're a good man."

"Kat is a woman, Kate. She understands her own mind and has since I've known her."

"You're right about that," Kate said. "She always has."

"Then I don't understand."

Kate didn't either, and her confusion came out as anger. "I just don't think it's the right time. She's too young even if you don't think so. No. Not now. I don't have anything else to say about it."

She didn't hear Kat come in the room and was startled when she spoke.

"I am not too young, Ma, no younger than you when you first loved my father. Would have married him if you'd had the chance."

Kate's head whirled around. Her eyes were startled, round owl eyes, pools in her face.

John got up, put his arm around her. "It's not a good time, Kat."

"Yes, it is. It's the perfect time. Ma, John and I are going to be married. In fact, we're already married ... by Cherokee custom. I gave him corn. He gave me venison. We were wed, and there's nothing you can do about it."

Kate blanched. Except for two circles of red on her cheeks, she was white.

"That's silly, Kat. You can't be married by an ear of corn and a piece of meat."

"Who are you to denigrate Cherokee customs? We're going, John. Will you go get Waya, please, and Harley?"

When he was gone from the room, Kat walked to stand in front of her mother. She waited until Kate looked at her and then spoke. Her words were deliberate, distinct and chosen with thought.

"I'm not sure what's happening with you right now, so I'm going to forgive you for your cruelty. This isn't you, but it is me. And you know very well that I'm certain about my love for John and his for me."

She paused, hoping her mother would come to her senses, come back to who she had always been. When it didn't happen, she continued.

"He is the other half of me, of my spirit. I loved him before I knew him because he is everything I love, respect, understand. We were married in the woods, and that's good enough for me. I only wanted a church wedding for you and the rest of the family. That will be your call."

She turned and walked out. John and Harley were waiting outside, and Waya rolled unsteadily toward her, already attached to his charge.

Her eyes were dry, her heart sore. John put an arm around her, and she was comforted. No words were needed.

Harley watched the interplay and saw pain in two sets of eyes. The conversation in the kitchen obviously hadn't gone well. Something was bothering Kate. He had noticed it a while back. She hadn't been herself since . . . well for some time.

"You know," he drawled. "I'd kind of like to stick around here for a bit. Do you two mind?"

"Of course not. Do you want us to come back for you?"
"No. It's a great day. I'll walk home later."

He found Kate upstairs in Dot's room. She was standing next to the baby's bed watching her sleep. She hadn't heard him, and he felt like an interloper watching Kate when she was unaware of his presence, like he was peeking through a window at her while she undressed. Minutes passed and Harley cleared his throat to let her know he was there.

Startled, she turned abruptly, her hand to her heart. "I thought you left."

"No. I wanted to spend a little time with you. I don't get to see you often enough since Dot came."

Kate nodded and looked back down at the sleeping baby. "She's a good sleeper. She likes her thumb and her bed. That's good for me 'cause I'm too old for this."

"Are you feeling old, Kate?"

She didn't look at Harley but smoothed an already neat blanket.

"I am old, Harley. So are you."

"Never," he whispered. "And neither are you."

Kate turned to leave, and Harley took her arm.

"How about a little picnic in the woods? Some bread and cheese and maybe a bit of cognac?"

"I'm busy, Harley. I can't just leave Dot and Sammy to play in the woods." She pulled away from him and strode heavily down the stairs.

"Kate," he called after her. "What's wrong?"

"Nothing, I just have things to do."

"I'm going to be nosy, Kate. Did you just refuse to give your permission for Kat and John to marry?"

"Yes. I did. And that *is* my business, Harley. But I did refuse. She's too young to know what she wants."

"And you, when you were her age, did you know?"

"That was different. It was Mark."

He let her go and searched out Mel. He was in the barn with Becca and Jeannie, cleaning stalls and feeding the calves. He heard Jeannie's high pitched squeals of delight before he got there. A calf was sucking on a bottle she held, and Jeannie was in baby-critter heaven.

Harley stood at the door taking in the image. It was peaceful and cheerful. A farming family doing what they love and caring for each other. Mel handed Jeannie another bottle, and she held it out to a second calf who was waiting not so patiently. It butted against the rails of the calf pen, bleating like a lamb.

"I don't think that animal knows it's a cow, Jeannie. Listen to it."

"He thinks he's my baby, Harley. Don't tell him he isn't; it'll hurt his feelings. Want to feed him?"

"No, but thank you. I'll just watch for now."

"I didn't know you were staying. I'm glad."

"Me, too, Copper Top."

"Were you looking for me?" Mel asked. "I was just puttering here with the girls, but they've got it under control, so I can leave."

"Would you want to walk a bit?" Harley asked.

Mel nodded and handed Becca another bottle. "Back in a bit," he told her.

When they were down the road a ways, Mel commented briefly on the great weather and then came straight to the point. "Is this about Kate? If you have questions, so do I. What I don't have is answers."

"Hmmm . . . so I'm not imagining things."

"Nope. I don't know what's going on in her sweet brain, but she isn't content. I've asked about it, but she says she's fine."

"Is she well? Physically, I mean."

"I think so. She's just . . . not happy. I don't think she's ever been happy, here. At the farm. But I thought she'd adjust eventually."

Harley thought about it. Considered Mel's words. He pondered the years she and Mel had been married. Things began to coalesce.

Mel asked a question, and Harley raised a finger, said "Wait a moment, please."

Mel walked silently, his thin frame casting a long shadow on the dirt road. He hadn't put on the lost weight or regained the lost muscle. He was lean, and his breath was still raspy. He wouldn't admit to ill health, give it a place in his existence. If he said it was true, it might be, so he didn't.

Harley watched the shadow, and ideas were set in motion. He began to understand Kate's odd behavior. "Think about this," he said to Mel, growing more excited as his understanding grew.

"This isn't a pretty picture, but it's the truth and hard to hear, I imagine." He turned to Mel and unconsciously picked up his pace. "I'm just gonna talk this through, and you can tell me what you think about it. That okay?"

When Mel agreed, Harley began and didn't stop for over a mile.

"Right after you and Kate married, Kat left, moved immediately back to the cabin; Rachel got pregnant, married, and left the baby to Kate's care; the Spanish flu epidemic attacked the nation, and Kate cared for her sick family and friends, watched them die. They left her, too. Oh yeah, and the war. A little thing like war. Jamie was already gone, and Robbie, Charlie and others left; and when life finally got back on track, Rachel appeared with a second baby to be raised by Kate and left, and the son of the man who nearly raped her and killed her dog, showed up and abducted her daughter. She didn't leave Kate, but she was taken away from her."

He paused for breath, reflecting on Kate's anguish over Clayton. "She felt responsible for Kat's abduction. She lamented her lack of accountability as if it was her fault. Like she should have done something a long time ago, the first time the monster tried to step foot into the cabin. She should have done something. For all her brave words about taking care of business, she'd been passive, invited me to stay with them, and went about her days as if nothing had occurred. Then Clayton took Kat, could have raped or killed her. In Kate's mind, it would have been her fault."

"But that's ridiculous. She wasn't responsible for those men," Mel said, aghast by Harley's words, not believing.

Harley went on like Mel hadn't spoken. "She's been the caretaker, and people keep leaving or dying on her, ever since Mark left. She can't do anything about it. Now she has two new ones to raise, to care for. She's frightened."

Mel had listened, mostly without interruption and was silent, thinking, when Harley paused for breath. Geese honked, filled the sky with their joy, and late migrating mallards flew overhead in imperfect v-formations. The lead duck flew point like a soldier, out in front of the others to assess the terrain and keep the rest safe. Heading south, following the direction of one duck.

Harley looked up, watched the formation change, ebb and flow, but always following the leader and saw Kate. She was point. She had taken on the responsibility for everyone's care, to see them safely across whatever sky they flew. He broke into Mel's quietude.

"She didn't choose point position," he said, indicating the overhead mallards. "She accepted it out of necessity when Mark died and left behind four daughters. That was the beginning."

"Are you crazy, Harley? What on earth do ducks and geese have to do with Kate?"

"See how they follow one mallard duck? One Canadian goose? Like a point soldier."

"Of course, they always fly in a v-formation."

"Kate has been lead duck for so long, she's forgotten how to fly in line behind others, forgotten how to give up point. Or she never knew how, and now she's afraid to let go of point and try it."

"Well, let's say you're not as crazy as you sound. She's unhappy. What can I do to make her happy?"

"I don't know."

"Great ... all that for a 'don't know?'"

"Understanding is the beginning, and I think we're on the right track. Let's give it some time. How about a Christmas party out at the cabin? A real sledding, skating party like we had ... Damn. I almost forgot."

"What?"

"The last sledding party we had was when Mark agreed to see a doctor in Grand Rapids. When they found out he had cancer and then had surgery. You were there," Harley said.

"Well, that's out then."

"No. No, it isn't. That is just what we'll do. As long as Kat agrees. It's her house, too."

"Alright," Mel agreed, but hesitantly. "I guess we'll have a winter party. When?"

"I'll get back to you, but I'm thinking two weeks. On Saturday."

Chapter Twenty-seven

Winter 1919

Jack and Ruthie came out early to help with the party preparations and stopped to get Ellen, Eldon and Verna on the way. John, Jack, Harley and Verna left to gather fire wood; Ellen tucked her charge, Eldon, into a chair in front of the fire.

"This is spectacular," he said. "I'd give up my twelve-room house for this cabin. No wonder Kate loves it so much."

"Kat loves it, too," Ellen said. "And John and Harley. We all do, actually."

"How about a cognac?" he asked.

"How about a tea? It's not yet noon."

"Okay, but it *is* a special day you know," he said with the Woodward charismatic grin. Waya stood on his hind legs begging to be a lap wolf, which promptly happened. He curled up and fell instantly into dreamland on the lap blanket.

"That's Waya. Yes, it is special. I'll bring some tea."

Ruthie joined Kat at the stove to put the finishing touches on the venison pot roast Kat had ready to go over the hearth coals.

"I have apples pared and sliced," Kat told her, "but I saved the crust for Grandma to make. Hers is the best."

"I heard that, Kat. Are you sweet talking me into work?"

"Yup. Is it working?"

"It's yes - not yup, girl. And yes, it worked," she said, grinning. "Where's your rolling pin and pastry cloth? Have you and your handsome man set a date yet?"

Ruthie spun around and then leaped at Kat, folding her in a bear hug. "You're getting married? When? Why didn't you tell me? Why didn't Kate say anything?"

Kat's glance roamed the ceiling, to Eldon and Waya, over the floor, looking for the best response. She rubbed her forehead.

"What's wrong, Dear?" Ellen asked. "Is there a problem?"

"Yes. The problem is Ma. She won't give permission, and John won't marry me without it. I told him he was a crazy Cherokee."

"You didn't!" Ruthie gasped.

"Of course I did. I spoke the truth! He is."

"Well, now. Did your mother say why?" Ellen asked.

"She gave a ridiculous reason. I'm too young to know what is best for me."

Both Ruthie and Ellen laughed out loud.

"Really? She said *you're* too young after her mourning period of ten years waiting for Mark? Starting at sixteen!" Ruthie said.

"Don't worry, Sweetie. I'll talk with her."

"Do that, Grandma, 'cause I am already married. I gave him corn. I don't need *her* permission to lie with *my* husband. Just John's. Crazy Cherokee! I gave him corn, damn it!" She slapped the brick of lard on the counter and reached for the bag of flour.

Ruthie's eyebrows raised, and Ellen shook her head, indicating 'don't ask.'

"Would you like a little wine while we work?" Ruthie asked. "I brought some of my own."

"Now, I just told Eldon he had to wait."

Ruthie held up a bright red bottle and wiggled it in front of them. Ellen laughed, and Kat said, "Why not? Yes - - not yup, Grandma. I think I will partake."

"Yup, me too," Ellen said with a devilish grin.

They were laughing and on a second glass when Willie and Rob pulled into the clearing, right behind Mel's buggy. Jeannie leaped out before the wheels quit rolling, giving a whoop of delight.   Becca followed, then turned to help Sammy down.

He imitated Jeannie's whoop of joy. He was happy to be here. The cabin had been his and Jeannie's home twice for extended periods when flu victims were at Mel's house. Sometimes he missed it.

When he talked about it, Mel shook his head, thinking there was something disturbing about the cabin, something otherworldly. It got to people, had a hold on them that was unlikely for an inanimate object, four walls and a roof. What did everyone see in -- love about -- the cabin?

They blew inside like a winter tornado, all talking at once, stomping snow, hauling in casserole dishes and baby supplies. Dot was immediately passed around, but she had other ideas and demanded to be put on the floor to show off her falling skills. She did it well. Crawl to a chair. Haul her chubby butt up, hang on to walk, and fall down. It was always good for cries of delight and applause. If not, she could yell. Hollering worked, too.

"Are we about ready to head outside? Skate -- sled? Have a bonfire?" Becca asked.

"It's up to Kat. She's the hostess here," Kate said. "How are things in the kitchen?"

"We are done, ready to go. Grandma and Aunt Ruthie are terrific. They're maniacs with a rolling pin and lard."

Kat hadn't said anything specific, but Kate felt slapped. Maybe it was her eyes. They regarded directly and held on to her mother's too long, waited for Kate's to turn away before they moved on.

"Eldon and I'll sit with Dot. It'll be good to get to know her," Ellen said.

"Are you sure, Mother? She won't be too much for you?"

Ellen's back went up, and she stiffened. "What are you talking about? I take care of this big baby every day," she said, slapping Eldon's shoulder. "I haul his wood and groceries, clean his monstrosity of a house, do his laundry, and fix his meals. Do you think I can't care for a little baby for a couple of hours? What is wrong with you?"

Kate had the sense to look chagrinned. She hadn't meant to insult her mother, didn't know why she had or what was wrong with her. She didn't know anything, anymore. She felt scrunched in the middle, not child, not parent, not needed as parent. She loved and cared for two who could be snatched back in a moment if Rachel decided she wanted them back.

"I'm sorry, Ma. Truly. I didn't mean you weren't capable. Of course you are. I'll just get her things."

She hustled to the stash of paraphernalia they'd brought in earlier and shuffled through it, unshed tears stinging her eyes as she bent to the task. She pawed around longer than needed, waiting for her eyes to dry before going back to her mother with diapers and other necessaries.

"Here, and I *am* sorry," she said.

"Forget it, Kate. It's done with. Go play with your big, handsome husband and your family. Let me have this little girl."

Ellen sat next to Eldon and rocked Dot who settled in for a snooze.

"My charge is fuzzier than yours," Eldon said.

"True. Mine has a diaper."

Eldon's face paled. "Do you think? Would he?"

Ellen raised her eyebrows. "Don't know."

They raced down the frozen creek, looking out for open spots where spring water kept ice from forming. Harley slid most of the way on his bottom. Jack skated in circles around Mel, taunting him all the way.

"For a big guy, you're not much of an athlete, are you?" He grabbed Kate's arm and sped off with her. "Got your girl now!"

"Catch us if you can!" she shouted, having too much fun at Mel's expense.

"Go, Mel. Catch him!" Jeannie shouted. "You can do it!"

Wolf tore off after them, almost knocking them both off their feet as the skaters skidded to a stop, and the animal just skidded into them.

Mel was not fleet footed on ice. He stood up, which was better than Harley was doing, but each step was an invitation to crash.

"As soon as I get these skates off, you'd better be on the run, my friend."

When they tired of skating, they dragged sleds and Mel's toboggan to Big Hill, named for its size as king amidst all the smaller, rolling hills surrounding the Hersey valley. With Mel in front catching most of the snow, Jeannie, Jamie, Becca and Kate behind, and Verna riding caboose, they flew down the hill, crashed at the bottom in a heap of arms, legs and laughter.

Mel found Kate in the snowy rubble and rubbed his cold nose on hers then licked her lips. "Ummm, cold lips good," he said. "Having fun?"

Wolf leaped around the heap of humanity, howling, stuck his nose on Mel's face and pushed.

She nodded and licked Mel's lips. "Yes, frozen lips are good, and I *am* having fun. You?"

"Yes. I am. This has been long overdue."

"Want to build a fire and get warm?"

"Not til we find a Christmas tree. Maybe two. One for Kat and one for us."

They collected the rest, sipped at frostbite medicine, and shuffled off in the direction of the world's best Christmas trees. Sammy alternately rode on Mel's shoulders and ran beside Jeannie. Jamie threw snowballs at Becca who pelted him back, harder, and then ran to hide behind a nearby tree. Jack strolled hand in hand with Ruthie. Harley and Verna brought up a straggling rear.

Kate watched and remembered the first time Jack had held Ruthie's hand. Harley had made them all hold hands as they left the cabin-- for safety, he'd said. They'd been looking for the perfect Christmas tree then, too. *God, how long ago was that?* she thought. "Damn . . . sorry," she whispered.

"What is it about the holidays that makes you cuss, Kate?" Mel said with a sly grin. "I've been saving you from becoming infamous in your sacrilege for years, now."

"Out loud, huh?"

He nodded.

"I was thinking about the first time Jack held Ruthie's hand. Harley made them. It was a long, long time ago. I think it might make me sad."

"Why, Kate?"

"I don't know. It just does. Were you with us or . . .?" Kate didn't finish. "I'm sorry."

"You don't need to be sorry, Kate. You can say it. I think Mark was with you then, and it's okay."

Kate didn't respond, just took Mel's hand in hers and walked on. Mel slowed his stride to let the others move ahead of them a ways.

"Something's going on with you, Kate. I wish you'd tell me what it is."

"Nothing. I'm fine. Really."

"You're fibbing, Kate."

"Stop it, Mel. You don't know what's in my mind, so quit telling me you do." There was irritation in her voice and her eyes. She chewed on her lower lip, then grimaced and closed her eyes as if she'd just been told a horror story and could block it out if she didn't see.

Mel faltered a step, surprised to hear bitterness, resentment in her words. He didn't know how to respond, how to make it better, just knew he wanted to. He had to. He wanted his old Kate back and wasn't sure where she'd gone -- or why. Was it him? Did she not want to be married to him? He was still weak from the illness, but he was the same man, the one who cherished her, loved her more than life.

Silence covered them like a cold fog, and Kate took his hand again in hers. She'd dropped it in her anger and felt remorse.

"I'm sorry, Mel. Truly. I don't know what's the matter with me."

"It's okay. Forget it and let's catch up with the others." They found their trees, teased as usual about who had to cut it down and sipped a toast to Christmas. Harley won the right to cut Kat's tree. They watched him kneel on the snowy ground, lean his heavy bulk under the tree and roll . . . and roll, down the slight incline, and on down the hill. Wolf chased him, leaped in the air and pounced.

"Where you going, Harley? Trying to get out of a little work?" Jack called. "You look like a snowball! Attack, Wolf!"

Wolf did and Harley defended himself, got up and waddled back up the hill. He tried again but his belly kept getting in the way. John gently took the saw from him and the honor of cutting the tree.

He whispered a few words before he cut, and Kat repeated them, giving respect and thanks to the tree for giving its life for their joy.

"Should we not cut this tree for a frivolous reason, John?" Kat asked, near his ear so she wouldn't be heard. He felt her warm breath on his neck, and heat invaded his body.

"Of course we should," he stammered and set her back a pace so he could work. "It wants to give us joy. And later, it will give us fire. And we thank it. As it should be," he said with a warm smile and an even warmer hug. "You're wise to question. I truly *love* that about you."

"Then you could marry me," she said, and added with Kat-like candor, "or just be with me -- your wife," she added, moving closer again, taking up the space between them.

"I *adore* that about you," he said, a meaningful look bringing to mind their bodies tangled in passion.

"What? What do you adore? Tell me," she whispered, her eyes on fire, sparkling with humor.

"You're hard to tease, Kat. You keep turning it back on me."

"Don't know what you mean. But I'll smother you with kisses right here and now, and pretty soon you won't care the reverend hasn't married us."

She moved away from him, and John shook his head, marveling at her. What a woman she was. He didn't know how to handle her most of the time. It wouldn't do any good anyway. Kat was her own person, her own woman. Had been since he'd known her. She knew her own mind, and he *worshipped* that about her.

They hauled the trees back, taking turns with the rope, and lit the bonfire they'd stacked in the clearing. They poured cordial and moonshine, Ruthie's wine and hot chocolate. They bundled up Dot and brought her out to join the festivities. Ellen and Eldon stayed inside. Let the youngsters freeze, the foolish children.

As the sun began its westerly slide, Kate took Dot from Ruthie. "She needs a change and to get warm. Bring them all in for supper in a little bit, please."

Inside, Ellen followed her daughter and great granddaughter to Kate's old bedroom where they'd set up a place for Dot to sleep. Kate unraveled her from the bundle of clothes and changed her, marveling to Ellen about the beauty of the baby.

"Was she good for you, Ma?"

"Of course. She was perfect."

"I'm sorry I insulted you earlier. I didn't mean anything by it."

"I know. You've seemed a bit out of sorts lately, though. Anything going on?"

"No, nothing more than usual. And I haven't been out of sorts."

Ellen stepped back and looked up at her daughter.

"I haven't," Kate repeated.

"Are you going to stomp your foot, too?"

"Don't treat me like a child, Ma. I'm not."

"You certainly aren't, but sometimes you act like one."

Kate hung her head, bent over Dot and nuzzled her bare belly. She blew a couple of belly bubbles and listened to Dot giggle.

"Why have you not given John permission to marry Kat?" Ellen asked, coming at it directly, the only way she knew.

It took Kate by surprise. She hadn't known Ellen was aware of Kat's fondness for John, let alone that they wanted to marry. She didn't answer right away, took time to formulate the right words.

"I don't want to discuss it," Kate said.

"Burying your head in the sand won't make it go away. Besides, John Crow is a good man. One of the best."

"Of course he is. That's not the problem."

"Then what is, Kate?"

"She's too young. That's all."

"Pshaw. Kat's never been young. And you were, too. Did your age change anything?"

"That's just it!" Kate hissed in frustration. "No one gets it! Why does everything have to change constantly? Why can't anything stay the same for a single, damn minute without changing? I can't keep up! I don't want to!" She ran out of steam and paused, saw her mother's sad eyes and regretted her outburst. "Sorry."

"For the cussword?"

"That, too."

Ellen sat on the bed and pulled Dot on her lap to dress her. Dot nestled into Ellen's arms and stuck her thumb in her mouth, content with her world. Kate watched and wondered where her mother found her resilience, her fortitude.

"I'll never have your grit, Ma. I used to think I'd never want to be like you. Should I not say that? I was wrong. How do I get to be you?"

Ellen smiled. "Where *ever* you are Will, are you listening? Kate wants to be like me." Turning to Kate, she added, "Would you say that again? I don't think I heard you correctly."

"Stop it. You heard me."

Ellen straightened and stood with Dot in her arms. She handed her to Kate. "This is yours," she said. "Oh, you didn't give her birth, but she is your charge and a change you must accept -- happily."

Ellen was quiet and thoughtful for moments, her eyes turned back in time. "Your father loved change, something I had difficulty accepting. He always wanted to move on, do something new. I hated it, but it was his life, almost more than I was. He grew bored and discontented with sameness. You have been like him in most ways ... except now. Change is not always easy, Kate, but it's inevitable. That I know, and

I've learned a lot over the years, much from our friend, Harley. Give those two young people your blessing. You will regret it if you don't. Kat won't take your ridiculous opposition lightly."

"I'm not ridiculous."

"About this, you are."

Before everyone left the party, Kat and John began packing for their rounds, sorting the herbs and salves, making sure the medicine bags held everything they might need. They'd leave before dawn.

It was something John had been doing since he began staying at the cabin. People depended on his care for miles surrounding Hersey, Reed City and Big Rapids. Sometimes Kat went with him, learned from him and more recently tended patients herself. She was a physician in her own right, and some of the ill or wounded felt more comfortable in her care than with John. She teased him when it happened, and he reveled in it.

"I didn't know you were doing this," Kate told her. "How long has this been happening?"

"Awhile. It's not something to get upset about. I'm working. Just like you did, Ma."

Kate stewed. "Damn, Kat. What else don't I know?"

"You don't know what you don't want to know, Ma. That's all. I'm going early, so I'll say goodnight to our company now."

They were already hitching their horses and buggies and passing out hugs. Kat and John stood together, hostess and host, with Harley on the fringe to wish the travelers well on their journeys home.

Kate pulled Mel aside while Becca and Jamie hitched Mel's team.

"What would you think . . . what would you tell me . . . if Dot and Sammy and I, and Jeannie, wanted to stay here with Harley for a couple of days? Just a couple while Kat and John are away. Keep Harley company?"

"What would I say, huh?" Mel tilted his head to look into Kate's eyes. He rasped his hands over late day stubble and studied her. He was a slender shadow, a thin reed standing tall by her.

"Do they know they want to stay here?"

"Well, no, but they'd have fun."

"I wouldn't tell you anything, Kate. I'd ask why, though."

"Why?" Kate faltered. She didn't know why. What could she say? I don't know. I just want to. That's why. I want to go back to when it was Harley and me, with the girls. When they were little, when they were mine. I want to work my ass off for them because I was all they had. I was their world. And they were mine. But she didn't say any of that. Tears came to her eyes and her back stiffened.

"Sure," he said. "Becca, Jamie and I will keep the home fires burning. You and Harley have fun."

He pulled her against his chest, and Kate could feel his heart pounding. He kissed her cheek, her hair. She felt the warmth of his breath, and tears threatened. Mel saved her with a pat on her bottom and a push toward the cabin.

"See you in a day or so." He swung his long legs into the buggy and clicked to the mares. Kate waved and Harley took her arm and led her inside.

They settled Sammy and Dot in Jeannie's room, and Jeannie volunteered to stay with them. She didn't want to be with the adults anyway because something just wasn't right. She was happier taking care of Dot and Sammy.

Kat went to her room after saying a stilted goodnight to her mother and hugging Harley, saying, "This is a three-day trip so expect us back on Tuesday." Waya followed Kat, watching every step, already protecting her from harm.

Harley nodded and Kate knew it was something they were used to, they'd done this before. She felt like an unneeded appendage, a third arm, an interloper.

This is my cabin! Her heart screamed. Mine! *You* are my child, mine!

Wolf nudged her leg, and she automatically reached to pat his head. "I love you, too. Thank you," she murmured.

John made a point of saying he was going to Rachel's old room. The attic space was his when he was here. Kate said goodnight, tried to make it warm, but it didn't feel warm or even more than polite.

Harley picked up the jug and pulled two glasses from the shelf. He brought them to the rocking chairs in front of the hearth and handed them to her. He stoked the fire, making white sparks and blue flames dance.

When he turned to sit, he saw the tears collect and not fall, saw her chest rise, the intake of breath, and he knew if he said anything at the moment it would be Kate's undoing. So, he sat. Poured. Rocked. Sipped. And time strode on, a slow healer but medicine, still, for the heart and soul, mind and body.

The fire dwindled, and Harley added logs to the blue embers. Their crackle and hiss were the only sounds in the room. He sat again and watched the flames grow, leap and curl around the new logs, a red and blue dance in the flames.

"Are you gonna sit here all silent and stoic, or are you gonna talk?" He sipped his drink and glanced her way.

Kate ran her fingers through her hair, rubbed her scalp and squeezed her head.

"There's really nothing to talk about, Harley."

"Hmmm," he murmured, nodding and rocking.

"Really," she insisted.

"See that bed by the wall?" he asked. "I'm about to fall into it and get some sleep. This old body is tired."

"Me, too. See you in the morning."

"While your dreaming, Kate," he said putting their glasses in the sink and turning to her, "dream up an answer to why you're here instead of at home with your husband."

"That's not nice, Harley. You've never been mean, why now?"

"But I've always been honest, and the same has been true for you, Kate. You're hurting people, without reason, and I can't for the life of me figure it out."

Kate got up, walked over to Harley and stared at him, anger stinging eyes. "And this is my home."

Harley raised his eyes and stared at her. He took a deep breath. "Now you're mad," he said. "If you're my Kate, you'll stomp your foot, recognize truth when it hits you in the face, and then admit it. If you've turned into someone else, you'll turn around and walk away. Go to your cold, lonely bed. Who are you?"

"You're talking nonsense, Harley! What truth do I need to recognize? Who am I hurting?"

"Kat and John, Ellen, your husband, and that's just for starters."

Kate turned and walked back to the rocking chair, sat hard in it, and pushed her foot irritably against the floor. The chair creaked loudly, a protest to Kate's violent rocking, a testament to her frustration.

Harley sat again, rocked slowly. Put another log into the waning flames thinking if he sat with her long enough, they'd talk about what was really bothering Kate, his Kate.

He looked around the room and noted the small changes Kat and John had made to the cabin. A picture of a Cherokee chief hung over the sink. A blue pottery bowl sat in the middle of the table, one John had given to Kat. A woven reed basket sat on the floor by the hearth. As Harley took note of the changes, a spark of a thought occurred, a glimmer of what might be a clue to Kate's unhappiness.

"Did you see the basket John brought?" he asked, pointing a toe toward the bright container. "It's colorful, no?"

Kate nodded but didn't respond.

"How about the picture on the wall?"

She nodded again.

"Did you notice the bowl on the table?"

"Yes, Damn it. I saw them all. What are you doing?"

"Just wondering if you noticed all the new things. That's all."

"Are you trying to upset me?"

Harley got up and poured himself a small cognac, lifted his glass to her, and raised his eyebrows in question. It felt like it could be a long night. Kate expelled a long breath of air and nodded.

"Why would pointing out things John and Kat brought to the cabin be upsetting?" he asked, and held out her drink, noticed her hand tremble when she reached for it. "Why would new things upset you at all?"

"Because . . . I don't know!" Kate pushed hard and the chair creaked louder.

"What do you have against John?"

"What makes you think I anything against him? I don't."

"Well, let's see. You fire up at the mention of anything to do with him. You adamantly refuse to give permission for them to marry. A perfectly logical, practical and truly blessed union of two people who love each other. Why would you sanctify that union? Hmmm. See my point?"

"She's too young."

"Hogwash."

"You're not thinking straight."

"You're not thinking at all."

Silence pressed in on them.

"You're a crazy old coot," Kate said, the hint of a grin on an otherwise frowning face.

"Yes, I am."

"And I'm getting old, Harley."

"Yes, you are. We all are. I, especially."

"I'll be half a century in a couple of years. I have a baby and a toddler. Does that make any sense to you?"

"The world doesn't have to make sense. You know that."

"What if I mess up again?"

"Just when did you first mess up?"

"Rachel."

Harley patted her hand and left it there. She let him.

"Rachel is absent, at least temporarily, but Kat's not leaving you, Kate. She's not going anywhere. Neither is this cabin. But some things you can't own. People. This place. They were never yours to own. You're just the caretaker for a time. Even your girls. How much did you want to run when your mother corralled you, tried to force you into her mold?"

"But it's not the same. What I love leaves," she said, her voice a sad whisper. "Somehow, it goes away if I relax and don't hang on with both hands."

"You can get white knuckled making fists, Kate, but the harder you try to hold onto people, the less likely they are to hang around."

Kate added a log to the fire and stood watching sparks fly up the chimney. How many days and nights had she tended this fire? How many nights had she spent in her father's rocking chair, loving this room, exhausted by work and worry yet content with her world? Do you only know contentment if you are worn out? If the weight of the family is on your shoulders? If the wolves at your door are not your friends?

"Why are you here, Kate?"

"Just visiting. I love this place. You know I do."

"It isn't your home anymore."

"Harley . . . I miss it. I miss my world. The way it was."

"You have a beautiful home, a big beautiful home, with a big beautiful husband in it," he said grinning, hoping against hope his words would lighten her mood.

Kate nodded but didn't speak. A lump grew in her chest and choked her.

"Are we going to go through everything tonight?" he asked. "Cause I'm going to get another sip if we are. Want one?"

She nodded again, a forlorn look in her eyes that went to his heart, a sharp knife twisted . . . and he bled.

"Aw, Kate," he moaned as he went to the kitchen counter. When he came back, there were wet tracks on Kate's face she didn't bother to wipe away. They continued to follow their salty trail on her cheeks, and Harley couldn't look.

"You need to talk, Kate. Tell me what is wrong. Now."

Kate took a long, deep breath. "I wish I knew. All I know for sure is I'm not happy. Worse than that; I'm unhappy. But only sometimes! Not always. I'm no longer in control of my own life, let alone anyone else's. How can I raise more children? I have no control! Over anything!"

She took a necessary breath.

"Are you done?" Harley asked.

"No! I'm useless at home. I miss mine. My home, not Mel's. I'm not necessary there. I'm just an appendage, and I want all my children, not two out of four and two new ones. I'm a failure, and I am getting old! I hate it! All of it!"

She paused, hung her head, and looked at her fingers twisted together like binder twine left out in a storm and blown hard against a barbed wire fence. Suddenly she giggled. "God, I'm awful." Then she giggled again and again. When Harley was sure she was really laughing, he joined her, and they laughed together, filled the night with noise.

"Is that all?" he said when he caught a breath. Then added, "Shhh, we'll wake the babies." And they started in again.

Chapter Twenty-eight

On the second morning, Kate was wiping circles on the window panes and staring out at the snow, asking herself what she was doing here. Wolf put his feet on the sill and looked, too, blew hot air from his nostrils and painted pictures with his nose in the steam.

"Old habits die hard, don't they Wolf? You always drew pictures on the glass just like the girls."

She cooked in her old pots, cleaned her old table, but it didn't feel the same. She went to bed in her old room and lay wide eyed and awake, wondering if the bed was much bigger than her old one. She shifted, lay on her side and then on her back. She punched her pillow.

"Move closer, Wolf. I'm cold," she complained. Wolf rolled a brown eye and stayed where he was.

She nudged him with a foot. "Come on, you lazy wolf."

But he wouldn't, and she couldn't get warm or to sleep.

In the morning, she was at the window again, looking outside for something that wasn't there when Harley came to stand next to her.

"So, you're in your own home. Is it the same?" he asked, trying hard to keep *I told you so* buried, forever unspoken.

"Maybe if I had more work to do, like laundry or . . . something."

"I'm sure that's it. If you want to scrub floors, I'd be happy to get out of the way," he said, hiding the grin growing behind his whiskers.

"No. You know what I mean, something I have to do because I have to, not because I need something to do. Damn it, Harley. Quit laughing at me!"

"I wouldn't laugh. Not at you. Maybe with you if you would laugh, too."

"Okay. It isn't the same here now."

"Anything else?"

"Pushy hobo, aren't you?"

"I am."

"Yes. I've had long nights to ponder because there surely wasn't any sleep to be had. I have a stupid wolf who doesn't take direction very well."

"Maybe he didn't like what you were telling him."

"Well, never mind. Sorry, Wolf. You know I didn't mean that. You're smarter than all of us put together. I need to go home. I've been dumb and mean. I have some apologies to make."

"And Kat?"

"Yes. I'll be back to speak with Kat and John. Will you keep Jeannie and the babies until I get back?"

"With glee."

She hitched the mare and let her have her head. Kitty danced in the snow, a foxtrot for young fillies, not old mares, but she was feeling the joy of the day. The sun was warm on her face, and the fragrance was fresh, of new snow and white pine. She slid from the saddle, dropped the reins, and found Mel in the milking parlor on his three-legged stool. Kate stood a long time in the doorway watching and listening to the comfortable squirt of milk hitting the sides of the pail.

She didn't see Becca and wasn't surprised. This was where Mel loved to be. He'd probably given Becca a break so he could be here alone. Milking was his therapy, the gentle cows his reassurance the world was as it should be, still spinning on its axis, still moving in its slow, methodical way around the sun.

She walked in and put her hands on his shoulders. Mel didn't turn or stop the rhythmic movements of his hands. Kate put her cheek on the top of his head and waited.

When he was finished, he lifted the bucket, patted the cow away and turned to her. "I've missed you," he said, his words a soft, murmuring caress.

"I've missed you."

"Enough to come home?"

"More. As soon as Kat and John get back, we'll be home. I need to see them first. But I couldn't wait to tell you I'm sorry. I'm really sorry."

Mel dropped the bucket and scooped her up in his arms. He buried his face in her neck and stayed there, his arms hard and tight around her. She felt the pounding of his heart on her breast and his deep, ragged breath in her hair. She knew fear. What would she do if she lost him? How would she live? What if her stupidity had driven him from her? She wouldn't blame him.

"I'm so sorry," she said again. "I don't ever want to hurt you, or lose you. I want to explain, well . . . the best that I can. I don't even understand me."

"No explanations necessary. And you could never lose me. I'd keep finding you, Kate. Don't you know that by now?" Mel's voice was raspy with tears he'd never shed, and the sound hurt her worse than any real, bloody wound. He kept his face buried.

"I need to explain. There are things I need to talk about, need for you to understand. But I have to understand them first, and I don't, yet. I am getting there, I think. Is that okay?"

"Is it something I'm doing?" he asked, finding he really did need to know because fear was a cold hand squeezing his heart.

"No. I just need to come to terms -- with this Kate -- this other, older Kate -- the one who can't control the whole world and everything in it. There's more, but nothing scary."

Mel waited, listened for more. He processed her words, her face, the simple fact she was here. Moments passed. He was okay, but questions battled peace without answers.

"Should I ride with you?"

"I'd love that. Let's get Becca, too. We have a little celebrating to do. If you want to finish up here, I'll go find her."

Mel apologized to his girls as he rushed through the rest of the milking. "I'll do better tonight," he told them. "Sorry."

312

In the buggy under warm blankets they laughed all the way to the cabin. They knew something was in the air, but Kate wouldn't say what. It was going to be a surprise.

"You have to wait for the news. It won't be long. And I need some time alone with John when we get there, okay?"

"Sure, but isn't John Kat's beau, Ma? And don't you think it's rude to Mel?"

"Brat. My children are all brats!"

The table was set with linen and decorated with an evergreen centerpiece. Crystal goblets waited next to small china plates.

Kate stood stunned. "Where did all this come from? The beautiful glasses, the china?"

"I have things," he said with a phony pout. "I," he said, pulling on his suspenders and puffing out his chest, "am a hobo with means. I didn't just jump off the train, you know. Well . . . I did, but not yesterday. It was quite awhile ago, as a matter of fact. You remember? I was in a sidecar, waiting for . . ."

"Okay, Harley. I get it," Kate said interrupting further comment about riding the rails. "Kat isn't back yet?"

"Due any time, I suspect."

Mel and Becca came in and stared at the table, eyes round with wonder. Becca added a 'wow,' and Mel asked for Sammy.

"I've missed that squirt. Where is he?"

"Out of my hair for the moment. Jeannie, our very own resident mother hen, is reading to him in her room."

"Nice table, Harley. What's the occasion?" Becca asked. "What are we celebrating?"

"No worming it out of Harley, Becca. Not fair," Kate said. "I told them it was going to be a surprise, Harley, so mum's the word."

"The answer is yes. I believe we are, Becca," he said, but didn't elucidate, and Becca understood him well enough to know when he couldn't be urged to talk. A silent Harley was contradictory to the natural world, but sometimes he liked ambiguity, and this was one of them. You could see it twinkling in his eyes.

Mel escaped to Jeannie's room, and they heard Sammy's squeals when he saw Mel in the doorway. In moments, Mel was on all fours and Sammy was riding him around the room.

"I think Mel makes a great horse," Harley said. "Should have been one long ago."

"He *is* crazy about that boy," Kate said.

"And *that girl* will have him wrapped around her itty-bitty finger, too. Soon, I'll bet."

"Are you trying to make a point, Harley?"

"I think you'll figure it out for yourself. You've got a good head on your shoulders."

"High praise from the exalted one."

Harley waved a wooden spoon in the air, swung his arm downward in a swooping bow.

"I like that. Exalted one. It's taken a lot of years, but you've finally got it!" he teased.

She heard them ride into the clearing, unhitch, then take the horse to the back of the cabin. Kate told Harley she needed to greet them, talk to them privately.

"I think that's a grand idea," she heard as she left the cabin, pulling her wrap tight around her shoulders against the winter cold, against eating cold, leftover crow. Kate hoped she was making the right move. This was just one of the many directions she wasn't sure about. Indecision was rampant. Where was her bat woman's radar when she needed it?

As she walked toward the back, she heard them talking about their trip and the patients they'd treated, sounding like they'd been together for ever, *and maybe they had,* Kate thought. They did seem to know each other well, right from the beginning when he'd tended to Jeannie's wounds several years back.

"You made the right choice giving old Joshua the blackberry root last time. His joints look better already," John said.

"Thanks. He looked pretty good, and it can't hurt him. I think he mixes it with moonshine, but at least his breath is tolerable now," she said with a laugh. "How's yours?"

"Stop that. Behave, wicked woman." Kate heard John say as she was just about to enter the shed. She came to a standstill just outside the door, waited a moment, then knocked and walked in.

Kat held her ground near John whose face began to glow lightly pink under his bronze skin. Waya, the wolf pup, yipped and stood in front of Kat.

Kate ignored the embarrassment, petted Waya, and went straight to the point.

"I apologize to you both for being stupid," she began.

Kat kicked at the straw on the shed floor. "You can't help it, I guess."

Kate's head jerked toward her daughter. "Don't sass, Kat. It isn't becoming."

Wolf stuck his head in the doorway, glared at Waya and nudged his way inside to position himself in front of Kate. It was a wolf stand-off.

"You sound like Grandma."

Kate snorted, a laugh turned bleak. "Isn't it funny how that happens? I'm trying, Kat. Let me finish, please."

"What did you want to say, Kate?" John said. "We're listening."

"I can't get over having grown daughters. I didn't want them to grow up. I still don't, I guess..." Kate wavered, not sure where to go with what she wanted to say, how to say it. "I think I'm not good with change. No," she admitted on a long exhale. "I know I'm not. It seems my life is constantly shifting, and I'm not the one propelling it, well, most of the time. I can't control the changes or direct them, or stop them anymore."

"No one really likes it. Adjusting is difficult." John said, trying to ease Kate's struggle.

Kate looked up at him, admired him, a tall, handsome man. His heritage was written on his face, in his eyes, his bearing. He wore his inheritance well, like a proud insignia.

Kat slipped her hand in his, an act of support and defiance. It was not dismissed by Kate, nor disapproved.

She is her mother's daughter, Kate thought, just as she, herself, had been her father's. Will would have approved of Kat, would have trained her to defy convention, with both feet planted on the ground or striding west . . . or east, or whatever direction the head pointed the feet.

"Your Grandma says I'm ridiculous, and Harley says I'm mean. I don't know what I am, except wrong. And it doesn't feel good. John asked for my blessing and I refused. I am truly sorry, and I hope you forgive my stupidity."

"There's no need for forgiveness, Kate. I imagine it's hard to give your children in marriage, especially if they are young, as Kat is. But I will cherish her, always. She is Selu. My Selu."

"I know that . . . not the Selu thing, but that you will cherish her. And it's fairly obvious she is in love with you."

"That is true," he said, and Kate laughed, the first real one since entering the shed to talk with them.

"Which do you say is true? That she's in love or that it's obvious?" Kate asked.

"Both. She makes her thoughts and wishes known."

"Excuse me," Kat said, stepping between them. "I'm here. I didn't leave."

"We both see you, Kat. Do you accept my apologies? You haven't said much, and I am sorry."

"Swear-sorry or sorry-sorry?" she teased.

Kate was happy to hear it, and knew they were all right. "Sorry-sorry . . . damn it." She put her arm around her daughter, and Kat hugged back, apologizing for her own rudeness. John's laugh rumbled as he hugged them both.

They ambled to the cabin, arm in arm, easy with each other and content that it was so. Inside, Harley waited with a smile and a raised glass.

"Celebrating?" he asked.

"Yes, we are Harley," Kat said. "Ma has been redeemed, and John and I will do the regular church wedding just like normal people. Although it's silly."

"Why do you say it's silly, Kat?" John asked. "It's an important tradition."

He smiled at her because she amused him. She was irreverent, succinct, unafraid, and beautiful. And she didn't know how stunning she was. Kat was tanned by her hours outdoors, toned from her labors, and her straight blonde hair slid down her back in a silky mass. How she could be unaware of her beauty was a puzzle to him. Perhaps it was because she didn't care.

"It's silly because I already gave you corn," she said, and the smile she gave him held knowledge and promise.

Kate didn't know why, but she blushed. "I'm gonna get Mel and the girls and Sammy. Then let's have that toast, Harley."

Jeannie leaped at John, flinging her skinny little arms around his neck, when Kate told them the news. She'd loved him for years, ever since he'd fixed her broken leg and asked to keep a lock of her copper hair in his bag of precious possessions. He had talked with Jeannie like an adult, consulted her about her own medical needs. They'd bonded.

"You're gonna be my brother!" she cried. "That is so exciting!"

"Brother in law," Kat said.

"Same thing. I love it. You're my Indian brother!"

Mel eyed Kate, questioning her outward happiness. He strolled to her and put an arm around her shoulder, watching for concealed signs of stress or discontent.

"I'm happy for you both," he said to the new couple, "and wish you unending joy."

"My turn," Harley said, splashing small amounts of clear liquid in several glasses. "This is some of Will's saved, treasured, and hidden, special moonshine." When everyone had a glass, and Kat had poured lemonade for Jeannie and Sammy, he raised his glass.

"Here's to Kat and John, to their bond, their love and to trading in two blue blankets for a single white one."

John interrupted. "How do you know Cherokee wedding tradition, Harley?"

"You never know what this old hobo knows, John. Now, please . . . and to bliss in this cabin once more, and to little feet running around and . . ."

"Harley," Kat said. "Finish, or I will."

"And to the impatient bride," he added, looking directly at her and raising his eyebrows. Kat blushed, a pretty rose hue under her tan, and gulped her drink.

"Smart ass," she said. "Sorry."

Harley wasn't affronted. "You are definitely your mother . . . in soooo many ways."

"I repeat, smart ass," Kat said.

Harley grinned, patted his belly and asked if anyone else had a toast to make because if not he could do more.

Mel stepped in to keep Harley from having to toast again and poured a tiny amount more in the glasses. He raised his.

"Kat and John, you're worth more than both your weights in precious gold. You showed your courage, your mettle, when we battled Spanish flu, when you tirelessly doctored this family and the whole town without fear for your own safety. I, like most of Hersey, will forever be grateful to you. You are separately remarkable, and together you are formidable. I'm happy to be part of your union and your family."

Eyes misted as Mel spoke, his own included. Kate's mist rolled down her cheeks, and she let it.

Kat broke the silence. "You're worse than Harley." But she crossed the room and embraced him, her face in his neck, hiding her own dew.

"If I ever decide to give up the reins of toast making, I'll call you, Mel. That was mighty pretty."

Chapter Twenty-nine

Seven women

The Congregational Church bell rang. Its peal slid over snow covered hills, resonated against snow laden trees, and came back to rest at the white steeple where it began. Thick snow tried to suck up the ringing but couldn't. The bell's song was stronger.

Mrs. Tate was at the organ, practicing the bridal march, and her music melted with the tolling of the bell. It sounded joyful and mournful at the same time, a blend of lament and hymn of praise.

John Nestor pulled the bell rope. He thought of the work that had gone into getting the steeple bell. Ellen and Kate had worked tirelessly earning money from bake sales and bazaars. Ruthie, too, but she'd been pretty young then. "God, it's ancient history," he said to himself.

He stood in the steeple bell tower where you could see every home in Hersey, out over the houses to the hills beyond, and remembered pulling the bell rope for Kate, twice. He had tolled this bell for Willie and Mary, Jack and Ruthie, many, many others, but Kate was his favorite, and her daughter, Kat, was a close runner up. She was moving up fast and closing in on her mother's heels for the top spot in John Nestor's heart.

He pulled the thick rope again and pondered, nostalgic. According to him, the best wedding ever had been Kate's to Mark. She had waited for him -- in spite of every warning to the contrary. Ten years she waited. And Mel had waited through it all for her. Their nuptials, Mel's and Kate's, were the second-best wedding. "I wonder if the magic's in the waiting," he mused with a chuckle, talking to the bell's peal. "Cuz Mel waited almost thirty years for Kate."

Holly greens with bright red berries lay on the altar, and ribbons brightened the aisle. He had tied the bows himself. His wife had died during the epidemic, leaving him to try and figure out life without her. She'd been part of his for most of the years he'd been alive, and he thought of her when he did the things she loved. She'd always decorated the church for weddings, and now John continued her work.

She was becoming Kat Crow. He laughed at the name as the bell rope pulled his feet from the floor then let him down again. The rhythm of it had a physically pleasing sensation. *Kat Crow has charm,* he thought, even if it was comical. And John Crow has magnetism, charismatic appeal, the man not the name. He laughed again.

"I'm a crazy old man!" he shouted from the bell tower. "A daft madcap!" His voice echoed across the roof tops, and bounced back to him. Mrs. Wellington looked up at the steeple from Main Street in front of Sadie's Saloon and chewed more frantically. He saw her jaw move faster as she watched, or just imagined he saw because he knew it would be. And he laughed again, for the sheer joy of the day and the odd, delightful old lady.

"I love you, Mrs. Wellington!" he shouted down to her.

Kat, her sisters, grandmother and mother were at Jack and Ruthie's. They had gathered there for the wedding preparations. It was three blocks from the church, an easy journey.

Kate pulled at the sash and tweaked the lace, fussed with the bow at the back. Ellen pulled at Kate. "Leave the girl alone. She's fine. She looks perfect."

"Ma," Kat said. "Why don't you, Grandma and Aunt Ruthie go have a little glass of wine and let Becca, Jeannie and me finish getting ready?"

"Don't you need me?" Kate asked, hardly believing she was dismissed.

"You've just about finished me," she said, spinning around for Kate's review. She wore her mother's wedding dress, the one she'd worn when she was Mark's bride, and it was a perfect fit. She was her mother, twenty years ago.

Kate saw herself, remembered her own eager joy, and saw it reflected in Kat's eyes. The future was blissful on your wedding day, as it should be.

Looking at Kat, Ellen saw Kate in the wedding dress, too, and then saw herself marrying Will. God, how she loved that man! She was crazy with love for him, still was today.

"Come on," Ruthie said. "Let's get out of here and go sip wine."

Ellen put her arm around Kate, knew what she was thinking. She'd been there.

Their thoughts ran the same tracks; weddings did that, brought contemplation, recognition of mortality and the passing of sand through the hourglass, the marking of time. A wedding made you stand still, made you pause, if only for a moment, and reflect. You couldn't keep busy enough to run from truths because you were sitting or standing, waiting for the bride and groom and the reverend. Nothing to do but think about children growing old enough to marry. That makes you older, the other passing generation.

Maybe that's what causes wedding tears. They weren't shed for joy, for the bride and groom's happiness. They rolled down cheeks for life gone before, for life hovering on the doorstep, but at the back door leaving, not the front stoop coming in.

"One thing is for sure," Ellen said. "This family knows how to love. Are you getting shorter?" she asked, turning to Kate.

Kate's eyes grew into round saucers. "Me? Me getting smaller? Hell no! That's you! Not me!"

She tramped down the hall to the kitchen. "Ruthie! Ma thinks I'm getting short!"

"You are! It's what we do."

"The hell it is!"

Ellen laughed. Hard. She was having fun -- even if it was at Kate's expense.

Ruthie tipped the bottle of her special red, splashing wine into three stemmed, crystal glasses. Kate took hers to the window and stood to watch a woodpecker boring a hole in the nearby tree, a severe contrast in color to the snowy

laugh. The jokes they made, the tears they shed. They were tied together with invisible twine made of blood and tears and life.

"Am I you, Ma? Are you your mother?"

"I hope so, Kate. If we didn't want that, why would we bother to instill our values in our children? But you're not an exact copy."

Kate nodded, thoughtful. "Will Becca and Jeannie be me? And Kat? Rachel?"

"There are differences. Perhaps not as many as there are similarities, but they're there. You always knew exactly what you wanted," Ellen told her daughter. "You were always so sure. And your kind of certainty wasn't in me at all. I only knew I wanted your pa. He was the one thing in my life I was completely, emphatically sure of, except for loving my children," she said with a laugh. "You were different, and there were times when I thought I didn't know you at all,"

"I know. There were times when I thought that, too. Pa walked me through it."

"Your pa was a wonderful man. And Kat is your replica. Will would adore her. Spoil her with love. Like he did you."

Kate couldn't speak around the lump in her throat, so she nodded.

"I wish he could see us all now, be with us," Ellen said.

"Mark, too. I hope he and Pa are watching together, sharing a sip of celestial moonshine. I wish I knew."

Kat, Becca and Jeannie came into the kitchen while they were still at the window.

"What's out there?" Jeannie asked. "Can I see?"

"Sure. Come here Copper Top," Ruthie said, pulling Jeannie in front of her. "Becca, stand by Grandma, and, Kat, get next to your mother."

"I need to get Dot first. I hear her squawking," Becca said.

Becca returned and they did as Ruthie said. When they were settled, no one could speak. The window pane was filled with beautiful Hughes women, all looking at each other, eyes roaming from one face to the next, looking for . .

. they didn't know what they searched for. Maybe for a sense of themselves in the eyes of others? A kinship born of blood? Or were they looking for something setting them apart, making them their own person instead of part of something larger, a family; generations of women who knew one another better than they sometimes knew themselves?

"I like your hair, Aunt Ruthie," Jeannie whispered, and everyone nodded. Ruthie's hair waved agreement.

"You look beautiful, Kat," Ruthie said.

"It's Ma's gown. It's gorgeous."

"It's you in it, Kat," Kate said. "*You* are beautiful."

"You are too, Ma and Grandma," Becca said.

"And you, Becca."

"Dot looks like Rachel all dressed up," Jeannie said. "Look at her hair and eyes."

Their words were soft, as if spoken in an empty, hallowed church where reverence and respect were sacrosanct, the icons sacred. In this old window pane, the icons were the girls and women, themselves *together*, and their images were blessed by love . . . for one another. No one wanted to move away, break the spell.

Mel drew up in a buggy decked out with white ribbons and bells. He was captured in the spell of what he saw and sat in the winter cold, watching the women in the window, wondering at their stillness. He didn't want to move. He stared at the vision they made outlined by the wooden frame, wanted jealously to keep the picture for himself, forever.

Jack's buggy came from the stable, wearing gigantic blue bows and bells. He parked behind Mel, got out and walked over. He looked at Mel, followed his line of sight, and found the picture holding his attention.

"Wow," he whispered and climbed in next to Mel.

"That was articulate, Jack."

"Aren't they something?" He pulled a flask from his breast pocket, uncorked it and took a deep pull, then held it toward Mel who nodded and did the same.

"Four generations of perfection."

"Perfect when they're not talking, like now," Mel teased, handing back the flask.

"This reminds me of a time Mark and I got pretty drunk in my buggy on the way back from looking for his kids. Left Jamie at the orphanage. That was hard. We finished two flasks that night. Almost fell out of the seat looking for bats. Well, I was looking at Mark who wanted to be a bat."

"A bat? What's with this family and bats?"

"They want to be sure of their directions . . . like bats."

They didn't look at each other as they talked, but stayed focused on the window and the women in it.

"Wish I had a picture," Jack said, sipping again and handing the flask to Mel.

"Me, too. And nobody knows the right direction. We just hope. We're not bats," Mel said. "Most of us would like to be and aren't. Kate included."

"I'd like to have seen her cowering when one flew out the chimney at her. Bat woman at her best."

Mel turned Jack's way, glanced at his buggy and gave him a wry grin, glad for a lighter bit of humor. "Have you lost your mind?"

"Jealous?" Jack asked, pointing at his gigantic blue bows. "In decorating, bigger is better, not where men are concerned, though." He punched Mel in the arm. "See? Don't cry now, little boy."

"We'd better go in. I get the bride and her sisters, right? Isn't that what they decided?"

"Yes, but you never know. That was yesterday."

The girls and Kate went straight to the choir room at the back of the church to do last minute repairs and to wait. Kate patted, tucked and fussed until Kat shoved her out the door.

"Go, Ma. Go get a seat. I'm ready."

Jack and Mel ushered the guests to their seats and argued about who got which guest like two bratty little boys.

Finally, Mel walked Kate down the aisle to her front row seat. He whispered in her ear.

"You are just as lovely today as your daughter. Do you know that?"

"You're a liar. Thank you," she said, her eyes wet with the threat of tears.

"You okay?" he asked.

She nodded, but she wasn't sure. Change. More change. Damn change.

Jeannie peeked out of the choir room door to watch the guests as they came in and commented on them all. Then she gasped.

"Look, quick! Look at Verna!" Kat ran to the door as fast as she could in her long dress and funny shoes.

She laughed and stared, then whispered loud for Verna's attention. She came to the door they were holding ajar and peered in.

"Look at you, Urchin, all dressed up. You're beautiful," Verna said, her ice blue eyes squinting shut in a wide grin.

"Me! Look at you! Wow!"

Verna twirled to better show her finery. New blue velvet trousers with a matching vest over a fine white lace shirt.

"I've never seen anything like it!" Kat gushed. "I could get married in your outfit."

"You'd have to rip it off me first. I had it specially made for today."

"I love it! You are something else, Verna."

"And you Urchin. I'd say something mushy, but I hate that. If I wanted a kid, which I don't, it would be you."

"Thanks, Verna."

"Welcome."

When Jack and Mel saw Verna, they fought over her.

"You got Kate," Jack whined. "The least you can do is let me have Verna."

"I'll give you Mrs. Wellington and Agatha Pennington. Two for one."

While they argued, Verna took off by herself, strolled down the aisle and nodded to every shocked face like it was her party. She strode up to John, who waited at the altar next to Jamie, chatted with them, and turned to stare at the folks seated in the pews. They stared back and shook their heads in wonder at Verna's audacity. But they always did. Today was no different.

"She's a barmaid at Sadie's," they whispered. "She doesn't know any better."

"She knows," Betsy Dunn said. She had a soft spot for anyone with guts. She didn't have any and knew it. "She doesn't care. Good for her."

Jack and Mel, startled to see she'd gone on her own, raced to the open doorway just in time to see her turn to face the congregation.

"Oh, Lord," Mel said. "Is she gonna preach?"

"She would be interesting, more so than the reverend, I'm thinking."

"You've got that one right."

John waited with the singular, customary nervous anticipation only grooms experience. He was bronzed elegance and looked ten feet tall in a long-tailed coat and white, shirred shirt. His sleek, black hair was tied back and glistened in the light of the altar candles. He glanced toward the back of the church, anxious to begin.

Becca and Jeannie were waiting at the entry for the music to signal their march down the aisle when Harley slipped into the choir room. He had deliberately delayed until they were gone.

Kat stared, her mouth open when she saw him. His golden curls glowed in the candlelight; his closely shaved, cherubic face glistened. He pranced into the room and turned in a slow circle, showing off the reason for her shock. He watched her eyes, enjoying the moment.

"Your clothes!" She was sure they were the ones her mother had washed, dried and pressed all the years she'd lived at the cabin. Since then, Kat had done the honors, keeping the tradition alive. The man who owned the cabin, where they'd lived forever, deserved that respect.

"Why are you wearing *the man's* clothes?"

He bounced, "Nice fit, huh? I'm impressive."

"You shouldn't be wearing them. Ma won't like it. They're his. For when . . . if . . . he comes back."

He held out his arm to walk her down the aisle.

"I'm not going anywhere until you answer my question."

"He came back, Kat. A long, long time ago. The day your Pa got off the train and took an old hobo with him to the Hughes house."

Kat stared, trying to comprehend. "How do you know?"

"Well . . . I know because I'm *the man.*"

It was a good thing Kat wasn't the fainting sort, though she did put her arm on his for support as she processed what Harley was saying.

"You're *the* man?"

Harley's curls bounced when he nodded.

"Why didn't you say anything?"

"It seemed better not to."

"I need to sit a minute."

"You need to go get married."

"I'm already married," she said stubbornly, the real Kat coming out through the finery, the white cloak of a gracious woman.

"I know . . . You gave him corn."

"Yes. Now all we need is a white blanket, and we're good."

"So, let's go."

"Why now, Harley? Why did you wait til now?"

Harley had the good sense to look repentant. "I wasn't sure how to do this. I own the cabin and the woods around it. Have for a great many years."

"Then . . . I don't get any of this. You lived in a cold room in Grandma's barn for years. Like a hobo. You let everyone think of you as a hobo!"

"Yes. Kat, we can go into this later. I wanted to give you this now. Before you marry. It's yours. Not yours and

John's, as much as I like and admire him. Yours. And your mother's if you wish to share it with her."

He handed her a legal document wrapped in a narrow blue ribbon. "You don't need to open it. It's the deed to all of it. Something blue."

"No!" she shouted, backing away from him, hands up palm out as if warding off an attacker.

He pulled on the string around her wrist from which hung a finely crocheted white sachet. Once it was opened, he slid in the rolled deed, then closed it back up and held out his arm.

"We'll talk it out later, Kat. I love you. Let's go because John loves you too, and right now you can bet he's on pins and needles wondering what's keeping you."

Kat took Harley's arm and moved to the door, hearing the strains of the bridal march increase, decibels trying, she thought, *to hurry them along.* All heads were turned toward the back of the church in held breath and anticipation. Concern turned to delight when they saw Kat come toward them with a beaming Harley by her side.

"I love you, too, Harley. But you really are a crazy old coot."

"That's what your mother says. You're beautiful."

"You are a menace to the sane world."

"You are going to make unbelievable babies."

"You'll never get your hands on them."

"They're going to love me, too."

". . . yes . . . they will."

And the reverend said, "Who gives this woman to this man?"

With shameless tears rolling down his cheeks, Harley said, "I do." He kissed Kat's cheek and pulled her hard against him. Before he placed her hand in John's, he didn't threaten, didn't tell him he'd kill him if he didn't treat Kat right, none of the traditional fatherly words of terrible wrath. He used no words. He begged with his eyes only, and John understood.

"I will worship her like the river and the trees."

And Harley understood, believed him, and put her hand in John's.

Still teary eyed, Harley sat down next to Kate to witness Kat's wedding. He watched with intent, noting every inflection of their words, packing them into his memory for later reflection. Kate had a hard time concentrating on her daughter's vows and not Harley's clothes.

She looked at Harley, at Kat, back at Harley.

"Later, Kate. We'll talk later. This is Kat's wedding."

"Old coot."

Chapter Thirty

Kat's wedding

Reverend Fitzgerald included parts of the Cherokee wedding celebration according to John and Kat's wishes. One was garnering consent from Jamie, as the brother of the bride, to be responsible for training the children of his sister and her husband. He accepted and ceremoniously walked over to Harley to ask for his help.

"I can give what I have," Jamie professed, "but I only have so much. I am asking you for help, Harley."

"If I have to come a thousand miles," Harley said, "I will, if I am able."

Reverend Fitzgerald continued with the traditional ceremony. They said 'I do,' and Harley rose with a white blanket in his hands. He wrapped it around them both and drew it together in the middle. He kissed John's cheek and Kat's again.

"You are man and wife," he said. With a grin, he added, "but you already were, no?"

Mrs. Tate's fingers banged on the organ, escorting them out of the first set of doors. Rice flew, tears fell with groans of relief.

They met with friends and neighbors in the church basement just as young married couples had been doing since the church was built. Just as Kate and Mark had done, and Kate and Mel had, as Jack and Ruthie, Willie and Mary, Rachel and Charlie -- all of them and all of the village couples had done over many generations.

There were different endings, and the beginnings and middles were different, too. But the sentiment of the bride running down the steps was the same. Feeling beautiful, like a princess, and if you never wanted to be one before, being princess felt glorious today. At this time, for this brief moment, you were in a fairy tale. You were where every eye landed and who they secretly wanted to be. No one else mattered as much as you did, and Kat felt the secret thrill of Queendom.

John looked at her as if seeing her for the first time. His eyes revered, the hand at her back was gentle and strong, his gaze intimidated any who might come between. It gave her a thrill that traveled throughout her body, and she wished they were at home in the cabin -- the cabin she now owned! Hell with being queen. She wanted to be Selu!

"Damn, wish I hadn't thought of that!"

"You're still in the church, Kat."

"Sorry."

John Nestor greeted them in the basement. He'd decorated it for the occasion, too. He grabbed Kat and lifted her off the floor.

"Bless you, Kat. Congratulations!"

Others swarmed into the room, making Kat wish for escape. She didn't like groups of more than three, let alone thirty-three.

The basement room filled. People from miles around came to celebrate with John and Kat. They'd made many friends while caring for people who were sick, dying, broken or giving birth. They'd not asked money for their services when it was clear some didn't have any. They'd tended to their ills and made sure they didn't feel like it was charity. Instead, payment was bacon, jams, a crocheted shawl or promise of labor. Kat and John accepted with honor and a smile, letting patients know their payment was appreciated. Pride and gratitude brought them to the church today.

On a table in the center of the room was a gigantic pile of gifts, a shockingly wild variety of wedding presents. A bowl of eggs, a baby blanket, a brick of cheese, jams and jellies, and most unusual, a glass bowl of money. On the front of the bowl was a hand-written sign: *For the clinic. We love you, Kat and John.*

Kat poked John in the ribs. "Look at that, John!"

John's slow grin spread over his face, starting from the eyes and working its way down to his white toothed smile. "This is wonderful."

They made their way around the room, stopping at each person to thank them for coming, for their gifts, for their love.

Jeannie carried Dot in one hand and held Sammy's hand with the other. It was too crowded to let him loose. Becca took Dot and told her sister to make her way to the stairs.

"Let's go up," Becca said. "I can't stand it down here. It's too crowded. Besides, I need to ask you something."

When they were in the quiet of the entry, Becca leaned to Jeannie. "Did you see Harley?"

"Sure. He gave Kat away."

"I mean, what he was wearing."

Jeannie shook her head. "I guess I was just looking at Kat. She was beautiful. I hope I look as pretty when I get married."

"You will. You'll be beautiful, but . . . think, Jeannie," she said, growing frustrated. "What was Harley wearing?"

Jeannie put a finger to the side of her face to show she was trying to reflect, and Becca could tell when it dawned on her. Her eyes grew wide, her mouth opened. "Oh, my gosh! *The man's* clothes! Becca, he was wearing *the man's* clothes! Didn't he have anything else to wear?"

"I don't know. But it's odd. And they fit him . . . really well. He looked good."

In the basement, Kate was working her way through the crowd trying to get to Harley. Just when she'd get near, he'd go in the opposite direction. "He's deliberately avoiding me," she said.

"Why are you chasing Harley, pretty lady?" Mel asked, putting an arm around her waist. "You're a wild woman on a mission."

"Sorry. I wanted to talk with him."

"Can't it wait?" Mel asked. "He's staying at the farm tonight. You'll have plenty of time."

Kate nodded, annoyed and embarrassed. She wanted to know why he was wearing *the man's* clothes. She didn't want to wait.

Across the room, near the gift table, John Nestor clanged a glass for attention. When it was quiet, he looked for Kat and John, and motioned them to come forward.

"I'd like to make a toast. Does everyone have a cup of punch or coffee? If not, get one and I'll get started. I'm long winded so you'll have plenty of time."

There was an appropriate titter, and someone said he didn't know long winded til he'd heard Harley.

"I've heard that," Nestor said. "But this is my show, so he'll have to wait." He raised his punch cup and looked at John and Kat. "You will never know, not if you live for a thousand years, what you did for this village, for the people of Hersey, during the epidemics, afterwards, cleaning up the town, riding into the hills to tend to ailing folks, child bearing women. You can't know what your work means . . ." He had to pause. Memory choked him, his wife's death, others he'd known since childhood, his own illness.

"I'm so sorry. This is most definitely not a time for sorrow. This is a time for joy, Kat and John, for gratitude you have chosen to settle in Hersey."

"Here, here!" a man shouted.

Another said, "Well done, kids."

Nestor continued, "Among all the gifts from people who love you is this bowl holding money. It's intended to go for things you need in your clinic. We know how expensive all that medical stuff is. So . . . here," he said, handing the full bowl to John who moved aside and indicated Kat should take the bowl. "And if you haven't added to this bowl, you still can," he said, looking meaningfully around the room. "Do it. I mean it."

Kat finally held the bowl in her hands, out away from her body like it might explode or infect her. She stared alternately into the bowl and out at the expectant faces, not knowing which she feared more.

Applause erupted amid shouts of 'speech, speech!'

Kat shook her head, and John stepped forward, his arm around his wife. He towered over many of the men as he looked around at the faces turned toward him, waiting for his words. His dark hair and skin tone gave him a mysterious look, intimidating to some. Once they'd been in his care, their awkwardness gave way to admiration, respect, and, for some, mild reverence. You could hear it in the growing hush as he waited.

"Thank you for celebrating with us. Thank you for honoring this family with your gifts. We value you and wish to continue to serve. Knowledge was given to me by my grandmother and grandfather, clan medicine woman and medicine man. Kat was born medicine woman. She's your gift. The clinic is yours, not ours. We will work hard to care for it in your name."

He turned to Kat, his hand held out, palm up. She shook her head. "I don't want to talk," she whispered.

He pushed a little and Kat frowned. "Come on, Kat," the youngest Tate boy yelled. "Give us a little speech."

She grinned. "John is a gift to us all, but he won't live long if he keeps pushing me to speak to crowds. Thank you for everything. That's all."

Laughter erupted. Loud guffaws. Knowing Kat all their lives, her words didn't surprise anyone. Except there had been twice as many as anyone expected. Brevity was Kat's middle name. And, if you should know something, she shouldn't have to say it. Right?

They mingled while Mel and Jack loaded the presents, found Becca, Jeannie, Dot and Sammy. They dragged Kate away from well-wishers and crammed into Mel's buggy.

"We're just heading to Jack and Ruthie's," Mel told Kate. "It'll be tight, but it's only two blocks, and we'll snuggle to keep warm. Jack can bring the bride and groom. He insisted cuz he has fancier decorations," he said grinning.

"Where's Harley? I didn't get to talk with him. What about Ma and Ruthie?"

"Your ma and sister are already there getting dinner finished. Eldon, too."

"Robbie and Willie? And Harley and Verna?"

"Following."

They entered with a rush of cold winter air and giggles. "Change Dot, will you, please, Jeannie?"

"Yea, I always get the good stuff."

"Sorry. I appreciate you."

"I know, Ma."

Kate fussed around the kitchen, touched the perfect table just to be sure. Everything was ready; they were just waiting. Her mind was in turmoil. Kat was a married woman. She and her husband had a medical clinic. And Harley... It never occurred to her he wouldn't have clothes to wear to Kat's wedding, but did he have to wear those? He knew how she felt about them, what they meant to her. *Aarrrgh*!

"What can I do?" she demanded as she entered the kitchen.

"Nothing. Go have a glass of wine," Ruthie said. "Get out of my way."

"Pushy, aren't you?"

"Yes. My house, my rules."

"Ma, Ruthie's being mean. Make her stop," Kate whined, putting her arm around Ellen's shoulder.

"She's absolutely right. Her house. Her rules. Go have a glass of wine."

"You're both mean," she giggled. "I'll sing off key," she threatened.

"Oh, for heaven's sake. Give her something to do. She'll drive us crazy."

"I will take some wine first," Kate said with a grin.

Ellen slapped her with a folded towel and Ruthie handed her a glass of wine. "Get out. Really."

Kate went looking for Harley, who had arrived earlier with Verna. She found him alone, staring out the same window they'd gathered in front of earlier, what seemed like days earlier, maybe weeks or years. *I'm losing my mind,* she thought.

"I was here a bit ago with four generations of women. It was a sight to see."

"I'll bet it was. You are definitely a sight to see, every single one of you. In a group, you'd be awe inspiring."

"Want to tell me what's going on, Harley?"

He was quiet, so close to the window his breath fogged the pane.

"You remind me of Wolf," she said.

"I smell like an animal?"

"Don't call him that. He doesn't like it."

"Sorry. I smell like Wolf?"

"No, but we'd stand together in the cabin window looking out at winter, and he'd steam the window and then draw nose pictures."

"I could do that."

"Not necessary. I'm not sure why you're wearing those clothes, which by the way look good on you, but it's important they're clean and hanging by the door . . . for him. For the man who owns the cabin."

Harley pulled a long, deep breath.

"I am him."

"Him, who?"

Harley turned and looked at Kate.

She was stunned, took a deep breath and slowly shook her head. She didn't understand. It made no sense.

"But why, Harley? Why would you not tell us? All these years?"

"You have to know something else, Kate. I deeded the cabin and woods to Kat. She can do as she wishes with it, but I think she loves it as you do. Even as a girl, she loved it. Remember her insect prowls in the woods? Gardening even when she didn't have to . . ."

Kate nodded, knew what he said was true. Kat was at home there more than anywhere.

"I gave it to her today just before we walked down the aisle. We haven't talked since."

"Was she as shocked as me?"

"As I. Poor Ellen. She tried and failed."

"I can speak properly if I want. I don't want."

"Yes. Are you okay with what I've done?"

"It's yours, Harley. You can do what you wish with it."

"That isn't an answer to the question, Kate. Are you hurt by my actions?"

She put her arms around him and hung on. "It's an adjustment. I do love my cabin. Kat 's cabin, I mean."

"I thought hard about this, Kate. Can we talk more later? I'll be staying the night, as we planned, so John and his bride can be alone."

Kate nodded. "They're coming. I see Jack's buggy."

"Hard to miss with all that blue and clanging like a herd of cows wearing bells."

Minutes later, Kat and John strolled in, arm in arm looking radiant and followed by Jack and John Nestor carrying a camera complete with flash equipment.

"Don't pay any attention to me," he said. "Just go about your business, and pretend I'm not here." He began clicking, bulbs flashed in surprised faces, and he only stopped to add a roll of film.

"The greatest toy since my automobile," he told Kate. "Remember when Mark drove it?"

She did, vividly. It was the best of days for him, made him forget the pain for awhile. "He would love this, too. Men and their toys," she said, pointing at his camera, grinning.

Mel found them a glass of wine, poured punch for Becca, Jeannie and Sammy, and gathered them all for toasts. "Ruthie, Ellen," he yelled into the kitchen. "Get in here. We're about to toast to the bride and groom."

"Who's toasting? Harley?"

"Not yet. It's my turn first."

"Be right there. Then I have work to do in here," Ruthie called out, raising snickers at Harley's expense.

Mel lifted his glass. "Here's to Kat, my stepdaughter and John, my new son-in-law. Sounds funny."

He let every eye rest on him before he continued. "I never sired a child, but I have several I consider *my* children." He nodded toward Kat, then Jeannie then Becca, taking his time, savoring his words, tasting them on his tongue.

"You, young ladies, are children of my heart if not my blood. You have always been, and because of you I've been blessed. My newest children, Dot and Sammy, are as much a part of me as my arms or legs. Heaven help the man who . . . tries to cut off one of my arms. All of you . . . are precious in my eyes."

"Wouldn't want to do that," Jack added. "He's a rattlesnake when he's riled."

"You're interrupting, Mr. Bay."

"Yes I am. You're getting as longwinded as the old man." Jack looked at Verna whose glass was inching closer and closer to her mouth. "Better hurry it up. Verna's looking mean."

Jack had seen his friend's eyes, the tremble of his hands. He was giving him a pause, didn't want the dam to break. For his sake.

Mel took a deep breath. "As I was saying. For a man who didn't sire babies, I have collected the most beautiful, wonderful brood a man could have."

"Are you saying I'm a brood mare, Mel?" Kate asked.

"No. Well, maybe. And a great one, too. But, here's to Kat." He lifted his glass higher and directed it toward her. "To a woman I highly regard, for her wisdom, her intellect, her good sense. And to John, a man I would trust with my life. I would trust them both. Well, I did. Many of us did."

"Hear, hear," was repeated around the room.

"Kat . . ." he said, and she stood, taking the reins from him.

"Here's to us, to all of us." She drank from her glass and then traded with John and drank again.

"Whatever bugs you have, I want them, too."

"You always were looking for bugs," Kate teased.

"And you're always finishing toasts," Harley chortled. "For all your positive qualities, you surely are impatient."

Kat looked to see if Harley was insinuating again, saw that he was, and didn't care. "You're all long winded, and we were thirsty, right, Verna?"

"Bless you, Kat. We were parched, dying of thirst."

"Sit," Ruthie called out. "I'm putting it on the table."

"Okay, Harley, spill your guts," Verna said when they finally sat to eat and plates were filled.

He opened his eyes wide, phony innocence pouring from them. "What do you mean?"

"The duds, my good man."

"Oh, these." He looked at Kate, waiting for her nod of approval. Then at Kat.

All eyes focused on him, lingered there. Avid interest thickened the air.

"As you most likely know by now, these clothes, my duds in Verna vernacular, have been hanging by the door of the cabin for more than two decades."

"I thought I recognized them," Jack said, nudging Ruthie. "Didn't I?"

Ruthie nodded. "Me, too. I thought you just borrowed them. No?"

"No. I bought these . . . oh, about thirty years or so ago. Look pretty good still, don't they?" he said, patting his belly. "Still fit, too."

"That's because we've been taking good care of them for *the man*," Kat teased.

"I don't understand, Harley. Why did you buy clothes for the owner of the cabin?" Ellen said, confusion wrinkling her brow.

"Because he needed clothes."

"But . . ."

"The man!" Jeannie said. She leaped from her chair and raced to Harley. "You're the man! You're the man!"

"Give the girl a Cupie doll! You guessed it!"

The room exploded in talk. You couldn't hear the person talking to you for the one on the other side.

"Are you fibbing, Harley?" Mel asked.

Harley beamed, turned his head from one person to the next and nodded like he'd just been given the Nobel Prize. "Nope. I'm the man. Have been for just about forever."

"How is it no one knew you?"

Harley waited for the uproar to die down before he responded.

"I was a bit of a recluse when I came to Hersey, recovering from some things I won't go into now. The result was I kept to myself. When I felt like leaving, I left. Always intended to come back . . . which I did when I followed Mark from the train."

"But you didn't go to your cabin," Ellen said. "You came to our house."

Harley nodded.

"Mark needed to talk. Needed a friend."

"And you stayed. In the barn!" Ellen said, almost shouting by this time. "You stayed in a cold room in the back of the barn! Why?"

"Kate needed the cabin."

Ellen put an elbow on the table, a sure sign of her debilitated mental state. She rubbed her forehead and held it there in her hand. You could see her head shaking back and forth, saying 'no, no, not possible.'

"So what if Kate needed it. It was yours, not hers."

Heads turned, followed the conversation. Harley then Ellen, now Harley, now Ellen.

"You old fool. What's wrong with you?"

"Nothing, my dear Ellen. I enjoyed our time together. Didn't you? Conversations at your table. Learning from you. Laughing with you. If I hadn't wanted to be there, I would have left. If I had wanted or needed my cabin, I would have gone there. I was happier with the Hughes family. You're my family now. What is a cabin compared with that?"

Kate spoke up. "Harley didn't say anything because he thought I needed it more than he did. Also, that I wouldn't have stayed there if I knew the owner had returned. He was right."

Heads nodded in understanding. They knew Kate.

"I'm betting he stayed in the barn because we all needed him. He helped us all," Ruthie added.

"You helped this old hobo," Harley said.

"Hobo, my ass," Verna said. "You're no more a hobo than Mel, here."

"Well, I'm thinking of becoming one. Want to go with me, Verna?"

"When?"

"How about tomorrow? Kat is the new owner of the cabin and woods. She can do with it what she likes. I know she loves it. Think I'll take a little trip."

Shouts of 'No!' erupted, flew around the table. He held his hands in the air asking for silence. "I'll be back. I've promised to help Jamie school Kat's young'uns. Wouldn't trust anyone else to that job." He picked up his fork and shoveled food into his mouth, forcing others to do the same.

"Tell us your plans for the clinic, John," Jack said, picking up on Harley's cue to move on.

"We can really use the money the town donated. It's appreciated. We need supplies and equipment to stock and furnish the clinic. Hopefully we'll be able to keep the clinic open for the wounded and ill, the ambulatory patients, and Kat and I will still be available to travel to treat others who can't."

"Who will staff the clinic, then?" Mel asked.

Kat spoke up. "Our nurses. Our trainees. We want to build a school to train nurses and even doctors. Thanks to Grandma and her gift of a house, they can live in the upstairs and keep it open when we're on the road."

"We desperately need doctors and nurses," John added.

"What a wonderful idea," Ruthie said. "I wish I could help. Is there anything I might do?"

"Me, too," Ellen said. "I'm available. This is such good news I've been bursting with wanting to tell everyone. Bless you both."

"Bless you for your house, Mrs. Hughes," John said.

"Ellen," she responded, and Harley was amused to see a slight flush creep up her neck.

They're back, he thought and his heart was content. They're happy again.

"Actually, we can use you both," Kat said. "Our nurse trainees will probably be young and will need supervision when we're either away or busy or just gone home to the cabin."

Everyone's breath held, waiting to feel sorrow or pain or something, anything that happens when lightening jolts out of the sky unexpectedly or the word *cabin* comes up. You could hear the slow exhale of breath with the realization no one was going to die, or have a stroke, or even fall off their chair and live with the woodchucks under the floor.

A change just occurred and I'm alive, Kate thought. Everyone looks the same. I'm the same. Amazing.

"Will you train in traditional or herbal medicine?" she asked.

"Both," Kat said, and John nodded agreement. "The world needs both kinds, and John is trained in both, although my preference, in most cases, is Indian lore-based medicine, natural herbs and remedies." She saw a flinch or two and smiled. "It's okay. John knows he's Cherokee," she teased.

"I am?" he teased back. "Why didn't someone tell me? You married an Indian?"

"Brat!"

"Indian brat."

Nervous snickers went to cackles to chortles to guffaws, and it wasn't long until they were holding their bellies in laughter.

Harley looked around the room and relished their joy, remembered the many times they had shared belly laughs - - right from the first day he'd jumped from the train and landed in the Hughes living room. The day he'd been named 'pretty eyes.'

He waited until the last of the laughter died and then stood and raised his glass. "Here's to Kat. Wait a minute. I need a refill. Any of Will's superior shine around here?"

Jack went to the kitchen and brought back a jug. "It's not full, but it *is* Will's. Funny, it never seems to empty. Love that about this jug. I think an angel keeps refilling it."

He splashed a little in each glass raised toward him and sat. Harley began again.

"Here's to Kat, soul of my soul. Long ago when we were working in the garden, you explained to your mother about blighted beans. I told you then you were hiding your light under a bushel basket and invited you out. Do you remember what you told me?"

"I believe I said I liked it there."

"You did. But now, here you are, out from under the basket. You are a bright light, indeed, Kat. A light in my heart. A light in the dark forest."

He had to stop for a moment, suck in the gathering moisture. He heard throats clear, sniffles covered, and heads turn away. No one stopped him. No one interfered.

"I treasure you, Kat. Here's to you." He drank deeply and no one spoke.

Kat's tears fell uninhibited. They matched Harley's.

"I can't see," she said.

"I know."

"Who's going to build insect traps for me? Who'll make drying frames if you leave?" she said, her voice strangled and soft.

"I'll be back. This isn't a sad time, Kat. Be happy for me. I'm going on an adventure."

"But you're taking Verna. She's mine," Kat said with a wet chuckle.

"I'll just borrow her for awhile, then."

"Hey, you two. I'm right here. I have a mind. I have a tongue."

"We all know that, Verna. You've made that inordinately clear," Jack said.

"Well, listen to the little man use big words. Inordinately. See I can use it too."

"Yeah, but do you know what it means?"

She threw a spoonful of potatoes at him, and he threw one back. Verna followed it with squash and he did too. It was a free for all. Miraculously, no one hit Kat in her mother's wedding gown.

"I think I'll go change, Ma. Get out of the line of mashed potato fire. Want to help?"

Kate unfastened the thirty-two satin buttons at the back of her dress. Ellen had sewn every buttonhole, attached every button. It was still beautiful.

"Ma, I've been trying to find a way to ask you something."

"About the birds and the bees?"

Kat gave a sad laugh, and Kate noted the sorrow, worried she had hurt her daughter with her idiocy.

"I guess, sort of. When I was with Clayton, waiting for the jimson to work, I tried to keep him talking . . . to keep him away from me."

"I understand. I'm so sorry you had to go through that, Kat. You can't know how sorry I am."

"I think I might."

"What do you mean?"

"I'm just going to say it, 'cause I don't know any other way to ask. Did Clayton's pa hurt you? Did he rape you?"

Kate's breath sucked in, held there, and then rushed out as Kat's words finally kicked her in the stomach. She held a fist to her chest as if her heart would fall out if she moved it.

"Oh, God. He told you? How could he know?"

"So, it's true. A lumberjack told him a story, and he put two and two together."

"He only tried, Kat. He didn't succeed."

Kat put her arms around her mother and held her, the bond of pain and horror a steel band around them, binding them together beyond mother and daughter, beyond years together, beyond blood.

"Is that how Bug died? Protecting you?"

Kate nodded, and when Kat looked at her mother, her eyes were dry. Dark grief lay in their depths, but she didn't cry.

"And Uncle Jack. Did he . . . What happened to the bastard who hurt you?"

"I didn't ask, Kat, and neither will you. He told me I was safe, he was gone, and I believed him."

They were quiet for a time, both reliving the past and coming back to stay in the present.

"I'm so sorry, Ma."

"Thank you." Kate looked at her little girl and asked, "Did Clayton . . . did he . . .?" She couldn't bring herself to finish, too afraid of the answer.

"No. Thank God."

She took a deep, cleansing breath and Kat did the same. They smiled, finished removing the wedding gown, and hung it on a padded hangar.

"I'm sorry, Kat, for giving you and John such a hard time. I truly am. You are a wonderful young woman, and I mean woman, not girl. I don't know why I didn't want to admit it."

"Forget about it, Ma. It's done."

"Forgive me?"

"I do." Kat was quiet trying to figure out how to bring up another painful subject, the cabin. It was a tough one. She knew her mother loved the place. Had since the day she ran across it while rambling through the woods.

"I don't need to keep the cabin, Ma. I can deed it to you. Harley said so."

Kate's head drew back as she stared at Kat. "Why would you do that? It's yours. Harley gave you a precious gift."

"But you love it."

"And so do you. I live at the farm, now. You live at the cabin. I'll visit you there. Sometimes, I'll even spend the night -- especially when you have babies."

"Don't count any chickens, Ma."

Kate covered the dress with a sheet. She'd fold it later and store it in her cedar chest, keep it for Becca and then Jeannie.

"Are you sure?"

"I am more sure of that than anything, Kat. It may take me awhile to get it through my thick head that it's yours, stop calling it mine, but be patient. It's right. It's appropriate. I think you're the only person in the whole world I would give it up to. Don't tell your sisters." She laughed then hit herself in the side of the head. "Listen to me. It's not mine to give. It just feels like it. Harley wouldn't have taken it from me. He's the little Christmas boy he told us about years ago."

"The hungry homeless boy making a widow happy by letting her feed him?"

"Yeah, him. The angel unaware."

"No, according to Jeannie, it's Harley in angel's underwear!"

"That's right."

They were laughing when they went downstairs, reminiscing and happy.

Chapter Thirty-one

1920

Kat and John rode the mare home, she in front of him, wrapped in the white wool blanket. They'd been offered a buggy, but Kat wanted this, to feel him wrapped around her, to feel the horse move under her. They were unencumbered, part of the night. Snow fell in huge flakes, clung to the branches, to them, and she snuggled into his arms, felt his heartbeat pulsing at her back.

His lips pushed aside her hair and kissed her ear. *Ah, this is why I didn't want their buggy*, she thought. Warmth rushed through her. She pulled his arms tighter around her middle. Felt the butterflies.

"Do you have butterflies, John?"

"Always when you are near, Kat."

She nodded, pushed her head back to look at his face in the moonlight. She nibbled at his chin. "Your silhouette is godlike," she said.

"Only because you are my goddess," he told her, bending his head and sipping at her exposed neck.

"I have always loved you. Do you know that?"

"Yes. I've always known. I had to wait for you to grow up before I could love you back."

Kat smiled. Wicked thoughts flitted through her brain. "It used to upset you when I took my clothes off to disinfect, didn't it?"

"It did." John smiled, too, remembering. He'd held a blanket up between them to shield her as she undressed in the cleansing shed. It hadn't really been as much for her as for him. She didn't care ... or maybe she knew what she was doing. He'd been the innocent.

"You enchantress ... that was deliberate, wasn't it?"

"I don't know what you mean."

"You said you didn't know how to tease. You were teasing me!"

"No. I said I didn't know how to flirt. There's a difference, and, yes, I was teasing. I had to do something to get you to see me as a woman. Not a girl."

"I saw."

John pulled on the reins, and the mare stopped. He slid down and pulled Kat with him. Her arms went around his neck, and his hands slipped under the blanket, skimmed over her back, and pulled her hard against him. He thanked his ancestors for her, for her love.

She kissed his lips, his neck, felt the hard muscles of his shoulders and moved her hands down his back, felt him tremble. She yearned to have her skin melt with his, his breath mingled with hers. She thanked God for bringing him to her.

"No other," she whispered. "There could be no other."

"I agree, Selu. Let's go home."

Sammy and Dot burrowed into a pile of blankets in between Becca and Jeannie and were instantly asleep. Jeannie wasn't far behind. Kate sat between Harley and Mel, snuggled tight and warm. Only the outside arms were chilly. The lucky ones in the middle didn't realize it wasn't summer.

It was a quiet ride back to the farm. The few words spoken were whispers. Mostly they were content to watch the snowflakes and remember the day. Every once in a while, Harley checked Kate's face to see if she was really as good as she claimed. She looked serene. After saying goodnight to the young ones, Mel said goodnight to Harley and Kate.

"It was a long day," he said, kissing the top of her head. "You know where to find me. I'll be sawing some heavy logs."

Kate added one to the fire and moved the two rocking chairs closer, nodded to Harley and sat. They watched the flames, considered what they wanted to say to each other, what needed to be said, what didn't. Harley got up, poured two small cognacs and came back. He groaned lightly when he sat, and she heard a long, tired breath escape.

"Are you okay?" she asked.

"I am. I'm more than okay. I'm happy. You?"

"Me, too."

She sipped, felt the tingling burn all the way to her stomach and sighed.

"I don't want you to go, Harley."

He smiled at her, eyes sparkling in the light of the fire, hair aglow with the red of the flames.

"I know, but it's time."

"No. It isn't. What makes it time? Why do you want to?"

"It's a perfect time. I'm not needed right now. By the time Sammy needs a teacher, I'll be back."

Wolf got up from the rug in front of the hearth, groaned and walked over, put his head on her lap, and closed his eyes. "You got left behind today, didn't you, Wolf? Sorry."

He opened his eyes, rolled the brown one, and closed them again.

"I hope Waya behaved herself alone at the cabin today. She's pretty young."

"She's a wolf. I'm betting she knew what to do, but she'll be glad to have her mama home."

"I always flinch a little when I think about the cabin being someone else's home."

He paused, his eyes filled with years of life and joys and sorrows. "I would have given it to you in a second. Would you have accepted? Would you have lived there if I had told you the truth? The place you cared for, loved?"

He paused, letting his words sink in. "I don't think so. And would you have liked living behind the smith shop? You and your babies? Would it have been good for them?"

Kate was silent, trying to visualize how different her life might have been if Harley had admitted to being *the man*. To owning the cabin and its wondrous woods. Would she have taken it as a gift? No, she knew she wouldn't have. Would she have borrowed it from him? No. And he had known it. If he'd said anything, she would have left, moved out, wouldn't have known years of its joy, its serenity.

Kate hung her head. Pride. Her mortal burden. A horrible, wretched defect. You have to do it yourself, she scolded, or not at all. Tears came to her eyes as she remembered the times Harley had said, 'Just say thank you.' He'd said it to Mark many, many times, and to her. They hadn't learned. Well, she hadn't. Mark had done a much better job.

"Do you understand why I gave the cabin to Kat?"

"Some. Not all."

"You recognize you would have left the cabin had you known it belonged to me, right?"

Kate nodded, not wanting to. It seemed foolish now, but was true.

"Why do you think that is?" he asked.

Harley waited for a response. Sipped at his drink, put another log on the fire, and waited.

"Because I don't know how to receive help and say thank you?"

"Why do you think *that* is? It's important to understand the foundation of our quirks."

"I don't know, Harley."

He waited, and when the silence got to her, she repeated it and added, "Do you?"

"I suspect. That's all."

Kate was beginning to struggle with tears, and her frustration was evident in the fists on her lap, the white knuckles.

"Damn it, Harley. If you know, tell me. Sorry."

He snickered. "No you aren't. I love you girl. More than you understand. You and your daughters are my life, and I wouldn't have you hurting for anything. So I'm gonna tell you what I think." He got up, poured more cognac in his glass and sat again.

"I'm going to tell you a story about a girl who fell in love. We'll call her Annie. Our Annie was beautiful and open, interested in the world, loved it and everything in it. She wasn't afraid of anything. She'd get mad and stomp her foot, tell old biddies off and mean it. She had a heart as big as the sea. She didn't do anything halfway."

"So when Annie fell in love, she fell all the way, butterflies and all. She gave herself without a backward glance, totally. She was unreserved, free, uninhibited. It took courage to give absolutely because she gave up control of herself, her world. She gave it to love. She was vulnerable. It was a beautiful thing." Harley peeked at Kate who stared into the flames, unwavering. He continued.

"He died, and Annie was distraught, devastated. With his passing, her mourning was for far, far more than loss of him in death. It was for herself in life. She gathered her children around her, tightly, as if they'd be taken away if she didn't hold them close, guard them as only she could do. She couldn't trust anyone else to do it. She went through life with her arms folded across her chest, holding tight to her babies and her emotions lest she lose them. She believed she'd lose control if she felt things too much. She was afraid, and fear made her choices for her."

Harley glanced again and saw Kate hadn't moved.

"Change was terrifying, especially any change she didn't make herself, because change was equivalent to sorrow and loss. So Annie calculated every move, stayed emotionally separate, refused help from others because accepting help would entail debt, connection, a bond she wasn't prepared to allow because those entanglements meant she would be vulnerable again."

"The lesson Annie learned was *not* to give herself again: maintain control, don't give it away, and don't take help. Some lessons are hard to unlearn."

He waited, peered at her, watched the wheels turning. She finally took a sip of her drink and tried to speak. She rose and went to the window, looked out at the pure white night.

The snow looked cold and sterile next to the dark sky. Like she sometimes felt. She cleared her throat and tried again.

"But when Mark was alive and we were happy, you didn't tell us who you were even then."

"What happened to Annie?"

"She died and went to heaven with her love," Kate said with a snicker.

"Ah . . . Would you have stayed at the cabin?"

Kate shook her head. "No, probably not."

"Neither would Mark have. And I was needed at the time, your mother needed me to need her."

Kate laughed. It was true. Ellen wanted to be needed, and nothing looked needier than a hobo.

"Why is it so important, Kate? Is it because I handed the deed to Kat?"

"I'm not sure."

"You don't need the cabin. This is your home. Learn to love it, care for it the way you did the cabin."

"I do love it."

"Liar."

"I am not! I love this house."

"You love it as a piece of architecture. You just called it a house, not a home.

"That's not true, Harley."

"It is true, Kate."

"Is that everything?" she said, her voice as frosty as the winter night.

Harley got up and stood behind Kate, put his hands on her shoulders, and felt her tense. He rubbed gently until he felt the muscles ease a little and heard her breath slow down.

"Fire cracker," he said.

"Am not," she answered, giving a smile with her words.

"My reasons for deeding it to her are complex, Kate. One has only to do with Kat. She would live in a cave, a hole in the ground, because what is important to her is medicine, caring for people and John. Neither of them would take the time away from work to make a place to live. I can do that for her. She is remarkable, open, honest, unafraid, grateful, and compassionate. Finally, she loves the cabin and woods with a passion. Her affair with nature has been going on since she could crawl and pick up a bug. It will be with her throughout her time in this world, even beyond, most likely, because her light will shine on. In the forest and in the world."

"Everything you say is true, Harley. Thank you for saying it honestly. She is amazing. Her brain scares me sometimes."

He chuckled. "I know. She has me beat."

"Nobody can beat you, old coot."

"Okay, now I know you're not mad. Here's the rest. She accepts gifts. With open eyes and a glad heart."

"Yeah. She does. I don't. I know. I love you, Harley. Can I have more cognac? Let's talk all night."

He complied and sat. They rocked, added wood to the fire, and reminisced about her father, Will, and more about Mark.

"You're right about how I loved him. It was crazy. I would have waited for him til I was ninety. I wanted to be his wife, paper or not, but he wouldn't." She smiled and the glow on her face wasn't from the fire, but memory. Her heart fluttered. *Butterflies,* she thought. Still have butterflies.

Harley thought of Kat and John, their exchange of corn and venison, but he wasn't going to share it with Kate.

They talked about their time in Big Rapids and then coming home. They mused about Verna, who she was, where she'd come from, provided a magical past life for her, from Egypt with kings for brothers.

"Does she want to go traveling with you?" Kate asked. "Be a real hobo this time?"

"She'll go. Don't know if she'll come back with me, but she'll go."

They talked about Bug, the dog she'd had before Wolf came to stay, the one who died defending her. Tears fell, and she tried not to care, tried to hear Harley's words and learn about trusting and sharing. Harley raised his glass to her.

"Here's to us, Kate. To my friend, my love, my home, for I will always come back to you and our family. You've given me more than I can begin to express . . ." He paused, tears streamed from his eyes and his lips quivered. "You've given me family, a place to love and be loved, to care and be cared for, to need and be needed. You've been my beacon, the light in my forest."

Kate touched her glass to his and brought it to her lips. She sipped but she couldn't swallow. She tried again and gave up and left it there, swirling around on her tongue. When she tried once more, the muscles of her jaw twitched, squirted the cognac out and shot Harley in the face. He choked on his own, and it dribbled down his chest. They snorted and laughed and snorted again.

"Oh my God, this again," she said between gasps.

He held his belly as it rocked, and his face grew red. Kate knelt on the floor trying to catch her breath. As soon as she did, a laugh bubbled out, and they were off. When it subsided, they stood and shook it off, trying for sanity. Kate hugged him, held him for a long time.

"I'm going to bed now, Harley. Thank you. I love you."

"I love you, Kate. Go to bed."

Upstairs, Mel was awake and waiting for her. He noted her red rimmed eyes, her tremulous mouth and worried.

"Are you okay? I mean, about Harley leaving and the cabin? Everything?" He didn't know how Kate would feel about her cabin belonging to Kat.

She smiled, removed her clothes and climbed into bed. She slid the length of him and sighed. 'This is good. It's better than good.'

"I'm okay," she said. "We had a really good talk. I'll miss him and hope he comes home soon, but it's okay."

"I'm glad," he said, and pulled her closer, running his hands over her hips. "You feel good."

"So do you. I love you, Mel. And I need to talk with you."

She felt him nod and grow tense. "It's just something I need to say. Don't worry."

"I'm listening."

"When I say I have always loved you, I mean it, you know."

"Yes. I do know."

"Just listen. Don't talk, okay?"

Mel chuckled and nodded silently.

"It's important for you to understand some things, things that made me who I am, that changed me. I've struggled with them, and sometimes I haven't been nice."

She could feel him begin to disagree, to speak, and she put a finger over his lips.

"I've been lucky. I've loved two wonderful men. In two different ways. Not one less than the other. Just different."

She paused, wondering if she would forever change the nature of their relationship if she continued. But she thought about who she used to be, the woman who stomped her foot at the school board president, who stared fear in the face, and knew she had to be that woman again. She moved forward on a prayer.

"The love I had for Mark changed me. It was all encompassing. It made my heart thud until it hurt. It took over my days and nights, blinded me to the world around me, and at the same time brought the world into clearer focus, sharper, more glorious, with more sunshine. It filled my whole body with joy and sorrow. Butterflies took over. That's what I had with Mark. I felt all of that and more. I would have waited for him, for that feeling, all of my life. I had no choice. But it died with him."

"Does my saying all this hurt, Mel? I don't mean it to hurt."

He shook his head and Kate looked up at his face, searching for signs of a lie, a look that said she was doing irreparable harm, but he looked serene, thoughtful, and she continued.

"The love I share with you is different, but not less. It's solid, slow burning, built on faith in you and who you are. You are everything I love all rolled into one person. You have inner peace, strength and wisdom. You are truth, loyalty and compassion. I love your tenderness, and I love what we are together. It fills me with serenity; your harmony surrounds me day and night. When I wake up with you in the morning, I know you, and I know who you will be all day. When I come to bed with you, my sighs are from happiness and trust. I've loved you like this since we were young, since you first made me aware of passion. You continue to make me aware."

She ran her leg up over his longer ones and nestled tighter to him. He pulled her over his chest and caressed her back, felt the small shivers his touch created.

"I'm working on letting go . . . of my need for control. I did it once. I let go of everything and gave it to love. I've been afraid to do it again, and it has made me distant, made me push you away. It even made me long for the solitude of the cabin when it was just my girls and me. But I promise I'm aware of it and working on it. I'm trying."

"Kate," he said. "Look at me."

She did and saw love in his eyes.

TO MY READERS

I am so happy you read my book and hope you enjoyed it as much as I loved writing it. If you want to know how it all began, read *Elephant in the Room: a family saga.* The other Family Saga Series books are waiting for you, as well.

I would love to know your thoughts. You can go to www.julisisung.com. From there, you can talk to me, leave an email address so I can talk to you, or click over to Amazon or another book store to leave a review.

Struggling authors need reviews, so I thank you.

Made in the USA
Coppell, TX
06 December 2021

67316211R00203